CITY OF THE LOST

Will Adams has tried his hand at a multitude of careers over the years. Most recently, he worked for a London-based firm of communications consultants before giving it up to pursue his life-long dream of writing fiction. His first novel, *The Alexander Cipher*, has been published in sixteen languages, and was followed by three more books in the Daniel Knox series, *The Exodus Quest*, *The Lost Labyrinth* and *The Eden Legacy*. He writes full-time and lives in Suffolk.

Also by Will Adams

The Alexander Cipher
The Exodus Quest
The Lost Labyrinth
The Eden Legacy
Newton's Fire

CITY OF THE LOST

WILL ADAMS

HARPER

Harper
An imprint of HarperCollins Publishers
77–85 Fulham Palace Road,
Hammersmith, London W6 8JB

www.harpercollins.co.uk

A Paperback Original 2014
1

A catalogue record for this book
is available from the British Library

ISBN: 978-0-00-742426-9

Set in Sabon LT Std by Palimpsest Book Production Limited,
Falkirk, Stirlingshire

Printed and bound in Great Britain by
Clays Ltd, St Ives plc

MIX
Paper from
responsible sources
FSC
www.fsc.org
FSC™ C007454

To Hattie and Mark

PROLOGUE

Alashiya, Eastern Cyprus, 805 BC

She'd thought she'd have till dawn, but it wasn't to be. They came at dusk instead. From the ramparts of her palace, she watched them landing on the beach. Between the breaking of the waves, she could hear the muffled roars of their triumph and the jubilant clashing of spears on shields as they saw they were unopposed and realized that her people had abandoned her.

She didn't blame them for that abandonment. She'd brought it upon herself through neglect of her queenly duties. What cut her, what truly cut her, was that the man she'd neglected them for had abandoned her too. She could see his fugitive sails still, the splash of frantic oars. She thought scornfully: *Aeneas of the Teukrians*

1

indeed! No doubt he'd be telling himself comforting lies about how Sicherbas was her brother and could therefore be trusted to treat her honourably. She wanted, suddenly, for him to be confronted with the brutal truth of it. And, with him already so far distant, there was only one way to achieve that.

It was time.

Her palace was on three levels. The subterranean treasuries and storerooms, hewn out of raw bedrock. A ground floor of grand chambers with walls of ashlar masonry and roofs of cedar timbers shipped in from her childhood homeland. And, finally, the upper quarters of wood and thatch. The bottom level would never burn; the top would burn easily. It was the middle floor, therefore, that needed work.

Her sister Anna was waiting below with two lit torches. She, at least, had no illusions about what their brother would do if they fell into his power. Nor did she have any stomach for letting him regain his claimed treasure. That was why, when word had first reached this new city of theirs that he was on his way with his full fleet, pledging terrible revenges upon them both, they'd sent every man they had to chop down the surrounding forests and fill these rooms with timber.

She and Anna touched their torches to the largest stack now, then stood back to watch the contagion spread, flaming embers spitting and drifting to neighbouring chambers, where new fires quickly started. The smoke made her eyes water so that tears spilled down her cheeks. She wiped them angrily away lest Anna mistake them for self-pity. When the heat grew too much for them to bear, they retreated to the treasury steps, then hugged and wished each other well on their respective journeys. Once Anna was gone, she went alone down the steps into the vaults, fetched her sword from her armoury. *His* sword, more properly, for it was what they'd exchanged instead of vows. She used its blade and hilt to pry and hammer away the stone chocks, releasing cascades of sand from the walls, allowing the vast marble slab to sink slowly beneath its own unimaginable weight until it slotted neatly into place above her, sealing these steps off forever.

One entrance closed. One more to go.

Through dark and twisting corridors, she hurried to and down the long staircase. Usually, when she stepped out into the great cavern at the foot, it was already aglow with the myriad constellations of oil lamps in the walls. But her handmaidens had left with Anna and the others, to found their next new city on the Libyan coast, beyond even her brother's vengeful reach. And so, for once, this place looked gloomy rather than magical. She closed and barred the heavy bronze doors behind her. Now for the second entrance: the twisting cave passage down which she and Aeneas had first discovered this place while seeking refuge from a storm. The mouth was high above the chamber floor, reached only by a staircase pegged to the left-hand wall, where the camber was easiest. She climbed it to the top, then crossed the short bridge to the narrow slit in the limestone. She ducked her head as she passed through it into the shaft beyond, then climbed the crude steps hacked in the rock up to and beyond the trap-doors.

High above her, the night sky flickered orange. Her palace was ablaze. Her heart twisted with a kind of bitter triumph, knowing her lover couldn't help but see this pyre as he fled his cowardly way. But she had no time to waste. She hacked at the two ropes until they both cleaved and slithered off upwards like startled snakes, then stood there for a moment, panting from the exertion. Rumblings began, as though Mother Earth herself were hungry. Her engineers had warned her to be swift. She climbed back below the trap-doors then closed them flat across the shaft and fixed them in place with their locking-bars. She was barely done when it began, a soft pattering that abruptly turned into a thunderous deluge before being so muffled by the sand already fallen that it grew silent again.

Her tomb was sealed. As was her fate.

Back across the bridge and down to the cavern floor. She held her torch to the staircase until it caught and began to burn with gratifying vigour, a spiral of fire spreading gloriously up and around the gallery. Wood and rope fizzed and crackled; steps and struts clattered blazing to the ground. With no more need for her torch, she tossed it into the general conflagration then went to their bed and set the pommel of his sword into a corner so that it couldn't slip. Then she tore open her robes and pressed the tip of the blade sharp and cold against her stomach, pointing upwards beneath her breastbone towards her heart.

A last hesitation as she looked down. How many times had they lain here together? How many times had he talked of sailing towards the setting sun, of founding a new city of his own somewhere across the great sea? He'd called it destiny. She'd called it avoiding marriage. Now he'd got his chance at last. And no doubt, if it went well for him, his entourage would tell stories to make heroes of themselves, as survivors always did. But *he*, at least, would know the truth of it.

And, one day, maybe the world would too.

ONE

I

Daphne, Southern Turkey

They said this was where the Trojan War had started. They said that it was here, among Daphne's wooded hillsides, glades and waterfalls, that Paris had awarded his golden apple to Aphrodite, rather than to Athena or to Hera, thus winning himself Helen, the most beautiful woman in the world, and precipitating the Greek armada and ten years of brutal, bloody war into the bargain.

Iain Black smiled as he took another sip of his sweet strong tea. Men going crazy over a beautiful woman. How far the world had come. 'Now *her*,' he said, nodding along and across the road to the steps outside the black-glass fronted Daphne International Hotel. '*She's* more like it.'

7

Mustafa glanced over his shoulder, snorted in amusement. 'What is it with you and scrawny women?' he asked. Then he flushed as he realized what he'd said. 'I'm sorry. I didn't mean to—'

'It's okay,' Iain assured him. 'Anyway, she's not scrawny. She's elegant. There's a difference.'

'Elegant!' retorted Mustafa. 'Can't you see what she's wearing?'

Iain laughed. He liked her clothes, the student chic of them, the way they showed off her figure without seeming to. A plain blue sweatshirt, baggy cream cheesecloth trousers, well-worn tan sneakers. Silver rings on her fingers and her left thumb, a back-to-front baseball cap through which poked unruly tufts of her straw-coloured hair, and a pair of John Lennon shades with shiny dark blue lenses. 'Give her a break,' he said. 'She's on holiday.'

'A woman should always make the most of herself,' said Mustafa. 'Especially a woman who can afford to stay in a place like that.'

'You're a chauvinist and a snob, my friend,' smiled Iain.

'Yes,' agreed Mustafa.

The woman was carrying a tattered blue-vinyl day bag. She now half drew a bulky manila envelope from it so that she could check its address. She put it back, looked both ways, turned left and headed away from them, towards the main road. Iain watched her out of sight with a mild pang of regret, not for her in particular so much as for the companionship of an attractive woman. It had been too long; that was the fact of it. And he was ready again, he suddenly sensed it inside himself. Yet this was hardly the time or place. With Butros Bejjani and his entourage on their way, he needed his game-head on.

He checked his laptop again, the feed coming in from the various cameras they'd set up to monitor the approach roads and the hotel lobby. No sign of them yet. 'How are we for time?' he asked.

'Another half hour at least,' said Mustafa.

Iain nodded at their empty glasses. 'More tea?'

'Need you ask?'

He picked up their glasses and took them inside, the door banging closed behind him. An elderly thin German woman with hennaed hair, silver jewellery and an embroidered crimson scarf was agonizing between juices. When finally she'd plumped for lemon, Iain gave his own order and asked for the drinks to be taken out. Then he headed for the rest-room. He was on his way in when it happened, a thunderous boom and the rest-room door slamming sideways into him like a small truck, throwing him down onto the white tiled floor. He rose with difficulty onto hands and knees. His ears were muffled yet he could still hear alarms outside, people screaming. The years of training and service kicked in, so that instead of panic he felt the familiar calm coldness spread through him, almost as though he was watching it happen to someone else.

He tried to stand but his balance was off and he fell back down. He didn't let this bother him but kept trying until he succeeded and made his way unsteadily out. There was glass, debris and dust everywhere. The waiter was down behind the counter, groaning softly. The German woman was on her side, her scarf splayed like blood around her throat and head. Her eyes were open but dazed and he couldn't see any injuries, for she'd been protected from the worst of the blast by the solid side wall which—

Mustafa.

He hurried outside. A glimpse of hell, daytime turned to night by a canopy of noxious black smoke. A blue van with shattered windows was blazing furiously. Dust and fragments of stone whispered down around him like dry rain; and even as he watched, a misshapen and charred sheet of once-white metal crashed from a nearby roof onto the cobbles. His eyes watered with dust and toxic smoke. He had to squint to see. The café's forecourt had been cleared as if by a giant arm. He went to the edge, looked down. The air was clearer here. Three cars had tumbled all the way down the steep slope to the tree-line of the valley beneath. Tables, chairs, sunshades and other debris were scattered everywhere. Great chunks of rubble, the tossed cabers of telephone poles, the black serpents of their wires. And there was Mustafa, two-thirds of the way down. The gradient was so steep and the ground so loose that he set off little avalanches with every step, earth cascading around his ankles. Mustafa was on his back, wheezing from the effort to breathe. His cheek was lacerated and bleeding and his left arm looked badly broken below the elbow. Iain knelt beside him. He'd dealt with trauma often enough in the army, but that didn't make it easy. He unzipped Mustafa's leather jacket. His white cotton shirt beneath was sodden with blood. A piece of shrapnel had torn into his friend's gut and gone to grievous work inside, releasing that hateful sick sweet smell. He looked up the slope in hope of help, but there was no one, he was on his own. A shredded cotton tablecloth fluttered like defeat a little way off. He made a wad of it, pressed it over Mustafa's wounds, bleakly and increasingly aware that it was futile, a gesture, that his friend was losing blood too fast for anything short of a miracle to save him. And he didn't believe in miracles.

Mustafa groaned and opened his eyes. He lay there for a moment, taking it in, assimilating what had happened to him, what was about to happen. He felt for and took Iain's hand, looked him in the eyes. 'My wife,' he said softly. 'My daughters.'

'You're going to be fine,' Iain told him. 'Help's on its way.'

He shook his head. 'My wife,' he said again, more urgently. 'My daughters.'

Iain blinked back tears. 'I'll see they're all right. I give you my word on it.'

11

Mustafa nodded faintly, satisfied by this pledge. 'Who did this?' he asked. 'Was this us?'

Iain grimaced. For eighteen months now, Turkey had been caught up in a spiral of violence that approached a state of war. Not just the overspill from Syria, a few miles south of here, but also from Kurdish separatists, Islamicists, Armenians and even Cypriots who'd taken advantage of the growing chaos to press their own particular causes. Yet that this should happen outside this hotel today of all days was too big a coincidence to ignore. 'I don't know,' he said.

'Find out,' said Mustafa.

'I promise.'

'Find out and make them . . .' He grimaced in pain or shock. He gave a little cry and clenched Iain's hand tight. His left leg twitched briefly, as though trying to kick off a slipper. Then he stiffened and his body arched for a moment or two before something seemed to puncture inside him and he relaxed again and was still.

II

Georges Bejjani was tapping a cigarette from its soft pack when the bomb exploded a short distance ahead. He didn't see the blast itself, for it took place on a side road and thus was obscured by the black glass exterior of the

Daphne International Hotel. And, because it was a fraction of a second before the first sound reached them, he thought momentarily that he was suffering some kind of weird hallucination, perhaps an optical illusion caused by sunlight and the midday haze. But then a silver 4x4 came back-flipping out onto the road and he heard the sudden thunder of it, and alarms began tripping all around them as a canopy of thick black smoke spread low across the sky.

Faisal slammed on the brakes, began instantly to turn. He was trained, after all, for such emergencies. But the traffic had been squeezed into a single lane by an unloading lorry and an oncoming van screeched to a halt right beside them, pinning them in. A fist of stone punched the passenger-side window, buckling the frame and turning the glass seawater green for a fraction of a second before it shattered and fell away. Debris pattered and then pounded upon their roof like a sudden squall of hail. Even while it was still coming down, Georges whipped out his mobile to call his elder brother. 'Bomb,' he said, the moment Michel answered. 'Get Father back to the boat.'

'Are you okay?' asked Michel.

'We're fine. Just get him safe.'

'On our way now,' Michel assured him. 'Was it for us?'

'I don't know. It went off ten seconds ago. But it was right outside the hotel.'

'Then it was for us,' said Michel.

13

'I'll check into it.'

'Be careful.'

Georges snorted. 'Count on it,' he said. He turned to Faisal and his bodyguard Sami. 'Let's take a look,' he said. 'But we're out of here before the police show. Okay?'

They ran forward in a crouch, wary of a second device or of gunmen waiting to ambush the first responders. Childhood in Lebanon was a harsh teacher. Dazed people appeared like a zombie army from the smoke, clothes torn and ashen, faces bloody and smeared. The smoke grew black as night, choking and eye-burning. They passed cars on their roofs and sides, reached the front of the stricken hotel. Only the right-hand side of the road here had been developed, affording hotel guests uninterrupted views of Daphne's gorgeous valley from the balconies. But the bomb had chomped a vast bite from this road, tarmac and hardcore tumbling in a great rubble avalanche down the hillside. The resultant crater had also been partially filled with shattered black glass, broken masonry and other debris from the hotel itself. A forearm protruded from beneath a chunk of grey concrete at such a grotesque angle that Georges couldn't be sure it was even still attached. The block was too heavy for him alone, but Faisal and Sami helped him lift it high enough to reveal the man beneath. They looked away, sickened, let the masonry fall back down.

In the distance, sirens. Police, medics, maybe even the

army. They were near to a war zone here, and this whole region was prone to earthquakes. They'd have experts and heavy lifting machinery. Staying here wouldn't help anyone, would only invite the kinds of questions he wished to avoid. He needed to find answers before returning to the boat, but this wasn't the place. Sami looked meaningfully at him. He gave the nod and they ran together back to the car, then pulled a sharp turn in the road and drove away even as the first emergency vehicles raced past them to the site.

III

The shameful truth was that fine music bored Deniz Baştürk. Two years in the steelworks had done damage to his ears and left him with coarse tastes: music to dance to, to drink to, lyrics made for bellowing. When his son Orhan had told him that he wanted to transfer to the Ankara State Conservatory to study it, therefore, he'd thought – or perhaps more accurately hoped – it was a joke.

But such were the perils of falling in love with an artistic woman.

On the concert platform, his son packed his oboe away into its case, took a zurna from his music-bag instead. He'd been granted the rare honour of choosing a piece to perform, to showcase his own talent. But what it was,

Baştürk didn't know. He frowned inquisitively at his wife Sophia; she gave him in return only an enigmatic smile. The lights dimmed a little. The players took up their instruments. His son put the zurna's reed to his lips, readied his fingers for the first note. Baştürk found himself tensing, hope fighting fear. If this was what his son wanted, it was what he wanted too. But he'd learned the hard way, these past six months, that aspiration wasn't the same thing as ability.

The first notes, so soft he could barely hear them. Baştürk made sure to keep his hands and expression relaxed, but his feet were clenched like fists beneath his seat until with a shock he not only recognized the piece but then quickly realized that Orhan had mastered it completely, that he was good; and now the other instruments joined in and the music began to soar raucously and joyously and he knew it was going to be okay, his son would have the life he coveted, and he sagged a little with the relief of it, and he took and squeezed his wife's hand, and he felt quite ridiculously proud.

Now that he could relax, the music went to work on him. It was a personal favourite of his, conjuring childhood memories of his own father, of being carried on his shoulders at protest marches, of watching him holding union crowds enthralled with his fierce rhetoric. Then the music hit its first melancholic passage, and it took him with it. For it had been a mixed blessing to have such a man for a father, dooming him to a life of falling short. And he *had* fallen short, he knew. He'd let his father down. He'd let his wife and son down. He'd let his country down. He felt, again, the almost crippling sense of inadequacy that had blighted him so often since he'd started his new job.

A door banged behind him. He looked irritably around at this disruption of his son's performance. Shadows conferred in those urgent low voices that were somehow doubly intrusive for being hushed. On stage, the players hesitated, uncertain whether to treat this as a rehearsal or a full performance, before staggering to an ugly, ragged stop. Baştürk slapped his knee in anger then got to his feet. 'I thought I said no interruptions.'

'Forgive me, Prime Minister,' said Gonka, his senior aide, hurrying down the aisle to him. 'But there's been an incident. A bomb.'

'Oh, no,' he said. 'Not another.'

'I'm afraid so,' she nodded. 'In Daphne. And I wouldn't have disturbed you even so, but the press have found out you're here. And they're already gathering outside.'

TWO

I

There was nothing more Iain could do for Mustafa, and others might need his help. He made his way down the slope to the cars that had rolled to its foot. The first two were empty, but a middle-aged woman was strapped unconscious behind the wheel of the third, a green Peugeot settled on its roof. He couldn't see any flames but its interior was clouding with smoke. The doors were all jammed shut, but its passenger-side window had partially buckled so he smashed it with a stone until it caved. He took a deep breath then wriggled inside. He released her seatbelt, took her under her arms, hauled her out and laid her on her back. Her pulse was weak but she was alive and breathing unaided.

He clambered back up the hillside. It was steep enough

18

to make his calves and hams ache. Shrieks of pain and wails of grief greeted him. The smoke had cleared to reveal the blast's full devastation. A great bite had been taken out of the road in front of the Daphne International Hotel and its black-glass frontage had shattered and fallen away, exposing a honeycomb interior of ruined rooms, of broken baths and toilets dangling grotesquely from twisted pipes. The scale of damage, and the lack of any residual smell of cheap explosive, suggested to him military-grade ordnance. And not some stray shell from the Syrian war: it would take a large missile or a truck-load of Semtex to wreak this much—

A cracking, splintering noise ripped the air, sending the fire-crews and search-and-rescue teams scurrying for safety. Then, a second or two later, the hotel's left-hand wall simply sheared away and toppled forwards into the general rubble, bringing the rear wall down too, throwing up more clouds of noxious dust and reducing still further any hope of finding survivors.

Ambulances were now arriving in large numbers. He led a pair of paramedics down the hill. While one of them treated the Peugeot driver, he and the other strapped Mustafa onto a stretcher and carried him back up to the top, loaded him onto an ambulance. He asked to go along with him, but the paramedic gave an expressive little shrug. It wasn't an ambulance right now, but a body-cart; and they needed all of it. 'Did he live around here?' the man asked.

'Istanbul,' answered Iain. He nodded at the wrecked hotel. 'He was staying there.'

'Wife? Family?'

'I'll call them myself,' said Iain.

'We still need to know who they are.'

He summoned up Layla's number on his smartphone, wrote it along with Mustafa's name on the back of one of his own business cards, then added the name of his Antioch hotel should they need to contact him. The paramedic thanked him and moved off in search of further grim duties. Remarkably, it was only now that he remembered what he and Mustafa had been here to do. Or, more precisely, remembered the footage that would have been streaming into his laptop right up to the moment of detonation. If his hard-drive had somehow survived, and the footage could be recovered, it could prove vital to the investigation. On the other hand, if the police discovered it for themselves it would be a nightmare to explain away.

He went back down the slope to where he'd found Mustafa then searched in an ever-widening spiral until he spotted an edge of the toughened black casing protruding from loose earth. He pulled it free. Its screen was shattered, its hinges broken and its casing pocked by shrapnel, but it could have been far worse. He carried it obliquely back up the slope to his hire-car, locked it away in his boot. His next job promised to be harder. He took out his phone again. No signal. The masts had to be overwhelmed. He walked away in search of coverage. Still nothing. A wicked little voice whispered that the paramedics or the hospital would take care of it for him, maybe even handle it better than he could. They'd be calm, clinical, practised.

In Istanbul, last year, Layla had cooked a feast in his honour, to thank him for bringing good employment to her husband. Their two daughters had sat either side of him upon their divan while he'd read them stories from the lusciously illustrated copy of the *Thousand and One Nights* he'd brought as a gift.

A signal at last. Tenuous but undeniable. He felt light-headed as he dialled Mustafa's home number, like the first hint of flu. The phone had barely rung before Layla snatched it up. She began talking Turkish so fast that it was a struggle for Iain to follow. He tried to slow her. When she recognized his voice, she burst into sobs of relief. 'You're safe,' she said, switching to English. 'Thank God you're safe. I've been watching on the news. I've been so worried. Where's Mustafa? Is he with you? I've been trying his phone.'

'Layla,' said Iain.

There was silence. It stretched painful as the rack. 'He's hurt,' she said. 'He's hurt badly, isn't he?'

'Layla,' he said again.

She began to wail. It was a desperate, inhuman sound, like an animal being tortured. He didn't know what she needed from him, whether to respect her grief with silence or to tell her what he knew. He decided to talk. It would be easy enough for her to shut him up if she wanted. He described their morning in the café, how he'd gone for more tea immediately before the blast. He told her how he'd knelt beside her husband in his last moments. She wept so loudly that it was hard to believe she could hear him, but he kept talking anyway, about how Mustafa had seized his hand and asked him to look out for her and their daughters. He told her of his promise, reiterated it now. Her sobs abruptly stopped. 'Layla?' he said. He'd lost signal. He felt sick and bruised and drained and guilty all at once as he walked around trying to reacquire it. When finally he succeeded, to his shame he couldn't bring himself to call Layla again. He called the London office instead, asked for Maria. Maria had known Mustafa a little, had a wonderful gift of empathy. He braced her for bad news, told her what had happened. He asked her to get in touch with Layla, arrange for her and her daughters to fly down to Antioch if she so wished, plus whatever else she needed; and also to start the paperwork on Mustafa's life insurance.

'Are you okay?' Maria asked. 'You yourself, I mean?'

'I'm fine,' he assured her.

'You don't sound fine.'

'I just watched Mustafa die,' he told her. 'I thought I was past all this shit.'

'I'll talk to Layla,' she promised.

'Thank you,' said Iain. 'And put me through to Quentin.'

'Now?'

'Now.' He went on hold. His boss picked up a few moments later. 'Maria told me,' he said. 'I can't believe it. Are you okay?'

'I'm fine.'

'What are you going to do? Are you coming home?'

'No. I need to be here for Layla.'

'Layla?'

Iain clenched a fist. 'Mustafa's widow.'

'Ah. Yes. Of course. Layla.'

'Listen, Quentin,' said Iain. 'Before Mustafa died, he asked me if we had anything to do with the blast. I promised him I'd find out.'

'How could you even think such a thing?'

'Because I don't know who our client is,' said Iain. 'Or what they wanted from this job.'

'You do know our client. Hunter & Blackwells.'

'They're *lawyers*, Quentin,' said Iain. 'Who do they represent?'

'They had nothing to do with this. Take my word for it.'

'No,' said Iain.

'I beg your pardon?'

'I said no, I won't take your word for it. Not on this. I need to know who they are and why they're so interested in the Bejjanis.'

Silence. 'Very well,' said Quentin, finally. 'I gave them a pledge of confidentiality, but under these circumstances, I think I can ask permission to share. Though I make no promises.'

'I do,' said Iain angrily. 'Either you tell me or I'll make it my business to find out. And they really don't want me going after them, not in the mood I'm in.' He ended the call, rubbed the back of his neck. His first few months at Global Analysis had been such a relief after the army: stimulating, demanding and rewarding, yet no one getting killed or even hurt. This past year or so, however, it had turned increasingly sour. The secrecy. The offshore accounts. The relentless push for profits. The downright nastiness of some of their clients. That was why, for several months now, he'd been making vague plans to set up on his own, maybe invite Mustafa and a few of the others to go with him. Yet he'd done nothing concrete about it.

And now this.

II

Turkish Nicosia, Cyprus

Taner Inzanoğlu made a point of walking his daughter Katerina to and from school every day he possibly could. He did it partly because his car was old and unreliable, and partly because petrol was so expensive. But mostly he did it because it was such a relief to get away from his writing and other work for a while; a relief to spend time with Katerina and not feel guilty.

The afternoon was sunny and warm, yet pleasantly fresh. The perfect spring day. He bought them each a raspberry-flavoured ice-lolly. They licked them as they walked through the park, tongues sticking to the frosting and turning ever redder. She told him about her day, her friends, the lessons she had taken, the inexplicable splinters of knowledge that had somehow lodged in her mind. They finished their lollies. He took her wrapper and stick from her, put them in a bin. Then he broke into a run. 'Race you,' he shouted over his shoulder.

The course was well known to them both. Through the trees, around the swings and the exercise machines, back to the path. 'I can't believe you beat me,' he protested, as he collapsed panting onto the grass. 'What kind of daughter would beat her own father!'

The way her eyes crinkled when she laughed reminded him so vividly of her mother that his heart ached almost as though it had just happened. With the pain came the usual premonition: that something calamitous would overtake her too, that he'd be equally powerless to stop it. He reached up and hugged her and pulled her down onto the grass beside him. 'What is it, Father?' she asked.

'Nothing,' he said. His anxiety wouldn't go away, however. If anything, it grew worse. They'd barely left the park before his mobile rang. He checked the number, was relieved to see that it was only Martino. 'Hey, my friend,' he said. 'Don't tell me you're cancelling tonight?'

'Aren't you watching?' asked Martino.

His heart stopped. 'Watching what?'

'The bomb. In Daphne.'

Taner turned his back on Katerina so that she couldn't see his face. 'How bad?' he asked.

'Bad. Really bad.' He paused a moment, then added what Taner had most feared. 'And they're saying that a warning was called in. They're saying it was us.'

III

The police had already started taking statements from possible eye-witnesses. Iain gave his name, details and a bowdlerized version of his day to a slab-faced officer with an implausible belly. A few paces away, the woman he'd earlier joked about with Mustafa was struggling to make herself understood by an officer with limited English. When he was finished, therefore, he went across and offered to translate. Her name was Karin Visser. She was twenty-seven years old. She was Dutch but had been studying and working in America for the past four years, which explained both her accent and her impeccable English. She'd been travelling around Turkey with her boss Nathan Coates, a retired oil executive, and his head of security Rick Leland. The two of them had been in Nathan's room all morning, in some kind of meeting. No, she didn't know who with. No, they hadn't been in Daphne long. They'd only arrived from Ephesus late the night before, had been due to fly on to Cyprus the day after tomorrow, then back to the States at the end of the week. No, she hadn't seen anything out of the ordinary. She'd gone for a long walk that morning, had returned to the hotel thinking the meeting would have finished. But it had still been going on. She opened up her day-pack to show the manila package inside, and explained how her boss had given it to her to have couriered, insisting that she see to it herself rather than merely trusting it to reception. She'd been on her way when she'd heard the blast and run back. That was when . . . She waved an expressive hand to indicate the destruction. The policeman thanked her wearily and asked her to let him or his colleagues know before she left the area, then went off to conduct his next interview.

'Are you okay?' Iain asked her.

'I'm fine,' said Karin. But her hand was trembling slightly and her eyes glittered. 'It's just, they were my friends, you know. And I've never been through anything like this before.' She shook her head. 'I feel so useless. I feel like there are things I should be doing.'

'Like what?'

'I don't know. To do with Nathan and Rick, I guess. I mean did you see the hotel? Nathan's room was right above that crater. I mean *right above it*.' Her tears finally started flowing. She brushed them away with the heel of her left hand. 'They have to be buried under God only knows how much rubble. There's no way can they still be alive. So what do I do? Do I call their families? Or do I wait until it's confirmed? And is it up to me to arrange for them to be . . .' She closed her eyes, unable to complete the thought. 'And then there's stupid stuff. I left my passport in my room safe, for example. My cards, my driver's licence, nearly all my cash. I assumed they'd be okay there.'

'Someone from your consulate will be here soon,' Iain assured her. 'By tomorrow at the latest. They'll deal with the police and the authorities for you. They'll arrange to have your boss and your colleague flown back home. They'll issue you with a new passport. They'll make sure you have money and a flight.'

'But what about until then? God, I know this is trivial, but where do I go? What do I eat? Where do I sleep? How do I get around? I don't know a soul in this place and I don't speak a word of the language and my friends are dead and I don't have anywhere to stay or enough money to pay for a room and I don't know what I'm going to do.'

'Hey,' he said. 'Don't worry about it. I'll get you a room at my hotel.'

'I told you. I don't have any money.'

He touched her arm gently. 'I'll put you on my tab,' he said. 'You can pay me back when you sort things out.'

'Are you sure?'

'Of course I'm sure.'

She wiped her eyes. 'Thank you so much.'

'It's fine.'

There was nothing more to keep them here, so he led her to his car. It was barely five miles to Antioch, but the roads were so chaotic that it took them an hour. He parked up the cobbled street from his hotel, led her inside. The receptionist stared at them in astonishment. 'You were there?' she asked.

Iain touched Karin on the elbow. 'My friend here was staying at the Daphne International. She needs a room. Oh, and she's lost her passport and her cards, so can you please put her on my account for the moment.'

'I'm so sorry,' said the receptionist, 'but we don't have any rooms left. The phone's been going crazy. Journalists and TV people and police. Everyone's on their way. And the other hotels are the same. We've all been referring inquiries to each other. I honestly don't know of any rooms left in the city.'

Iain glanced at Karin. Sharing a room with a stranger breached all kinds of company protocols, but she was visibly at the end of her tether. 'We can go hunting, if you like,' he said. 'Or there's a spare bed in my room.'

She shook her head. 'I couldn't possibly.'

'Just for tonight. We'll sort something better out tomorrow.' The receptionist smiled at this happy solution, tapped Karin's details into her terminal, gave her a spare card-key. They took the lift up. He fixed them a drink each, spilled a pack of chocolate-covered nuts into a saucer. Karin sat heavily on a bed and checked her mobile, but the masts were evidently overwhelmed here too. He nodded at the bedside phone. 'Use that,' he said.

'It's to Holland. To let my parents know I'm safe. Then to America.'

'For fuck's sake,' he said. 'Owe me.' He half held up his hand to apologize for his irritability, but Karin didn't even seem to notice. He went into the bathroom, put his hands upon the sink, rested weight upon them. It was a risk of being single too long that you lost your soft edges. He checked himself in the mirror: a mess of sweat and dust and blood. He fetched clean clothes from his wardrobe, stripped and took a shower, vigorously soaping off the dirt and blood and sweat, watching the grey-brown mess of it circle the plug and then vanish. He dialled the heat up as high as he could take it then turned his face to the spray almost as if to purge himself of something, or perhaps in penance for the fact that, yet once more in his life, an operation he was running had turned so utterly to shit.

THREE

I

They found a storage room crammed with pianos and other instruments in which to brief Deniz Baştürk on the bomb before he went out to face the press. Discordant notes thrummed and pinged each time someone changed position or rested a hand on a keyboard, making it even harder for him to absorb what he was being told, fretting at the ordeal ahead as he already was.

Hard to believe that he'd actually once enjoyed dealing with the media. As an economics professor of reasonable repute, brought into the Ministry of Finance in the wake of the global financial crisis, his first interviews had almost exclusively been policy-dense one-on-ones with sober-minded financial journalists. He'd enjoyed the intellectual challenge of making his case persuasively, and he hadn't needed to worry much about ambush, partly because he was essentially an honest man, but mostly because access was too valuable a commodity to the press to be wasted on a hit against someone as obscure and technocratic as himself. But then had come his unexpected elevation to the top job, and everything had changed.

Enough. His aides knew nothing more and if he didn't go out soon the murmuring would start, that he was hiding. He led the way himself, marching through the lobby and striding boldly out the automated glass front doors, because you had to look in command even if you didn't feel it. It had turned darkly overcast outside, exaggerating the eruption of flashbulbs from the several dozen reporters and photographers crowded in the small courtyard and on the steps up to the street, almost like he was in an auditorium of his own. He felt exposed without a podium to stand behind; his usual one not only had a concealed step to make him appear taller, but its considerable girth also helped disguise his own. There was nothing for it, however. He took a moment to compose himself and to adopt a suitably sombre expression then spoke the usual platitudes about the nation's thoughts being with the victims and their families, giving them his word the perpetrators would be caught.

'You've been giving your word for six months,' said Birol Khan of Channel 5. 'Yet still they bomb. Each worse than the last. The Syrians, the Kurds and now it seems the Cypriots. It's like they're competing with each other.'

'That's an unnecessarily alarmist way of—'

'Alarmist? These monsters murdered thirty people. And you call me alarmist?'

He held up a hand. 'That's not what I meant. These . . . *perpetrators* are criminals. This is a security problem, not a war.'

'It *feels* like a war. It feels like we're under attack *all the time*.'

There were murmurs of approval at this. These weren't merely journalists. They were civilians too, people with their own fears, with loved ones of their own. Until recently, the troubles had been sporadic and largely confined to the Kurdish south-east, but now attacks were taking place with increasing frequency and violence all across the country. No town or village felt safe any more. No public space or office. And it was impossible to protect everywhere. He cast a guilty glance over his shoulder. Since his son had started here, the Academy had added layers of security, courtesy of the state. He himself was escorted by at least six secret service bodyguards wherever he went. His cars were armoured, his office and both homes protected by rings of steel. How would he feel if it was his own family in jeopardy and no progress was being made? He suffered another flutter of inadequacy. The country needed a proper leader, not some floundering economist. 'The police are doing the best they can,' he said weakly.

'That's the precise problem,' shouted out Yasemin Omari, a gadfly TV reporter who mistook rudeness for speaking truth to power.

'They've made a great many arrests.'

'Yes. Of people the Interior Minister doesn't like.'

'That's a ridiculous allegation.'

'Some say he can't catch the bombers because he's fired his best officers and replaced them with incompetent loyalists. Others say he's deliberately slow-pedalling the investigations to make you look bad. Which do you think it is?'

'I think he's a dedicated public servant doing an excellent job under extremely difficult circumstances.'

'Your current Chief of the General Staff helped take down the Kurdish separatists last time it got like this. Why not put him in charge?'

'Because counterterrorism is a civilian task. Besides, the Minister and the General are already in close contact. We operate a joined-up government.' Laughter made him flush. 'I assure you,' he said.

'You *assure* us?' taunted Omari. 'Everyone knows those two hate each other. When was the last time they even spoke?'

'We have just suffered the most terrible atrocity,' he said sharply. 'Do you seriously expect me to reveal details of our investigation on national television?' He shook his head as if in dismay then pushed his way through the pack and up the steps to the waiting cars. A heartfelt sigh the moment they were safely inside. 'Get the Interior Minister and the Chief of the General Staff for me,' he told Gonka, as they pulled away. 'I want them in my office.'

'Yes, Prime Minister,' she said. 'When?'

He turned so that she could see his face. 'When do you think?' he asked.

II

Karin was on the phone when Iain finished his shower, being talked at by an American man with an abrasively loud and patrician voice. '. . . need to let me know the moment my father's death is confirmed,' he was saying.

'Of course,' said Karin. She glanced up at Iain. 'But I have to go now,' she said. 'Again, I'm really sorry for your loss.'

'I'll bet you are,' said the man, sounding remarkably chipper for someone who'd had such grievous news. 'Waking up like this to find nothing on the night-stand.' The phone clicked; there was dial-tone. Karin grimaced as she replaced it in its cradle. 'Nathan's eldest,' she said.

'He seemed to take it well.'

'They aren't the closest of families.'

Iain nodded. If she wanted to talk about it, she'd bring it up herself. 'You look exhausted,' he said. 'Enough with the phone calls. Have a bath. A nice cup of tea.' He fetched an olive T-shirt from the wardrobe, tossed it to her, then fished some Turkish lira banknotes from his wallet. 'For clothes and food and shit. Whatever you need.'

'Thanks,' she said.

'My pleasure,' he said. 'And if there's anything else . . .'

She took a deep breath. 'Does that extend to advice?'

'Sure. About what?'

Karin had brought her day-pack up to the room. Now she took the bulky manila envelope out from it. 'You remember what I told that policeman? How I went out walking all morning. Then I went back to Nathan's room only to find him still in his meeting, and how he gave me this to post.'

Iain frowned. 'You want me to run it down to reception?'

'No. It's nothing like that. It's just that I've been thinking about something. About why we were even here.' She bit her lower lip briefly, as though torn between discretion and the urge to share. 'If I tell you something in confidence, will you keep it to yourself?'

'Of course,' said Iain. 'What?'

She showed him the package's address label. It was made out in neat turquoise handwriting to a Professor

Michael Walker at the Egyptian Institute of Archaeometry in New Cairo, Egypt. 'The thing is,' she said, 'I know Mike. My boss Nathan used to sponsor his institute, you see, so I've dealt with him a fair bit over the phone. He's an archaeologist, essentially, but he specializes in scientific techniques like carbon-dating, thermoluminescence testing, spectrum analysis, that kind of thing. How old is this parchment? Where was this amphora fired? What's the mix of metals in this ingot?'

'Okay,' said Iain.

'Nathan was fascinated by the ancient Greeks,' said Karin. 'Particularly the Mycenaeans. The ones Homer wrote about. We were in Troy a couple of days ago, for example. Then we came here. You won't know this, but some people believe the Trojan War started in Daphne.'

'Sure,' nodded Iain. 'Paris awarding Aphrodite the golden apple.'

'Yes. Exactly.' She looked so impressed, he decided not to confess that Mustafa had told him this that same morning. 'But you saw the place. It's not exactly Ephesus, is it? Though, to be fair, Nathan also co-sponsors excavations at an old Hittite city called Tell Tayinat, which is only a few miles from here, by the Syrian border. But that's off-season right now. There's no one there.'

'Am I supposed to be following this?'

'Sorry. I'm thinking out loud. You see, when I was arranging our itinerary, this was the only leg of the trip that Nathan insisted on, even though there was nothing for us to do here. We had to arrive last night, we had to stay at the Daphne International Hotel, and we couldn't leave for Cyprus until the day after tomorrow.'

'Ah,' said Iain.

'And Nathan only decided to make this trip two weeks ago. You don't know him, but that's completely out of character. He likes to have everything just so.' She gave a little grimace. 'He *liked* to, I should say. Spontaneity was never his thing. Yet suddenly he decides to come here. And you should have seen how excited he's been these past few days. And that hotel! It was nice enough, yes, but Nathan was *rich*. I mean *really, really rich*. I could easily have found us something far nicer, like the place we had in Istanbul, you should have seen it. But no, he insisted on that specific hotel. And then this morning he tells me that he and Rick have a meeting, and that I should go out and not come back for at least two hours.'

Iain nodded. 'So you think your whole trip here was in fact cover for this meeting?'

'Yes. Yes, I do.'

'Do you know who it was with?'

'No.'

'But you suspect someone was offering him artefacts for sale, right? And that this package for your friend Mike in New Cairo contains samples he wanted tested?

To authenticate the pieces before he handed over any cash?'

Karin grimaced. 'Nathan never cared too much about provenance,' she said. 'At least, that's not fair, he *did* care, he cared a lot. But he thought it worth pushing the boundaries a little if it meant getting important pieces back into the public domain. He donated all those sorts of acquisitions to museums, you see. The black market's still illegal, though, however honourable your intentions. And he told me once that he almost got caught here in Turkey several years ago. So what do I do? I can't see how telling the police would help the investigation, but what if it could? Yet if I tell them about it, and they use it to trash his reputation, I'd hate myself. Or what if they accuse me of being his accomplice? I wasn't, I swear I wasn't. It never even occurred to me until a moment ago. But how could I possibly prove that?'

'So post it to this Walker guy,' suggested Iain. 'You'd have done it anyway.'

'But they're bound to be keeping an eye on those sorts of places, aren't they? What with the bomb, I mean. Or what if Mike notifies them himself after he receives it? It'll look like I was trying to hide it. And I showed it to that policeman, remember? What if he asks for it?'

'Why would he?'

'I don't know.' She sounded a little close to the edge suddenly; shock often got to people in unexpected ways.

'Maybe to find out who Nathan was meeting. To identify his body or something. What would I do then?'

He took the package from her, packed it away in his holdall at the foot of his wardrobe. 'Okay,' he said. 'You were badly shaken by the explosion. I took it from you to carry. What with everything else, you never even gave it another thought.'

'But I—'

'You never even gave it another thought. If anyone asks for it, which they won't, frown and say you think maybe I have it. If they ask me, I'll give it to them and your boss' reputation will have to take a hit. That's all. But it won't happen, I promise you. Nor will anyone come after you. They've got far more important things to worry about.'

She let out a deep breath. 'Thanks,' she said. 'And not only for this. For everything. I honestly don't know what I'd have done without you.'

'Just glad I could help,' he said.

III

A smallholding near Gornec
The Turkish Republic of Northern Cyprus

Zehra Inzanoğlu was breaking up soil in her top field when she heard the engine. It sounded strained and urgent, with a different pitch to any of her neighbours' vehicles. Nor did it sound much like the hire-car of one of the hapless tourists who sometimes got themselves lost up here while trying to find some imaginary shortcut across the mountains to the north coast.

She rested her mattock against her thigh, brushed dry earth from her hands. The car crested the low rise and came into view. It was old, pale blue and patched in places with grey filler and black tape, and her heart gave a little skip of recognition as it pulled to a stop on the hardened mud track near the steps to her cottage. Then the driver door opened and her son Taner stepped out.

He was taller than she remembered. He'd filled out in the chest and shoulders too. When she'd last seen him, it had been possible to think of him as a boy, *her* boy, though he'd been twenty-four, married and about to become a parent himself. But he was a man now, beyond question. She walked down the path towards him, but stopped several paces short and held her mattock out like a pikestaff. 'What are you doing here?' she asked.

He tried a smile. 'I need help, Mother,' he said, spreading his hands. 'I need *your* help.'

She shook her head slowly. He was flesh and blood so saying no to him could never come easily. But the choice had been his. She and her husband had made the consequences of his betrayal perfectly clear. 'You should have thought of that before.'

41

'I'm not asking for myself,' he said. He turned and beckoned to the car. The passenger door opened and a girl of perhaps ten years old climbed out. She was wearing a school uniform of royal blue with yellow bands, and her hair was of a lustrous black that tumbled in glossy curls down to and beyond her shoulders. Her mouth was mutinous and her eyes were bloodshot from rubbing or weeping. Even so, she looked so strikingly like how Zehra's younger sister had looked at that age that it was a punch in her chest. 'This is your granddaughter Katerina, Mother,' said Taner. 'Katerina, this is your grandmother Zehra.' They stared at each other for several moments, uncertain what to say or do, so that in the end it was Taner himself who had to break the silence. 'I need you to look after her for a few days, Mother,' he said.

'Why?'

'Because I'm about to be arrested.'

That caught her attention. She tore her eyes from her granddaughter. 'Arrested?'

'The bomb.'

'What bomb?'

'On the mainland. Haven't you heard?'

'I don't listen to news.'

'It killed many people. And they're blaming me and my friends.'

'With reason?'

He flinched as though she'd slapped him. 'Of course

not, Mother,' he said. 'I *detest* violence. But plenty of people don't like what we stand for and this is their chance to shut us up.'

Zehra nodded at Katerina. 'Why can't her mother look after her?'

'Athena's dead, Mother. She died last year.'

'Oh.' Despite herself, despite her promises, she felt an unexpected pang of pity for her son, for there was no doubting that he'd loved his wife, and she knew what it was to lose someone you loved. 'Don't you have friends?'

'They're going to arrest them too. They'll arrest all of us. They made that absolutely clear after the last time. So it's either you or sending her to stay with her mother's family in Paphos.' He gave her a shrewd look. 'And if I send her there, how can I be sure they'll ever let her come back?'

Zehra sniffed. She knew he was trying to manipulate her, but it was the truth too. Greek Cypriots couldn't be trusted, which was precisely why she'd warned him against marrying one in the first place. She was about to point this out when she heard other engines approaching. 'I told them I was coming here,' explained her son. 'I didn't want them to think I was trying to run.' He went to Katerina, crouched down before her so that she could see the seriousness on his face. He murmured something. She shook her head. He murmured it again, more force-fully. She took a couple of half-hearted steps towards

Zehra then stopped and looked around. 'Please, sweetheart,' he said. 'For Daddy.' She nodded and went unhappily over to Zehra. 'Be kind to each other,' he said. Then he turned and raised his arms above his head and walked up the short hill to meet the two black SUVs now cresting it. They pulled to a stop either side of him. Doors opened. Six uniformed and plain-clothes policemen got out. They cuffed him roughly and bundled him into one of the SUVs, climbed in either side. The drivers executed a neat ballet to turn in the constricted space, then headed off. Taner looked back through the rear window, his palms pressed against the glass, but then they were gone, leaving only the fading noise of their engines and thin clouds of settling dust.

Zehra turned and looked bleakly at her granddaughter. Her granddaughter looked bleakly back. What now? It was Katerina who made the first move. She clenched her eyes, opened her mouth, and began – at a quite appalling volume – to howl.

FOUR

I

Iain turned on the TV while Karin was in the bathroom. He only meant to watch for a minute or two, to get the latest on the bombing, but it proved strangely compelling. The picture, unsurprisingly, was still blurred, but between the various channels it was beginning to come in to some sort of focus. An unidentified white van or truck had been seen parked outside the hotel, though he couldn't recall it himself. A phone call claiming credit had been made to a local newspaper within a minute or two of the explosion. Thirty people were confirmed dead, with at least as many more unaccounted for.

He was still watching when Karin came out of the bathroom, tucking his olive T-shirt into the waistband of her trousers. 'What are they saying?' she asked.

'They're saying it was Cypriots.'

'Cypriots?' She frowned in puzzlement. 'Why?'

'Apparently they rang in a warning.'

'No. I mean why would Cypriots want to bomb here?'

Iain muted the TV. Cyprus was one of the world's more intractable problems; explaining it was hard. 'You know it's partitioned, right?'

'Turks on the top,' she nodded. 'Greeks on the bottom.'

'Right. Except that the Greek bit is actually independent.' The island had been a tug-of-war between Turkey and Greece for three thousand years. Then the British had taken over for a while, until forced out by insurgency in 1960. An uneasy independence had lasted until 1974, when a botched coup backed by Athens had provoked the Turks into invasion, seizing the northern third of the island before stopping. As Greek Cypriots in the north had fled south, so Turkish Cypriots in the south had fled north, creating a *de facto* partition. At first glance, the Turks got the better of the deal; their nationals accounted for one in five of the population, but they now controlled a third of the island, including the main resorts, the ports, the water resources and the fertile central plain. But sanctions had since devastated tourism and trade, forcing Ankara to pump in billions of lira every year to keep the place running. Worse, Cyprus had blighted Turkey's international reputation and hobbled its application for EU membership. 'The UN's been trying to negotiate a settlement from the start,' he told Karin. 'But without much success. You can understand it: well over a thousand people vanished without trace during the fighting, and have never been found. Tens of thousands of others lost their homes and businesses and belongings, so there's still a lot of bad blood. But then this new guy Deniz Baştürk became Turkish Prime Minister. He made it clear that Cyprus would be his number one foreign policy priority. There's this place called Varosha. It's a district of Famagusta, a city on the east coast of Cyprus. It used to be one of the top resorts in the whole Med until the Turks seized it, but it's been completely abandoned ever since and now they call it the Lost City. Anyway, it's been one of the major sticking points, because the Greek Cypriots have always insisted it be handed back before negotiations can begin in earnest, which the Turks have refused to do, because giving Greeks something for free is unthinkable. But then Baştürk came in and made noises about handing it over, which caused such an uproar among Turkish nationalists that Baştürk had to back down. That, in turn, provoked hard-line Cypriot reunificationists into setting off bombs, in the hope of persuading Turks to change their mind and let Varosha go.'

'And so they murdered thirty people?' asked Karin. 'But that's crazy.'

'Since when has crazy ever stopped bombers?' He touched his left ear. 'Suds,' he said.

'Thanks.' She checked a mirror, wiped them away, then ran fingers through her hair, spiking it a little, but with evident dissatisfaction. 'You don't have a comb, do you?'

Iain ran a hand over his buzz-cut. 'Do I need one?'

'I guess not.' She held up the banknotes he'd given her. 'Then maybe I should go do some shopping,' she said.

II

'Hush, girl,' said Zehra Inzanoğlu, as her granddaughter stood on the road and continued to bawl. 'Enough.' But Katerina didn't stop, except to take in more breath so that she could howl all the louder.

Indignation roiled Zehra's heart. How could her son do this to her? She was too old. Her parenting was done. Yet what could she do? She looked around. She couldn't see any of her neighbours watching but she knew they would be, if only because she'd be watching them were their situations reversed.

And still Katerina howled.

Village life was a delicate affair. Everyone knew each other's business, yet they also soon learned where they could and couldn't tread. But then something new came along and suddenly all those tacit boundaries broke down, and people would ask their intrusive questions again. They'd make judgements. Zehra couldn't face that again. She just couldn't. Besides, a girl of Katerina's age should be at school. Yes. The thought was clarifying to her. She needed to return her to her home, find someone there to look after her. The Professor, perhaps. They wouldn't have arrested *him*. And it would serve him right for introducing her son to that Greek whore in the first place. Her chin jutted with the rightness of it.

The bus wouldn't run again that day, she couldn't afford a taxi and asking a neighbour for a lift would mean having to explain and thus justify herself. She'd rather die. She went instead to her son's car. His keys were still in the ignition; his wallet and mobile phone were on the dash. The car was a manual, however, and Zehra had only ever driven automatics. On the other hand, she knew the basic principle: you started them in second gear and then drove them as though they were very, very bad automatics.

She went inside to pack a bag, in case the Professor wasn't home. When she came back out, Katerina was still bawling. Her persistence was astonishing. 'Hush,' she said crossly, belting her in to the passenger seat. 'I'm taking you home. That's what you want, isn't it?' But Katerina just carried on. Bitter thoughts filled her mind as she climbed behind the wheel, turned on the ignition and tried various combinations of pedals while heaving at the gear-stick, until finally it slotted into place. Then she took her foot off the brake and began bunny-hopping on her way.

III

A police horse whinnied in the street outside the Prime Ministerial offices, then did a little leftwards dance before lifting its tail and venting its bowels in a massive, noisy movement exactly as Deniz Baştürk was getting out of his car, providing the pack of press photographers across the street with the perfect visual metaphor for his premiership. And no one to blame but himself, for the horses were his idea, a way to increase security without making it look like they were turning into a police state.

A car pulled up behind. Iskender Aslan, his Minister of the Interior. 'Prime Minister,' he called out, hurrying to catch up. 'May I ask what this—'

'Inside, Iskender.'

'But I—'

'Inside,' said Baştürk.

They found the Chief of the General Staff waiting in the antechamber. General Kemal Yilmaz typically wore suits in Ankara, as befitted a civilian city, but he'd been supervising exercises when the call had come, and so was in uniform today. 'All those ribbons,' mocked Aslan. 'You must be very brave.'

'They award most of them to anyone who serves,' replied Yilmaz. 'I'm sure you have plenty of your own.'

'Gentlemen, please,' said the Prime Minister. He motioned them through into his private office, made their aides wait outside. This wasn't the kind of talk that wanted witnesses. 'Nine mass-casualty bombings in three months,' he began, walking to his desk. 'Twenty in the past year.'

'The terrorists are to blame for that, Prime Minister,' said Aslan. 'Not my ministry or the police. We're doing all we can. And we're making real progress. We have already made a number of highly significant arrests in Cyprus this afternoon.'

'Ah, yes, all these highly significant arrests of yours. You tell me about them after every bomb. Then you quietly release them a week later for lack of evidence. So what good are these arrests when the bombings don't merely continue, but get worse? They're saying thirty people. Thirty people!' He sat down, as much to calm himself as anything, then looked back and forth between them. 'You may have seen me on television earlier. I assured the nation that we operate a joined-up government, that you two were already working together on this. Is that even faintly true? Are you working together?'

The two men glanced coolly at each other. Their mutual

loathing was an open secret. 'I saw your briefing, Prime Minister,' said General Yilmaz. 'As you made clear, counterterrorism is rightly a job for the police, not the army.'

'And we don't need the army's help,' added Aslan. 'All things considered, we're making commendable progress in—'

Baştürk slapped the table. 'Commendable progress!' he mocked. He let silence fall again, then said: 'I don't care what history you two have. I don't care about turf wars or saving face. This is a crisis.' He dropped his eyes a little, for all three of them knew that this was merely his own exercise in arse-covering, so that his earlier statement wouldn't be proven a lie. 'General Yilmaz helped defeat the terrorists last time it got this bad. He knows the Syrians and he fought in the Cyprus campaign. So I want you to take advantage of his experience, Iskender. Is that clear?'

'But we—'

'Is that clear?'

'Yes, Prime Minister.'

'Several of my old team are still in the service,' Yilmaz told Aslan. 'Perhaps I could have them seconded to you? To observe and advise only. That way we wouldn't overstep any constitutional boundaries. And, who knows, your team may even find their new perspective helpful.'

'Minister?'

Iskender Aslan flushed. If he said yes and things

improved, people would credit the army. If things continued or got worse, it would be because he hadn't accepted enough help. But he had no choice. 'Of course, Prime Minister.'

'Excellent,' said Baştürk, hurrying to his feet and walking Aslan to the door before he could think up some objection. 'Thank you so much for coming by. Now I need a quick word with General Yilmaz on that other matter.'

'That other matter?' frowned the Minister. 'But I thought we'd agreed to leave it until—'

'Did you?' asked Baştürk politely. He closed the door on him then turned back to the General. 'Now, then,' he said. 'Let's talk riots.'

FIVE

I

Iain walked Karin down to the hotel lobby and pointed her to a nearby shopping street, then asked at reception about overnighting a package to the UK. He'd missed his window, however, so he asked instead for directions to a computer repair store, got sent across the river along the hospital road. A grizzled shopkeeper was hauling down rusted shutters with a hooked stick, a cigarette almost sideways in his mouth, as though he'd walked into a wall. He eyed Iain gloomily, but invited him inside. The place was dimly lit, as seemed appropriate for the computer morgue it resembled, shelves crowded with innards and peripherals. It would be easiest to have the man try to recover the footage for him, but it was too risky, so he bought himself a new laptop instead, plus a screwdriver and various other tools, then returned to the hotel.

Karin was still out shopping. He cleared space on the dressing table, opened up both laptops and transferred his old hard drive into the new machine. It wouldn't boot. That, sadly, was the extent of his computer skills, so he called the office, got put through to Robyn. 'I just heard,' she said. 'Poor Mustafa. I can't believe it. He was so nice.'

'I didn't know you knew him,' said Iain.

'I put him on our system.'

'Of course.' Iain rubbed his neck wearily. 'Listen,' he said. 'My laptop got pretty badly banged up. I'm sure you can imagine. But there's stuff on it I need.'

'What kind of stuff?'

'Footage.'

A moment's silence. 'My God. You think you got it?'

'It's possible. I'd like to find out.'

'Overnight it to me. I'll start on it first thing.'

'I missed last post,' he told her. 'And this needs doing fast. Can't you talk me through it?'

'You'd need a new laptop.'

'Already got one. And I've tried switching drives.'

'No luck?'

'No luck.'

'Then you're going to need some more equipment. And it won't be quick. Recovery could take a day, maybe longer.'

'I'm only after a few video-files.'

'It doesn't work like that. What we'll have to do is we'll have to send in a special program to copy every bit of salvageable information on your old hard drive over to your new one. Think of it as like a photographer at a crime scene. You don't know where the vital clue might be, right, so you photograph everything. But you won't have to stand over it or anything. The program will run by itself.'

'Okay. What will I need?'

'Get Skype if you don't already have it. And an external web-cam too, so that I can see what you're up to. Plus a CD-writer and some blank CDs and a—'

'Whoa!' he said. 'I need to write this down.' He fetched a pad and pen. 'Okay. Shoot.'

'An external web-cam. A CD-writer. Some blank CDs. An external hard-disk drive with as much capacity as you can get, because you're going to be sending everything to it. Oh, and does your room have a fan?'

'No. Air conditioning. Why?'

'You'll need to keep the disks cool. They'll seize up otherwise. Buy two computer fans to lay on top of them. And a couple of mouse-mats, to stop them vibrating.'

'What about software?'

'I'll email it to you. Burn it onto a CD then boot up your new laptop with it. Call me back once you're ready.'

'It won't be until morning. The shop's closed.'

'Try me on my mobile if I'm not in. And don't go yet. Maria wants a word.'

'Fine.' He sagged and fought a yawn, the day's adrenalin finally ebbing away. 'What about?'

'I think there's some issue with Mustafa's insurance.'

'Oh, hell,' he said, sitting up straight again. 'Put her on.'

II

'Riots, Prime Minister?' asked General Yilmaz.

'You know, I imagine, that the public service unions have called for a Day of Action this Friday to protest against the new wage and pension cuts.' It was why he'd gone to the Academy that afternoon: his son's concert was on Friday night, and so there was a chance that duty would keep Baştürk from it. 'Most of the other major unions have declared their support. And now various opposition parties have endorsed it too. There will be large marches and rallies here in Ankara and in Istanbul, and smaller ones all across the country. And they keep revising the estimates of attendees up. Because it's not only about pensions and the economy any more. It's about the bombs as well. People see us as ineffective. They see us as weak. So there'll be plenty of trouble-makers out to take advantage: anarchists, Marxists, criminal gangs, everyone with a grudge or a fondness for mayhem.'

'Then cancel the rallies.'

'On what grounds? We're supposed to be the party of the people, and the people are suffering. Deny them this opportunity to vent and it will only make things worse. Anyway, that's not the issue right now. The issue is that, what with everything else they're dealing with, the police are likely to be under extreme strain that day. Our friend the Minister insists that this proves how under-resourced he is, how he needs more officers. But it's only one day, and we're all having to make do with less.'

Yilmaz looked unhappy as he saw where this was heading. 'My men are soldiers,' he said. 'They aren't trained to police marches. You know that.'

'Yes. But they are trained to protect strategic sites, correct? And to provide personal protection to important figures? A great many police officers are currently employed on such duties. The Minister assures me that, if your troops were to take over various such tasks for the day, he could put enough additional officers on the streets to make the difference.'

Yilmaz frowned. 'Are you telling me you want this done, Prime Minister? Or are you telling me that you want me to draw up contingency plans in case it needs doing?'

'The latter. I don't like this any more than you do. But we need to be ready, in case.'

'As you wish, Prime Minister. I'll see to it myself.'

'Thank you, General.' Baştürk allowed himself a wry smile. 'If only my cabinet colleagues were as helpful as you are.'

'Are they not?'

'They want my job.' He let out a heavy sigh. His ministers were all potential rivals, so he couldn't talk of this to them; and he hated to worry his wife or his old friends with his woes, so he rarely got the opportunity to unburden himself. 'Let's face it, I only got this job because the last guy went so fast that none of the others were ready or quite strong enough to seize it for themselves. So they compromised on me as a kind of caretaker, because they knew I'd be easiest to get out later on.'

'I'm sure that's not true, Prime Minister.'

'We'll get on better, General, if you don't humour or flatter me.' Then he smiled. 'Or not to excess, at least.'

'Forgive me, Prime Minister,' said Yilmaz. 'I find it hard with politicians to know what constitutes excess.'

Baştürk laughed a little too loudly. The Chief of the General Staff made for refreshingly candid company, but he was also in mild awe of him, of his uniform and his war service, and he very much wanted him to like him. But he quickly turned serious again. 'I'm not under any illusions, you know. I can't fire any of my main rivals without sparking a civil war in the party. My government wouldn't last a week. *I* wouldn't last a week. I don't have the support. Nor can I go to the people. They think I'm competent and likeable enough, but they don't respect me, they don't love me, they wouldn't miss me.' He looked up for Yilmaz's opinion of his analysis. The General nodded fractionally. He felt himself droop a little, for it was only human to want such a bleak assessment rejected. 'I have a few months at the most to get done the things I want done. Maybe not even that. Sometimes I think I can hear the footsteps behind me. So if you should happen to hear anything . . .'

'If I hear anything, I will of course report it to the proper authorities.'

Baştürk gave a strained smile. 'The proper authorities are the ones that scare me.' He glanced meaningfully at the door. 'Our recent friend is a *very* ambitious man. In my more suspicious moments, I can't help but wonder if he's not tolerating or even encouraging a certain level of disorder simply to undermine me.'

Yilmaz frowned. 'Surely he'd only be undermining himself.'

'Except that in every interview he gives he insists that his problem is lack of powers and men. Yet every time we give him more of either, he uses them to bed himself further in, win himself more allies. When I think of all the information he now has access to . . . On each one of us.'

Yilmaz pursed his lips. Then he said: 'You are not the only person seeking to do the best they can for the institution they are privileged to lead, Prime Minister. I don't have to remind you of the modern history of the army in Turkey. Four coups in fifty years. Five, by some measures. Over three hundred officers and their associates recently convicted of attempting another. Those incidents have tarnished our reputation badly. Some would say disgraced it. As you know, the reason I was offered my current position – and the reason I accepted – was to make sure that nothing of that nature could ever happen again. That has to be my overriding purpose. If it should be suspected for one moment that the army was once again involved in deciding who should and shouldn't lead Turkey, that we were taking sides . . .'

Baştürk sighed. 'Yes,' he said. 'You're right. Of course you're right.'

'But if I can find a way to help without overstepping . . .' added Yilmaz.

'Thank you.' He shook his head despondently. 'You don't know what this job is like. No one does. Not until you sit at this desk for yourself.'

'Look on the bright side. You may not have it for much longer.'

Baştürk laughed a second time, albeit more ruefully this time. 'Thank you, General. I needed that.'

III

Iain was on hold for the best part of a minute before Maria came on. 'Hey,' she said.

'Hey yourself. What's up?'

'I've been on with Layla. Her sister can look after her daughters, but only for one day. So I've booked her a return flight tomorrow. She'll be arriving really early, but I said you'd meet her at the airport. I hope that's okay?'

'Of course. What time?'

She read out flight details. He jotted them down. 'There's something else,' she added, lowering her voice. 'I didn't tell Layla, but there seems to be an issue with Mustafa's insurance.'

'So Robyn said. What?'

'You know how all you guys need special coverage for whenever you go on missions? Well, we changed policies for our overseas associates at the start of the year, and I'm not sure—'

'We did *what*?'

'We changed policies. And the new one is basically workplace only. I don't think Mustafa's covered.'

Iain didn't speak for a moment. He didn't trust himself. The work they did was nothing like as dangerous as serving in a war zone, but it was dangerous enough. Their regional client-list read like a *Who's Who* of oil-and-gas oligarchs and other power-brokers, all engaged in fierce competition with each other, seeking information that they could use as leverage or even as weaponry to destroy; and although incidents of lethal violence were rare, they were far from unprecedented. 'Was this Quentin?' he asked finally.

'I don't know for sure,' she said reluctantly. 'But I think it must have been.'

'Put me through to him.'

'He's left for the day.'

'Then put me through to his mobile.'

'Iain, I'm not sure that's so wise right now, not until I've made sure—'

'I said put me fucking through.'

She gave a sigh, put him on hold. Quentin came on a few moments later, sounding as cheerful as ever, over Mustafa already. 'This'll have to be quick, old chap. I'm on my way to a meeting.'

'Is it true about the insurance?'

'Is what true?'

'That you downgraded our overseas offices all to workplace only?'

'Downgraded is a *very* loaded word,' said Quentin. Iain could hear someone angrily tooting a horn in the background. 'All I did was update our policies to something more appropriate to our new structure.'

'More appropriate,' said Iain. 'Cheaper, you mean.'

'This is a business I'm running, not a charity. Income is down. We're only profitable at all because I clamped down on unnecessary overheads.'

'Unnecessary?' exploded Iain. 'Since when has insurance been unnecessary?'

'You've no idea how expensive those policies were.'

'Yes. Because this is a dangerous fucking business we're in, particularly out in the field.'

'Uh, oh,' said Quentin. 'Tunnel.' The phone went dead in Iain's hand. He glared at it for a moment then made to hurl it against the wall, controlling himself only just in time.

'What is it? What's wrong?'

He looked around in surprise to see Karin in the doorway. In his distraction, he hadn't heard the door. 'My colleague,' he said. 'The one who was killed this morning. There's a problem with his insurance.'

'Oh, hell. Does he have family?'

'A wife. Two daughters.'

'Oh, hell,' she said again, coming over to touch him on his arm. 'What will you do?'

He shook his head. He couldn't face thinking about it tonight, not after everything else. 'I'll sort something out, I guess. But not right now. Right now I need something to eat. Fancy joining me?'

'Yes,' she said. 'I do.'

IV

It was dark by the time Georges Bejjani returned to the small fishing port of Kapisuyu. Lights on the boats and around the harbour walls reflected charmingly upon the ruffled water, while the light breeze made steel cables tinkle like wind-chimes against the masts of the pleasure boats. He walked briskly to the *Dido*'s berth, found his elder brother Michel waiting impatiently on deck. 'Where the hell have you been?' he demanded.

'Hospital.'

'Hospital?' Michel frowned over Georges' shoulder to look for Faisal and Sami. 'Is one of the guys hurt?'

'No. They're fine. They're parking the car.'

'Then why hospital?'

All his life, Georges had looked up to Michel. He was his elder brother, after all, and heir apparent to the Bejjani Group. But then Michel had let himself get played by a third-rate Mexican conman on a fictional property deal in Acapulco, losing the bank several hundred thousand dollars and making an international laughing stock of them all for a few months. The succession had thus been put in doubt, and suddenly Georges had discovered in himself an unexpected ambition. 'Perhaps I should explain to you and Father together. No point going through it twice.'

'Father's on with the executive committee. He won't want to be disturbed unless it's—'

'He'll want to be disturbed for this. Where is he? His cabin?' He didn't wait for an answer but made his way along the starboard deck to his father's suite. As Michel had indicated, he was on a conference call. He held up a finger to beg their silence for a moment then told his management team he had to go and that they'd pick it up again tomorrow. Then he rang off. 'About time,' he told Georges. 'Where have you been? Why didn't you call in?'

'The coverage in Antioch is terrible,' said Georges. Which was true enough, but he'd also turned off his mobile for tactical reasons, so that he'd have the chance to present his ideas and discoveries in person.

'Well? What have you learned?'

Georges sat in an armchair and stretched his legs out in front of him. In this world, the trick was always to look in command. 'I'm sure you've heard how they're saying the bomb was Cypriots. In which case, we don't need to worry about it. We can leave it to the police.'

Michel sighed theatrically. 'It's really taken you all afternoon to work that out?'

'We only need to worry if it *wasn't* Cypriots,' continued Georges imperturbably. 'We only need to worry if the bombers really were after Father. Imagine for a moment that that's the case. We all know how hard it is to kill a well-protected target with a car bomb, even one *that* big.' Every Lebanese citizen was painfully familiar with assassination techniques. 'You can't simply set a timer and then leave. The kill zone is small and you have to make sure your target is in it when you detonate. That means having line of sight not just on the bomb itself but on all the possible approaches too. And the only way to guarantee that is by being on the spot. Which makes it a dangerous business, because you'll be in the danger zone yourself should it trigger early for any reason. And, if this one was meant for Father, then by definition it triggered early.'

Butros nodded thoughtfully. 'You think the bomber was caught in his own blast?'

'I thought it worth exploring,' agreed Georges. 'So we tailed an ambulance to Antioch hospital, where they've taken all the victims. Then it was a matter of finding a friendly nurse willing to sell us a casualty list.'

'And?'

'One of the dead men was called Mustafa Habib,' said Georges. 'Executive manager of the Istanbul branch of a British company called Global Analysis. According to their website, they provide business intelligence services to multinational corporations.'

'Company spies,' muttered Butros. He glanced at his elder son. 'Are they the ones your London friends warned you about?'

'They only told me they'd been approached themselves,' answered Michel. 'They didn't know who if anyone had been hired.'

'Anything else?' Butros asked Georges.

'Mustafa Habib wasn't alone. He had a companion with him. This companion gave his card to a paramedic in case they should need to contact him. His name is Iain Black. He is director of Global Analysis's Middle-Eastern operations. Which makes it all but certain they were in Daphne on a job.'

'A job!' scoffed Michel. 'They were there for us. They set that fucking bomb.'

Butros shook his head. 'What kind of assassin takes business cards on a hit with him? What kind of assassin would then give one to a paramedic?'

'You're not suggesting it was coincidence, are you?' protested Michel. 'I don't believe it.'

'Nor me.' He brooded a few moments before he came to his decision. 'Michel,' he said. 'Get in touch with your London friends. Have them find out what they can about this man Black and his company Global Analysis. Their clients, their reputation, their range of services. But discreetly, discreetly. I don't want them knowing we're onto them.' He turned back to Georges. 'I want to talk with this man Black myself. I want to look him in the eye when I ask him what he was doing at the hotel. I want to look him in the eye when I ask him if he tried to kill me.'

'You're not leaving the boat, Father,' said Georges. 'Not until we know what's going on.'

'Then perhaps we should invite him here for lunch tomorrow.'

'As you wish, Father,' said Georges. 'But what if he says no?'

Butros smiled thinly. 'I really wasn't thinking of that kind of invitation,' he said.

V

Iain and Karin chose a restaurant close to the hotel, too weary to explore further. They sat upstairs on an open roof terrace of polished terracotta tiles hedged by potted cypresses. Few tables were taken; the atmosphere was subdued. Every so often voices would be raised in anger, not only against the bombers, but also against the perceived feebleness of the government's response. Everyone seemed agreed that someone new was needed to take up the fight; someone with the stomach to do whatever was necessary to restore order. And everyone seemed keen to take part in Friday's Day of Action.

They ordered beers that arrived already poured into miniature brass tankards, to protect the sensibilities of their more devout customers. They clinked them together in a dull toast then tried some small talk, but it proved hard work and Karin soon fell into an introspective silence.

'Tell me about him,' prompted Iain.

'About who?'

'Your boss. His assistant. Whichever one it is you're thinking of.'

Karin shook her head. 'I really didn't know Rick all that well.'

'Nathan, then. What was he like?'

'He was fine. He was nice. He was *rich*.' She gave a sad smile. 'I don't mean that in a bad way. It's simply that some people have so much money it becomes part of who they are. You can't describe them without it.'

'How do you mean?'

'I don't know. I guess I used to think of money as something you bought stuff with. That the more money you had, the more stuff you could buy. But it's not like that, not when you're born into an oil dynasty, as Nathan was. At that level, it's more like a force. Like gravity. It shapes the world and everyone bends to it, whether they want to or not.'

Iain looked curiously at her. 'Including you?' he asked.

'You know us Dutch?' she said. 'How tolerant we are. Live and let live, all that shit? Well, my family isn't like that. Not one bit. My parents are very Calvinist. They raised us to think a certain way: that money was slightly disgusting, that hard work should be its own reward. And so I worked hard. I studied history at Leiden. I got a good degree, good enough that I was offered the chance

70

to go study at the University of Texas in Austin. They had an excellent programme there, right in my area. I was offered a partial scholarship too, so that at least my tuition was paid for. But it's still an expensive business, being a student in America. I had to take on a crazy amount of debt, which my parents were *not* happy about, let me tell you. Anyway, I got to know Nathan while I was there, because he was the one sponsoring the programme. It was on the Homeric Question, you see, which was his thing too. And he saw how stretched I was with my studying and my bar-jobs, so he hired me as a sort of PA to help him manage his collection and deal with museums on his behalf, that kind of thing. But the work was pretty light and really it was another way for him to support my research, you know?'

'Yes.'

'So eventually I got my doctorate and then Leiden offered me a job. It wasn't exactly what I'd wanted but it was a start, a foot in the door. For some reason, however, Nathan decided he wanted me to stay and work for him full-time. He offered me twice what Leiden were. I said no. So he offered me quadruple.'

'He must have thought highly of you.'

'Yes. But I think also he wanted to demonstrate something. I'd been so *pleased* at the Leiden job, you see. And my attitude towards money always amused him. The *rectitude* of it. All that hard work bravely done shit. This will sound awful, but I think he wanted to corrupt me a little. And he had so much money that my salary was effectively meaningless to him. Like filling a thimble from his lake. So he kept offering me more and more until finally I said yes. It was all that student debt; suddenly I could pay it off.' She sat back in her chair as their main course arrived: succulent charred lamb kebabs garnished with yoghurt, onions, tomatoes and eye-watering peppers. 'But the thing about a big salary is that you start taking it for granted. You think it's what you're worth. So instead of paying down your debt, you rent yourself a nice apartment, you lease a car, you fly home four times a year. Which was stupid, because no one else would ever have paid me half what Nathan did. I was his friend as much as his employee. I was his escort for openings and family events. It got so that people began to talk. I tried to ignore all that. I mean, Christ, he was as old as my grandmother. Literally.' She took a deep breath, looked defiantly at Iain. 'Last Christmas, he asked me to marry him.'

Iain nodded. He'd guessed something of the sort. 'What did you say?'

'I said no. I told him I was fond of him, but not like that. He kept at it. It seemed almost like a game to him. He kept making exploratory little advances. Like he'd buy me gifts small enough that I'd have been churlish to refuse them. But then the next gift would be a little bigger, so how could I fuss about that after accepting the one before. Or he'd touch my elbow in public. Then my shoulder and my back. Or he'd tease me and call me pet names. That kind of thing. And whenever I tried to draw a line for him, he'd joke about my salary, only not altogether a joke, you know. Once you've grown used to a good income, the prospect of losing it is a bit like vertigo.'

'I can imagine.'

'Anyway, it got so that everyone took it for granted that we were secretly engaged. You should have seen the looks his children used to dart at me. Like they *hated* me.'

'Ah,' said Iain. 'That dickhead on the phone earlier.'

'Julian. Nathan's eldest son. It's hard to blame him too much. Even by his own telling, Nathan must have been a truly shitty father. He whored around until his wife finally had had enough and walked out on him, taking the kids with her. They grew up angry with him, as you can imagine; justice matters so much when you're young. But then they grew older and realized where the money was.'

'So they came crawling back?'

'And he despised them for it, I think. Even though he'd inherited the company himself. And, God, he could be cruel. He'd get them to tell stories against themselves and against their mother, that kind of thing. Muse aloud about leaving everything to some absurd charity or other, or marrying again and starting a new family.'

73

'But now they'll get to inherit after all,' observed Iain. 'No wonder Julian sounded like he was off to pop some corks. After all that worry.'

'Yes.'

Iain allowed himself the faintest of smiles. 'You don't suppose he could have been worried enough to have had his father killed, do you?'

SIX

I

Karin looked at Iain in consternation. 'Have his father killed? What are you talking about?'

'Someone set off a bomb today,' said Iain. 'You said yourself the crater was directly beneath his room. Maybe it really was Cypriot reunificationists out to inflict carnage for the cause. But isn't it possible that it was a murder made to look like terrorism? That your boss was the real target?'

'No.' She shook her head emphatically. 'His children aren't angels, but they're not like that. They *couldn't* be. Anyway, Nathan only decided to come here two weeks ago. And he didn't tell his family until a couple of days before we left. You'd need far more time than that to set up something like this halfway across the world.'

'What if they had more time? What if they had weeks? Even months?'

'Aren't you listening? He only decided to come two weeks ago.'

Iain reached across the table to touch the back of her hand. 'Don't get mad at me. I'm only speculating. I don't know Julian and these others. I owe them nothing. But I do owe Mustafa the truth. So put yourself in the shoes of one of Nathan's sons. He hates his father for all the shit he's made him eat. He sees him falling for you and now he's panicked too. Maybe he's a gambler. Maybe he has a high-maintenance mistress. He *needs* his inheritance. He needs it *now*. So he decides to act. But getting at his father isn't easy. Rick was his *head* of security, correct? Not just a bodyguard. So he obviously took his personal protection pretty damned seriously, right? Getting to him in America was sure to have been hard. And he'd likely have been near the top of the suspects list. But what if he could lure Nathan somewhere he'd be vulnerable? He's a collector. Dangle the right piece in front of him and he'd be on the first plane. And if he was killed by some random atrocity while he was here, no one would look at it twice.'

She shook her head. 'And all those other people? Collateral damage?'

'He wouldn't necessarily have planned it that way. He could have hired a hitman and left the method up to him. It wouldn't be the first time. Some of the gangs here are notoriously ruthless. There's this group of ultra-nationalists called the Grey Wolves who . . .' He frowned, sat back in his chair, scratched his neck thoughtfully.

'What is it?' she asked.

Iain didn't answer at once. There was something darkly familiar about all this, he suddenly realized: about the worsening terrorism, the hapless government response, the growing public clamour for decisive action. But surely all that belonged to Turkey's buried past. 'Nothing,' he said. 'A weird déjà vu, that's all.'

'What about?'

'I can't really talk about it.'

She tipped her head quizzically to one side. 'You have a past,' she said.

'Who doesn't?'

'Tell me.'

'I'd rather not.'

'I told you mine.'

He sighed and splayed fingers on the starched white tablecloth. 'I was in the army kind of thing for a few years.'

That made her smile. 'The army kind of thing?'

'Afghan, Iraq, a bunch of other places. I saw the usual horrible things. I did the usual horrible things. It got to me. I left. Now I'm a business consultant. Nice, safe and boring, you know. All that shit well behind me. Until today. Until Mustafa.' He shook his head. 'Let's not talk about it, eh? Not tonight. There must be happier topics.'

'Fine,' smiled Karin. 'You lay off Nathan's kids, I'll forget the army kind of thing. Deal?'

'Deal.'

'Then what do we talk about?'

'How about this Homeric Question of yours,' said Iain. 'Surely it can't get any safer than that.'

II

The drive to Nicosia was gruelling. Zehra Inzanoğlu kept so far to the left-hand lane that her passenger-side wheels sporadically left the tarmac altogether and she'd bump her way over mud and loose chippings for a second or two before correcting herself, sometimes too sharply. Cars, minivans and lorries sped past in a blur of head-lights, tooting resentfully at her slow crawl. She tried once to change up to third gear, but metallic harpies screeched at her from beneath the bonnet and she veered dangerously from her lane and almost side-swiped an overtaking bus whose indignant blare unnerved her all the more and turned Katerina stiff as a shop mannequin in the seat beside her.

Zehra had intended to drive straight to the Professor's house and thrash it out with him that night, but she was simply too shattered by the time they reached Nicosia's outskirts. She therefore followed signs to her son's neighbourhood instead then had Katerina direct her in. His apartment block was run-down and ugly, its car park a patch of deeply rutted earth. The lift wouldn't answer repeated summons so they trudged wearily upwards with their bags instead. Zehra's spirits sank as they climbed. How could anyone choose to live in a city? Lift doors opened and closed continuously above her. She could hear men whispering. Something wasn't right. She called out. Footsteps came scampering down towards them; two youths in leather jackets with collars up, cans of spray-paint in their hands, their laughter now echoing up from beneath.

A red plastic chair was lodged between the lift doors on her son's floor, stopping them from closing. The landing lights were poor, the red spray-paint moist and dripping. Instantly, Zehra was swept back forty years. Then, the slurs had been aimed at her father, not her son; and in Greek, not Turkish. Yet the message was the same. And an immense gloom settled upon her, a sense of troubles not her own, yet which threatened to snare her even so.

III

'The Homeric Question,' said Karin doubtfully. 'Are you sure?'

'At least tell me what it is. Maybe I'll be able to answer it for you. Or is that what you're scared of? That I'll put you out of a job.'

'I'm out of a job already.'

'Shit. Sorry. Yeah.' He raised his empty tankard at a passing waiter to request refills. 'But tell me anyway.'

'It's not that simple,' said Karin. 'For a start, it's really a series of questions rather than a single one. Who was Homer? Where was he born? When? Where did he live? How old was he when he composed his various works? Which of the places he wrote about had he visited? Who and what were his sources? Was he a woman?'

Iain laughed. 'Really?'

'Really. And was there only one of her, or was it a family enterprise, passed down from parent to child?' She sat forward in her chair as she got into her subject, her cadence quickening and her eyes brightening; and Iain could soon see exactly why Nathan had bid so fiercely for her services. Enthusiasm became harder to generate yourself as you grew older, but you could still warm yourself on the radiated enthusiasm of others. 'Or maybe Homer was simply an honorific title, like "bard",' she said. 'There are some reasons to think that the *Iliad* and the *Odyssey* were composed by different people, for example.'

'Like what?'

'Style. Vocabulary. Attitudes towards races. Homer praises the Phoenicians in the *Iliad*, for example, but then derides them in the *Odyssey*. And the *Odyssey* also pokes fun at the *Iliad*, which is odd if he wrote them both.'

'Maybe he didn't take himself too seriously,' said Iain.

'Of course,' she agreed. 'There are all kinds of explanations. That's why people like me argue about it. But there are other questions too. More to do with the general history of the era. The ones I studied for my thesis, and which Nathan was particularly interested in.'

'And what are those?'

'How his books were even possible. You see, the Trojan War, if it really happened, which is a big debate all in itself, took place towards the end of the Late Bronze Age. Somewhere around 1200 BC, give or take. Yet the *Iliad* and the *Odyssey* weren't composed until the Early Iron Age: 800 BC at the earliest, more likely nearer to 700 BC or even later.' It wasn't merely enthusiasm either; it was command, authority. Iain had always had a weakness for smart women confident in their expertise. Watching Karin now, he had a sudden, vivid flashback, waking up weak and dazed to find a tall woman of angular beauty standing beside his bed in a loose white medic's coat, frowning down at him as she jotted notes upon a clipboard.

'So we've got this gap of around four hundred years to explain,' Karin was saying. 'And not any old years. There was a terrible dark age between the Late Bronze and the Early Iron. Do you know about this?'

He'd collapsed, apparently. On a flight back from

Pakistan. And, because he'd been delirious with some strange fever, and thus liable to say something indiscreet about his mission, they'd summoned a specialist in exotic diseases with an appropriate level of clearance. 'Assume I know nothing,' he told Karin. 'You can't go far wrong that way.'

'Okay. Then this is one of the great mysteries of the ancient world. During the fourteenth and thirteenth centuries BC, the eastern Mediterranean was reasonably stable. Roughly speaking, Greece and the Aegean were ruled by a loose confederation of Mycenaean kings; the Hittites ran Turkey; the New Kingdom Pharaohs had Egypt and Israel; and the Assyrians ran Syria, Iraq and Iran. Then something terrible happened. The trouble is, we don't know what. Archaeologists call it the Catastrophe, but mainly that's because it sounds cool and what else can you call it? But, whatever it was, it scared the shit out of people.'

Her name had been Tisha Morgan. A professor of microbiology brought in from her London research institute to diagnose his condition, then cure him of it. Scrawny, Mustafa had called her. And maybe so. But what Iain had mostly noticed about her at the time was how fully she'd committed herself to his cause. It was why she'd gone into research, she'd later confided to him; because she'd been prone to get too attached to her wards, and therefore took it too hard when she lost them. 'How can you tell?'

'By excavating old cities like Tiryns and Mycenae,' explained Karin. 'They *massively* strengthened their fortifications. They built huge storerooms and dug deep wells or secret underground passages to nearby springs. All classic signs that they feared something bad. But it did them no good. They pretty much all got sacked and burned. And this wasn't only in Greece. Same thing across the whole eastern Med, from the Hittites here in Turkey all the way down to Egypt. And no one knows what or who or why.'

With Tisha's help, he'd soon overcome his fever. Getting over her, however, had proved somewhat harder. After his discharge from hospital, he'd fought the urge to go see her, telling himself he was being stupid, that there was no way they could fit into each other's lives, that there were plenty of other women out there. But he couldn't shake the feeling and finally he'd succumbed. He'd visited her at her institute. They'd taken coffee together in a nearby café. The next day too. On both occasions, she'd mentioned her surgeon boyfriend about once every minute, in that half-conscious way people touch a lucky charm in times of stress. But it had done her little good. 'You must have some idea,' he said. 'I mean, didn't the Greeks invent history? Surely they had something to say about it?'

'Not as much as you'd think,' said Karin. 'They kind of glossed over it, skipping straight from the age of heroes to the archaic age, despite the centuries in between. But then they weren't very good with chronology. There are hints of a mysterious tribe called the Dorians invading from the north of Greece, setting off a cascade of displaced people in which each went pillaging the next. A lot of people think that the Trojan War was part of it. And maybe the *Odyssey* too. There's a bit in there that seems to describe a famous battle fought by the Egyptians against invaders known as the Sea Peoples. Trouble is, there's no real evidence of these Dorians, or of any new arrivals. The opposite, if anything.'

Their marriage had lasted three wonderful years. He'd become a father, which had changed him in ways he'd never have imagined possible. He'd been inside Iran when this idyll had abruptly ended, courtesy of an overworked truck driver on a damp and foggy night. The importance of his mission and the difficulty of exfiltration had persuaded his handler neither to inform him nor to pull him out early. It had been the correct tactical decision, the decision he'd probably have made himself had the roles been switched, yet it had been a betrayal all the same. And though he'd returned to active service afterwards, in an effort to slough off his encasing grief, his heart had never again been in it. He'd begun to cast a jaundiced eye not merely at the fine expressions of intent behind his missions, but at the consequences of them too. And he'd grown to hate the things he'd seen. His own bereavement, to put it crudely, had sapped his will to maim and kill. And so he'd quit.

'You see, what's so remarkable is how little changed. Three to four hundred years of absolute turmoil, yet the Greek world emerged from it still recognizably Greek. The Hittites were succeeded by neo-Hittites, the Phoenicians by more Phoenicians, the New Kingdom Pharaohs by Late Period Pharaohs, the Assyrians by neo-Assyrians. All still in the same places, worshipping the same gods, speaking much the same languages, crafting the same kinds of goods with the same materials and techniques. So maybe a terrible region-wide famine caused a bunch of local resource wars; except we can find precious little evidence for that either. Earthquakes, then, except that earthquakes simply don't happen on that scale. They may take out an island or a province, but not the whole Mediterranean.'

Life after the army had proved hard for Iain. Without Tisha and Robbie to give him purpose, a dreadful lassitude had set in. He'd lain on his sofa, drinking beer, watching daytime TV, loathing himself for not having been there when his family had most needed him, sinking into the downward spiral that had claimed so many of his former comrades, half of whom now seemed to be Born Again, while the other half were drunks. A long, hard look in the mirror one hung-over morning had finally jolted him into action. He'd cut out the booze, got himself fit, sent his CV to anyone in the market for his particular skills, eventually joining Global Analysis. And time had done its usual healing. These past few months, in fact, he'd finally begun to feel better about the world. Like glimpses of blue sky on a dull day, an unfamiliar sensation would sometimes spread right through him, and he'd realize to his mild surprise that it was happiness. Yet, in one way, he hadn't moved on at all. Despite the efforts of well-meaning friends to fix him up, the few dates he'd been on since Tisha had had all the spark of a wet match struck against a wet box; so that tonight was the first time in years that he'd felt even the possibility of flame. 'How about a tsunami?' he suggested.

'Maybe,' nodded Karin. 'Except much of the destruction happened inland; and, afterwards, people settled on the coast, which you'd hardly do if you were scared of tidal waves. Besides, these cities were *burned*. I know you might expect earthquakes to knock over candles and oil lamps and so start fires, but actually it doesn't work that way because—' She broke off, however, looked around. They'd been talking so long that the restaurant was empty, except for staff leaning wearily against the walls, waiting to close up for the night. 'We should go,' she said.

'Yeah,' he agreed. 'We should.'

SEVEN

I

It made for a long day, wondering whether you'd killed one person, five people, fifty. But, once Asena and Hakan had found themselves caught between police roadblocks, they'd had no alternative but to hole up in a tumbledown farmer's hut and wait them out.

The roadblock had lasted only a couple of hours beyond nightfall. No stamina, these rural police. They'd got back on her Kawasaki and headed on their way. A first drizzle at the forest fringes quickly turned into a downpour that made the track treacherous with mud and puddles and sodden leaf litter. With Asena's rear tyre a little bald, and Hakan riding pillion, it kept sliding out of her control, so that they both kept having to thrust out their feet to stay upright. But they arrived at last at the lair of the Grey Wolves, eight large wooden huts hidden from spy planes and satellites by thick camouflage nets. She drove past the armoury, gave the engine a final roar as she pulled up between the horse-box and the other trucks, enough to bring Bulent, Uğur, Şükrü, Oguzhan and various others out of their cabins, most holding waterproofs above their heads. 'Well?' she asked, embracing them briskly in turn. 'What news?'

'A success,' nodded Bulent, but soberly.

Asena felt a twinge. Success was such a loaded term for operations like these. 'How many?' she asked.

'Thirty-one so far,' said Uğur. 'Thirty-one and counting.'

'Thirty-one?' protested Hakan, appalled. 'But you promised me we'd—'

'That was a bomb we set off today,' said Asena sharply, before he could finish. 'Not a fucking hand-grenade.'

'I know. But—'

'One, two, ten, a hundred?' snapped Asena. 'What does it really matter? This is a war we're fighting. A war for the soul of our nation. Or have you forgotten?' She glared around at them all, daring one of them to challenge her authority. No one did. She stalked into the main cabin, poured two fingers of raki into a glass then splashed in water to turn it cloudy. Lion's milk, they called it: *aslan suku*. She held it up as if in a toast then knocked it back and poured herself another. She could hear Hakan muttering with the others outside, but right now she didn't care. Let them grumble if they must. As long as they obeyed.

The glass casings of the oil lamps, blackened with soot, threw eerie shadows on the wooden walls. These cabins were fitted with electric lights, but they only used their generator once a day, to recharge batteries and put a chill on the deep freeze. She rinsed her plate, poured herself a third glass of lion's milk. The rain had stopped, but still drip-dripped rhythmically from the eaves. Wolves howled in the distance. They were in good voice tonight. Usually the sound cheered her with its hint of camaraderie, as if some higher power was letting her know the justice of her cause. But tonight it merely made her feel all the more alone.

The Lion and the Wolf.

The milk wasn't going to be enough. She needed to talk to the man himself. She needed his assurance that those thirty-one lives and counting had been necessary. She went to her room, set up her satellite phone, pinged out an encrypted message. Ten minutes dragged by. Nothing happened. His job kept him absurdly busy and he had to be extravagantly careful about how and when he contacted her. She understood this intellectually yet she resented it all the same. The things she was doing for him, he should find the time. Today, of all days, he should find the—

Her screen blinked. A black box appeared. In the box,

his face, grey-lit and jerky and craggy, yet so handsome withal that he still had the power to lift her heart. 'My love,' she said.

'What is it?' he asked, glancing at his watch.

His brusqueness hurt her. 'I only wanted to know if today went as you'd hoped,' she said. 'And if there were any ramifications we needed to know about.'

'Today went as hoped. There are no ramifications you need to know about. I'll notify you through the usual channels if that should change.'

'Only you never said this morning what it was we—'

'It had to be done,' he said. 'That's all you need to know.'

'Thirty-one people,' she said. 'Thirty-one and counting.'

'It was necessary.'

'So you said. But why?'

'I can't tell you.' He looked uncomfortable for the first time. 'Please trust me.'

She shook her head, but only because she was unhappy. 'I hate this,' she said. 'I want it to be over.'

'It won't be much longer,' he said. 'A few months at the very most and then we'll be together forever, with everything we've worked for. Our nation will be free again. And your father too, don't forget.' He checked his watch again. 'But right now I have to go.' He softened the message with a smile. 'You may have heard that a bomb went off today.'

'Call me tomorrow,' she said.

'If I can.'

'No,' she said. 'Call me tomorrow.'

He nodded seriously. 'As you wish.'

She reached out and touched his cheek upon her screen. 'The Lion and the Wolf,' she said.

He nodded and touched his own screen. 'The Lion and the Wolf.'

II

Somehow, during the course of their meal, sharing a room with Karin had become an issue for Iain to manage. They fell into a slightly awkward silence on their way back to the hotel. Their footsteps synchronized on the pavement, that heel-and-toe cadence that sounds weirdly like heartbeats. The receptionist gave a curious frown as she wished them good night, and the lift seemed a bit more cramped than it had while coming down earlier.

He let Karin into the room ahead of him, the better to follow her cues. She invited him to use the bathroom first. He did so. When it came to her turn, he heard the toilet flushing, the running of a tap, the vigorous brushing of her teeth. She came out wearing his olive T-shirt, its hem hanging loose around her thighs like some skimpy miniskirt. 'Christ,' he said. 'Never looks like that on me.'

'The lights,' she said.

He switched them off. She slipped beneath her duvet. The room was on the hotel's top floor and had a sloped skylight in place of a window. The weak moonlight and the white net curtain that drooped across it meant that all he could see was various gradations of darkness. He turned onto his side to face her, propped himself up on an elbow. 'So you were telling me about earthquakes,' he said. 'How they don't cause fires like you'd expect.'

'Wasn't I boring you?'

'Are you kidding? I'll never get to sleep until I know.'

He heard her laughter, then rustling as she too turned onto her side. Strange to think that they were facing each other a few feet apart, yet blind. 'Okay,' she said. 'These places were mostly built of stone. Their citadels, at least. Even if an oil lamp tipped over, there was nothing to catch fire, certainly not enough to spread. Sometimes a conquering army would want to burn a city as punishment, or to send out a message, but actually it was a real production. They had to cut down nearby forests and drag the trees into the city then spread them around the houses before it would catch. A lot of work, especially when you consider a city was a valuable thing. Even if you didn't want to live there yourself, you could squeeze the citizens for tribute. So why burn it? Yet we have numerous examples.'

'A game of tit for tat?' he suggested. 'Only it got out of hand.'

'That's one theory,' she agreed. 'But these places are scattered all over the place, so it's hard to fit them to a pattern. Usually, in history, you can build a narrative that makes some kind of sense. It may be wrong, but it helps you think about it until something better comes along. Not with this. And, even if it did, it still wouldn't explain how *brutal* the Dark Ages were. Everything collapsed. Cities were abandoned, and not only the burned ones. There was a *massive* depopulation. In some places, the lack of archaeological remains suggest that populations fell by ninety per cent or more. *Ninety per cent!* And this lasted twenty generations, give or take. Think about that: How much do you know about your family twenty generations ago? Especially as this wasn't normal, settled life, but nomadic scavenging and hard-scrabble farming under constant threat of raiders stealing your winter stores. Yet somehow, at the end of it, Homer managed to depict the Trojan War almost as though he'd been there.'

'I thought you said the Trojan War may not even have happened.'

'Yes. But the world in which it was set existed. He knows the names of Mycenaean kingdoms that no longer existed. He depicts their armour and weaponry, their ships, tactics, gods, rituals, terrain and burial customs. He's not perfect, sure, and there's plenty of later stuff mixed in, but he's still far more accurate than he had any right to be. How?'

The room was as dark as before, yet suddenly he glimpsed something like movement in the darkness, almost as if Karin were reaching out her hand to him across the narrow aisle. He reached out, curious, to check; but it proved a mirage. Nothing but empty space. 'And that's the Homeric Question?' he asked.

'Yes,' she said. 'That's the Homeric Question.'

EIGHT

I

Iain slept poorly that night. It had been a while since he'd shared a bedroom, and he found himself vaguely unsettled by Karin's proximity, her breathing, the occasional rustle of her bedclothes. But his restlessness had other causes too. Twinges in his ribs each time he shifted reminded him of the battering he'd taken from the restroom door. Unhappy thoughts of Mustafa and the day's other victims interwoven with older memories of similar scenes in different places. And, underlying it all, the fear of oversleeping, of being late for Layla. It was almost a relief, therefore, when it neared time for him to get up. He turned off his alarm-clock in anticipation so that Karin could sleep on. He rose, washed and dressed as quietly as he could, then wrote her a note to assure her she was welcome to stay on as long as it took to sort herself out.

The sky was milky with dawn, the roads so empty that he reached Hatay Airport in barely twenty minutes. The terminal seemed disconcertingly normal, as though yesterday's carnage had never happened. Layla was on the first flight in. He met her by the gate. Her eyes were raw from weeping and she cried again when she saw him waiting. He put his arms around her and murmured what small comforts he could think of until she'd composed herself again.

They were silent on the drive in. Layla was lost in private thoughts and he couldn't think of anything to say. The hospital was an ugly green block on Antioch's western fringe. He parked in an adjacent street and led her inside. They asked directions to the morgue, an unmarked low grey building standing all by itself. Layla took his arm to stop him before they went in. 'Was yesterday anything to do with you?' she asked. 'With your work, I mean?'

'They're saying it was Cypriots.'

'I know what they're saying. That's not what I'm asking.'

Iain sighed. 'I don't know,' he told her. 'Not for certain.'

'It's possible, then?'

'Yes. It's possible.'

'Find out. I need to know.'

'Yes.'

'Thank you.' She opened the morgue door then stood there blocking him for a few moments, her head down, as if debating with herself whether to speak or not. 'When we were on the phone yesterday,' she said, at last, 'suddenly you weren't there any more.'

'I lost coverage. The masts were overloaded.'

'Yes. I thought that was it. But you didn't call back. I waited and waited and you didn't call back.'

'I told you,' said Iain. 'I'd lost coverage.'

'You called Maria,' she said. 'You asked her to get in touch with me. How did you manage that without coverage?' She waited for him to answer, but he looked helplessly at her. 'There's no need to wait,' she told him. 'I can take a taxi back to the airport when I'm done.'

'It's no trouble,' he said.

But Layla shook her head. 'I'll take a taxi,' she said.

II

The reports on Global Analysis and Iain Black had arrived from London during the night. Michel Bejjani printed out copies for his father and brother to digest along with their breakfast. He handed Georges his with a certain satisfaction then scooped up a generous dollop of *tahini* with a strip of pita bread and gestured for some coffee.

Until recently, there'd been no question about his and Georges' respective futures within the Bejjani Group. Michel didn't just have seniority, a Cambridge degree and a Harvard MBA, he also had the look, temperament and connections of a top international financier. All Georges had, by contrast, was a certain innate shrewdness and a bullish forcefulness that together suited him perfectly for security and the like. It was humiliating, therefore, that there was any question about the succession, but his father had the old-fashioned attitude that a company leader should be able to handle all aspects of the business. That was why Michel had been on the lookout for a way to dent Georges' reputation in such matters; and this man Black was his opportunity.

The report on Global Analysis was extensive. It included its latest balance sheet and accounts, its scope of operations, key clients and an executive summary that portrayed a company with a once-stellar reputation now hit by rumours of cash-flow problems, perhaps on account of an ill-fated joint venture between the founder-owner Quentin Oliver and a shady Uzbek oligarch.

The report on Iain Black was even more detailed. By happy chance, Black had sent his CV to all the leading business intelligence companies a couple of years before, including RGS, the agency the Bejjanis sometimes used. Black had ultimately opted to join Global Analysis, but in the meantime RGS had been interested enough to commission a head-hunter's report, which they'd kept on file. It included eight photographs of him, both by himself and in company. They showed a tall, powerfully built man in his early thirties; and with a certain presence, to judge from the way other people arrayed themselves around him.

His British father and Jordanian mother had met while working on a pipeline project outside Amman. They'd later worked together on similar projects in Turkey, Pakistan, Egypt and elsewhere, giving Black a suite of useful languages, a comfort with exotic places and – thanks to his mother's genes – a valuable ability to pass for native in most Middle-Eastern countries. Back in England for his teens, joining the army out of school, serving with distinction in Afghanistan and Iraq. But then suddenly his file went dark. His records for his last seven years were classified, and the head-hunters had had to make do with unconfirmed reports of secondment to a shadowy military intelligence unit running special ops across the region, from Pakistan to Iran, Somalia and Libya.

Michel watched with satisfaction his father's eyebrows rising as he read, and the finger Georges tugged inside his collar. He didn't wait for them to finish, therefore, but said instead: 'We need to call this morning off. It's not fair to expect Georges to take on a man like this.'

'What are you talking about?' scowled Georges.

Michel turned to Butros. 'I'm the first to acknowledge what a fine job Georges does running security, Father. But we need to be realistic. We're bankers, not men of war.'

'This is ridiculous,' said Georges. 'He's one man. I'll have Sami and Faisal and the whole crew with me. We can take him easily, I assure you.'

Their father held up a finger for silence. He thought for half a minute or so then turned to Georges. 'Your brother is right,' he said. 'This isn't a job for you.'

'But, Father—'

'This is a job for *him*.'

Michel's smile grew a little strained. 'With respect, Father, that wasn't what I meant. What I meant was—'

'I know what you meant. But you've been assuring me that Mexico was a one-off. It's time for you to prove that.'

Silence fell. It was Georges' turn to smile. Michel felt a sudden unwelcome squishing in his gut, but he knew better than to let it show. 'And so I will, Father,' he said. 'And so I will.'

III

Zehra rose early to prepare a light breakfast for herself and Katerina. After last night's harrowing drive, not all the demons in hell would ever get her back behind the wheel of her son's car, so she had Katerina show her the way across the park to her school. She said goodbye to her at the gates and promised to meet her there again that afternoon.

It was a promise she had no intention of keeping.

A bus to the Old City, then on foot to a small enclave of handsome whitewashed homes just inside its walls. Two policemen were on duty outside the Professor's house. She hesitated but then steeled herself. 'I'm here to see Metin Volkan,' she told them.

A scar from upper lip to left nostril made the nearer policeman seem to sneer. Or maybe he really was sneering. 'And you are?'

'Zehra Inzanoğlu.'

'And what are you to him? His cleaner? His lover?'

She ignored their laughter. 'We were children together.'

'That was a while ago, I'm guessing.' He took her bag, rummaged through it, holding individual items up for mockery before thrusting the whole thing back at her. 'Go on in, then,' said his companion, opening the door for her. 'You'll find your sweetheart in his study.'

Zehra didn't know where that was, but she wasn't about to ask. She opened doors at random, therefore, until she found him at a desk in a brightly lit, book-lined room, making notes in green biro upon a sheaf of stapled papers. Professor Metin Volkan, formerly a noted historian but now best-known as leader of One Cyprus, the political party he'd founded to press for reunification of the island. He looked up irritably from his work but sprang to his feet the moment he recognized her, hurried around to greet her. 'My dear Zehra,' he said. 'How good to see you. But what are you doing here?'

'My son came to visit me yesterday,' she told him, launching into the speech she'd rehearsed on her way here. 'Before they arrested him. He asked me to look after his daughter. But it's impossible, I can't, I'm too old. She needs to be here, near her school, near her friends.' She thrust out her jaw. 'You'll have to look after her for me.'

'*Me?*'

'Yes. You.'

He looked at her as though she were crazy. 'What do I know about looking after a schoolgirl, Zehra? And did you really not notice those policemen at my door? I'm under effective house arrest. It'll be a miracle if I'm not under full arrest in the next few days. The moment they find anything on me, anything at all . . . Anyway, she's *your* granddaughter, not mine.' He shook his head in bafflement. 'What happened to you, Zehra? You used to be so *kind*.'

'She's one of *them*,' spat Zehra.

'One of them?' frowned the Professor.

'Yes,' insisted Zehra. 'One of *them*. A Greek. Like her mother. That whore you introduced to my son. So this is *your* fault. Your fault, your responsibility.' She folded her arms emphatically, as if her position was unarguable.

Volkan nodded. 'I'm sorry about what happened between you and your son. I truly am. But it wasn't my fault. Nor was it even your son's. All he ever did was fall in love.'

'Then whose fault was it?' demanded Zehra.

'Yours.'

She looked incredulously at him. 'Mine?'

'Yours and your husband's.'

'Those monsters raped and murdered my sister,' she said furiously. 'They broke my father's legs and they stole our home and land and everything we'd ever owned. We had to run for our lives. We had to take refuge in a concentration camp. *You* had to take refuge there too, in case you've forgotten. And now you're telling me that it was *my* fault?'

'Athena did all those terrible things to you? Remarkable, considering she hadn't even been born at the time.'

'Not her. Her kind.'

'Her kind!' he retorted. 'So all Greek Cypriots are accountable for the sins of those few, are they? Even the ones who weren't yet born back then? Does that work both ways, I wonder? Did you know that Athena's family came originally from Kyrenia? That they were refugees themselves, only in the opposite direction, fleeing from *us*? Do you have any idea how many hundreds of them vanished during that time? And did you know her own uncle was one of them? That he was photographed surrendering to Turkish troops yet he was never seen again?'

'Good,' snapped Zehra. 'I'm glad.' Volkan didn't say anything to that. He didn't need to. Her cheeks grew hot all by themselves. 'They started it,' she said weakly.

'Yes,' he said. 'They did. But before they started it, we started it. And before we started it that time, they'd started it once before. Go back to the beginning of time and you'll never run out of other people starting it. So the question isn't who started it. The question is who can finish it.'

'You?' scoffed Zehra.

'No,' said Volkan. 'Not me. Your son, perhaps. More likely your granddaughter.'

'Don't call her that.'

'Your flesh, Zehra. Your blood.'

'I'm too old,' she said. 'I don't live here. I made a vow to my husband . . .' She faltered at the feebleness of her own protests. 'What am I to do?' she asked plaintively. But it was an admission of defeat.

He put a hand upon her arm. 'It may not be for long. With luck they'll release your son soon enough.'

'With luck?'

'We have good lawyers,' he said. 'They're working hard on his case. On everyone's cases. But you have to understand what's going on here. These arrests have nothing to do with investigating the bomb or capturing the real culprits. They're all about reassuring the Turkish people that the police are active, that they're making progress, and most importantly that they're making life miserable for people like us. To release your son and the others now would be to admit that they have nothing, and they can't do that, not without risking an outcry.'

She gave a long sigh. She knew the truth of this. It was how life was. 'And you swear that neither you nor my son had anything to do with the bombings?'

Volkan shook his head. 'How could you even ask such a thing? We make a lot of noise, your son and I, because we want desperately for Cyprus to be one island again, independent of Turkey, Greece and Britain, and ruled by its own citizenry under its own constitution. But we reject utterly the use of violence.'

'I still want your word,' she insisted. 'I want your word that you know nothing about it.'

'I give you my word,' said Volkan. But there was just a hint of something else in his voice: of hesitation, of doubt. And they both heard it. And, to judge from his expression, it seemed he was every bit as taken aback as she was.

NINE

I

Antioch was slowly rousing itself from its slumbers as Iain headed back in from the hospital. Perhaps that was why the countless minarets looked, from this vantage point, so like the nails in a fakir's bed. For all the city's rich pre-Islamic history, few traces of it were left. An early Christian church on its northern fringe; and, a little further out, a single pillar of giant stones and crumbling mortar rose from the foot of a precipitous gorge to hint at the one-time vastness of its ancient walls. But now, like so many modern Turkish cities, it was all office blocks and apartment buildings painted in sickly sweet pastels, like some Soviet suburb with a Miami makeover.

Last night's computer shop wasn't yet open. He parked

and wandered for a while. It was between seasons right now. The chilly wind that swept down from the snow-capped mountains to the city's north-west was countered by the warmth of the morning sun. Men in sweaters and thick jackets polished shoes beneath colourful sunshades. Hawkers flogging winter snacks set up next to others selling iced drinks. Men in mirror shades, stubble and fat-collared shirts stood in small clusters on street corners. He walked an accidental gauntlet of shopkeepers sluicing down their pavements, passed through an alley of shabby workshops where two mechanics fought like emergency-room doctors to bring an ancient jalopy back to life. Children waged hose-pipe wars beneath cat's cradles of electric and telephone wires, while laundry flapped like indulgent parents on the overlooking balconies.

The shutters were finally up when Iain returned to the computer shop. The owner was in boisterous spirits this morning, greeting him like a long-lost friend and insisting he share his pot of spiced tea. They chatted of football as they drank, then Iain passed him Robyn's list and he put together a box for him. Karin was up and gone by the time he returned to the hotel. She'd left her things in his room, he saw, along with a note to tell him she was off to Daphne in search of her consul but hoped to see him later. He hung out his 'Do Not Disturb' sign, bolted the door, cleared the dressing table and laid out his new gear. He downloaded Robyn's software, cut it

107

onto a CD, rebooted his laptop, then called her on her mobile. 'I'm ready,' he told her. 'Now what?'

She talked him through the set up, had him start recovery. 'Let it do its thing,' she told him. 'Check it from time to time. If it freezes, give me a call.'

He thanked her and rang off. He watched it for a while, but he soon tired of that. He felt restless and a little hungry. The hotel would have stopped serving breakfast by now, but he was in the mood to stretch his legs anyway. A café at the top of town, a selection of newspapers for the latest on the blast. He wrote admonitions in English and Turkish to leave the computer equipment alone, and placed them so they couldn't be missed. Then he made up both beds, left the 'Do Not Disturb' sign on the doorknob and headed on his way.

II

Michel Bejjani and his team had been in position for a couple of hours before Iain Black finally re-emerged from his hotel. Michel, sitting in the café across the street, looked away at once lest he be spotted himself, then gave a surreptitious nod to Faisal across the backgammon board, and to Sami and Ali who were sharing a water-pipe at a nearby table. He cupped a hand over his earpiece to cut down on the café's ambient noise then murmured into his microphone hidden beneath his collar: 'That's him now.'

'Got him,' said Yacoub, who was with Josef in the first SUV, parked a short distance up the road.

'Me too,' confirmed Kahlil, with Sayed, in the second.

Black paused on the front steps. He took out his phone, chose a number, made a call. He began chatting cheerfully away then crossed the road and walked obliviously straight past them. The moment he was out of sight, Michel checked to make sure his taser and GPS transmitter were both on, then got to his feet and gestured for the others to follow him.

Acapulco had been an aberration, an uncharacteristic lapse of concentration. He was every bit as capable of running this kind of operation as Georges, should the need arise.

It was time to prove that to his father.

III

'We had nothing to do with yesterday's bomb,' Professor Metin Volkan assured Zehra. 'With any of the bombs. I swear this to you on everything I hold dear. I started One Cyprus because I believe passionately that reunification offers the best future for the people of this island. But it only works if there is peace and trust. And you can't achieve peace and trust with bombs, no matter who you target.'

'But . . .?' asked Zehra.

A grimace, a little flicker of the eyes. 'When you asked your question a moment ago, it reminded me of something, that's all. Of someone. A man. He came to one of our rallies. To two of them, actually, though we only spoke once.'

'Where?'

'In Famagusta. Both times in Famagusta. You know the Eastern Mediterranean University? In a lecture hall there. That was one reason he stood out. He was much older than the other students. Not that there were so many of them, mind you. What with the bombs starting to go off, and people thinking we had something to do with them.'

'This man,' prompted Zehra.

'Yes. He stood to one side and watched. Very still, very quiet, very intense. He spooked me a little, if I'm honest.' He nodded towards his front door to indicate the two policemen outside, the power structure they represented. 'I assumed he was one of them, there to take names, scare people off, find things to use against us. But nothing came of it so I forgot about him. Until he showed up at our next Famagusta rally too. This was maybe three or four weeks ago. There'd been another bomb by then, the worst until yesterday's, so that even fewer people were there, for all that we denounced the bombings furiously at every opportunity we got. Anyway, he came to talk to me afterwards.'

'And?'

'He asked me the same question you did. And he asked me to give him my word too. That's what made me think of him. I told him what I told you: that we were men of peace who deplored the use of violence; and, moreover, that our involvement in a bombing campaign wouldn't merely be vile, it would be stupid too, because he could see for himself how people were turning against our cause. He didn't seem surprised. It was more like it was confirmation of bad news, like a second opinion of cancer. I asked him what was going on. I told him that if he knew anything he had to go to the police. He said he knew nothing, he simply wanted to make sure he could trust us before contributing. He asked me what we needed. I didn't want him around the campaign, if I'm honest, so I told him we needed money. He promised to see what he could do. That's all, I swear. I haven't seen or heard from him since.'

'Then why do you think he had something to do with Antioch?'

'I don't. If he'd been a bomber, why would he ask me for my assurances?' He must have realized how weak this sounded, for he added: 'But there was something about him. Like he was dead inside. If ever I've met a man capable of that kind of horror, it was him.'

'Cypriot?'

Volkan shook his head. 'A mainlander. But here a long time, to judge from his accent. An old soldier, if I had to guess. He had that look.'

Zehra nodded. After the Turkish army had successfully annexed Northern Cyprus, they'd awarded many of the homes, farms and businesses abandoned by Greek Cypriots to veterans of the campaign, in part to thank them for their service but mostly to tie the island ever more closely to the mainland. 'Do you have photographs?'

'Nothing official. People were already edgy enough about being seen with us. But I think someone filmed it for the university's website.'

'Who?'

'I don't know.'

'Can you find out?'

Volkan scowled angrily. 'Do you really not understand what's going on here, Zehra?' he asked. 'I'm considered an enemy of the state. I'm being watched *all the time*. As are my friends and associates. As you may be too, simply for coming here this morning, unless they consider you too obviously harmless. They monitor my Internet and email; they listen to my phone calls. Anyone I touch I taint. They're waiting for an excuse to take me in. *Any* excuse. And what if I'm right about this man, that he is involved in some way? They'll use him to incriminate us all.'

'So you'll do nothing? Is that what you're saying?'

An insult too far. He snorted almost contemptuously. 'If you want something done, Zehra, maybe you should do it yourself for once.'

Zehra lifted her chin. 'Very well,' she said. 'Maybe I will.'

TEN

I

Michel Bejjani and his men tailed Iain Black into Antioch's main market, a tangle of cobbled alleys and roads thronged with shops and stalls and shoppers. It was so labyrinthine that the only way to keep your bearings, when the sun went in, was the way the city everywhere sloped down to the Orontes river.

It said in the head-hunter's report that Black had made multiple solo trips inside Iran, seeking information on the regime and its nuclear programme from dissidents, while also advising insurgents on their tactics.

Michel watched him banter with a silversmith about a brooch and a pair of earrings, then buy a punnet of strawberries from a barrow piled so high that the fruit was squishing beneath its own weight, little pools of

114

sticky red juice gathering on the cobbles below. A call came in on his phone. He spoke briefly, checked his screen, put it away again, meandered onwards.

It said in the head-hunter's report that Black had been in Libya all through the Qaddafi uprising, making sure Western weaponry got to the right people, and teaching them how to use it too.

He came to a busy road, waited for a break in traffic. The two SUVs approached from his right, tracking his GPS transmitter on their SatNavs. Josef raised an eyebrow at Michel as he drove by, but it was far too busy for a snatch. Lights turned red ahead. Traffic congealed. Black weaved between cars to the far pavement then hurried up a steep flight of narrow stone steps into the city's old quarter. Michel clenched a fist with quiet satisfaction. This part of Antioch was crowded with colourful yet dilapidated slum housing, walls slanted at impossible angles, roofs repaired with sheets of corrugated iron, balconies made from wooden planks strapped to scaffolding poles. The kind of place where people knew to mind their own business. The kind of place almost designed for ambush.

The steps kept corkscrewing wildly, stealing Black from view. He walked so briskly that it was an effort to keep up. They had to step aside as a group of rowdy school-boys charged gleefully past, satchels bouncing on their shoulders. Another turn of the steps and then the staircase forked, with no sign of Black on either prong. Michel gestured Sami and Ali left while he and Faisal went right. Barely twenty paces along, however, they came to a dead end. A strangled cry in his earpiece was followed by a thud and then by silence. He felt a sudden dread as he ran back around. A booted foot protruded from a recessed doorway. He drew his taser, advanced cautiously, heart pounding in his ears. Sami was lying unconscious on his side, dribbling saliva from his mouth, while Ali lay face down beside him.

A short buzz of electricity behind. Faisal yelped and then went down. Michel raised his taser as he whirled around. Too late. His wrist was seized and twisted so hard that he cried out and let it go. His hair was grabbed; nodes were pressed against his throat. Their coldness and menace made him whimper. He had to fight to hold his bladder.

'So who the fuck are you idiots?' asked Black, in an offensively measured voice. 'And why have you been following me?'

II

Famagusta was an hour by bus from Nicosia. Zehra got off by the main gates of the Eastern Mediterranean University. A campus map steered her to the registrar's

116

office, but she found several people already waiting there, and they looked so ridiculously young and exotic that Zehra instantly lost her nerve and fled, wondering what on earth she was doing there. But she knew what she was doing there. Volkan had got beneath her skin. She meant to prove something to him, and she could scarcely back down already.

There was an Internet café across the street. Zehra had never used the Internet herself, had only gleaned the vaguest idea from television of how it worked. But it seemed a place to start. A large, gloomy room with cubicles against the walls in which teenage boys in headphones yelled curses at the cartoon violence on their screens. Thankfully none of them paid her the slightest attention. An overweight young man had his feet up on the reception desk. 'Yes?' he asked, without looking up from his comic.

'I'd like to see the university's website please,' Zehra told him, putting a half-lira coin down on the counter, as though to buy a ticket for the movies.

The young man snorted in amusement, but took pity. He put away his comic, slapped his mouse, brought his monitor into life. 'What bit of it?' he asked.

She gave a helpless shrug. 'The news. From a month ago.'

He brought up a new page on his screen, turned it for her to see. 'What story?'

'There was a rally here.' She lowered her voice. 'Professor Metin Volkan.'

He raised an eyebrow, clicked a link. A new page loaded. A clip of Volkan mouthing silently began to play. Four paragraphs of text ran down its side and there were thumbnail photographs of four other speakers beneath. Her heart gave a little skip when she saw the third of them. 'My son,' she murmured, touching the screen.

The young man nodded. 'That's what you're looking for? Your son?'

'No. What I'm looking for isn't there.'

'Whoever took this is bound to have filmed more than they posted,' he said. 'If they've kept it, and you ask them nicely . . .'

'And how do I do that?'

He scrolled back up for the reporter's name, gave her a big grin. 'How about that?' he said. 'Andreas Burak.'

'You know him?'

'Know him? I follow him. Everyone does.'

'Follow him?'

He held up his phone. 'On Twitter.' She shook her head in bewilderment. He might as well have been speaking Chinese. 'Never mind,' he said. He ran a search of the university's directory, dialled a number. 'Here.' He handed her his phone. 'You speak to him.'

III

Iain had known he was under surveillance from the moment he'd left the hotel. In his line of work, it was second nature to notice people looking hurriedly away. He'd seen, too, the man's loaded glance at the second table, the way he'd cupped his hand over his ear and murmured into his collar. A posse, then, and an incompetent one at that.

The prudent move would have been to retreat inside the hotel. But Mustafa was dead and so fuck prudence. Besides, he was pretty sure he recognized Michel Bejjani. The Bejjanis were bankers, not gangsters. If he couldn't handle this lot, it was time to get a new job.

His meander through the market had revealed their numbers and disposition; it had also given Maria time to send file photos of the Bejjanis to his phone, to confirm their identities. He'd told Maria what to do should he disappear then had led them into his ambush. He yanked Michel's head fiercely back by a hank of hair. 'I won't ask again,' he warned him. 'Who the fuck are you?'

Bejjani wailed pitifully and held up his hands. 'Michel Bejjani. I'm Michel Bejjani.'

'And why were you following me?'

'You were in Daphne yesterday,' he said. 'My father wanted to know why.'

'You think I set off that fucking bomb?' said Iain furiously. 'It killed my friend.'

119

'We know. We know. My father himself asked what kind of assassin would give his business card to a paramedic. But still: you were there because of us. My father wanted to know why, and who for.'

'Then why not ask?'

'Would you have told us?'

Iain nodded. It was as he'd figured. 'Call him,' he said.

'Call who?'

'Your father.'

'But I—'

Another yank of his hair. 'Now.'

Michel fished his phone from his pocket, dialled the number. Iain took it from him. 'This is Iain Black,' he said. 'I'm with your son Michel. He says you wanted to talk to me.'

A moment or two of silence. Butros Bejjani was reputed to be as sharp as knives. 'Yes, Mr Black,' he said. 'I was hoping you'd join us for lunch.'

'To eat it or to be it?'

Bejjani laughed. 'You'd be my guest, Mr Black. My *honoured* guest. If you know anything about me, which I think we both know that you do, you'll be aware that I take the obligations of hospitality most seriously. Besides, if you weren't as eager to discuss yesterday's horrors with me as I am with you, we wouldn't be having this conversation, would we?'

'Okay,' said Iain. 'Lunch it is.'

ELEVEN

I

The road out of Antioch was cramped with roadworks, a dual-carriageway reduced to a slow slalom of single lanes. They passed an apartment block in mid-demolition, lumps of concrete hanging bizarrely like dreadlocks from bent and rusted reinforcing rods. But finally traffic loosened. They crossed a ridge and the crescent bay of Samandag lay beneath them. They drove north along a coastal strip, whose hotels, cafés and shops were either closed or lightly used. It was early season still, and bombs weren't good for business.

They passed out of the town. A sandy track split the beach from a scrubby hinterland of farm buildings, overgrown plots and polythene greenhouses. They overtook four boys playing Ben Hur on a pair of pony-carts. They crossed a small inlet bridge. It grew prettier. The sea somehow looked warmer here, the sand more golden, the apple and cherry blossom brighter, groves jewelled with lemons and oranges. A flight of white birds frolicked and whirled, weaving joyous patterns against blue sky and green hillsides. They reached a fishing village with a walled harbour of dinghies, smacks, even a coastguard gunboat. But the *Dido* was a class apart, the largest and most gorgeous catamaran Iain had ever seen, its twin hulls of dazzling white fibreglass set with perfectly polished black windows. A slightly built man with thinning silver hair and pale blue-grey eyes was waiting for them on deck. Butros Bejjani. He was wearing blue deck shoes and cream cotton trousers and a collarless white linen shirt with mother-of-pearl buttons, and he held his hands clasped lightly behind his back. He smiled drily at Michel's dishevelled state then turned to Iain. 'Thank you so much for coming,' he said.

'How could I refuse?'

'Any fault was mine, not my son's. I was upset by yesterday's horrors. Yet I shouldn't have let it get to me as I did.' He turned his gaze on Iain. 'It's just that I like to look a man in his eye when I ask him whether he tried to kill me.'

'Happens a lot, does it?'

'More than I would wish.' He gestured at a man in blue flannel trousers and a yellow linen shirt standing in the shadow behind him. 'My son Georges,' he said. 'He went ahead of me into Daphne yesterday, to make sure it was safe. He was driving a black 4x4 with tinted windows, exactly like the one I was in myself, both of which we'd hired through one of our Turkish subsidiaries. He was barely a hundred metres from the hotel when the bomb went off.'

'I was closer than that. My friend was closer still.'

'I know, Mr Black. And I am truly sorry for your colleague. So I do not believe you planted or triggered the bomb yourself. On the other hand, you weren't there for pleasure, were you? You were there on a job. You were there, specifically, because a client of Global Analysis hired you to spy on me.' He gave a nod to a crewman, and they cast off at once, began to burble backwards out of their mooring. 'So it must have crossed your mind that perhaps they wanted you there for more than just spying. It must have crossed your mind that perhaps they hired you to find out for them when I was within range of their device, perhaps even to use you as scapegoats in the aftermath.'

'I won't tell you who our client is, if that's where this is heading,' said Iain, following Bejjani up steps to another deck where a table was sumptuously laid with heaped platters of mouthwatering Lebanese starters beneath a canopy of white silk. 'But I will tell you this: I'm going to find out who killed my friend, whatever it takes. Then I'm going to make them pay. Even if they are a client.'

Bejjani nodded as he motioned for Iain to sit beside him. 'And will you keep me informed of your progress?'

Iain considered this. 'If it turns out you were the target yesterday, then yes. I don't hold with assassination. And I'll also let you know what you need to do to protect yourself. Beyond that, I make no promises. Not until I know more.'

'Very well.'

'And you? Will you tell me what you learn?'

Bejjani spread his hands. 'I am a simple banker, Mr Black. I wouldn't know how even to start such an investigation. But should any relevant information come my way, I will, of course, gladly share it with you.'

'Like who you were going to meet in Daphne yesterday?'

'Any *relevant* information. That is not relevant.'

'And you're sure about that, are you? You were quite right earlier when you suggested I'd done my homework on you. One of the things I discovered is that enough people mean you harm that you rarely leave Tyre these days, let alone Lebanon. Yet here you are. So how can you be certain that your meeting yesterday wasn't a trap?'

Bejjani frowned slightly. To Iain's surprise, it seemed he genuinely hadn't considered this possibility before. But then he shook his head. 'It wasn't a trap,' he said.

'You're sure?'

'As sure as I can be of anything. But should that change . . .'

Iain nodded. Bejjani would no more give up a client than he would – especially as his were rumoured to include Mexican cartels, Russian oligarchs, Arabian royalty and Chinese kleptocrats. 'Okay,' he said. 'That seems fair.'

'Good,' smiled Bejjani, reaching for a wicker basket of bread and the nearest bowl of hummus. 'Then let us eat.'

II

Zehra stood in the doorway of the Salamis Road fast-food restaurant and looked for Andreas Burak. The place was full but only one man answered the description she'd been given: a heavy-set forty-something sitting by himself, spooning up lunch with one hand while he tapped away at his phone with the other. She went to stand by his table and waited for him to force-swallow an outsized chunk of spit-roasted lamb. 'So you're Taner's mother, eh?' he asked.

His question took her aback. When she'd referred to her son on the phone, as a way to explain her interest in his footage, she was sure she hadn't mentioned his first name. 'Do you know him?' she asked.

'I met him a few times,' shrugged Burak. 'He always spoke fondly of you.'

'No he didn't,' said Zehra.

'No he didn't,' acknowledged Andreas. He gave her a transparently false smile that was somehow disarming even so. 'All these arrests,' he said. 'It's hard for a man to know who he can trust.' His phone vibrated. He checked it briefly, frowned, set it back down. There was something slightly manic about him, as though trying to do one thing too many, and failing. 'So you wish to see my footage of that rally, yes? Why that one? Your son gives lots of speeches.'

'I can't tell you.'

'You can if you want to see my footage.'

She met his gaze frankly. 'You don't want me to tell you. I assure you.'

He picked up his can of fizzy orange, sucked it through his straw until it made rude noises. But then he came to a decision. 'With me, then,' he said. The booth was narrow. He had to edge sideways out of it, push himself to his feet. He led her out then down an alley to a litter-strewn road of shabby housing. He didn't talk to her or even look at her, but rather checked his phone like a nervous tic. Occasionally he'd snort or laugh. Twice, he stopped to tap out some new message. Zehra grew increasingly irritated, but it was hard to shame a man who wouldn't even look at you. He led the way into the lobby of an apartment block, let the door slap back in her face. He belched inside the lift as they were going up to the top floor, filling the cramped space with pungent smells. His apartment proved surprisingly plush and spacious. A work-table against the facing wall was cluttered with computer equipment. 'I'll need a minute,' he said. She nodded and stood beside him. 'No,' he said, pointing her at his balcony doors. 'Out there.'

She sniffed as she went out. She knew all too well the things men got up to on their machines. The view from his balcony, however, drove such thoughts from her mind. The city had somehow vanished. Instead, a lake of wading birds surrounded by swaying walls of rushes, then grassland all the way to the sea. 'Belongs to the army, of course,' grunted Andreas, coming out to join her, as if everyone had the same question. 'Those bastards always grab the best land for themselves. Imagine what we Cypriots could do with it if we were allowed.'

'Ruin your view, for a start.'

Andreas laughed loudly. 'That's what your son said.'

She looked sharply at him. 'Taner was here?'

'I teach new media at the university, among other things. Plus I run the news section of the website. That makes me a journalist of sorts. Being a journalist means I have to *appear* neutral; not that I have to *be* neutral.'

He led her back inside, had her sit, played footage of the rally. A huge banner above the stage declared CYPRUS FOR THE CYPRIOTS, while a thin man with a high-pitched voice talked about DNA-testing and how Greek and Turkish Cypriots were one beneath the skin.

'I want to see the audience,' said Zehra.

Andreas fast-forwarded. On stage, the thin man charged comically through his speech. The camera panned around a mostly empty auditorium. She leaned in and squinted but saw no one old enough to match the Professor's description.

'Who are you looking for?' asked Andreas.

'No one.'

'If you tell me, maybe I can help.'

The thin man finished with a raised fist. The camera tracked him off the stage past several other attendees, including a brief glimpse of an older man in a worn leather jacket, with short grizzled hair and a three-day beard. But it was his eyes that gave him away, the deadness in them. 'Stop,' she said. 'Can you go back?'

'Of course.' He played the footage in reverse. The man reappeared. 'Hell's teeth!' he muttered. 'He looks a charmer. Who is he?'

'I don't know.'

'Sure!' he scoffed. But he didn't push it. 'You want a copy, yes?' He put a rectangle around the man's face, enlarged it, sharpened it, sent it to his printer. He folded the page in half before handing it to her. 'You should be careful with men like this,' he warned her.

Zehra nodded soberly. 'I will be,' she said.

III

The breeze was light but the catamaran was so slick it still sliced through the gorgeous Mediterranean afternoon, heading north-west towards Karataş. No sign of women or children on board, though Iain knew that all three Bejjani were fathers as well as husbands, confirming for him that this trip was pure business.

Course followed course, each with its own wines. After the starters came red snapper in a sharp chilli and coriander sauce; succulent spit-roasted lamb so salty and fatty it would make a dietician blanch. Baklava and kanafeh and then thick sweet coffee that Butros Bejjani poured himself from a golden coffee pot into fine-white porcelain cups that seemed incongruous on a boat as built for speed as this, and which rattled in their saucers as they headed back to harbour, tacking into the breeze.

Conversation was a dance: they each tried to lure the other into indiscretion, but they were all skilful enough to waltz back to safe ground without being rude. And Butros took the opportunity to show himself better than his reputation as banker to the underworld would imply.

He enthused about the sports teams he sponsored, the hospitals he supported, the Moustafa Farroukh landscapes he'd donated to the Beirut Art Centre. His love for Lebanon was obvious, even if his stated hopes of a brighter and less sectarian future came across as somewhat pious. In short, he treated Iain like a journalist to be charmed, and made sure to tell him nothing.

An irony, then, that by telling him nothing, he told him all he needed to know.

Iain sat back in his canvas chair. It creaked luxuriously, as if it had enjoyed the meal as much as he had. 'So then,' he said. 'Tell me about Dido.'

Bejjani's bland smile didn't flicker for a moment. But his eyes did. 'I beg your pardon?' he said.

'Your boat,' said Iain. 'What made you call her the *Dido*?'

A faintly rueful smile played on Bejjani's lips, as though he suspected he'd been rumbled. 'I'm from Tyre,' he said finally. 'Home of the Phoenicians, the greatest seafarers the world has ever seen.' He waved a hand at the expanse of Mediterranean that lay around them, at the harbour mouth they were fast approaching. 'Dido was their most celebrated princess. What else would I call my boat?'

Iain nodded. When first he'd heard that Bejjani was heading to Turkey for a meeting, he'd taken it for granted that it had to be with a very important client. Why else would he risk leaving Tyre, after all? Yet once Karin had told him of Nathan Coates' purpose, he'd begun to suspect another possibility. What were the odds, after all, of two billionaires having unrelated meetings in the same hotel on the same day? Besides, Butros Bejjani didn't merely support Lebanese sport, medicine and art. His most generous gifts had been of Phoenician artefacts to Lebanon's National Museum. Yet no mention of those over lunch, almost as though he'd not wanted to draw attention to them. Iain looked levelly at him. 'Have you ever heard of Nathan Coates?' he asked.

'Nathan Coates?' Bejjani looked genuinely puzzled. 'Who is he?'

'A very wealthy American oilman,' said Iain. Crockery rattled on the table as they nudged the harbour wall, and crewmen hurriedly yet quietly secured them to their mooring. 'An avid collector of historic artefacts, just like yourself. More to the point, he was in a meeting in the Daphne International Hotel yesterday when the bomb went off. He was almost certainly killed in the blast, along with his head of security and the black market dealer he was there to see. So let me take a wild guess: you were heading into Daphne to see these same artefacts and maybe buy them for yourself.'

Bejjani was silent for several seconds as he considered this information. 'I'm afraid you're mistaken,' he said finally. 'I've never heard of Nathan Coates, or of this mysterious dealer of yours.'

'Yes, you have,' said Iain. 'Maybe not of Coates, but of the dealer, for sure. Who was he? What was he selling? Phoenician pieces? Mycenaean?'

Again Bejjani gave himself time to think. Again he decided to play coy. 'I have no idea what you're talking about,' he said. 'Now, if you'll please excuse me, I have phone calls to make. My bank doesn't run itself, you know.' And he smiled politely and put down his napkin and rose to his feet to indicate that lunch was at an end.

TWELVE

I

Georges Bejjani walked Iain Black to the SUV. He thanked him for coming then told Sami to drive him to his hotel or wherever he wanted to go. He smiled broadly until they were out of sight then he whirled around and marched back on board to where his father and brother were waiting. 'Artefacts?' he asked incredulously. 'All this for *artefacts*?'

Butros gave Georges a sour look then beckoned him and Michel to join him in his cabin. 'To start with,' he said, closing the door, 'our recent guest confirmed he was in Daphne yesterday because of our meeting. That he didn't know who it was with strongly implies that the leak is on our end. Our security is therefore compromised. So please think in future before you speak loudly enough for the whole world to hear. Do you understand?'

'Yes, Father,' said Georges. 'I'm sorry. But I still can't believe you thought it worth risking your life for—'

'Michel,' interjected his father. 'Perhaps you might get the search for our leak underway.'

'Now?'

'Yes. Now. I'd also like to know more about this man Nathan Coates. And please arrange to have our recent guest watched too. He's seen our faces so you'll need to hire someone new, someone local. But make sure they can be discreet. We don't want them spotted too.'

'What should I have them watch for?'

'Anything. Everything. What he does, where he goes, who he talks to. If we're very lucky, he might even steer us to his source.' He waited until Michel had closed the door behind him then turned to his younger son. 'What is it with you?' he asked. 'Can you possibly be unaware of the opportunity I'm offering you right now? I thought that's what you wanted: to lead the Group.'

'I do, Father. But I don't see—'

'Because you don't think. Or, at least, you think like a corporal rather than a general. You see the world as a series of skirmishes to be won. Forget skirmishes. Skirmishes don't matter. What matters is the *war*.'

'What do artefacts have to do with war?'

Butros sighed. 'Do you know why history bores you, Georges?' he asked. 'It bores you because you think it is about the past.'

Georges laughed, thinking his father had made a joke. Then he realized he was serious. 'I'm sorry, Father,' he said. 'I don't understand.'

'Clearly. Which is precisely why I can talk to your brother of these things, and not you.'

'Give me a chance. I'll try, I promise.'

'Very well.' He went to his wall-safe, punched in a code. He swung open the door and took out a blue box that he passed to his son. 'Here,' he said. 'Look at this.'

George pulled back tissue paper to reveal a curved shard of charred pottery beneath, inscribed with faded ideograms. He shook his head in puzzlement. 'What is it?' he asked.

'Part of a storage jar or cooking pot.'

'And it's significant somehow?'

'These characters are Phoenician,' replied Butros, running the tip of his little finger across them. '*Early* Phoenician. As you can see, these characters are difficult to read, but this symbol here is a signifier of royalty; and these other characters appear to comprise the name Ishbaal, or something similar, meaning "child of Baal" or "servant of Baal" or the like.'

'Ishbaal,' frowned Georges. 'Who was he?'

'There are several plausible candidates. According to Jewish history, their first king, Saul, was succeeded briefly by his son before David seized the throne. This son was called Ishbaal, though later Bible editors refused to countenance a king of Baal as king of Israel, so they retrospectively changed his name to Ishbosheth – man of shame. But I think this piece is later than that. There was a very small quantity of organic residue on this shard that I had carbon-dated. Almost exactly twenty-eight hundred years old, they tell me. Think of that.'

'I don't . . .'

'There was a king of Tyre called Eshbaal who died in around 860 BC. That's a little early. His daughter was the notorious Jezebel, the one who married the Jewish King Ahab. Many think her name is a corruption of the feminized version of Ishbaal. And there'd have been no need for the Jews to change *her* name, after all, as it was precisely for worshipping her different god that they put her to death and fed her to the dogs.'

'You think this piece once belonged to Jezebel?'

'I think it's possible. But the carbon residue was from later still. So it's possible that the piece was passed on to one of her heirs. Her niece, say.'

'Her niece?'

Butros looked up. 'I meant what I said over lunch,' he told him. 'We have Phoenician blood, you and I. And not just any Phoenician blood, but the blood of Tyre. Our ancestors showed Solomon how to build his temple. They devised the alphabet and shared it with the world. They circumnavigated Africa and were first across the oceans. They led the Mediterranean out of its centuries of darkness, and founded many of its greatest cities. Yet does the world honour us for this? No. Egypt and Greece get all the credit instead. Do you know why?'

'Why, Father?'

'Because our past is invisible, that's why. Because our ancient cities have become our modern cities. Tyre is Tyre. Sidon is Sidon. Beritus is Beirut. We've built over ourselves so often that we have nothing left to show for it. No Petra, no Giza, no Troy, no Ephesus. And what little we do have is Roman. *Roman*! Nor do we have any great icons to make up the loss. No Rosetta Stone. No Phaistos Disc. No Mask of Agamemnon. We're a nation without a visual narrative, without an image of ourselves. That's why we're always divided, because in our heads we see our differences before we see our common heritage. We see Christian against Muslim, north against south, coast against mountain. This division makes us weak, and weakness makes us ripe for conquest. But if we could find our narrative again, if we could find our identity . . .'

Georges looked doubtfully down at the shard. 'And you think this could do that?'

'No,' said his father, taking back the box. 'This is nothing. Just a fragment from an old pot. But if it leads us where I think it could lead us, then yes, it could be everything.'

137

II

Iain returned to the hotel to find Karin still out. He bolted the door then checked his laptop. Recovery complete, it told him. He dismantled and packed away the peripherals then ran a search of video files. A list appeared on his new laptop's screen. He ordered them by date, clicked on the most recent. The screen went black. He feared it had suffered an aneurysm of some kind. Then footage began to play. It was from the laptop's integrated camera, so the resolution was relatively poor and the hotel entrance looked further distant than it had in truth been. It was also corrupted in patches, as was the audio of him chatting cheerfully away with Mustafa. Yet, all in all, it was better than he had any right to expect.

The hotel's main car park had been to its rear, but several bays were marked out either side of the front steps, for taxis, delivery vans and the like. The blast crater suggested the bomb had been to the left of the steps as he looked at it, so that was what he watched. Time passed. Vehicles came and went. He fast-forwarded until he saw Karin approaching. She walked up the front steps then paused to let a helmeted, black-clad motorcycle courier in ahead of her. Several minutes went by. Karin came back out. Her day-pack was now bulky with its package. She stopped on the steps to check its label, while

Iain and Mustafa bantered about her. Then she looked around and walked briskly out of shot.

On the recording, he offered Mustafa more tea. Glasses clinked as he picked them up. The café door opened and then banged closed again. On screen, meanwhile, the leather-clad and still helmeted motorcyclist came back out. To judge from their build and gait, it looked like a woman. She walked along the front of the hotel, looking up at balconies. She stopped beneath one, took two paces backwards, then turned and beckoned to someone out of shot. A plain white truck now drove past the camera then reversed up against the hotel. Iain sat forwards. This was surely it: the bomb being delivered. The low resolution and the glare from the windscreen obscured the driver's face. The door opened and a man jumped down. His jacket was zipped to his chin, its collar was up, and he was wearing a plain black baseball cap and mirror sunglasses. He had leather driving gloves on, too, and was carrying a dark blue motorcycle helmet. He slammed the door behind him, walked briskly around the front of his truck and vanished from view. A bang as the café door shut again. The motorcycle nosed out onto the road. The leather-clad woman leaned forwards, looking both ways before pulling out. The man was riding pillion, his helmet now on, tapping at a phone in his left hand. They vanished out of shot.

Iain braced himself. The seconds ticked by. The truck

seemed suddenly to bulge and lift. The screen went topsy-turvy and then black. The file ended. He replayed the last few minutes again, stopping and starting in hope of getting a better look at one or other of their faces. Without reward.

He opened the second file. This one had footage from a camera Mustafa had planted beneath an armchair inside the hotel's lobby. It had been to plant it, and others on the floors above, that Mustafa had booked himself into the Daphne International, despite the slight risk that the Bejjanis, or whoever they were meeting, would take their security seriously enough to have the hotel's guests checked out. Which was also why Iain had opted to stay in Antioch instead of Daphne, for his presence would have been far more likely than Mustafa's to set off alarms. Those other cameras had relayed their footage to a server in Mustafa's room that had, of course, been obliterated in the blast; but they'd had this particular stream sent to his laptop as well, so that they'd have at least some advance warning when Bejjani came to leave.

The cameras had no microphones. They were too easy to check for, and might have given their surveillance away. The video was therefore synchronized with his laptop audio. Unfortunately, all he saw was Karin, the motor-cyclist and various other staff and guests walking to and fro. The third camera had been set up on the main Antioch road, because that was the direction from which they'd expected the Bejjanis to arrive. But neither the motorcyclist nor the truck had come that way. Now for the fourth and final camera, attached to a telephone pole across the road from the hotel. The motorcyclist arrived, parked, went inside. Time passed. She came back out, walked along the front of the hotel, then turned and guided in the truck. The driver got out, shoulders hunched and head bowed. The woman straddled her bike and rocked it off its stand. The man had his back to the camera. He took off his cap and sunglasses and stuffed them in his pockets. Then he made to put on his helmet.

'Look around, you bastard,' muttered Iain, leaning closer. 'Look around.'

The café door banged at that moment. The man couldn't help himself, he glanced over his right shoulder. Iain stared at the screen almost in disbelief. 'Got you,' he said.

THIRTEEN

I

Iain froze the crucial frame then zoomed in on the man's face. The resolution wasn't great but it caught his short, dark hair, his high, wide forehead, his weak chin and the crescent scar by his left eyebrow. Not perfect, granted, but surely recognizable to a friend, colleague or relative.

What now?

He had to get this to the investigating team, of course, but that was easier said than done. They were bound to ask why he'd been filming the hotel; and while private surveillance wasn't exactly illegal, you didn't want to have to explain it to the police in the aftermath of an atrocity like this. They'd make his life miserable, force him to name his client, probably deport him from Turkey, maybe even ban him from ever returning. So he needed to remain anonymous.

The media had been pushing hotline numbers and other ways to get in touch with the investigating team. He quickly found an email address for them. The last section of footage from the fourth camera, from the arrival of the motorcyclist up to the moment of the blast, contained everything they'd need. If he sent it from a bogus Hotmail account set up via his new computer, ISP confidentiality would normally make it untraceable. But this was a terrorism case and so the rules were different. He couldn't risk using the hotel wi-fi, and he was liable to be remembered if he used a local Internet café. And if he used Tor or one of the other programs people like him used to cover their digital tracks, it might prompt the police to look for someone with his particular skill-set and so steer them straight to him.

He needed another way.

The day he'd arrived, he'd wandered around the market, had taken coffee in a café with free wi-fi. He'd used his old laptop but he remembered the password. He checked his watch. The market shut down at night. The café was certain to have closed. But such places often left their routers running overnight. It had to be worth a shot. He zipped his laptop into its bag then hurried down and out.

II

Such food as her son had had in his apartment, they'd eaten the night before. Zehra therefore had Katerina show her to the nearest shop after collecting her from school. Plastic crates of tired produce looked as limp as she felt after her long day, but there was still enough for a meal or two. The first molohiya of the year was in. She added vine leaves, an onion, a pepper, a lemon, two small potatoes, a tomato, a garlic bulb, a few pinches of fresh herbs and a single chicken thigh, which was all her purse and arms would allow. The checkout woman eyed her sourly as she weighed each item in turn but Zehra paid her no mind, except to watch the scales to make sure she wasn't cheated.

Back in the apartment, she gave Katerina the molohiya to prepare. Katerina looked dumbly at her, as though she'd never even seen it before. Zehra frowned. 'It's molohiya,' she said. 'Don't tell me you don't know how to prepare molohiya.'

Katerina shook her head. 'No.'

Zehra sighed. She found a knife and showed Katerina how to hold it so as not to cut off her fingers, then chopped the dark green leaves into long thin strips. 'Now your turn,' she said.

Katerina bit her lower lip in concentration as she worked. Her fingers were tiny and boneless compared to

144

Zehra's own gnarled, arthritic stubs. But she kept at it until she was done, when she looked up with such shining eyes that it was a thump in Zehra's chest. 'Are we having this tonight?' she asked.

'No, child,' said Zehra, more severely than was warranted. 'It's too bitter. It needs to soak.' She filled a pan with water, tossed in the leaves. Then she took out the chicken thigh, two potatoes, the vine leaves, an onion, a lemon and a selection of herbs. 'These are for tonight. Do you want to help?'

Katerina nodded eagerly. 'Yes, please.'

'Very well,' said Zehra. 'Then those potatoes aren't going to peel themselves, are they?'

III

Incident Investigation HQ, Daphne

Inspector Ozgur Karacan leaned back wearily in his chair and covered his face with his hands. Another brutal day. It wasn't just that the bomb had devastated his home town and killed two old school-friends working in the hotel, it was that the investigation into it was such a shambles. Part of that was excusable. A large team had had to be put together in a rush. It comprised local, regional, and national officers as well as specialist technical teams and gendarmerie under the broad authority of the Turkish National Police Counterterrorism Authority, all working hand-in-hand with the National Intelligence Organization. Each had overlapping areas of responsibility and conflicting reporting structures. Each had had to procure for itself suitable workspace and accommodation. To add even more confusion, a lieutenant colonel had arrived that afternoon from the Office of the General Staff. He'd claimed his brief was to observe and advise only, but no one believed that for a moment. With so many competing interests at work, it was no surprise that already people were manoeuvring crudely for what little credit was going, as well as to avoid blame. And so it had become painfully clear to him exactly how the terrorists had run their campaigns with such impunity, and why—

'Inspector,' said a woman.

He looked around. Melisa Avci, no doubt with yet another piece of nonsense from the incident hotline. 'What now?'

'Footage,' she said. 'It came in a minute ago. You can see a white truck backing up against the hotel. You can see the driver's face.'

Karacan stood, electrified. So much police work was about luck; but this was extraordinary. He followed her to her desk. She played it for him. He watched the driver park his truck and get out. He watched him walk around the bonnet. Then he watched him glance around. Even as he exulted, he struggled to make sense of it. The camera must have been directly across the road from the hotel, yet that whole area had been wide open, to afford the hotel's guests uninterrupted views. There'd been no CCTV cameras in the vicinity; it was about the first thing he'd checked. And what tourist would film the front of a hotel?

'Fantastic work, Melisa,' he told her. The hotline was soul-destroying work, what with all the whackos calling in their theories, so she deserved full credit if only for stamina. Within minutes, the room was filled with braided uniforms. A *jihadi* video, they all agreed. Perhaps sent in by a turncoat of some kind. But what to do with it? Some wanted to give it to the media in hopes of a quick identification and arrest. But others cautioned against alerting the bombers to the breakthrough and thus giving them time to cover their tracks. So up again it went, to the Minister himself. In the meantime, there was plenty to be done: licence plates to check out, emails and footage to examine, suspect photos to be searched for a match.

Ozgur Karacan's jaw trembled as he fought a yawn. The notion of a *jihadi* video made little sense to him, but back-to-back twenty-hour days meant he was in no state to offer anything better. His first boss had once told him that the best next move in a hard case was often a good night's sleep. Never had that advice sounded sweeter than right now.

FOURTEEN

I

The shower was on when Iain returned to his room. Karin was back. He stowed his laptop beneath the dressing table then turned on the TV both to catch the latest news and to alert her to his presence. Yet she still looked startled to see him when she came out a few minutes later, a white hotel towel wrapped around her chest.

'Sorry,' he said.

'Yes,' she said. 'How dare you barge into your own room like that?' She grabbed clean clothes and vanished again, re-emerging several minutes later. 'God, I needed that,' she said.

'Tough day?' he asked.

'My Dutch consul guy is an angel,' she said. 'But the Americans are such pricks.'

Iain laughed. 'Is that a general observation, or did something specific happen?'

She sighed. 'I have this thing called an EB-1B visa. It's a green card for researchers and academics and the like. But it was with my passport in my hotel safe. The thing is, Nathan arranged it for me before I could go to work for him. And now that he's dead they're saying they can't issue me a new one, not unless I have another offer of work. I mean Jesus! You'd think they'd give me a little leeway. All my stuff's over there. My apartment!'

'Hell. What will you do?'

'I don't know,' she said. 'Hope, I guess. The police have already recovered a bunch of the hotel safes, apparently, and their contents have been fine. If they find mine, and my passport and green card are okay, then I can at least defer it for a while.'

'I'll keep my fingers crossed.'

'You'd better. All my bank cards are in there too. If things don't sort out soon, it may be a while before I can repay you.'

'Yeah. My two hundred lira. It's all I've been able to think of.'

'I hate owing people things.'

'So I guess you won't want dinner tonight, then?'

'I don't hate it quite *that* much.'

'Great,' he said. 'Then let's get out of here.'

II

The storm was brutal, lashing the Grey Wolf camp with the kind of fury that made one believe in ancient gods, pinning Asena inside the main cabin. To make matters worse, Hakan just wouldn't shut up. His family lived less than an hour away. He wanted to go see them. She told him no but he wouldn't let it go. He droned on so long that he drove the others off, even through the deluge. He insisted she owed him for delivering the bomb. He swore blind that he wouldn't give anything away. But there'd been something perilously close to remorse about Hakan ever since he'd learned the death toll, and she simply didn't trust him. 'Enough!' she cried. 'Enough!' She made sure she had all the vehicle keys and retreated to her room.

It wasn't yet time for the Lion to call, and he was rarely punctual anyway, but she set up all the same. To her surprise and pleasure, he came on early. But then she saw his expression and sensed trouble. 'What is it?' she asked.

'You went to Daphne yourself, didn't you?' he said angrily. 'I told you not to.'

'I have to make the men respect me. They won't respect me unless I prove myself.' Then she frowned. 'But how did you know?'

'We received footage this evening. Of you and your friend outside the hotel.'

'What? *How?*'

'We don't know that yet. We're working on it.'

She thought back. 'It can't be too serious, can it? We used false plates. We never showed our faces.'

'Your idiot friend did. Before he put on his helmet.'

'Shit.' She bit a knuckle. 'Is he identifiable?'

'You'll be able to judge that better than me. I've just sent you the clearest shot.'

Asena checked her inbox, opened the attachment. Not perfect of Hakan, but close enough. If it got wide coverage, someone was bound to finger him. Then they'd tear his life apart. He was the one who'd known of this remote forest camp, because he'd hiked here as a child. He'd even put her in touch with the former owners. They'd therefore have to leave tonight. They couldn't take Hakan with them, however, not if this picture got out. Yet nor could they leave him here. 'How long have we got?' she asked.

The Lion shrugged. 'It will come out eventually. If not from us, then from whoever sent it in. For all we know, the media already has it.'

Her heart squeezed. She felt hatred. 'Who did this to us?'

'We're working on that. And we'll find out, I promise. But right now we have a larger question.'

Asena nodded. When you were plotting to overthrow a government, a certain flexibility of planning was essential. There were simply too many uncontrollable externalities, from the economy and popular opinion to unforeseen political and world events. All you could do was work to make conditions as favourable as possible, then strike hard with everything you had when the moment was right. And while they weren't there yet, they were close. 'We're not calling it off,' she said flatly. 'Not after everything we've already done. And postponing will just give them more time to find us. I say we move it up.'

The Lion looked pleased. It was evidently his view too. 'Put those stories out,' he told her. 'We'll aim for Labour Day next month. And please make sure that your idiot friend can't cause us any grief.'

'Leave him to me.' She touched his cheek upon her screen. 'The Lion and the Wolf,' she said.

'The Lion and the Wolf.'

His box went black then vanished altogether. She stared at the picture of Hakan still on her screen. How to handle him? With so much blood already on her hands, she wanted, if possible, to let him live; yet it would be crazy to risk everything they'd worked so hard to—

A floorboard creaked behind her. She whirled around. Hakan himself was standing there, wearing his wheedling expression, evidently come for one last plea. But then he saw the photograph of himself upon her screen, and he must have realized the implications at once, for the blood drained from his face and his expression changed before her eyes to one of mortal terror.

FIFTEEN

I

The restaurant that night proved very different: low-ceilinged, intimately lit, with small tables set obliquely to each other and no scruples about alcohol. Their waitress stood with one foot hooked behind the other as she took their order, like a ballerina about to curtsey. 'Listen,' said Iain, once they'd agreed on red wine and mezes. 'Remember what I said last night about your boss' kids? Forget it.'

'I already had. They're whiners, not doers. But why the change of heart?'

'I met a man today. I can't tell you about him, I'm afraid. But he was here for the same reason as your boss. If that meeting had been a ruse, they'd hardly have invited rival bidders, would they?'

'Huh. Another Homer buff?'

'Not exactly. Dido and the Phoenicians. But that's all part of the same thing, right?'

'Sort of.'

'Sort of?' frowned Iain. 'But Dido had a fling with Aeneas, didn't she? And Aeneas was at Troy.'

Karin pulled a face, as though she saw quicksand in their path. 'It's not quite as simple as that,' she said. 'Yes, Aeneas fought at Troy. Yes, he also had a famous love affair with Dido. But the dates simply don't work. The Trojan War was around 1200 BC, like I said last night; yet Dido wasn't even born until around 850 BC. And that's assuming she existed at all, which is far from certain. Her name actually means "wanderer", which is a classic sign of folklore.'

'But I thought she founded Carthage.'

'Yes. Maybe. Except the earliest graves they've found there date to about thirty years after her time. More to the point, they're *poor*.'

'So?'

'So that doesn't tally with the legend,' said Karin. 'Dido's husband was famously rich. Her brother Sicherbas, the king of Tyre, grew so jealous that he had him killed, then he tried to force Dido to marry him instead to get his hands on all that gold. But Dido was too smart for him. She pretended to dump it all into the sea as an offering to the gods, but actually she stashed it on her fleet of ships then looted her brother's treasury and sailed off with the lot.'

'Good on her,' laughed Iain.

'Yes, but like I said, the first settlers in Carthage were poor. So what happened to all that gold? It was actually one of the great mysteries of the ancient world. Nero tore up half the Tunisian coast looking for it.'

'Any luck?'

'Still out there,' smiled Karin. 'A spare afternoon and a metal detector. We could be rich.'

Iain laughed and refilled their glasses. The wine was raw and left a pleasurable warmth in the throat and chest. 'Seriously, though, where did the story of Dido and Aeneas come from, if the dates were that far off?'

'The Greeks weren't very good at chronology. They had nothing to measure dates against. So they pretty much glossed over the Dark Ages altogether. Besides, the Trojan War was a huge part of their mythos. They all wanted a piece of it. You wouldn't believe how many ninth- and eighth-century cities claimed they'd been founded by some returning Homeric hero or another. Besides, Carthage and Rome went on to become the great rivals of the ancient world, so a doomed love story between their founders made perfect material for a story. The beautiful, exotic princess falling so hard for the hero's war stories that she threw herself onto his sword when he sailed off – what's not for a man to like?'

'I've got war stories,' said Iain.

'I'll bet you do,' laughed Karin. They held each other's gaze a fraction longer than was polite, but then she shook her head and looked away.

Iain reached for the wine, refilled their glasses once again. A single drop spilled onto the white tablecloth, staining purple as it spread. When you'd lost the love of your life, it felt like betrayal even to look fondly at someone else. It felt like betrayal of his dead son, to cheat upon his mother. But four years had passed, and it was time.

II

Hakan was first to react. He snatched up the keys to Asena's motorbike then ran from her room and slammed the door behind him. She grabbed her M-16 from her bottom drawer, slapped in a new magazine as she went after him. But the door had jammed shut and she couldn't open it so she went to her window instead, lifted the sash, dropped herself down onto the waterlogged earth outside.

An engine sputtered and then caught. She ran around the side of the cabin, shoes squelching, just as Hakan opened the throttle and pulled a sharp turn, spraying her with muddy water. She fired three times but he didn't slow down. Doors banged open behind her. Men ran out shouting. She wiped her eyes, struggling to see in the darkness. Hakan was evidently blind too because he flicked on his headlight, revealing himself near the top of the rise. But it was steep there, and the storm had turned the earth to mud so that his back wheel span uselessly. He climbed off to push it up the last few metres. She ran after him, stopped, aimed, fired. He cried out and clutched his shoulder. She fired again. He went down and the bike fell upon him. She walked up to him, her gun at the ready in case he had a final trick; but all he had were upheld hands and the pleading terror of his eyes.

The others caught up with her. Ali looked bewildered when he saw it was Hakan. 'I assumed we had an intruder,' he said.

'They have a picture of him at the hotel,' she told him. 'They have his face.'

'They have his face?'

'This place is blown,' she said. 'We have to leave.'

Ali nodded at Hakan. 'And him?' he asked.

She looked down. His mouth was a tight grimace as he braced himself for the *coup de grâce*, yet there was a glimmer of hope in his eyes that she was a woman and therefore maybe not quite hard enough for this kind of work, that she'd persuade herself she could afford to let him live. She shook her head with genuine regret as she aimed down at his forehead and pulled the trigger twice more. 'He'll be staying here,' she said.

III

Iain settled the bill, held the door open for Karin. It had turned colder outside, a storm brewing. The wind was in their faces, gusts stiff enough to throw them slightly off balance and mean that they had to turn towards each other and raise their voices to be heard. A young woman sending a text on her phone overtook them, her head bowed, her long black hair streaming behind her like something from a cartoon. They reached a T-junction. Iain put his hand upon Karin's elbow to steer her left. Then he kept it there afterwards. She hesitated for a moment or two but pulled away from him and shook her head. 'I really don't think this is a good idea,' she said.

'What isn't?'

'You know what.'

'I like you,' said Iain. 'Is that so bad?'

'I like you too. Honestly I do. But we live on other sides of the world. There's no future to it.'

'All the better.'

Karin laughed, but not for long. 'I don't do flings. Not any more. They make me unhappy. Besides . . .' She spread her hands to indicate the bombing, the friends they'd both lost. 'Does it feel right?'

Iain nodded soberly. 'No.'

They were silent the rest of the way back to the hotel. He felt deflated. As they waited for the lift, the receptionist called them over. 'Good news,' she said. 'We've had a cancellation.'

'Excuse me?' said Karin.

'We have a free room for you, if you still want it.'

'Oh,' said Karin. She looked uncertainly at Iain. 'That *is* good.'

'Not tonight,' said Iain. 'It's too late tonight. How about tomorrow?'

'Yes,' said Karin. 'Tomorrow.'

They took the lift up, stared diligently at the doors. Iain took the bathroom first again to leave it clear for Karin. She turned off the lights herself before slipping into bed. The storm started outside, announcing itself with a sweep of rain against their skylight. It quickly grew closer and fiercer, then suddenly erupted all around them. Lightning shuddered above; rain slammed like machine-gun fire into the glass. The thunder was so loud that Karin sat up at one particularly violent clap, hugged her arms around her knees. 'Christ that was close,' she said.

'Yes,' he said.

'Yesterday must have got to me worse than I thought.'

There was something in her voice, a hand reached out. On instinct rather than calculation, Iain threw back his duvet and crossed the narrow divide between their beds, climbed in beside her.

'What are you doing?' she said.

'Just while the storm lasts,' he said.

'No.'

'I won't try anything,' he said, sliding his hand down her arm to her elbow, feeling the warmth of her, the goosebumps on her skin. 'We can play football rules, if you like. You can be ref.'

'Football rules?'

'Sure. You're Dutch. You must have come across the beautiful game.'

He could hear the smile in her voice. 'Not in this context.'

'Okay. Then how it works is, first offence, you can give me a yellow. If I talk back or do it again, it's a second yellow and I'm off.'

'And I can give you a straight red, yes?'

'If I do something completely outrageous, sure. Which I won't.'

'And you'll go at once? Without protest?'

'You're the ref.' She had her back to him. He put his arms around her, fitted himself to her contours. 'Take my hands,' he said. 'That way you can be extra safe.'

She put her hands tentatively in his. He spread his

fingers to let her interlace. 'While the storm lasts,' she said. Another lightning bolt struck even more loudly. This time Karin didn't even flinch. He smiled to himself, and wondered whether he was the one who'd been played. If so, he was glad enough of it. Her neck was by his mouth, the curve of it as it flowed into her shoulder. He couldn't help himself, he kissed her gently.

'Hey!' she said. 'I felt that!'

'I didn't do—'

'That's your first yellow, mister.'

'A yellow!' he protested. 'But I barely touched you!'

'It's a yellow,' she insisted.

'But—'

'One more peep and you're off.'

'But—'

'One more peep!' Her body trembled with suppressed laughter. For a moment he hankered to hug her tight, to feel again the reciprocated affection of a desirable woman. But he held himself back, and when the storm finally abated, and the room began to grow a little grey with dawn, Karin was sleeping peacefully in his arms, and the warmth where their bare legs touched was like sunshine on his skin.

SIXTEEN

I

Inspector Ozgur Karacan turned his pillow to its cooler side then slapped it three times like a mouthy suspect until it had the shape he wanted. He rolled onto his front and rested his face sideways upon it with his hands up either side, trying to surrender himself back to sleep. But his father was snoring upstairs and the bakers next door had opened their doors so that he could smell their bread and hear their banter with their first customers, and his mind began inexorably to hum and whirr again with yesterday's unanswered questions, and he knew in his heart it wasn't going to happen.

It was that damned email and its attachment. He couldn't get it out of his head. The consensus view of a *jihadi* video struck him as self-evident nonsense. For one thing, Cypriot reunificationists were not *jihadis*. And even if they had decided to film their handiwork, then surely they'd have known better than to film from inside the blast zone.

His pillow was already too warm. It promised to be a muggy day. He flipped it over again, but it was no good. The trouble was, he knew, making progress on the email and the footage required people who understood computers and the new digital age. He was of the wrong generation, that was the fact of it. A dinosaur in an age of . . .

With a slight start, he realized he'd been thinking about it wrong. He shouldn't be trying to work out who had *sent* the footage. He could leave that to the IT guys. He should be trying to work out who had *taken* the footage. That traumatic first afternoon, the witness interviews he and his fellow first responders had conducted. Everyone shocked and bewildered, except for the burly Englishman with the excellent Turkish, the only one close to the blast who'd been sharpened rather than dazed by it. He never had explained satisfactorily what business it was that had brought him to Daphne.

Tiredness left Karacan in a blink. He threw back his bedclothes and reached for the uniform folded neatly on his bedside chair.

II

Karin woke to find Iain still lying beside her in her bed. She wasn't quite sure whether to be pleased or dismayed by this development. Certainly, she'd felt a powerful hankering for his companionship last night, which was why she'd first refused a room of her own then had offered him the opportunity to join her in her bed. She liked him a great deal, was attracted to him, and was immensely grateful for everything he'd done for her. Yet her life was such a mess right now that she needed no further complications. When you had important decisions to make about your future, you wanted your head clear.

She removed her hand from his, edged carefully from the bed. She washed and dressed and came back out to find him still dozing. She turned on her smartphone to check her messages. That done, she tried to log on to the password-protected website that the police had set up to publish bulletins for people affected by the blast. The page was running some script that kept freezing her phone. It had played up the same way yesterday, so she'd ended up using the hotel's guest computer down in reception. She was about to head off down there when she noticed Iain's laptop zipped away in its bag beneath the dressing table. She sat down beside him on the bed, shook him gently by his shoulder. 'Hey,' she said.

He turned onto his back, stretched, smiled fondly up at her. 'Hey yourself.'

'Listen,' she said. 'There's this website I need to check. Is it okay if I use your laptop?'

His expression didn't flicker, yet somehow she got the sense he was suddenly on alert. 'I wish I could,' he said. 'But I've got client information on there. It's absolutely against company protocol to let anyone else use it.'

'Of course,' she said. 'No problem. They've got one down in reception.'

'If you tell me the website address . . .'

'It's honestly no problem,' she assured him. 'I'll be back in ten minutes. We'll have breakfast.' She smiled and left the room, took the stairs down to reception. The computer was free. She sat down and typed in the address. No updates had been posted since last night. Instead of ending her session, however, she stayed where she was. Iain's story about client information and company protocol had been a lie. She wasn't quite sure how, but she was certain of it. So what was on his laptop that he didn't want her seeing? Was it merely embarrassing or something more serious? And, realizing how little she truly knew of him, she opened a new browser and began to Google him.

III

Butros Bejjani was taking breakfast on deck when Michel appeared, reading a folder of documents in the ostentatious manner of someone wanting to be asked about them. He ignored him, therefore, returned to his coffee and his correspondence, until finally Michel couldn't contain himself any longer. 'Remember that detective you had me hire to watch Iain Black,' he said.

'What about him?'

'It was a her,' said Michel. 'And she's sent her first report.' He moved the bowl of *manakish* and the jug of mango juice, then laid out six photographs of Iain Black with a tall European-looking woman. 'Black and this woman went out together last night. They ate dinner then returned to their hotel.' He touched a photograph of them all but holding hands as they walked through the foul night. 'As you can see, they're on friendly terms. *Very* friendly. They're even sharing a room.'

'So the man has a girlfriend,' said Georges, joining them on deck. 'So what?'

Michel smiled faintly. 'Her name is Karin Visser,' he said. 'She's a Homer specialist. Until two days ago, she was personal assistant to Nathan Coates, the American who Black himself said had come here to bid against us.'

Butros looked with renewed interest at the photographs. There clearly was something between the two of them. But what? How long had it been going on? And what did it mean for his own plans? Until now, he'd been content to wait here for a few days in case the seller had somehow survived the blast, or had a confederate. If they were dead, after all, he'd have all the time in the world to find the site for himself. But these pictures changed all that. Nathan Coates presumably had been sent the same materials he had. If Visser knew of them, and had teamed up with Black, then suddenly he was in a race. 'They're in it together,' he said flatly. 'They're going for the treasure themselves.'

'That's certainly how it appears, Father,' agreed Michel. 'But it's not all bad news. Maybe we can even turn it to our advantage.'

Butros raised an eyebrow. 'How?'

'This man Black is highly skilled and can call on unusual resources. There's a good chance that he'll find the site, even if we can't. Unfortunately, he's already demonstrated that he's likely to spot us if we try to track him. But this woman Visser has no such talent. And, if they're in this together, then following her by definition means following him too.'

'If they're in it together,' pointed out Georges, 'then Black will spot us following her.'

'Not necessarily. Our London friends have developed an app for Android devices like this one here.' He tapped a photograph of Karin Visser checking her smartphone at the dinner table. 'Load it on to her phone and it will send us copies of all her texts, emails, conversations and browsing activity. It will also send us her GPS coordinates every fifteen minutes. And she'll never know a thing.' He smiled broadly. 'That way, if they do find the site first, they'll lead us straight to it, like truffle pigs. Then we simply haul them back by their collars and say thank you very much.'

Butros laughed at the image. 'And how exactly do we get this app onto her phone?'

'If yesterday proved anything,' said Michel, 'surely it proved that Georges is far more suited to such tasks than I am.'

Butros turned to him. 'What do you think?' he asked.

Georges nodded. 'It's worth a shot.'

'Yes,' agreed Butros. 'It is.'

IV

Iain cursed himself as he turned on his laptop. As he'd feared, he'd left thumbnails of the four video-files visible on his desktop. He hadn't worried about them because his laptop was password protected; but passwords offered little protection against a friend who asked nicely. Now Karin no doubt suspected him of something shameful or even nefarious. Just when things had been going so well.

He moved the video-files to a secure folder, wiped away all traces of them. Then he checked his inbox. He had two emails from colleagues. The first was from Quentin, a curt message that if he still wanted to know who their client was, he should call a certain London telephone number, ask for Richard Brown and cite reference number 26301. Iain recognized the phone number instantly as the main switchboard number for the SIS. So their client was British Intelligence. It wasn't the first time. They often used outside help where deniability was important or where they lacked good sources. But why their interest in Bejjani? He could only imagine it was on behalf of the Americans, perhaps in an effort to get at the Mexican cartels for whom he laundered so much money. Whatever, he wouldn't find the bombers there. The CIA might conceivably take out a hotel if the target were important enough, but they'd never risk it in an ally country like Turkey.

The second email was a long and distressed message from Maria. Layla had called three times asking for details of her husband's life insurance, yet he hadn't been covered under the new policy, and Quentin was refusing point-blank even to discuss it with her, or to acknowledge Global Analysis's responsibility. She couldn't stonewall Layla forever, nor could she file a false claim. What should she do?

Iain rested back his head and stared up at the skylight.

He'd planned to stay in Antioch as long as his clients wanted. But maybe it was time to go home. The trouble was, Quentin was clearly struggling for cash, and he had no way to force him to do the right thing. Besides, he had his other promise to fulfil: to find Mustafa's killers and make them pay. He sighed heavily. What a mess. He'd known Mustafa for eight years, since working with him on a counterterrorism mission that had straddled the Turkish–Iraqi border. They'd got on from the first, had become firm friends. When he'd decided to open an office in Istanbul, he'd only seriously considered one candidate for the job. He'd thought he'd be doing him a favour.

A shower. Fresh clothes. They did little to cheer him. Karin wasn't yet back. He was about to go look for her when he heard soft footsteps on the corridor carpet outside. They reached his room and stopped. Then nothing happened. Maybe she'd forgotten her key. He went to the door, opened it. It was hard to say who was the more surprised, he or the squad of armed and body-armoured policemen poised outside with a battering ram. He tried, instinctively, to close the door on them, but they were too quick for him, too many and too strong. They charged their way in and threw him to the ground, spinning him onto his front then cuffing him and hauling him roughly to his feet and frog-marching him to the door and out.

SEVENTEEN

I

Karin was still at the lobby computer when the police arrived in numbers at the hotel. While most hurried upstairs, two stayed by the front doors and tried with bright false smiles to intimate that all was normal, when clearly it wasn't. Even so, it came as a profound shock to see their colleagues come back down again, a scrum of them surrounding a handcuffed Iain. He looked quite incredibly composed, all things considered, just as he had in the aftermath of the Daphne bomb. He looked around the lobby as he passed through it. His eyes glanced her way but didn't settle on her even for a moment, as if trying to convey the message that this was his crisis and that she should stay clear. She stood to watch through the window as they bundled him into a squad car. Sirens turned on; a three-car convoy sped away.

Several police officers remained behind in the reception area, joking and laughing with the release of tension that accompanies the successful conclusion of a hazardous mission. She could only imagine that they suspected him of having some connection to the bombing. It seemed absurd to her, but what did she really know of him? Her searches on Google had turned up little, for there were no photographs of him and Iain Black was too common a name for her to be sure of anything.

She had visions, suddenly, of being pointed out to the police, of being arrested as a suspected accomplice, of interrogation and incarceration and tangled explanations falling on deaf ears. She logged out of the computer and hurried from the hotel while she still could, more in need of her passport and her own money than ever. She glanced behind as she climbed the short hill to the bus-stop, but no one was following. She caught a minibus out to Daphne and made her way to the warehouse the forensic team had sequestered to process debris from the hotel. Fatma saw her by the doors and came across. She was her liaison officer, thanks to her good English. From a distance she looked deathly pale, but it turned out to be plaster dust. She had bad news: the bodies of Nathan Coates and Rick Leland had been recovered overnight. Karin nodded. She'd already accepted the certainty of their deaths. Fatma waited a moment or two out of respect then added that they'd also recovered a number of safes, including hers. They'd open it for her just as soon as their locksmith arrived.

Karin bought water and fruit from a nearby shop then breakfasted on a bench beneath blossom trees. She felt like she should be grieving for Nathan and Rick, but she had too many problems of her own. The warehouse door opened. Fatma called her over. They walked together down a long corridor to a large storeroom where a man in grimy blue overalls stood by a sturdy work-table. 'What room number?' asked Fatma.

'One one five,' she told her.

The safes had their numbers written in black marker pen on their rears. The locksmith found 115, unscrewed a front panel and tried to pick it open. The mechanism was fried, however. He fetched an electric drill. The screech was hideous. Karin covered her ears and looked away. It saddened her to see the stack of battered safes and know their contents would likely never be reclaimed. The door popped open. She stooped to look inside. Her belongings were all there, dusty but unharmed. Relief flooded through her.

Fatma checked her against her passport photo, then wrote up and printed out a receipt. 'Thank you so much,' said Karin, signing it. 'Is that everything?'

'Your friend Nathan Coates,' said Fatma. 'We need someone to sign for his belongings too.'

'Oh,' said Karin. 'Of course.'

The locksmith began to drill. Karin felt a sudden twinge of alarm. What if Nathan had already bought an artefact from his mysterious dealer? What if he'd stowed it in his safe? How would she explain *that*? The door opened. She craned to look. It was empty. Her heart-rate settled back down. 'Oh, well,' she said.

'Now for Mr Leland's,' said Fatma. Karin braced herself again. She hadn't much liked Rick, to be honest. He'd mocked her accent, had had her make him drinks and the like. Then Nathan had fallen for her, and he'd become resentful of her, even jealous. But there was no disputing how heavily Nathan had relied upon him, especially when anything murky needed doing, say like holding black market artefacts on his behalf. Her mouth was dry as the door opened, but again her fears proved unfounded. A bunch of keys, a black-jacketed notebook and a sheaf of travel documents. Her involuntary loud sigh of relief prompted Fatma to glance quizzically at her. 'My friends,' explained Karin.

'Of course,' said Fatma. 'I'm so sorry for your loss.'

II

The police took Iain down to a windowless basement room with a broken air-con unit, damp white walls scratched with defiant graffiti, and a pair of dark blue moulded-plastic chairs set to face each other. They uncuffed him and sat him on one of them then left him alone again.

Arrest was an unavoidable risk in his line of work. He'd previously enjoyed the hospitality of Afghan, Libyan and Sudanese police forces, compared to whom the Turks were champions of the rule of law. He had powerful friends and extensive contacts to call on, should the need arise. But, when all was said and done, this was still an investigation into a terrorist atrocity in which dozens had been killed or badly injured, so he had to assume the normal rules suspended.

The door opened. His interrogation team filed in. Apparently he warranted four. The first, who sat down in the chair opposite, was the only one in uniform. Iain recognized him as the inspector who'd taken his statement after the bomb. The second was a low-ranking bruiser who stood behind Iain in an obvious effort to intimidate him, while the remaining two stood against the walls either side. Both wore expensive dark suits that implied senior rank, but otherwise looked very different. The one to Iain's left was badly out of shape. He had grizzled gelled-back hair and a bushy Stalin moustache that he kept stroking, as though to imply that he'd gladly consign Iain to the Gulags should the opportunity arise. The man to Iain's right, by contrast, had the shaven scalp and lean and hungry look of a career soldier: military intelligence, if Iain had to guess.

'So then,' said the inspector. 'Tell us about the footage.'

The trick in situations like this was to stick as close to the truth as you could. The more lies you told, the greater the chance of one of them being discovered. So Iain explained what he did for a living, and for whom. He told them about Mustafa and how he'd recruited him from the National Intelligence Organization. He told them how they'd been hired to find out who Butros Bejjani was meeting in Daphne, which was why they'd been filming the hotel. He told them how his laptop had been badly damaged by the blast, but that he'd recovered the video-files yesterday afternoon and had immediately sent the crucial clip in from an anonymous account, lest he get into trouble for conducting the surveillance in the first place.

'Why were you watching this man Bejjani?' asked Stalin.

'I told you. It was a job.'

'For whom?'

'They're called Hunter & Blackwells,' said Iain. 'They didn't tell me what their interest was, but I'm sure they'd tell you if you explain the circumstances.' He was sure of the absolute opposite, if he was honest, but there was no harm bluffing.

'Did you send them the footage you recovered?'

'No.'

'Why not? They were paying you, weren't they?'

'Not for that.'

'So who else has seen it?'

'No one.'

'Are there copies?'

'On my laptop and my old hard-drive. Both of which you now have.'

'What about in the sent folder of the email account you used?'

'I deleted it. Hotmail accounts aren't exactly secure.'

The inspector rose from his chair. He left the room and returned with Iain's laptop. 'Show me,' he said. The station had its own wi-fi. Iain logged on to it then complied, showed them the empty sent folder. 'Now let's see your proper email account,' said the inspector.

'It's private,' said Iain. 'But I assure you—'

'Monday's bomb killed over thirty people,' said the inspector. 'Including two friends of mine. It will be easy to get a warrant if you insist. But then I will make you pay for it. How does a week in one of our cells sound?'

Iain shrugged. The laptop was new and it was basic trade-craft not to keep anything sensitive or incriminating in one's email. He logged in to his company account then turned the laptop around to let the men browse. 'Satisfied?' he asked.

Stalin nodded at the door. The four men all left, taking

his laptop with them. It was another half hour before the door opened again and Stalin came back in alone. He sat in the facing chair. 'The two bombers you filmed are foot soldiers,' he told Iain. 'We want to catch them. Of course we do. But our priority is to catch the people behind them. The ringleaders, if you will.' There was an evasive look in his eyes as he talked, giving Iain the strong impression that he wasn't sharing the full story. 'Should news of this footage leak out, it will give those ringleaders time to cover their tracks. Should they successfully evade us, they'll recruit new foot soldiers to bomb more hotels and murder more of our citizens. I will not let that happen. So I ask again: are there any other copies of this footage?'

'No.'

Stalin glared at him for maybe ten seconds. But then he relaxed. 'I spoke to a friend at the National Intelligence Organization. She vouched for your colleague Mustafa Habib. Your office and your client both broadly confirm your account of your mission. We therefore accept that you were here on surveillance and that you filmed the bombing by chance. We also accept that, under the circumstances, you have been tolerably helpful. However, running surveillance is a clear violation of your tourist-visa status, and there have to be consequences for that.'

'Consequences?'

Stalin smiled thinly. 'Frankly,' he said, 'our overriding

concern is that word of this footage doesn't get out prematurely. With that in mind, we have decided to offer you a choice. Your first option is to acknowledge your visa violation and agree to leave the country of your own volition. There is a flight from Hatay to Istanbul this afternoon, for example, from where you can easily catch a plane on to London. Do that, keep your mouth shut about the footage, and after an appropriate interval – six months, say – you will be welcome to return to Turkey.'

'And option two?'

'We hold you in one of our cells until we catch the bombers. Then we charge you with obstruction of justice, perhaps with conspiracy too. Even if you are acquitted, I will make sure you are deported and barred from ever returning, which I imagine might prove problematic for a man with Middle-East Director on his business card.'

Iain nodded. 'I'm thinking option one.'

'Good. Then let's get you to the airport.'

III

Zehra was in a black mood. After walking Katerina to school earlier that morning, she'd gone straight back to Professor Volkan's, ostensibly to get his positive identification of her photo, but in truth to prove she wasn't useless. His shrug, however, had said it all. *A photograph*.

So what? And so here she was again, back in Famagusta for a second day, tramping the streets in an effort to find him.

Old men in checked shirts and spacious trousers played dominoes and backgammon outside a café. She weaved between them, showed her picture to a woman sweeping out the inside. The woman held it at arm's length, squinted and shook her head. 'Who is he?' she asked.

'He owes me money,' said Zehra.

'Good luck then.'

A broken wind turbine span uselessly in an overgrown lot. Zehra knew how it felt. Yet the man had to live somewhere. Two rallies he'd been to, both in Famagusta.

A bench at a bus-stop, reprieve for throbbing feet. The loudspeakers of a twin-spired mosque began to blare. As a child, Zehra had been intensely devout, like religion was a competition; but she'd witnessed the suffering of too many good people since, and the triumph of too much evil, to waste time with it any more. Yet somehow this muezzin's recorded wail seemed to call directly to her. She pushed herself wearily back to her feet and continued on her way.

IV

They buried Hakan out in the woods then divvied up the weapons and the explosives between the trucks and

and also to confirm her own bookings for tomorrow. She'd need to talk to their Cypriot car-hire people too, as the booking would be in Rick's name. She checked his travel documents to see which company he'd used, then she sat there in shock.

It had been a gorgeous spring night in Houston the year before, out on the terrace with Nathan and Rick. The garden in full bloom, the electric hum of nocturnal insects. Nathan had been in full courtship mode at the time, compensating for the age-gap with stories to demonstrate his status and virility, including an anecdote about a Bronze Age cauldron he'd tried to buy in Istanbul several years before. The trip had almost ended in disaster because the antiquities police had been tipped off to the obscene quantity of Turkish lira he'd had to raise at short notice. Raising cash fast was a nightmare, he'd confided, particularly with modern money-laundering regulations. But it was what dealers insisted on, so what could you do? He'd actually changed strategies as a result, keeping large stashes of dollars and euros in safety-deposit vaults in black market hotspots like Athens and Rome. But that had had its own drawbacks too. He'd grinned at Rick. 'Tell her about last year.'

A bright false smile from Rick. 'Are you sure that's wise, sir?'

'You're such a pussy. Okay, I'll tell her. Remember all that shit when the euro almost broke up? I thought for sure the fucking Greeks were about to slap on capital controls; maybe the Italians too. And me with over half a million euros in an Athens strongbox, as much again in Rome, all about to become worthless! So Rick here went to work. He flew over, drew it all out, took it up to Stuttgart instead. I mean, you can say what you like about the Germans, they weren't going to default, were they?'

The thing was, Rick hadn't flown in to Turkey with Nathan and Karin the week before. It had been his job, after all, to make sure Nathan was safe. He'd therefore flown in a week early to scope out their accommodations and the places they planned to visit, travelling their route in reverse from Cyprus up through Turkey to Istanbul, where he'd met them off their plane. Karin had assumed, therefore, that he'd flown directly from Houston to Larnaca.

But not according to his itinerary.

No. According to his itinerary, he'd flown via Stuttgart instead.

III

Asena identified Iain Black easily, thanks to his police escort. She bought a glossy magazine for cover then sat nearby and watched him. Buying herself a ticket at short notice had been no problem. She always travelled with a spare passport and a choice of plastic, and the London flight had been wide open. The trickier part would be to make friends with Black in such a way that he'd think it all his own doing.

He bought newspapers, read them for a while. He looked around thoughtfully. He got up, consulted a screen, went to talk to an airline supervisor. Then he came back to chat to his two policemen. They seemed to come to some kind of agreement. He picked up his holdall.

It was her cue.

She picked up her own bag and went to join the check-in queue ahead of him. When he arrived immediately behind her, she gave him a mildly flirtatious smile, as if she suspected he'd deliberately followed her, and was flattered. The queue was short, the service efficient. In no time she was being beckoned forwards. She dropped her purse, spilled a few coins. By the time she'd picked them up again, Black had been called to the desk alongside her. 'London,' she said to the check-in woman, handing across her passport. Then she smiled again at Iain and gave him an interrogative little arch of her eyebrow.

He smiled warmly back at her as he handed over his own passport. 'Tel Aviv,' he said.

NINETEEN

I

The policemen escorted Iain to his departure gate, where he joined the line for hand-luggage checks. He nodded farewell to them but they sat on a metal bench across the corridor, intent on seeing this all the way through. His bribe had bought him a change of destination. Charm evidently cost more.

He took off his belt to pass through the scanner, unzipped his holdall and parted his clothes for a woman security officer with a broken front tooth. A flash of manila at the bottom of his bag gave him a start, and he feared for a moment that his two policemen had set him up. Then he remembered Karin's package, taking it from her after the blast and stashing it in there himself. He was waved through. He went to a far corner to open

192

it. There was a toughened black plastic case inside, the size and weight of a hardback, with a handwritten note taped to it.

> *Dear Mike,*
> *I think we're finally homing in on our Virgil Solution!*
> *Nathan*

The case had twin clasps. He opened it up. There were eight sealed glass jars embedded in protective grey foam inside, along with a memory stick. The jars were labelled A to H and each contained a small shard of pottery, a lump of corroded metal or fragments of charred wood.

Boarding was announced. He still hadn't arranged to be met in Tel Aviv. He called Maria from a payphone for Uri's contact details. He tried him on his mobile first, got straight through. 'Hey, mate,' he said. 'It's Iain. You up for a visit?'

'To London? Always.'

'No. Me to you. In fact, I'll be landing at Ben Gurion in about two hours.'

Uri laughed. 'Thanks for the notice, mate. What's this in aid of?'

'You heard about Daphne, right?'

'Shit, yeah. Terrible thing. Mustafa was good people. But why would that bring you here?'

'One of the victims was Israeli.'

'So they've been saying. That history guy, yeah?'

'That's the one. Can you run a background on him? Doesn't have to be too deep. Work history, where he lived, family, friends and colleagues. You know the score.'

'I'll get on it now. Anything else?'

'I could use a spare phone or a laptop, if you've got one. I keep losing mine.'

'I'll see what I can find. What about actual help?'

'This is an off-piste kind of thing,' said Iain. 'Quentin won't be happy.'

'Fuck Quentin,' said Uri. 'Mustafa was one of us.'

'Yes,' agreed Iain. 'He was.'

II

Zehra's feet were by now in an openly mutinous mood, rapidly gaining support from her thighs and back. Yet she pressed on all the same until she reached the edge of the Forbidden Zone itself – the lost city of Varosha.

It had to be at least forty years since she'd been here last. Her uncle had worked in the kitchens of an expensive restaurant on the seafront, and they'd sometimes come to visit him on holidays. Varosha had been so glamorous back then, dazzling with film stars and European royalty, with millionaires and sporting legends. On one visit, she'd even seen Elizabeth Taylor coming out of the Argo hotel in a gorgeous blue dress and a wide-brimmed white hat.

It wasn't like that any more.

Tall apartment blocks lay derelict, their windows broken, their façades riven by gigantic cracks. A cross had collapsed onto its side atop an Orthodox church, and its terracotta dome was sieved with holes where tiles had fallen in. Houses were overrun by vegetation, while cacti pressed up against the perimeter fencing in the forlorn manner of prisoners in a concentration camp. She remembered what Professor Volkan said about all those people who'd gone missing during the war, whose bodies had never been found, and suddenly this place appeared to her their symbol: not a lost city so much as a city of the lost. It gave her the chills, and she was glad to turn away from it again.

She came across a general store. The owner grunted when she showed him her photograph. 'What do you want with *him*?' he asked.

She looked up in surprise. After so many failures, you stopped expecting success. 'Do you know him? Does he live here?'

'Why do you ask?'

'He owes me money.'

'Sure,' scoffed the shopkeeper. 'To you and those men in the cars, I'll bet.'

'What cars?'

'The ones watching his house. Three days now. What's going on? What's he done?'

'Nothing. He owes me money.'

The man shrugged it off, gave her directions. She reached a patchwork of fields, orchards and allotments. The houses were in small clusters here, but there was one all by itself that matched the shopkeeper's description: compact and shabby white, with a wooden lean-to against its side. It was set in a little citrus grove with a pair of tattered polythene greenhouses nearby, vegetation sprouting like straw from old mattresses. A rutted track connected it to the road, and a black SUV with tinted windows was parked near the junction.

She shuffled past the SUV, muttering to herself like a crazy woman. Two men were in the front, both wearing dark glasses and looking monumentally bored. Neither paid her any attention whatsoever. But the man in the back gave her a long, hard, piercing stare. Then he laughed scornfully and looked away again. She reached the next junction, turned right. The moment she was out of view, she bent double and fought for breath. It had been years since she'd suffered a panic attack. She'd thought herself over them.

As a young woman, the local PASOK thugs had eyed her in a different way, yet with that same fusion of entitlement and contempt. One day, four of them had pounded on their front door and demanded she come out. Her father had gone out instead to remonstrate. They'd beaten him into unconsciousness then forced their way inside. She'd hidden in the narrow space behind her wardrobe. For the next twenty minutes she'd had to listen as they found her mother and younger sister instead. Their cries haunted her still, as did the knowledge of such men. And the truth was that she'd been in hiding from their kind ever since.

Zehra didn't know why such men would bother to watch the small white farm-house in the shadow of the lost city. Nor did she much care.

She was out.

TWENTY

I

Israeli immigration was usually a bugger for Iain, his passport being so clotted with visas and entry stamps of hostile neighbours that his arrival was treated almost like a taunt. But this time they waved him through. Uri was waiting the other side, a year older, a year balder, a year fatter. 'A word with a mate,' he grinned, as they hugged.

'I knew there had to be a reason I recruited you.'

He was parked short-term, a powder-blue Mercedes soft-top. He popped his jeans button and lowered his zip to give his gut room to breathe. 'My trousers keep shrinking in the wash,' he said.

'Sure. That's the only possible explanation.'

Uri tossed him a smartphone. 'Yours for the trip, but I'll need it back. And those pages on the dash are all I could find on your man Jakob. Seems clean enough. Born in the States but moved here young. Taught archaeology up in Haifa. Wife died a few years back, no kids. Lives up near the Lebanese border. I'm assuming you could use a driver, right?'

'You're a prince among men, Uri.'

'Tell me something I don't know.' He glanced over his shoulder, screeched backwards from his spot. 'Your turn,' he said. 'The fuck's going on? What's this guy got to do with Mustafa?'

'I'd tell you if I knew. I'm chasing shadows here.'

'Then tell me about the shadows.'

'Give me a moment. There's something I need to do first.' He hauled the samples case from his holdall, plugged the memory stick into Uri's smartphone. It contained a number of image files that he began copying across. 'Okay,' he said. 'Ever heard of the Bejjani family?'

'The bankers?' frowned Uri. 'Sure. How do they fit in?'

'About a month back, we got hired to find some dirt on Butros. He's a bugger to get close to in Tyre, as you can imagine, but one of Mustafa's old colleagues tipped us off to a meeting in Daphne the day before yesterday. Butros Bejjani doesn't go to meet people. They go to him. So this had to be a *major* swinging dick, right? We reported back to our clients, who turn out to be British intelligence, though I didn't know that at the time. They asked us to find out more.' The image files had all loaded, so he began looking through them. The small screen made it hard to see clearly, but the first two showed a pair of wheeled suitcases lying open on a floor, each containing what he could only presume to be artefacts, wrapped for safekeeping in clothes and tissue paper and bubble-wrap. 'So I flew in, hooked up with Mustafa, set up some cameras outside the hotel and settled down to watch.'

'Which was when the bomb went off?'

Iain nodded. 'The thing is, we got Bejjani's meeting wrong. He wasn't there for a client. He was there sniffing after some black market artefacts. He's a sucker for Dido, apparently; for anything Phoenician.' He continued going through the image files as he talked, which showed the various artefacts unwrapped and held in a patch of sunlight for the photographer to shoot. They were mostly shards of pottery and the like that meant little to Iain. But, every so often, there'd be a glimpse of something different: the floor or the bed or the hands of the men holding the pieces up. There were at least two of them. Both were elderly and deeply tanned, but they were wearing different coloured shirts. One wore a gold wedding ring, the other had a faded forearm tattoo half-hidden beneath his cuff. 'The thing is, Bejjani wasn't the only bidder. An American oil gazillionaire called Nathan Coates and his head of security were with the dealer when the bomb went off. They were both killed in the blast, and presumably the dealer too. So maybe the bomb was planted by Cypriots, like the police are saying. They've bombed before and apparently they sent in a codeword. But the Cypriots are denying it furiously and – let's face it – codewords aren't exactly top secret. And the more I look into it, the more it's looking like a hit.'

'On who?'

'That's the question. My first thought was this guy Coates. He's rich, his kids hate him, the bomb was parked directly beneath his room. But that didn't pan out. So then I thought Bejjani. Maybe even our clients. That didn't work either. Then this morning I learned that three antiquities police officers were killed in the blast too, which can't be coincidence. They *had* to be there for Coates or Bejjani, either to investigate them or to sell them the pieces. So now I'm thinking that maybe *they* were the target. That someone got wind of their investigation and freaked out and used the Cypriots as a scapegoat.'

'Murdering over thirty people while they were at it? Isn't that a bit extreme?'

'Are you telling me you haven't witnessed worse?'

Uri grunted. 'Not for at least a week. So how do you see it?'

'I don't yet. But if these antiquities police were the real target then the bombers presumably got scared of where their investigation might lead. It's *possible* Coates or Bejjani could have provoked that strong a reaction, but I can't honestly see it. Which leaves whoever was trying to flog them the pieces.'

'And you think it was this guy Jakob?'

'He's an archaeologist interested in roughly the right era. He was in Turkey supposedly to visit a place called Tell Tayinat. And guess what: Nathan Coates not only sponsored the excavations there, but it's off-season at the minute. Why would he choose now to visit?'

'It's a cover story,' said Uri.

'It's a cover story,' nodded Iain. 'And I intend to find out what he was hiding.'

II

Karin tried hard not to brood on Stuttgart and safety-deposit boxes stuffed with currency. But she couldn't help herself. She kept returning to Rick's itinerary. He hadn't merely changed planes there. He'd arrived in the morning, had spent the night there, then had flown on to Cyprus the next afternoon. So surely he'd taken out at least *some* of that cash to have on hand should Nathan decide to buy. But what had he done with it?

Along with his travel documents, Karin had Rick's notebook and keyring. She started with the notebook: thirty-odd pages filled with sketched plans of their lodgings in Nicosia, Daphne and Istanbul, plus various sites they'd intended to visit, annotated with arrows, question marks, exclamation points and brief notes in a shorthand she didn't recognize. Most of his keys were standard car- and house-issue, but one looked significantly more sophisticated, exactly how she'd have expected a safety-deposit box key to look. A paper tag was attached to it by a thin white thread. On one side of the tag someone had written SGAMA 16a. On the other, they'd written a date. She double-checked against Rick's itinerary and, yes, it was the day he'd flown from Cyprus into Turkey. She sat there in disbelief for a moment or two. A fortune in cash that no one else knew about. And the key to it in her hand.

Karin was an academic by temperament and training, not particularly motivated by money. But it was one thing not to covet it in the first place, another to be unmoved when one's income was snatched away, when one found oneself jobless, deep in debt and with uncertain prospects. Nathan's heirs were already set to be multimillionaires, and Rick had no close family. She had a right to this money. It was severance.

The afternoon was gorgeous, perfect for walking. There were bank branches scattered either side of Antioch's Orontes river. She entered all those she came across, looked around. None of them had vaults that she could see, or offered any explanation for the letters on the tag. She continued hunting until the working day ended and the banks closed, and she realized how tired and hungry she was. At a courtyard café, she ordered tea and a pastry, took a table beneath a willow tree and tried to make sense of Rick's shorthand.

Two men arrived, boisterously shouting out their orders as they took the table behind her. She shifted her chair to give them more room. She became aware of a presence by the café entrance: a slim girl in a white-and-yellow summer dress darting timid looks at her. Karin smiled in invitation. She came shyly across, sat down, began speaking tangled English. A young American man, it transpired, had backpacked through the region three months before. He'd meant to stay a day; he'd ended up staying a week. They'd become friends. *Good* friends. Her furious blush implied just how good. It had been fun. But now he thought of it as more than fun. He kept sending her letters speaking of his love for her and pledging to return. She didn't want him to return. Her time with him was over. She had a new friend now. She'd tried to tell him this in her letters, but he kept writing. Perhaps this was her own fault, because while she'd wanted to be clear and firm with him, she hadn't wanted to be cruel.

Karin smiled. 'You want me to help you write a letter?' she asked.

The young woman nodded eagerly. 'Is it possible?'

'Of course,' Karin assured her.

The young woman had a pad of paper with her. Karin took it from her then encouraged her to speak her mind. She fashioned her thoughts into a draft, then cleaned it up and handed it over.

'Will he be hurt?' asked the young woman.

'Not as much as if he moves here first.'

The young woman laughed. 'Thank you so much. It's been such a worry.'

'My pleasure,' said Karin. 'And good luck.' The buzz of having helped a stranger energized her. It was time to get on again. She waved for her bill, reached for her day-pack. It had shifted while she'd been talking, she was sure of it. She looked around. The table behind was empty. Her heart sank to her boots. She closed her eyes. And having only got everything back a few hours ago too! She picked up her day-pack to see the damage. To her surprise and relief, everything was still there: her purse, passport, mobile, cash and Rick's keys too. She smiled and gave her chest a little pat. Just another typical westerner, wasn't she? Always so quick to misjudge.

III

The motorway north was fast but dull. Iain used the time to read through the briefing pack that Uri had put together on Jakob. He'd come to Israel to study Hebrew back in the 1970s, had never returned. He'd joined the faculty at Haifa University, had quietly become a respected field archaeologist and academic, specializing in the close links between early Hebrew, Phoenician and Proto-Canaanite. The pack included copies of papers he'd written on various seal-stones found on Mount Carmel, on Baal worship, on architectural styles under Omri. But though these were in English, they were written for an expert audience and Iain found them dense and hard to understand.

They turned west into a setting sun, reached Jakob's home just after dark. A low, hunched cottage, part of a small hamlet. No lights were on, no car was parked outside. No reason to expect otherwise, but it seemed only courteous to start here. He got out and knocked. No one answered. Across the road, however, a door opened and a grey-haired woman came out, a double-barrelled shotgun held aslant her chest. Iain tried a smile and spread his hands wide. She said something he didn't understand, Hebrew not being one of his languages. Uri got out slowly, raised a conciliatory palm, then held a brief conversation with her. 'She thinks we're journalists,' he told Iain. 'What do you want me to tell her?'

'How about the truth?' she mocked, in heavily accented English.

'We're not journalists,' Iain assured her. 'But we are here to investigate the bomb that killed your neighbour Jakob. Did you know him?'

'I worked with him for twenty years. I was his neighbour for ten. Of course I knew him. But why investigate here? The bomb was in Turkey.'

'I know,' Iain told her. 'I was there.'

The gun was lowered. 'You were there?'

'A good friend of mine was also killed. If I hadn't gone to get us more tea, I'd have been killed too. So you can see why I want to find the people who did it.'

'Then go to Cyprus.'

'I don't think it was Cypriots. I think that's just a cover. I think it really had to do with some black market artefacts.'

Up came the gun again. 'Are you implying Jakob was involved in the black market? Is this a joke?'

'He was an archaeologist,' said Iain. 'He had access to interesting and no doubt valuable—'

'Stop this,' said the woman. 'You didn't know Jakob, so I will excuse you this insult. But the idea is absurd. He hadn't been on a dig in years. Even if he had been, never in the whole history of the world has a man been less interested in money than Jakob. And why fly to Turkey to sell these mysterious pieces? Why not invite buyers here?'

Iain had considered this. 'I think he needed an auction to push the price up. One of the bidders was a Lebanese banker called Butros Bejjani. Bejjani is a controversial figure. He wouldn't have been allowed inside Israel without—'

'Enough!' she protested. 'Enough! Not just selling arte-facts now, but to the Lebanese!' She broke her shotgun, beckoned them across. 'Come,' she said. 'Let me show you Lebanon.' They went into her house, followed her upstairs then up a wooden ladder through a trap-door onto her flat roof. She pointed to lights twinkling on a distant hill. 'That is Lebanon there,' she said. 'They lob shells at us, from time to time, when they get restive. Ten years ago, one of them killed Jakob's wife. And now you'd have him sell them Israel's heritage?'

Iain rubbed his chin. Her certainty was persuasive. Yet he still couldn't believe Jakob had been in Daphne by chance. An alternative occurred to him. 'How about this, then?' he said. 'The other prospective buyer was an American collector called Nathan Coates who sponsored the dig Jakob supposedly went to Turkey to see. They were interested in closely related fields. Say they knew each other somehow. Say they got to like and respect each other. Then Coates is offered some important pieces slightly outside his own area, but bang in Jakob's, so he asks him along to appraise them before he spends big money on them. And bear in mind that Coates always donates such pieces to museums. Under those circum-stances, can you see Jakob helping?'

'Under those circumstances, yes. But Turkey wasn't his area.'

'What was?'

She grimaced. 'It's not easy to explain. The early history of the Jewish people, I suppose one might say, with particular reference to the United Monarchy.'

Iain shook his head. 'The what?'

'The Tanakh tells us that we, the Jewish people, first came here as nomads with Abraham from Ur. There was a terrible famine, so we moved to Egypt. We were enslaved there during the Sojourn. We escaped in the Exodus. Led by Moses and then Joshua we returned here to our Promised Land. We settled across it in tribes led by judges. Division left us weak. Our enemies took advantage. We grew fed up with this and so banded together under our first king, a man called Saul. This was the start of what we call the United Monarchy. But Saul proved ineffective and was ultimately replaced by a young shepherd turned warlord named David.'

'Ah,' said Iain. 'Him I've heard of.'

'The father of Israel,' she said. 'Our champion and national hero. Charismatic, smart and ruthless, as every great king should be. He united Israel, defeated our enemies, established our capital at Jerusalem. His son and successor Solomon was proverbially wise and rich. He built our first temple and founded cities across the land. It was Israel's first flowering, a glorious era of prosperity, abundance and high culture. But it didn't last. Solomon died, Israel split and the United Monarchy ended.'

'And that was Jakob's speciality? That period from Saul to Solomon?'

'In a sense,' she said.

'In a sense?'

'There's long been a vigorous debate about how much of the Tanakh is true. Some scholars believe in every word. Others reject it almost entirely. Most fall in between, broadly holding it to be a mix of truth and folklore that becomes increasingly unreliable the further back you go. The Babylonians certainly invaded in 586 BC, for example, and the United Monarchy is typically seen as broadly historic too, though many of the stories about David and Solomon are clearly folklore. It was only before that, with the Sojourn, Exodus, Abraham and the rest, that its historicity was truly controversial. But a strange thing happened when we archaeologists started trying to reconcile the stories in the Tanakh with the physical record of the twelfth to ninth centuries BC. Because what we found shocked us.'

'And that was?'

She smiled. 'Israel *before* the United Monarchy was rich and prosperous, with a material culture every bit as fine as that later attributed to David and Solomon. And Israel *after* the United Monarchy mapped neatly onto the Bible accounts of Ahab, Omri and the rest. But the period of the United Monarchy itself . . .' She shook her head. 'Nothing.'

'Nothing?'

'Nothing. No David. No Solomon. No cities, no palaces, no conquests. Just some scattered hill-tribes struggling grimly to survive. That's all. This whole period, this founding narrative of our nation, this flowering of heroism, wealth and power, was in truth the poorest and most desperate in Israel's entire history.'

TWENTY-ONE

I

Her name was Hannah, she told them, as she brewed a pot of mint tea in her kitchen. She had worked alongside Jakob at Haifa. Then, when his wife had died and this house had become available . . . She looked defiantly at them both, daring them to comment.

Considering her obvious fondness for him, her stoicism at his loss was impressive. But she'd known where he'd been staying in Daphne and so had been braced for the worst even before confirmation had come. She talked of him as they drank tea. Uri tapped his watch surreptitiously, but Iain wasn't quite ready to leave yet. 'You know about artefacts, I assume?' he asked.

'I'm an archaeologist,' she shrugged.

He went to the car to fetch the samples case, the

memory stick. The smartphone screen was too small for her old eyes so she led them through to her study, brought the photos up on her monitor. She sagged a little when she saw one of the men holding a piece for the camera. 'Jakob,' she said.

'You're sure?'

She touched his ring. 'Ten years a widower, and still he wouldn't take it off.'

'I'm so sorry.'

She shook her head to clear it, frowned back at the piece he was holding: a ceramic bowl festooned with lines and patterns. 'Geometric,' she said. 'Probably middle geometric, though you can never tell for sure with geometric.'

'Important?'

'Unusual for southern Turkey, and in remarkable condition; but common enough in itself.' She went through the pictures one by one, identifying the pieces as best she could. Most were pottery, either geometric or a style she called black-on-red, but there were a few other pieces too: a brooch encrusted with semiprecious stones, a pitted dagger, several seal-stones and some seal impressions too. Tenth to eighth century, as best as Hannah could tell, mostly in exceptional condition. More to the point, she didn't recognize any of the pieces, which implied that – if authentic, at least – they came from somewhere new.

Iain nodded. So it hadn't just been a few choice pieces

that had lured Coates and Bejjani to Daphne. It had been the possibility of a whole new site. She opened another picture now, a different man holding a clay oil lamp, and something snagged his eye. He took the mouse from her, zoomed in on the man's forearm. The faded tattoo beneath his shirt cuff was finally large and clear enough to make out. It showed a wolf. A grey wolf.

'Hell,' muttered Uri, with a glance at Iain. 'Did you know they were involved?'

'I was beginning to wonder.'

'What are you talking about?' asked Hannah.

'You don't want to know,' Iain told her. 'Really, you don't.'

'You think this man is one of the bombers?' she frowned.

'No,' said Iain. 'He was killed in the blast. But the group he's connected with . . .' He looked back at the screen. It was finally taking some shape in his mind. A Grey Wolf who'd needed shutting up before the antiquities police could arrest and interrogate him. But why? What had he known that was so dangerous? With startling clarity, Iain realized suddenly that this man was the key. Find out who he was and why he'd had to be killed and he'd have Mustafa's murderers. And, banned from Turkey as his way, his best hope of finding him was surely to first find this site. 'These pieces,' he asked Hannah, gesturing at the samples case. 'Where did they come from?' But she shook her head. The styles were

Eastern Mediterranean, she told him, but too diverse to be specific. A trading centre of some kind, perhaps. Maybe on Cyprus or one of the other islands. Iain scowled. 'There has to be some way to find out.'

'You could test your samples,' she said. 'The composition of clay varies significantly from place to place. The same goes for metal and paint and pollen.'

'Can you do that here?'

Hannah smiled. 'No. You'll need state-of-the-art equipment for that level of analysis. There's a lab in Tel Aviv we used to use. It won't be quick or cheap, but I could give you their number if you'd like.'

'It's okay,' said Iain. 'I've got a better idea.' It was getting late. They thanked her and returned to the car. While Uri turned the Merc, Iain found his Antioch hotel receipt then called the switchboard and asked for Karin. Slightly to his surprise, they put him through. 'Yes?' she said.

'Hey,' he said. 'It's me. Iain.'

'Hey yourself,' she said. He could hear gladness in her voice, the creak of bedsprings as she sat down. 'How are you? What's going on? They said downstairs they'd taken you to the airport.'

'I'm calling from Israel,' he agreed.

'No!' She gave a little laugh. 'Why?'

'Things got a bit fucked up,' he admitted. 'I was only ever in Turkey to look into that Lebanese guy I told you about; the Dido fan. Turns out he was there to meet the same guy your boss was. But we didn't know that at the time, so we set up cameras around the hotel. They caught the bombers parking their truck. I sent the footage in to the police. I sent it anonymously, but they managed to trace it back to me.'

'They deported you for that? But why? You helped them.'

'They said it was because I'd violated my visa. But I don't know. The whole police investigation stinks, if I'm honest. It's like they're trying to avoid finding the truth.'

'Are you serious?'

'Remember those Grey Wolves I mentioned our first night? I keep seeing signs of them. Word is that the Turkish police are infested with them. And the thing is, whenever they've been involved in shit like this in the past, it's been a sure sign of something bigger coming down the pipe.'

'Like what?'

Iain hesitated. As long as Karin remained in Turkey, there was a risk that the police would pick her up and interview her. 'I'm still working on that,' he said. 'Which is why I called. Remember that package Nathan gave you to post? The one I took from you after the bomb?'

'Christ! I'd forgotten all about it. Where is it?'

'I've got it here. I brought it with me in all the chaos this morning. I had to check what was in it before I boarded my flight, make sure it was benign. It's samples, like you said. Pottery and shit. The thing is, I want to get them tested. Apparently you can tell where the clay and metals originally came from.'

'Yes,' she said. But she sounded extremely doubtful.

'I know it's a long shot, but I'm pretty sure that the bomb was meant to kill the guy selling those pieces. So I need to find out who he was and why he needed shutting up. This is my only lead. But I can't take the samples to just anyone, not without inviting awkward questions. That's why I was thinking your friend Mike Walker in Cairo. He was expecting them anyway.'

'Yes. Of course.'

'Only if I ring him up out of the blue and start yapping about black market artefacts . . .'

'You want me to call him for you? Tell him he can trust you?'

'Could you?'

'I'll do it now,' she said. 'When can you get them to him?'

'If he's okay with it, I'll fly them down tomorrow.' He gave her his number so that she could call him back, then hung up.

Uri slid him a look. 'Who was that?' he asked.

'Just some girl.'

'Sure.'

It was another minute or two before Karin rang back. 'Mike's fine with it,' she told him. 'He's actually pretty excited.' She read out his contact details. 'He's got his in-laws staying, so he can't put you up or anything. But he said to let him know your flight number and he'll pick you up from the airport.'

'I'll call him when I'm booked.'

'Let me know if you find anything.'

'Of course. Give me your mobile.' She did so. He jotted it down. The conversation had reached its natural end, but he didn't want to let her go, and she seemed in no hurry either. 'How about you, then?' he asked. 'Get your stuff back yet?'

'This morning. You'll have to give me your address so I can pay you back.'

'Your passport and green card too?'

'Everything.'

'Brilliant. So it's back to the States, is it?' He tried his best to sound pleased for her, but didn't quite succeed.

'Not straight away. It didn't seem worth changing my bookings, so I've got a couple of nights at the Nicosia Grand. Then God knows what I'll do. Nathan was a fluke. I'll never get a job like that again. And, honestly, it was the only thing keeping me over there.'

'Holland, then?'

'If Leiden will still have me. Otherwise I'll have to start sending out résumés.'

'Come to London,' he said. 'They're crying out for Homeric specialists there.'

She laughed. 'Is that right?'

'It's all anyone ever talks about.'

'Don't tempt me. I'll take you up on it.'

'I hope you do.' His directness caught her by surprise. Silence stretched a little awkwardly, but he was in no mood to retract. 'I want to see you again,' he said.

'I'd like to see you too,' she said. 'But I've got to sort America out first. When I get back.'

'Sure,' he said.

'Good night, then.'

'Good night.' He ended the call, tucked away his phone.

'Just some girl, huh?' grinned Uri.

'Just some girl,' agreed Iain.

II

Asena arrived dispirited at the Grey Wolves' Istanbul safe house. She reported her failure with Iain Black to the Lion but agreed with him that they should carry on with their plans regardless. She duly fed the three stories and supporting materials to the journalists they'd identified, then ate a light meal and fell exhausted into bed.

The night was warm; the city noisy. Sleep eluded her. She was tossing restlessly when her phone began to buzz. Her eyes were gummed; she had to squint to read. The Lion wanted to talk again. She threw on a shirt and went up onto the roof to set up her satellite phone. 'What is it?' she asked.

'Your friend Iain Black,' he said.

'What about him?'

'I had our Antioch team check deeper into him. They went back to his hotel and made the staff talk. It turns out that Black was sharing his room with some Dutch woman he met after the blast. It further turns out that she's still there. So they put a tap on her phone.'

Asena stiffened. 'She called him?'

'He called her. Two hours ago. They spoke twice. I'm sending you the transcripts now. As you'll see for yourself, he now constitutes a definite threat. We need to deal with him urgently.'

'He's in Israel,' said Asena. 'No way can we set up that kind of operation in Israel at this short notice.'

'That's the thing,' said the Lion. 'He's flying on to Cairo in the morning. We have friends in Cairo. Suppliers. You can get at him easily there.'

Asena grimaced. 'Is this absolutely necessary?'

'Read the transcripts. It's absolutely necessary. And I warn you that there may be other work too, specifically the Dutchwoman I mentioned. It depends how much Black has shared with her. Perhaps if you could persuade him to tell you somehow . . .'

Asena fell silent. When she and the Lion had started out on this enterprise, it had been to remedy the grotesque injustice inflicted on her father and so many others like him. She'd felt righteous, therefore, certain that the scales of justice tilted heavily in their favour. But every episode like this brought them closer and closer to the level. 'I *hate* this,' she said. 'I want it over. I want us to be together again.'

'We will be. Soon. If we keep our heads.'

'Yes.'

'The Lion and the Wolf,' he said.

She sighed and touched her screen. 'The Lion and the Wolf.'

TWENTY-TWO

I

The first story was published in plenty of time to be picked up by the main breakfast shows. But because it appeared on the blog of an opposition muckraker, or 'citizen journalist' as she styled herself, with a history of bombshell announcements that went phutt, it received a cautious and sceptical response. But then she published the supporting documentation and suddenly it had legs.

The claim was simple: Turkey's Ministry of Tourism had spent vast sums improving the roads and other infrastructure of certain Mediterranean resorts, and also offering generous tax incentives to encourage privately funded projects. One such project had been granted a stretch of prime national parkland south of Bodrum to develop into an eco-resort. Instead, however, a small number of opulent villas had appeared; and now it tran-spired that the Minister of Tourism owned one of these himself via an offshore holding company, though he had no family wealth to speak of, and its market value was far beyond his salary. To make matters worse, the Minister had been making his name by denouncing corruption and calling for shared sacrifice. His own sacrifice, it seemed, had involved taking bribes of luxury villas in exchange for prime public land, huge tax subsidies and the licence to profiteer.

TV reporters went out onto the street to solicit reac-tion. *They're all the same*, people fumed. *They're all in it for themselves. One rule for them, another for us. No wonder we're all getting poorer.* And they were agreed, too, on whether the Minister would ever stand trial for it: *not a chance*.

II

The annual *khamsin* had started blowing in Egypt. Iain landed at Cairo International Airport in a see-saw of such brutal crosswinds that for once he was tempted to join in the general cabin applause for their safe arrival. He cashed some Egyptian pounds near passport control then found Mike Walker waiting in arrivals, holding up a sheet of foolscap with his name scrawled in purple marker pen upon it. He was tall, thin, angular and younger than Iain had judged from his voice, mid to late thirties. 'Thanks so much for coming to meet me, Professor,' said Iain.

'Mike, please. And it's my pleasure. Nothing else on today. To be honest, I'd pretty much cleared the whole week for these pieces of yours.'

'Interesting, are they?'

'Not the foggiest.' He turned and led the way through the crowded and chaotic arrivals hall with characteristic British diffidence, murmuring soft warnings and wincing apologies to everyone he bumped. They made it to the doors then outside into the hot, dry wind, a yellowish smog of dust and sand gusting violently enough to make Mike hold his glasses in place and raise his voice. 'But when your main sponsor asks you to run some tests, you don't tell him about the slot you've got available the week after next.'

'Big supporter, was he?'

'Our biggest, by a mile. Frankly, I don't know how we're going to manage without him.'

'Maybe he'll have left you something in his will.'

'Yes. And maybe we'll have three Christmases this year.' They reached his car, climbed in, brushed themselves down with smiles of relief. Mike flipped his wipers to clear his windscreen then leaned forward to squint through the gloom as he pulled away. 'But we'll figure something out. This is Egypt, after all. If it's coming easily, then you're clearly doing it wrong.'

Iain laughed. 'That's always been my experience.'

They passed out of the airport. Conditions improved, but only marginally. Out on the open road, Mike proved a bolder driver than Iain would have anticipated, keeping up a decent pace and not being shy with his horn when anyone tried to cut in. But then an accident ahead brought traffic on the el-Nasr road to a complete standstill, and he sighed and ratcheted his handbrake and turned off his engine and raised his eyebrows at Iain as if to warn him that they were likely to be there awhile.

'So did you know Nathan well?' Iain asked him.

'Not particularly. We only met a few times. But we spoke on the phone a fair bit. I had to report in at least once a month, though much more often if something juicy was going on.'

'Juicy meaning to do with the Homeric Question, right?'

'Or the oil thing.'

'I'm sorry,' said Iain. 'What oil thing?'

'Oh. I assumed you knew. His family money came from fossil fuels. Fossil fuels fuck up the planet.' He nodded at the lorry in front of them, spewing exhaust fumes even though it was stuck in the jam with the rest of them. 'Most people in that business either shrug it off or reject the science. But Nathan had studied geology at Yale. He liked data. He understood models. He knew the climate really was changing. So he set about it in a different way. Specifically, he argued that the planet was naturally susceptible to large swings in temperature, so that the current rise was only a to-be-expected part of an overarching pattern. But if such climate fluctuations are standard, we should find evidence for them in the archaeological record. And we do. The medieval warm period. Various minor ice ages. And then there's the big one: the Catastrophe itself. The Mediterranean was plunged into hundreds of years of misery, ergo the cause of it must have been extraordinary. A lot of people – including Nathan – believe it involved climate change of some kind, most likely a prolonged heatwave causing droughts and widespread famine. But there was no proof of this, so he set out to find it. That was where we came in, of course. We were right here on the spot and already studying this exact period. So he gave us lots and lots of money for shiny new machines. But it's a rabbit warren, this kind of thing. You set off down one hole only to pop up another. And pretty soon Nathan got hooked on the Dark Ages themselves. And I do mean hooked. He spent well over a million dollars on it through us alone. Not to mention all the artefacts he bought.'

'Looking for his Virgil Solution?'

Mike threw him an uneasy glance. 'I beg your pardon?'

'He wrote you a note to go with his samples. Something about you guys getting closer to your Virgil Solution. Which is what, exactly?'

'No idea, old chap. No idea at all.'

Iain looked curiously at him. He didn't look the type to lie. Yet he just had. But he let it go for the moment. 'So these Dark Ages,' he asked. 'What exactly got Nathan so hooked?'

'Are you being polite? Or are you genuinely interested?'

'Let's call it fifty-fifty.' He nodded at the gridlock ahead. 'It's not as if we're going anywhere for a while.'

'Fair enough,' smiled Mike. 'Okay. Let me start with this: Alexander the Great died on the afternoon of the eleventh of June, 323 BC. That is to say, we know the hour of the day of the year. You may think that's trivial. But Alexander died while campaigning in a far-distant country. They didn't have fixed calendars back then. It was all "in the fourth moon of the fifth year of such and such a king . . ." Every time a new dynasty took over, the whole system was liable to be replaced. Rulers fiddled the records shamelessly, both to glorify themselves and to diminish rivals. Record-keeping was atrocious, and archives and libraries were constantly being destroyed. And the whole region was in constant turmoil. There were endless wars, famines, revolutions, earthquakes, eruptions and the like. Then, to cap it all, came the collapse of the Roman Empire, which precipitated a dark age of its own. Piecing the timeline of *that* back together is incredibly hard. So surely it's possible that we've missed a day here or there, maybe even a year or two. Some people argue we've lost *decades*. Yet I can assure you with total confidence that we know exactly when Alexander died. How is that possible?'

Iain smiled. 'I trust that's a rhetorical question.'

Mike jabbed a finger upwards. 'The stars, my friend. The stars. Alexander died in Babylon and the Babylonians kept incredibly detailed astronomical records. With modern computers and algorithms, it's easy to retrocalculate what was happening in the skies there two and a bit thousand years ago, then to test that against their records. And they match perfectly. So we know beyond reasonable doubt when Alexander died. And the Babylonians weren't the only astronomers. The Greeks and Romans and Egyptians all were too. Their records all confirm our chronology. What's more, they help us push our knowledge further and further back. There was a battle near the River Halys in eastern Turkey, for example. The two sides called it quits after a solar eclipse made them all think they'd made their gods angry. Retrocalculate solar eclipses for that part of Turkey and you get the twenty-eighth of May, 585 BC. That, unfortunately, is about the earliest specific date everyone agrees on. We can do months and years before then, but not days. When we get back to the Early Iron Age, even years become fuzzy so we move increasingly to ranges: the third quarter of the ninth century, that kind of thing. But once we hit the Dark Ages proper, everything falls apart. We can't date specific events in the Late Bronze Age with anything like certainty, not even to the nearest hundred years.'

'Karin told me the other night that the Trojan War took place in 1200 BC,' said Iain mildly. 'Are you saying she was wrong?'

'No, no. Not at all. At least, that's a very *unhelpful* way of thinking about it. To give you the short explanation, Karin was using something called the conventional chronology. We all use it, even though we don't necessarily agree with it, because it makes communication so much easier. Think of it as our collective best guess, if you like. But many of my colleagues think it's too low, which is to say they think we should push the Late Bronze Age fifty or a hundred years further backwards in time, so that the Trojan War would have taken place in around 1275 BC, say. But others think that it's too high, and that the Bronze Age should be brought forwards by fifty years or so, placing the Trojan War around 1150.'

'And that was the short explanation, was it?' said Iain. 'It wasn't so bad. What's the long one like?'

III

Karin spent the morning on the hotel computer running searches for safety-deposit vaults in the Antioch area. When she came up dry, she turned to variations of SGAMA, the cryptic initials on the tag of Rick's key, and other such long-shots. Again without success. Her departure time approached. She considered, briefly, switching to a later flight; but in truth she'd run out of ideas. And she was eager to leave too. Antioch had bad associations for her.

A taxi to Hatay Airport. A half-empty plane out across the Anatolian coast and over dazzling deep blue sea, then flying in over the accusatory finger of the Karpas peninsula. From Erkan Airport, she took a taxi south across the border into the Republic of Cyprus. Her passport was checked; she was asked intrusive questions. It made her wonder how Rick had brought across his Stuttgart cash. A significant risk, surely, especially with Nathan not even certain to buy.

Her hotel was on Archbishop Makarios Avenue, at the heart of Nicosia's modern city. She took the lift up to the top floor. Her room was vast and plush with a whole wall of smoked glass. She slid between doors out onto a spacious balcony with white metal furniture heavy enough to resist strong winds. She enjoyed heights. They made her toes tingle. She leaned over the balcony and looked down at the busy street below, the awnings and polished windows of chic boutiques and jewellers, a florist's shop and a pair of expensive-looking cafés with glassed-off areas of pavement. But it was none of those that really caught her eye. What really caught her eye was the branch of the Société Genève bank nestled in between them.

The Société Genève, Archbishop Makarios Avenue.

SGAMA.

TWENTY-THREE

I

In quieter times, the Turkish media might have made the scandal surrounding the Minister for Tourism's villa last them several days. In fact, it lost top billing before noon. And all it took was a holiday snap of two men drinking coffee together at an Antalyan café.

Alaattin Sahin was Chief Prosecutor of Adiyaman Province. More problematically for the government, he was also the Justice Minister's first cousin. His companion was a certain Karim Ghazi, a bag-man for the Kurdish separatists with two terrorism-related convictions to his name. And that the photographs were recent was apparent not merely from the men's appearance but also because the café in question had only been open eighteen months.

Sahin's immediate response was to deny that he'd been

in Antalya at all during the past three years. But an old press release was quickly published, promoting a panel he'd sat on at a conference there the year before. His story switched. Yes, he had been in Antalya that one day. When one sat on as many panels as he did, such things were easy to forget. And yes, he now remembered taking coffee, and how this stranger Ghazi had come to sit at his table, and how they'd exchanged a few inconsequential words. He'd thought nothing of it at the time, but in retrospect it was obviously a crude attempt to discredit him. But that line fell too when footage of the meet was published, showing them talking for over five minutes before Ghazi passed him a fat envelope that he checked and then pocketed. Now came a third story. The man had approached him at the café and had asked for help with a neighbourhood dispute back home. Yes, it had been a backhander, but everyone took backhanders. If you started dismissing people for taking backhanders, Turkey would have no employees left. But it had been too late by then. No one believed a word he said any more.

Journalists gathered outside the Justice Ministry, but no one came down to talk. They contented themselves, therefore, with asking rhetorical questions of their cameras: Did the Justice Minister himself know about these bribes? Was he involved somehow? Were the payments even meant for him? The innuendo finally got beneath his skin. He marched downstairs to address the media directly. After distancing himself from his cousin and announcing his immediate suspension, he dismissed the whispers against himself as self-evidently ridiculous. What, after all, could he possibly have to gain by talking to criminals and terrorists? It was his job to put criminals and terrorists in prison.

Exactly, went the murmurs. *And look how well that's going.*

II

A slew of sirens flashing past on the other side of the road signalled that the accident was finally in hand. Engines rumbled back on around them; traffic began squabbling over access to the single lane. With the *khamsin* still blowing hard, Iain let Mike concentrate on the task in hand. They finally got moving. They passed three cars with crumpled bonnets and rears, then a blue container lorry lying like a beached whale on the verge, and suddenly they were through. The road opened up and Mike quickly shifted through the gears, anxious to make up time despite the continuing sandstorm.

'The long explanation,' prompted Iain.

'Yes.' Mike gave himself a few moments to think, then said: 'The Dark Ages affected everywhere in the ancient world; Egypt every bit as much as Greece, Turkey, Israel and the rest. But if we were ever to solve the dating problem, this always looked the best place to start. For one thing, it was relatively out of the way, and so more stable than those other regions. Its climate also meant that its monuments and archives survived well. Most of all, the Egyptians kept the best records, including king lists. So after we'd cracked the language it was comparatively easy for early archaeologists to work out the order of the various dynasties, and how long each Pharaoh reigned for.'

From the fog of sand ahead, the ghostly silhouette of a modern city began slowly to emerge. And then, abruptly, they were upon it. New Cairo was thinly populated at the best of times, but the sandstorm had driven everyone indoors, and right now it looked almost post-apocalyptic.

'Take New Kingdom Egypt, for example,' continued Mike, slowing as he approached a junction. 'It started with a guy called Amosis I and ended nearly five hundred years later with Ramesses XI, which signalled the start of the Dark Ages here. But did those five hundred years run from 1800 BC to 1300 BC or from 1400 BC to 900 BC? No one could say, not for sure. The Dark Ages themselves were too messy for anyone to make sense of, so we desperately needed some astronomical anchor point from the New Kingdom that we could date exactly, like that solar eclipse I mentioned at the Battle of Halys.

Then, about a hundred years ago, an ingenious solution called Sothic cycles was proposed. The exact mechanism is quite complex, but – to simplify it outrageously – the Egyptian calendar had 365 days to a year, rather than 365 and a quarter. Their seasons therefore slowly shifted by one day every four years until their summers gradually became their winters, and vice versa; and then, eventually, after fourteen hundred and sixty years, they got back to where they'd started.'

Iain nodded. 'One Sothic cycle completed.'

Mike flashed him a pleased smile. 'Exactly. Exactly. Now, a guy called Meyer took it upon himself to trawl through Egyptian inscriptions looking for descriptions of coronations and the like that included some mention of the Sothic cycle. Because if he could work out at what stage of the cycle a specific event took place, then he could retrocalculate the date of that event with some precision. And in fact he found multiple examples, enabling him to come up with the first truly reliable Egyptian chronology. And because the Egyptians had traded with, and corresponded with, and fought wars against all the other great Mediterranean powers, Sothic cycles effectively gave us a framework to date the entire ancient world.'

'And they placed the Trojan War at 1200 BC?'

'Exactly. And, of course, things didn't stop there. We developed scientific techniques like carbon-dating, dendrochronology and ice-core sampling, and they not only more or less endorsed that model, they also allowed us to fine-tune it.' He allowed himself a wry smile. 'Our garden was coming up roses.'

'Ah,' said Iain. 'I sense a car crash coming up.'

'I trust you mean that figuratively and not as a comment on my driving,' said Mike, peering through the gloom for their turning. 'But you're right. A car crash puts it nicely.'

TWENTY-FOUR

I

The Société Genève branch was open-plan and muffled with plush red carpeting, armchairs around the walls for customers to browse lifestyle magazines in English, German and Greek. Three cashiers sat at generously sized desks of lacquered dark wood, while others worked in glass-fronted offices to Karin's left. But she could see no sign of a safety-deposit vault.

There was a queue of one. Karin doubled it. Two of the cashiers looked young and friendly; the third old and severe. She prayed for one of the former. Naturally she got the latter. 'Excuse me,' she said, sitting down. 'But I was told you have safety-deposit boxes here. Is that right?'

The woman nodded fractionally. 'For account holders.'

'May I see?'

'They are for account holders,' said the woman. 'Are you an account holder?'

'No.'

'Well then.'

She tried a winning smile. 'Can't I have a look? I only want to know if it will be suitable.'

'It's a safety-deposit vault. If you need a safety-deposit box, then I imagine it will suit you very well.'

'What about charges?' asked Karin. 'What about terms and conditions?'

With a weary look, the cashier dialled an internal number, spoke briefly in Greek. An office door opened and a portly middle-aged man in a shiny pearl suit emerged. He smiled brightly when he saw Karin, showing unnaturally bright white teeth, then hitched up his trousers and straightened his tie as he came across. 'You wish to know about our vault, yes?' he said. 'Perhaps we should discuss it in my office.'

'Thank you,' said Karin. She followed him through. They sat either side of his desk. With a courteous gesture, he invited her to talk. 'It's my grandmother,' she said. 'She died last week.'

'I'm so sorry.'

'She'd been ill a long time,' Karin assured him. 'Anyway, she lived near Limassol down on the coast. She owned lots of beautiful things. Beautiful *valuable* things. Paintings and porcelain and jewellery and I don't know what else.'

The fluency of her lies surprised her. She was better at this than she would have expected. 'The thing is, I don't want to auction it all off. These pieces were a part of her, you know. They hold memories. But I can't leave them where they are either, because I'm definitely going to put the house up for sale. It's *far* too big for me, though I am thinking of maybe moving here myself. Only I have my job and I can't relocate just like that.' She shook her head. 'I'm sorry. I must sound incoherent.'

'Not at all,' he assured her. 'You want to keep your late grandmother's most valuable and personal possessions safe while you decide what to do with them. A box in our vault is the obvious answer. Before you make your decision, however, you naturally want to know how much it will cost, what our facilities are like, what the procedure will be.'

'Yes,' smiled Karin. 'That's it exactly.'

He swivelled a little in his chair, steepled his fingers, looked up at the portrait of a stern-faced Greek Orthodox patriarch on his wall. 'I can *tell* you everything you want to know. But I can't show you, I'm afraid. It will seem strange, I know, but it is our strict policy here that only account holders can visit our vault. We know who they are, you see, because we've already run checks on their background. You'll forgive me, I'm sure, for saying this, but when a stranger comes into our branch from off the street – however charming they may be – we have no way of knowing for certain that they are who they claim to be.'

'I understand completely,' said Karin. 'In fact, I'm re-assured to know you take your security so seriously. But I presume I could open an account here? And that I could open a safety-deposit box after that?'

He spread his hands. 'Of course.'

'How long would it take? Only I'm due to fly back home the day after tomorrow, and I'd love to have this sorted out first.'

'Our new account checks are usually completed over-night, unless there are any . . . *issues*. Which I am sure there won't be in your case. If I take your details now, therefore, and you make a nominal deposit, I should be able to show you the vault first thing tomorrow morning. Then you can decide what kind of box you need, and for how long, and we will set it up for you. After that, you can bring in your grandmother's belongings whenever you like. As long as we're open, of course, and one of our cashiers is free.'

'Perfect,' smiled Karin, reaching for her passport. 'Then let's get started.'

II

Mike waited for a van to pass then turned into a street of large houses with imposing façades. He drove slowly, looking for a place to park. But everything was taken. He accelerated to the end of the road, turned left and left again. The buildings in this new street were less impressive, but at least there were spots free. Iain grabbed his holdall then got out, squinting against the sandstorm as he followed Mike around the corner and into the sanctuary of the Institute's lobby, where they both brushed themselves down once more.

'My office, first, I think,' said Mike. 'I can't operate without coffee.' He led the way along a corridor with labs on either side, a sprinkling of young men and women in white coats working diligently at gleaming machines.

'You had a car crash to tell me about,' prompted Iain.

'Yes,' agreed Mike, pushing between a pair of fire-doors. 'You see, we kept turning up these odd anachronisms, particularly here in Egypt. There's a notorious tomb complex in Tanis, for example, where a twenty-second dynasty Pharaoh built his tomb before a twenty-first dynasty one. Which is odd. And we found a cache of mummies in a sealed cave in Deir el-Bahari. If our chronology is right, then one of those mummies simply couldn't have been among them. But it was. And then there are all those Apis bulls missing from Saqqara.'

'If you say so.'

'It's not enough to overturn our model, of course, because history is messy, you expect anomalies like that.' He opened a door and ushered Iain into his office, cramped with filing cabinets and work-tables strewn with papers and samples. 'But it was certainly enough to make us look again at our assumptions. And, when we looked at Sothic dating again, it turned out to have a slight flaw.'

'Which was?'

'It was bunk, old chap. Complete and utter bunk.' He allowed himself a nervous laugh as he poured a generous helping of ground coffee into a fresh filter. 'At least, the *theory* is fair enough. But in practice it depends entirely upon the Egyptians never having adjusted their calendar. Not once. Not in thousands of years. Yet people were always adjusting their calendars. We know of several examples from the Ptolemaic and Roman eras alone. And before them came the Persians, the Nubians, the Libyans and a wretched intermediate period when Egypt disintegrated into rival chiefdoms vying for control. And we're supposed to believe that the calendar was never adjusted in all that time?' He glugged bottled water into the percolator then set it running. 'Not *once*? Even though the most important Egyptian season was actually called inundation because – as you might expect – it marked the annual flooding of the Nile. Except, of course, that it wouldn't. Yet no one noticed this, or did anything about it, for a thousand years? Perhaps it *could* have happened. *Perhaps*. But it's fifty-to-one against. And to base our entire chronology upon such odds . . .' He shook his head.

'So out goes Sothic dating?'

'Out goes Sothic dating. Unfortunately, our chronology was already set by then. Reworking it from scratch would have been a monumental task. Because, like I said, it wasn't only Egypt now. It was the whole ancient world. And we'd all kind of internalized the chronology as undergraduates. It's what our textbooks said and what our professors taught us. But then they would, wouldn't they? They wrote the damned books.'

Iain frowned. 'What about carbon dating and the other scientific techniques? Didn't you say they supported the conventional chronology?'

'I did, yes. Unfortunately, it's not as simple as that. Take radiocarbon dating. The original and still the best. But what holds true for it also holds true for dendro-chronology, thermoluminescence and the rest. Do you know how it works?'

'Not a clue,' said Iain.

'There's a variant of carbon called carbon-14 in our atmosphere. Radioactive but harmless. We breathe it in all the time, absorb it into our flesh and bone. We're both taking it in now. All living things are. But when we die, we stop ingesting it, and so it begins a slow transition into a more common isotope of carbon, carbon-12. We know the half-life of this process, so by measuring the ratio of carbon-14 to carbon-12 in a sample, we can deduce how long it's been dead. Simple, accurate, flawless. Or so people assume.'

Iain frowned at him. 'Are you saying it doesn't work?'

'Oh no. I'd hardly have made a career out of it if I thought that.' The percolator was choking on its last drops. He poured them each a cup, added two heaped spoonfuls of sugar to his own, then a dribble of milk. 'What I *am* saying is that its reputation for precision is sometimes better than its capability. For one thing, we need organic materials to test. But organic materials decay unless they're preserved in some way. One common method of preservation is charring, from being partially destroyed in a fire or being cooked. Yet exposure to heat can make wood seem older than it really is. Or take a wooden beam: date it and you can work out the age of a building, right? Except that beams last hundreds of years and were often reused, potentially throwing out calculations by *centuries*. Then there's confirmation bias. It's only human to accept data that fits your model while excluding that which doesn't. Two samples from Tutankhamen's tomb carbon-dated to nearly five hundred years after his death. Those results didn't fit the accepted model and so were discarded. But if every such anomaly is discarded then the models gain false credibility. And even that isn't the biggest problem. The amount of carbon-14 in the atmosphere varies significantly over time and place. We can't, therefore, use raw results. We have to calibrate them. Let's say our raw results indicate that a piece of wood is from a tree that died three thousand years before present. We check our charts for that time and place, calibrate the result, then declare that it's actually two thousand eight hundred or three thousand two hundred years old, or whatever.'

'Seems logical.'

'Yes. But think about it: How do we calibrate our results? Well, we're fortunate to have a vast bank of securely dated artefacts. How do we know they're securely dated? Because they're tied to particular Pharaohs whose dates we can be confident of, thanks to Sothic dating.'

'But you just told me Sothic dating was bunk.'

'I did, yes.'

Iain frowned at him. 'So calibration assigns dates by referring to a discredited chronological model? But that's ridiculous.'

Mike smiled broadly. '*Now* you're getting it,' he said.

III

Idleness didn't come easily to Zehra. She'd spent her whole life working her house and land and so felt uneasy when not usefully occupied. She washed a basket of clothes then hung them up to dry on the clothes-lines on the small balcony. Then she set about cleaning the apartment. She left her son's study until last. His desk had twin filing cabinet drawers. The top one was locked but the bottom one was open. It was packed with folders of columns, articles and speeches he'd written over the years, many of which were scribbled with annotations marking his dissatisfaction with them.

Curiosity tugged at her. She pulled one out to read. The light in his study wasn't very good so she took it into the living room instead. She quickly found herself offended and exasperated by her son's naïvety. She kept exclaiming in indignation and dismay. Yet, when she was finished, she went back for another and then a third.

One phrase in particular got beneath her skin. It came up in speech after speech, exhorting his audience to stand up and be counted. Fear was a border, he said. You could cross it in your mind.

How easy for him to say! He'd never experienced a unified Cyprus himself, as she had. He'd never seen what neighbour would do to neighbour when given half a chance. Who was he to call her a coward? Who was he to disparage those who chose peace and separation over fear and conflict? She put the last of the pages away. The sun had shifted, leaving the apartment gloomy. She felt agitated. She felt the need for fresh air, for sunshine on her face. It was still an hour until Katerina finished school, but she set off anyway then waited in her usual spot, in the shade of a dappled almond blossom across the road.

When you feared for your life, you made bad bargains, because being safe trumped all. But those same bad bargains meant you'd never be safe. Nor your children. Nor your children's children.

Something hardened inside her as she contemplated this. She wasn't quite sure what.

Parents arrived in cars, blocking her view. Doors banged. A first few pupils ran out the gates. A bell rang and trickle turned to flood. Katerina appeared with two friends, all speaking excitedly over the others. Something twisted in Zehra's heart, a mix of pain and pleasure that she hadn't felt in years. She thought of her late husband. She thought of her imprisoned son.

'Who were those two?' she asked, when Katerina came over. 'They looked nice.'

They *were* nice, enthused Katerina. They were working on a biology project together, growing beans in the school garden. She reached into her satchel and pulled out her digital camera to show Zehra various photographs she'd taken. Zehra found herself captivated, as much by the camera as by the pictures. The gadgets they had these days! She took it from her, turned it around in her hands.

Fear was a border. You could cross it in your mind.

An unexpected serenity settled upon Zehra as she crossed that border now. She would return to Famagusta in the morning. She would see inside the house of the man from the photograph, come what may. She passed Katerina back her camera. 'Teach me,' she said.

TWENTY-FIVE

I

Asena sat in the passenger seat of the silver Subaru and read yet once more the transcripts of last night's telephone calls between Iain Black and Karin Visser. It didn't get any better. The Lion was right: Black was close enough on their trail that he needed to be dealt with as a matter of urgency. The only question was how. She glanced across the street at the front door of the Cairo Institute of Archaeometry: no movement since Walker and Black had hurried inside half an hour or so before. She didn't know what tests they'd be running in there, but presumably they'd take a while.

She had time.

Hits were nothing new to Asena. She'd killed her first man – a loathsome creep of an army officer called Durmuş

Hassan – immediately before joining the Grey Wolves three years ago. She'd killed on multiple occasions since. It was shocking how easy it was, as long as you had patience, strong nerves and a robust plan. But abduction was far more challenging, as your target was unlikely to come willingly. That was why she'd brought Bulent and Uğur with her, and why their first order of business on arrival had been to visit the Lion's contact for weapons and other equipment.

Mike Walker had his in-laws staying. Black would need a room. New Cairo was a city reclaimed from desert. There were no tourist attractions here, and therefore no hotels. All those were in Cairo proper. It was far too far to walk there, and public transport was uncomfortable, unreliable and slow, especially with the *khamsin* blowing. After he'd checked in for the night, he *might* go out again to eat or to sample the nightlife. But she couldn't count on it. Ideally, therefore, they needed to take him between here and his hotel.

There were other problems too. They weren't doing this snatch for fun. The point of it was to pump Black for everything he knew about the Grey Wolves and their plans, and what he'd told others. They needed, above all, to find out how much Visser knew, and whether she'd have to be taken care of too. Black was certain to resist their questioning, so they'd need to make him talk despite himself. That was likely to get loud, and so necessitated privacy. Finally, she had to make him vanish afterwards in such a way that no one would connect it back to Turkey.

A flurry of sand blasted her window. A youth leaned into the wind as he hurried by, a red-and-silver silk scarf over his mouth to help him breathe. They all did that here. She remembered reading of a man lost in a desert storm who'd collapsed from heat exhaustion then had suffocated from inhaled sand. The germ of an idea came to her. Maybe she wouldn't need to make Black vanish after all. She checked the forecast on her smartphone. The *khamsin* was so named because it blew over a period of fifty days; and tomorrow was expected to be another. 'Keep watching,' she told Bulent. 'Let me know if anyone comes out.' She tilted her seat back, closed her eyes. Darkness helped her think. Her mind played with the variables like a child with a wooden puzzle. She tested ideas, refined them, tried to fit them together into workable combinations. It was fifteen minutes before she sat up again and turned around to Uğur, sprawled snoring across the back seats. 'Wake up,' she said, shaking him by his shoulder.

'What is it?' he yawned.

'You're coming with me,' she told him. 'We need to get a taxi.'

'Sure. Where are we going?'

'Nowhere,' said Asena. 'We just need to get a taxi.'

251

II

The third of the scandals was in some ways the least surprising. Yet, coming on top of the others as it did, it perhaps proved the most consequential.

For years, there'd been rumours that the Defence Minister had been taking massive kickbacks in return for the award of major arms contracts. He'd always denied these rumours furiously, stating flatly that, with all the audits and other checks, there was no technical possibility of profiteering from his office. But now an Istanbul newspaper published the confidential testimony of a US defence industry whistle-blower detailing several real-world examples of how such transactions worked, including a diagram showing how they'd funnelled money to the Swiss bank account of the Turkish Defence Minister himself.

Along with the news coverage, there was speculation too. Canny political journalists wondered aloud why three such juicy scandals should emerge on the same day. They pointed out that the Tourism, Justice and Defence Ministers were each members of different factions within the government. What seemed to be going on, therefore, was that either a tit-for-tat cabinet civil war had broken out or another faction altogether – perhaps the Interior Minister's, for example – was sabotaging potential rivals before making a play for the top job.

On the street, however, the reaction was both simpler

and blunter. Get rid of the whole rotten lot of them, was the verdict. Get rid of the whole lot of them and start again.

III

There was bad news for Iain when he handed Mike the samples case. 'How long before you'll have results for me?' he asked.

'It depends on the tests,' Mike told him. 'But I'd say allow at least a week.'

'A *week*?' frowned Iain. He'd assumed, from Nathan Coates's compressed itinerary, that it could be turned around in a day or two at the most.

'For the kind of analysis you want, yes,' said Mike. 'It's one thing to tell whether a particular piece is authentically old or not, which is all Nathan wanted to know fast. It's another to tell where clay came from, or where metals were originally mined, as you want. You've no idea how complex that level of analysis is.'

Iain grimaced. He was in no great hurry to return to London, but he could hardly hang around here for a week. 'Can't you give me anything?' he asked.

Mike pursed his lips. 'We'll prepare the samples now and run our first tests overnight. Who knows? Maybe we'll get lucky. But don't pin your hopes on it. Other than that, I can have my archaeobiologist check for pollen.

But again I wouldn't put too much weight on that. It's far too easy for samples to get contaminated.'

'Right now I'll take anything.'

Mike briefed his team then set them to work. Iain watched them embed tiny fragments from the samples in plastic discs and feed them into their spectroscopes for analysis. But it was largely a waiting game now. He made himself more coffee, borrowed a phone to book himself into his usual hotel in Central Cairo, then spent the afternoon reading dense articles about dating and archaeology in academic journals.

The lab assistants – like Mike himself – were all attached to the nearby American University New Cairo campus, and so lived nearby. They drifted off, one by one, until only Mike and his pollen expert were left. At six-thirty, Mike came to fetch him, looking decidedly pleased with himself. 'I have to lock up now,' he told him. 'More than my life's worth, being late for the in-laws. But we've found something for you. Or Soraya has, at least. Come take a look.' They went together to her lab, where a shy-looking woman in a hijab was standing by a high-powered micro-scope next to a computer monitor displaying an image of multiple spiked yellow balls. 'Pollen grains,' said Mike. 'Soraya got them from one of your shards.'

'And?'

Mike touched the screen with the tip of his index finger. 'This one here is henna. Nothing surprising about that. It's been grown all over the Eastern Mediterranean for millennia. But Cyprus was particularly well known for it. Homer even mentions it in the *Iliad*. Some people claim that's how the island got its name, because henna was *kuprus* in Greek. But that's not all.' He nodded at Soraya. She changed the slide and a cluster of small purple pods appeared on the screen. 'This is a variety of grass pollen,' he said. 'The thing is, Soraya recognized it. We found it on some samples last year from Salamis. These appear to be identical.'

'Salamis?'

'An old city on the east coast of Cyprus,' said Mike.

Iain nodded. 'That's where I should look?'

Mike shook his head emphatically. 'Just because we found it there doesn't mean it's only there. Anyway, like I said earlier, you should never put too much weight on one pollen finding. But it's interesting, certainly. A good start.' He checked his watch meaningfully. 'What say we reconvene in the morning, see what the night has brought us? You've got yourself a room, yes?'

Iain nodded. 'Near the Corniche.'

'I'd offer to drive you . . .'

'Forget it. I'll take a cab.'

'I'll run you up to the university. There are always a few cabs there.'

They locked up, headed out, hunched against the continuing *khamsin*. As luck would have it, a taxi pulled up just ahead and a woman got out to pay her fare, clutching her headscarf about her face. Iain waved to the driver. The driver nodded. Iain thanked Mike then hurried across to it. He tossed his holdall in the back then climbed in after. He checked his pockets for cash but pulled out instead Nathan's cryptic note to Mike. For some reason, he got the joke instantly this time. What more fitting answer could there be to the Homeric Question, after all, than a Virgil Solution? And not only that, he also realized what that solution must be, and that Karin and Nathan and presumably even Mike himself were all in on it.

He reached for the door to call after Mike and ask him about it only to find the woman blocking his way. There was something odd about her posture, the way she had her hand beneath the flap of her bag, almost as if holding a weapon of some kind. He glanced up at her in surprise. Her scarf had slipped slightly. It was the woman from Sabiha Gökçen. He didn't know precisely what was going on but he knew it was trouble. He threw himself at her but too late. Taser nodes thumped his chest and flung him twitching to the floor. He tried to cry out but his tongue was stuck in his throat. The driver reached around and plunged a syringe into his neck and he felt the blackness pulling up like a sleeping bag around him as the woman climbed in and the handbrake released and the taxi pulled serenely away.

TWENTY-SIX

I

Deniz Baştürk rubbed a hand wearily across his face. That Twitter and the other social media were ablaze with outrage at the day's three scandals was hardly a surprise. Under other circumstances, it frankly wouldn't have been much of a worry, either. Firestorms like this were common enough in Turkey, and they usually burned themselves out quickly enough. Unfortunately, tomorrow's Day of Action offered the people the perfect opportunity to take their anger out onto the streets. And current intelligence suggested that they meant to seize it. No one was talking about tens of thousands any more. Nor even hundreds of thousands. No. According to this latest estimate, the best part of a million people were expected tomorrow.

And that was in Istanbul alone.

Deniz Baştürk tossed the report down onto his desk and looked up at Interior Minister Iskender Aslan. 'And?' he asked. 'What exactly do you expect me to do?'

'I don't expect you to do anything, Prime Minister,' said Aslan. 'I'm merely keeping you informed.'

'Of course. But you can handle it, yes?'

Aslan was too experienced a politician to answer a direct question with equal directness. 'The organizers have been helpful,' he said. 'They seem sincere in their wish to keep things peaceful. But the usual trouble-makers are certain to try to cause mischief; and, as you know, these things can sometimes take on a life of their own. What we'd normally do, we'd bus thousands of reinforcements in from around the country, then flood the streets and squares with uniforms. But we can't do that this time because these rallies are happening everywhere. I've done all I can. I've cancelled leave. I've authorized unlimited overtime. I've told our regional offices to defer the usual paperwork and put everyone on the streets. General Yilmaz has been helpful too. His troops will take over protection of transport hubs and national monuments, allowing us to put those extra officers on riot duty.'

'So that's a yes, then,' said Baştürk. 'You can handle it.'

Aslan grimaced. 'You have to understand. Civil unrest is like a forest fire. You beat it in one place only to find it breaking out in a dozen others. Then suddenly it's everywhere.'

'What are you saying?'

'I'm saying that tomorrow may be difficult. I'm saying that I may need to take strong action. I'm saying that that action may include the arrest of hundreds of people, perhaps even important people, if they start inciting trouble. But I can't do that in the current climate unless I have your full and explicit backing.'

'You have it, Iskender. I assure you.'

Aslan smiled graciously as he picked up the intelligence report. 'Thank you, Prime Minister. Then I'll leave you to your work.'

II

Asena and Uğur led in the taxi with Bulent following in the Subaru. They headed out of New Cairo on the Ain Sukhna road. The sandstorm was finally subsiding a little, revealing the terrain as flatter and bleaker than she'd expected. But it would do fine. They took a spur road then bumped down a desert track until they found a patch of suitably soft sand. Black was still out cold, and would be for another hour yet. She took out and searched his wallet, pocketed a slip of paper with various phone numbers on it, then dropped his hotel receipt from Antioch on the floor. Holding his hand by the wrist, she dabbed his fingerprints on the door-handle, the window and the seat. Then she had Bulent and Uğur carry him to the Subaru and toss him in the rear.

Black's mouth was already covered with duct tape. Uğur used up the rest of a roll binding together his forearms and then his ankles. Bulent, meanwhile, drove the taxi out onto the soft sand and spun its wheels until it was stuck. He popped the bonnet, loosened a starter motor lead, closed it again. He locked the taxi then rejoined them, adding the taxi's keyring to the Subaru's as he came back across. They drove the Subaru deeper into the desert, bumping over the moonscape of pits and loose rocks for the best part of an hour. The wind died away. The ground grew soft. They reached a steep-sided dune valley turned almost to snowdrifts by luminous moonlight. 'This will do,' she said.

Bulent stopped, ratcheted the handbrake. He dragged Black out by his ankles while Uğur covered him with his silenced handgun. Asena crouched down beside him. His eyes were groggy slits as he lay on his back, just beginning to come round. She ripped the tape from his mouth and the sting of it brought him abruptly awake. She expected confusion and panic and pleading, but there was none of that. Instead, he looked around for a few moments then stared up at her with gathering focus and what might have been unnerving calm had she not held all the aces, and all the kings too. 'Hello, again,' she said. 'Remember me?'

'Refresh my memory,' he said, his voice a little slurred from the anaesthetic. 'I have a lot of stalkers.'

'Istanbul Sabiha Gökçen. You were supposed to fly to London.'

'I had a premonition. Seems like it was right.'

She waited for him to ask the obvious questions. He didn't. She sighed and said: 'I imagine you've guessed who we are and what we want with you. But in case there's any doubt, we're here for information. Specifically, I want you to tell me what you know about the Grey Wolves, and why you think they were involved in the Daphne bombing. I want you to tell me who you've talked to about it, and how much your girlfriend Karin Visser knows.'

His single blink at Visser's name was the first hint of weakness he'd shown. 'She's not my girlfriend,' he said. 'She knows nothing.'

'Convince me,' said Asena, 'and maybe I'll let her live.'

'Fuck you,' he said, with such disdain that she had a sudden fierce urge to hurt him. She took her hunting knife from its sheath and pressed it so hard against his larynx that it drew blood. He didn't so much as flinch. Her cheeks grew hot, as though she'd lost in some small way. A tough one, this. He'd need softening before he talked. She stood and beckoned Bulent and Uğur out of his earshot. Then she told them what she wanted.

III

Butros Bejjani was on the phone with a minor Saudi prince when his son Michel came into his cabin and signalled that he had news. He therefore hurried His Highness through his usual litany of excuses then made clear to him the consequences of default and put down the phone. 'What is it?' he asked.

'Our private investigator just called, Father,' said Michel. 'According to her contact in the police, Iain Black was arrested first thing this morning. He was interviewed in connection with the Daphne bombing, then deported.'

'Deported? What for?'

'She doesn't know, not for sure. But apparently there's a rumour that he was filming the Daphne hotel at the time of the blast. It would certainly make sense. If so, we have to assume that he told his interviewers about us. If they come to see us, explaining our purpose here could prove awkward.'

Butros nodded. Awkward was right. On the other hand, an awkward interview or two was a small price to pay for the prize he was after. 'What about Black's girlfriend Visser?'

'Yes, Father,' said Michel. 'That's another thing. She flew off to Turkish Cyprus this afternoon, as she was scheduled. So it looks as though we were wrong about her and Black working together.' He dropped his eyes.

'Father, it's been two days and still no word from your contact. Surely he must have been killed in the blast. And surely he left no confederates to carry on his work. The police are likely to be here soon. Who knows what restrictions they'll put on us. We have a reputation to preserve and a banking group to run. If we don't set off while we still can, then—'

'Yes, yes,' cut in Butros. Michel had a habit of rattling on beyond what was necessary. 'Very well. Give the order.'

'Thank you, Father. I'll do it now.'

The door closed. Butros scowled in frustration. *To be so close. To be so close and yet still miss out.* There had to be something he could do. He turned on his monitor, opened the video-file once more. He'd only had it two weeks or so, yet he'd already watched it at least twenty times. But he'd watched it, all those times, in anticipation rather than forensically.

He hadn't studied it for *clues*.

It was twelve minutes fifty-seven seconds long. It had been filmed on a digital camera then crudely edited. The first few seconds were a confused blur as the man – you could tell it was a man from occasional glimpses of his free hand and tattooed forearm – came to grips with his equipment. A flash of night sky, then dusty tarmac painted with faint stripes, like a long-abandoned car park. A rope ladder was fed through a hole drilled in crudely-laid concrete. Then the descent began, the ladder twisting and yawing as the man filmed beneath him, offering a brief glimpse of the front grille and bonnet of a truck or bus that must somehow have fallen backwards through some crevice into the site. Bejjani froze the footage and zoomed in but the resolution wasn't sharp enough for him to make much of it, largely buried beneath sand as it was.

He resumed playing the footage. The man stepped off the ladder onto a hillock of rubble presumably deposited there by the collapse of the car park above. He panned slowly around a huge ancient chamber, twin rows of rounded columns that faded into the distance, and beautifully smooth walls of ashlar masonry either side. He clambered down the hillock, his camera jumping and jolting as he went, catching incongruous flashes of modern litter as he went, sweet wrappers, a weathered plastic bag, an empty soda bottle. He ignored all those and reached down instead to tug free a crushed grey disk from the earth. When first he'd watched this footage, Butros had thought it a battered tyre-rim from the fallen vehicle. He'd been wrong. The man brushed it free of dust and sand then laid it flat on the ground to photograph. The photograph was one of several high-resolution stills that Butros had been sent along with the footage. He opened it now. Despite having been crushed flat, some relief-work was still visible, several men toasting each other at a feast. A silver mixing bowl, the kind for which the Phoenicians had been justly famous. Properly restored, it would make a prime exhibit for a middle-ranking or even national museum, and would be worth something upwards of half a million euros on the open market.

The man tossed it negligently aside.

The banqueting hall next, then the friezes. Nothing new in either. The footage now cut abruptly to a more cramped series of chambers. One had a carpet of broken pottery so thick that it crunched beneath the man's feet, like he was munching crisps. He crouched down to pick up and inspect various shards. Most were plain but a good number were black-on-red. He zipped several away in his shoulder-bag. One of these was currently in Butros's wall-safe, couriered to him two weeks earlier from an Antioch sorting office, along with the Ishbaal seal fragment, this footage, the still photographs and his invitation to Daphne.

Black-on-red ware was an enigma. It was found in moderate quantities in his home city of Tyre and elsewhere in Lebanon, Syria, Israel and Turkey, in contexts dating from the eleventh century BC onwards. Curiously, however, analysis of the shards suggested strongly that the vast majority of it had been made in Cyprus and then exported, even though black-on-red pottery hadn't been found in Cypriot contexts before the mid ninth century BC, over two hundred years later.

Butros sat back in his chair. He'd assumed, because the package had been sent from Turkey, and because the meeting was in Turkey, that the site itself would be in Turkey too – for why risk smuggling artefacts across a border unless you had to? But what if it was really in Turkish Cyprus instead? The woman Visser had just flown to Turkish Cyprus, after all. Maybe that was coincidence, for she was merely following her original schedule. But her original schedule had been set by Nathan Coates, who'd surely been sent a package very similar to his own, including this same footage.

It was a hoary joke of archaeology that it was largely the study of broken pots. For while bowls and jars and the like broke easily, their shards were virtually immortal. And, because styles changed every generation or so, those shards could be dated with some confidence. What was true for ancient pottery was equally true of their modern equivalents. He skipped back through the footage. He'd ignored the modern litter on his first pass. Maybe he'd missed a trick. The old plastic bag had faint writing upon it. He zoomed in on it until it blurred. It was too worn to read, yet the characters looked distinctly Greek. The soda bottle was badly weathered but still recognizably Pepsi. He opened a web-browser and ran a search. What a marvel was the modern world. It took him only a few minutes to find the information he needed. Pepsi-Cola had been truncated to Pepsi in 1962, a sans-serif font introduced. In 1973, the font had switched colour. Allowing a year or two for . . .

A great shiver rippled him, as though he'd walked through a ghost. He leaned back in his chair and bit a knuckle. Where else could a truck fall through a hole in a car park and yet remain undiscovered, except to his mystery cameraman, for forty years? He thought to himself: *My beloved Elissa; is that truly where you've been hiding all these years?* In something of a daze, he turned off his monitor and made his way to the bridge. 'A new plan,' he announced. 'We're going to Cyprus.'

'Cyprus?' scowled Michel, visibly irritated to have his orders overruled so quickly and publicly. 'Where, exactly?'

Butros smiled almost beatifically. 'Famagusta,' he told them. 'The lost city of Varosha.'

IV

After the day's hard winds, the night sky was luminously clear, constellations and galaxies with mythic names undimmed by passing headlights or the faintest urban glow. At another time, Iain would have found it beautiful. But right now all it meant to him was how completely he was on his own.

These three were involved in the Daphne bombing, he was sure of it. In fact, from the shape of her, he thought it probable that the woman was the leather-clad motor-cyclist herself. He watched them talk. The breeze was against him so that he couldn't hear what they were saying, but he could see enough of the taxi-driver's face to lip-read him a little. As best Iain could tell, he kept addressing the woman as Asena, almost as though it were an honorific. And maybe it was. The name 'Asena' had great resonance in Turkish folklore, from a Romulus and Remus-style legend of a female grey wolf who'd nursed and raised the founders of the nation. So what more fitting title could there be for a woman leader of the Grey Wolves?

She glanced around at him again, then pointed across the flats to a tall dune, for all the world telling a pair of deliverymen how to get her new sofa up her stairs. That they intended to kill him out here seemed certain. Daphne had proved their ruthlessness, and they couldn't risk him talking. He was therefore in a fight for his life here. And perhaps for Karin's too.

His forearms were clamped together so tightly with duct tape that his hands had numbed and he could barely wriggle his fingers. His shins were bound too, though less so, as though they'd run out of tape. He worked his arms and legs in an effort to loosen them, but the conclave broke up before he'd made any progress and they came back over.

The taxi-driver aimed down a silenced handgun at Iain. The second man, a thuggish lump of muscle with a shaven scalp, fetched a coil of rope from the back of the Subaru. He looped a slipknot over the tow-bar then wound the other end multiple times around and between Iain's ankles, securing it with another knot. Then he gave Asena the thumbs-up. She crouched beside him. 'It doesn't have to go like this,' she said. 'Just tell me everything you know about the Grey Wolves. You seem to believe that the bombing in Daphne is merely the prelude to something bigger. To what, exactly? Who have you told about your suspicions? How much does Visser know? And please don't lie: I'll know if you do.'

There was a bitter irony to the situation. Karin posed these people no threat. But if Iain told them that they wouldn't believe him, because it was in the nature of torturers to believe only what they forced out of you with pain. 'Fuck you,' he said.

She stood and nodded to the shaven-headed man. He got into the Subaru, started it up. The engine roared even as the brake lights flared red, so that his tyres spun wildly, spraying sand. Asena drew back her foot then kicked Iain in the pit of his stomach with savage force, winding him so badly that he gasped in air thick with sand, rasping down his throat and into his lungs. The brakes were released; the Subaru sprang away. The rope snapped taut, jolting through Iain's ankles, knees and hips, winding him for a second time. Then he was off, flailing after the Subaru like some hapless water-skier, stones stabbing and scoring his skin as he sucked in ever more of the sandy

269

air while still choking on that already in his system, coughing and gasping and suffocating. *He couldn't breathe. He couldn't breathe.* Yet on and on it went, beyond what was endurable so that he thought he was going to pass out, until finally the Subaru began to slow and stop, allowing him to turn onto his side and retch and cough and spit out the worst of it while at the same time trying to suck air down his raw throat back into his starved lungs.

It was perhaps half a minute before he'd recovered sufficiently to even think about anything else, before he could look around. They'd completed a circuit of some kind, were back to where they'd started. The taxi-driver was again on his right, aiming down his handgun. Asena was to his left, drinking in his pain, fists upon her hips. 'We can do this all night,' she said.

'You bitch,' said Iain.

Her mouth hardened. She nodded at the driver. The engine revved. As he began to pull away, she drew back her foot and kicked Iain again in his stomach. She kicked him as hard as before, but he was prepared this time, it winded him less badly. He turned onto his side and put his bound forearms up in front of his face to filter out what sand he could. They rode up a dune, ploughing furrows as they went, then returned to the crusted sand of the desert floor, where the battering was harder but the breathing was easier. He worked his arms back and forth against each other but the duct tape was still tight. He reached down for his belt instead, undid its buckle then gripped it between his fingers and rolled over to pull it free from its loops. Then he fed it back through its own buckle to fashion a slipknot of his own.

He was barely done when they began slowing for the end of the second circuit. He lay on his front and coughed and hacked and gasped exhaustedly, as if beyond the limits of his endurance. They came to a stop. He could see shoes either side. Asena crouched beside him. 'The truth,' she said implacably. 'Your last chance.'

'You sick ugly bitch,' he whispered.

She scowled and stood back up, gestured at the driver for another lap. The engine revved, the tyres turned, they began to pull away. Then she drew back her foot to kick him for a third time.

Now.

TWENTY-SEVEN

I

Iain spun onto his side to release his belt, fashioned into a makeshift lasso that he snared around Asena's ankle even as she kicked him. She looked surprised rather than alarmed as he yanked the slipknot tight. The Subaru was already accelerating away. She hopped several times before she fell. The taxi-driver ran after them, yelling and pointing his gun but too worried about hitting Asena to shoot. Asena, herself, was kicking out and twisting furiously, doing everything she could to force him to let her go, putting extraordinary strain on his fingers, dragging his arms back over his head. But when you had just one chance to survive, your body would find a way.

Asena took out her hunting knife. She hauled herself up by her own trousers into a sitting position then slashed at Iain's hands. She couldn't quite reach him, however, began hacking at the belt instead. And her blade was so sharp that the leather immediately started to fray.

Behind them, the gunman gave up his futile chase. He unscrewed his silencer and fired twice into the air. Brake lights flared. The Subaru slowed and stopped. Iain hauled Asena towards him by the belt. She stabbed at his face. He swayed aside then clubbed her so hard with the hammer of his bound hands that she slumped to the sand and dropped her knife. He picked it up between his clumsy paws and began to saw at the rope around his ankles.

The Subaru swung around. Its headlights picked out Iain attacking his bonds while Asena lay dazed beside him. The engine revved; it began to charge. It was almost upon Iain before he finally freed his feet. He feinted left then dived right. The Subaru blurred past, flicking his heel. He dropped the knife as he fell and was too dazzled by the headlights to find it again. The Subaru wheeled sharply, a bull looking to finish off a wounded matador. Iain's only hope was the dunes. He ran to and then up the nearest, working at his wrists as he went. The sand was so dry that it caved away beneath him with each step, slowing his progress. The Subaru swung around to build up speed before charging up the steep face. Iain reached the ridge first. His legs were sacks of cement as he ran down the other side. The Subaru crested immediately behind him, its headlights throwing his shadow onto the valley floor ahead. With no chance of outrunning it, Iain turned and ran along the slope then back up. The Subaru tried to come after him but the gradient was too steep for that and its right-side wheels lifted from the sand, forcing the driver to straighten up again, speed down to the valley floor and turn there. Headlights picked out Iain once more as he scrambled back towards the ridge. The engine roared. It came charging. Iain made it over the top and threw himself down. He finally tore his hands free of the duct tape. The Subaru went down through the gears as it struggled to the top. Its fused headlights separated into twin beams. Its bonnet nosed into view. Iain sprang to his feet and hurled himself at the door. It was locked but the window was down. He punched the driver with everything he had. The man grunted and slumped sideways. Iain hauled himself in through the window even as the Subaru began to bump down the dune. His foot caught on a seatbelt. The car began turning at a precarious angle. He freed his foot and brought his legs inside as they reached their tipping point. He grabbed hold of the driver's seat as the Subaru toppled onto its side then crashed onto the roof, rolling over and over down the steepest part of the slope. Iain's world span. He clung desperately to the seat. The Subaru finally came to a rest on its passenger-side doors, its windows buckled and frosted, its bodywork rocking and groaning and creaking. The driver lay unconscious among detritus that included Iain's wallet and holdall. He packed the one into the other then tossed them out the open driver window.

The battered Subaru looked a write-off, but he couldn't take the chance. He grabbed the keys from its ignition then clambered out, picked up his holdall, slung it over his shoulder. Two shots cracked out. He looked around. Asena and the taxi-driver were running towards him. He put the Subaru between himself and them then sprinted hard for a minute or more. He crested another dune then looped around to head back in what he figured was the way they'd come, because the road surely lay that way, and therefore Cairo too.

The moon was low in the sky, making silver glitter of the mica in the sand. 'Come back!' yelled Asena. The idea was so ridiculous that he almost laughed. But then she added: 'Come back or your girlfriend will pay. I vow this on my life.'

The threat got to him. Asena and her comrades had bombed Daphne; they were capable of anything. He turned and cupped his hands around his mouth. 'Do that and I'll take you down, I swear I will.'

'Then keep your mouth shut,' she yelled. 'Keep your mouth shut and she can live. But breathe one word and she dies.'

Iain hesitated. For a moment, he considered turning back and finishing this now, one way or another. But moonlight, the mismatch of weapons, the open terrain and the easy-to-read tracks he was leaving in the sand all stacked the deck too heavily against him, so he turned his back on them and began once more to run, putting distance between them, intent on taking the fight into another day.

II

The Offices of the Prime Minister were in the heart of the government district of Kizilay in central Ankara. Until recently, the road immediately outside the main entrance had been open to the public at either end; but the growing terrorist threat had led to its being walled off at its Güven Park end, while sturdy security gates had been installed at the other, with access being strictly limited to those with passes. Unfortunately, it seemed that such passes had been issued to every journalist in the land, and all of them were out there right now, waiting for him to leave for the night so that they could assail him with their questions.

Deniz Baştürk had hoped to wait them out. But it was getting on for midnight and still they remained. And if he simply slunk away in his car, they'd make it look like he was frightened, or had something to hide. 'Set up the podium,' he told Gonka. 'Tell them I'll make a short statement and take a couple of questions. But no more. And for God's sake have the car ready.'

'Yes, Prime Minister.'

He waited in his office until the time came. He checked himself in a mirror then strode boldly out. He briefly addressed the scandals engulfing his cabinet then switched to tomorrow's Day of Action, assuring the country that peaceful protest was welcome but that any efforts to cause trouble would be severely dealt with. Then he invited questions. 'Have you spoken to the ministers?' shouted out a man. 'Have you asked for their resignations?'

'I thought I made that clear,' answered Baştürk. 'Yes, I have spoken to them. They all deny the allegations categorically. They've each served this country well and so deserve the chance to defend themselves. But I promise you that the charges will be quickly and rigorously inves-tigated. And if they prove true, appropriate measures *will* be taken.'

The fusillade of flashbulbs made him blink. Sometimes he wondered if they coordinated it that way in order to make him look shifty.

'Three scandals in one day,' called out Yasemin Omari. 'Doesn't that suggest a government not only hopelessly corrupt but also in terminal crisis?'

'The corruption, if true, pre-dated my administration. As for—'

'You invited them to join your cabinet. What does that

say about your judgement? Or don't you think you should be held responsible for your choices?'

'No, of course I—'

'Then if you accept responsibility,' demanded Omari, 'what choice do you have but to resign? When can we expect a statement?'

He found a strained smile. 'You can have a statement right now. It's late and I wish you all a very good night.' He nodded to them then made his way over to his waiting car. Rarely in his life had he ever felt quite so conspicuous, yet so alone.

III

Iain ran at a decent pace for half an hour or so, then dropped to a more sustainable jog and finally a walk. It grew cold. He trudged on, hour after hour. Ahead, he could now see the soft orange glow of a city at night. Cairo, presumably. And then, behind him, the sky began finally to lighten with the promise of dawn. As if to welcome it, a gentle breeze picked up and gradually grew strong, hinting at further sandstorms ahead. Still no sign of a road, of anything. It puzzled him that they'd taken him so deep into the desert. Then he realized a possible answer that would also explain Asena's curious choice of interrogation technique. Forcing him to breathe in all that sand would make it seem as if he'd got lost out here during the *khamsin*, and suffocated. Though what might have brought him out here in the first place, he couldn't imagine.

A dark dot far ahead swelled into a car. He drew closer and saw last night's taxi. It appeared to be stuck in the sand. Its doors were locked. It was old enough to hot-wire if he got inside, so he looked for a rock to break its window when he remembered the keys he'd taken from the Subaru. He checked them now. One fitted and turned. He climbed in. His receipt from the Antioch hotel was lying on the passenger-side floor, which was odd, because he was sure it had been in his wallet. Asena or one of her friends must have left it there for some reason. But he had more urgent concerns. He tried the ignition but nothing happened. He checked beneath the bonnet, reattached a loose lead. Now it started. He tried to reverse out but it was stuck. He scooped sand away from behind the rear tyres then laid down stones to give them traction. This time he came free, made it onto harder ground. He swung the taxi around and headed along the track until he reached a road. He followed it to a junction then headed west.

The receipt kept catching his eye. Asena must have had some purpose in leaving it there. But what? He was on the outskirts of New Cairo before he realized a possible explanation. He pulled in, got out, went around to the boot. He checked that no one was watching then unlocked it and lifted it a little way. Yes. A man, presumably the taxi's real driver, was lying inside. His face had been beaten to an ugly pulp. His left arm looked broken, and there were ligature marks around his throat.

Asena's plan finally became clear. Crude, yes, but likely to have worked. Egyptian taxi-drivers were notorious for taking tourists off on magical mystery tours to perfume shops, papyrus dealers and the like. The police would assume that something of that nature had transpired, that Iain's protests had turned into an argument until finally he'd lost his temper and bludgeoned and strangled the poor man to death. Then he'd panicked and stuffed him in his own boot and driven him out into the desert to dump his body, where the taxi had got stuck in sand and broken down. So he'd left it there and legged it, only to get hopelessly lost in the sandstorm and swallowed by the desert.

What now?

Egyptian police weren't exactly known for subtlety. If he went to them with this story, they'd laugh in his face. Even if they did check into it, their obvious first move would be to call their counterparts in Turkey. Yet Asena clearly had connections inside that investigation. How else could she have known he'd be in Sabiha Gökçen Airport unless she'd been tipped off? How else could she have known so much about his conversation with Karin last night unless they'd put a tap on . . .

With a small shock, he remembered Karin telling him she'd be staying at the Nicosia Grand Hotel. If Asena's friends had been listening in, they'd know exactly how to get to her. He checked his wallet then his pockets and his pack for her number, but he must have lost it somewhere. He drove over to the Cairo Institute of Archaeometry, but there was no sign of Mike and he couldn't hang around so he wrote him a note warning him to be careful and slipped it under the door. Then he headed on into Central Cairo and parked beneath an overpass. He cleaned himself up in the rear-view mirror then put on fresh clothes from his holdall. He pocketed the invoice, wiped down the steering wheel and every other surface that he might plausibly have touched, then he locked up and walked briskly for ten minutes before waving down another taxi and taking it out to Cairo airport.

TWENTY-EIGHT

I

The orders had been issued the night before. As morning arrived, so fleets of armoured buses drove into city and town centres across Turkey. Tens of thousands of riot police set up steel barricades, while cells were emptied and paddy-wagons deployed in anticipation of hundreds of arrests. And it wasn't just the police on the move. Great convoys streamed out of army garrisons around Istanbul, Ankara and other major cities. Squadrons of tanks divided into troops then parked with maximum visibility next to major road junctions and by international airports, while units of light infantry went into towns and cities, establishing defensive positions outside government offices, national monuments, railway stations and the like.

People arriving for their day's work, or for the marches, grumbled about intimidation; but in truth most were glad to see the army, for they trusted them more than they did the police. Conscription meant that they'd all served themselves, still had friends and relatives in uniform. And the soldiers themselves took pains to diminish any sense of threat. They stayed well away from the main rally points and march routes, and they waved in solidarity, and assured them that their orders were only to protect and deter, and on no account to intervene.

Not unless something truly cataclysmic should happen.

II

Asena led the way back to the Cairo road, bowed down by the enormity of her failure. Every so often, she'd catch herself favouring her left leg slightly and it would make her scowl. Her ankle still ached from Black's makeshift lasso, yes, but the limp wasn't about that. The limp was self-pity.

The sun rose behind them, grew warm upon their backs. Yet still she had no signal on her mobile. She had little appetite for the calls ahead, but they needed to be made. 'Keep up,' she said to Uğur and Bulent.

'His leg's hurt pretty bad,' said Uğur.

'We need to catch Black.'

'Sure,' scoffed Uğur.

The insubordination rankled, but she let it go. They reached the place they'd left the taxi. It was gone. She glared at Bulent to remind him who'd added the keys to the Subaru's ring, but this fiasco was all hers. She'd underestimated Black. It was simple as that.

Never again.

They trudged on. Finally she acquired a signal. She pinged the Lion at once, knowing it would take him several minutes to call back. Then she rang Emre in Famagusta. 'It's me,' she told him, when he picked up. 'Where are you?'

'The safe house,' he grunted. He sounded half asleep.

'Then who's on watch?'

'Tolgay and the others.' He fought a yawn. 'We could always go join them if you reckon it needs all six of us to watch an empty house.'

'Your mission there is important,' she said tightly. 'I wouldn't have sent you on it otherwise. But this is about something else. You've all got clean passports, yes?'

'Of course.'

'Good. Then I want you to go to Nicosia for me.'

'Why? Is there an empty house for us to watch there too?'

'There's a young Dutch woman staying in the Nicosia Grand Hotel. Her name's Karin Visser. You're going to pick her up for me.'

'A young Dutch woman. Now you're talking.'

'She's to be a bargaining chip, so hold her somewhere safe until I can get there.'

'Consider it done.'

It was five more minutes before the Lion called. She talked him through last night's débâcle. When she was done, he was silent for half a minute. Like many great men, he had problems with his temper; but his voice was calm when at last he spoke. 'Will Black go public with this?'

'I don't think so. Not as long as he's worried about Visser.'

'But you're not sure?'

'No.'

Another silence. She knew what he was thinking. When plots like this started to unravel, you couldn't stop them, you could only buy yourself time; and not always very much of that. 'We'll have to bring it forward,' he said.

'How far?'

'All the way. We go today.'

'*Today?* Is that even possible?'

'You've no idea how our three scandals have stirred things up,' he told her. 'The Day of Action is going to be huge. Our men are everywhere. We have the perfect cover. Give us enough mayhem to work with, and we can do the rest, I promise you.'

It was Asena's turn to fall quiet. Her Grey Wolf packs were all primed and ready to go. A single coded message to her dozen top commanders would initiate a cascade of carnage and chaos across the country. Yet the suddenness of it, after these years of toil and planning; it didn't seem possible somehow. 'How much?' she asked doubtfully.

'Everything,' he said.

'The marches? The department stores? The train stations?'

'Everything.'

'Even the four horsemen? But what if he doesn't hold a press conference?'

The Lion grunted. 'He'll hold a press conference. Trust me. It's all he has.'

A deep breath. For better or for worse, by this time tomorrow their fates would be sealed. 'Very well,' said Asena. 'I'll issue the orders now.'

'The Lion and the Wolf,' he said.

'The Lion and the Wolf.'

III

Karin was barely through the doors of the Société Genève when the branch manager came out of his office to greet her, almost as though he'd been watching for her. He was wearing a girdle beneath his cotton shirt this morning, she could tell, and he smelled pungently of cologne. She immediately relaxed a little. This was going to be a breeze.

'Miss Visser,' he said, shaking her warmly by the hand.

'Well?' she said, giving her smile just a hint of the flirts. 'Did I pass your tests, or should I run for it while I still have the chance?'

'Of course you passed,' he beamed. 'Welcome to our bank. Do you wish to see the vault now?'

'If I may. My flight, you know.'

'I'll get the keys.' He led her to an empty office, opened a wall cabinet and pocketed a selection of keys hanging from hooks inside. A fire-door at the rear of the branch led to an internal stairwell. They went down. The basement was shabby and cluttered compared to the plush space above. The vault had a steel door fitted with lock and keypad. She turned her back so that he could tap in his code. He heaved the door open and ushered her inside ahead of him. It was smaller and less impressive than she'd expected, and one of the strip-lights kept breaking into fluttery spasms. The boxes were ranged around three walls. There was a plain pine table in the middle and a stepladder against the wall, presumably for reaching the highest boxes. Those were, sensibly enough, the smallest, and they grew progressively larger as they neared the floor. Each had two keyholes and a unique serial number. Karin looked around for 16a and was glad to find it on the bottom row, where the biggest boxes were.

The manager fished his keys from his pocket. Most had green rims and serial numbers, just like Rick's. But one had a red rim and no number. He selected this and one of the greens, then looked around for the corresponding box. He inserted and turned both keys, pulled the steel safety-deposit box inside all the way out. It was deeper than she'd expected, the best part of a metre long. He set it on the table, lifted its lid to show her that it was empty. Then he replaced it and relocked it. He held up both keys. 'This green one will be yours to take away,' he said. 'But the red one never leaves the bank. That way, even should someone steal your key, they still couldn't get at your belongings, not without first passing our identity checks.'

'May I see one of your bigger boxes?' she asked. He checked through his keys, selected one, opened one of the bottom boxes. It slid out on rails, like a filing cabinet drawer. He lifted its lid for her. She was surprised by how roomy it was inside. She could just imagine it filled with banknotes. 'Perfect,' she said.

'Then you'll take one?'

'Grandmother had a *lot* of stuff,' she told him sweetly. 'I rather think I'm going to need two.'

TWENTY-NINE

I

Taksim Square, heart of Istanbul. The city's main congregation point, large enough to accommodate huge crowds, easily accessible on foot, by Metro and passenger ferry, and therefore the natural place for rallies. Yet that wasn't the only reason for holding today's main rally here.

Taksim Square had history.

It was here that the Gezi Park protests had started, leading to the nationwide marches, demonstrations and clashes with the police that had so roiled the previous administration. But it went back far further and deeper than that.

On 1 May 1977, half a million people had gathered here, undeterred by rumours of likely trouble. Most had been union members, their families, friends and other sympathizers, but there'd been more belligerent elements too: anarchists and Maoists and members of the banned Turkish Communist Party. Everything had been going smoothly until reports had started spreading of snipers on surrounding roofs. Shots had been fired; the vast crowd had panicked. Fortunately, security forces had been there in huge numbers. Unfortunately, their crude use of sirens, armoured vehicles, rubber bullets and water canon had only made matters worse. In the ensuing stampedes, thirty-four people were crushed to death or otherwise killed. Yet only demonstrators were ever arrested, prosecuted or jailed, while the investigation into the botched policing was slow-pedalled so effectively that the statute of limitations passed before a single charge was brought.

As for the rooftop snipers, everyone on the street knew the truth of that. The Grey Wolves had been responsible. The Grey Wolves and the CIA.

II

Iain arrived at the airport intent primarily on getting out of Egypt before Asena could find a way to finger him for the murdered taxi-driver. But luck was with him, for there was a flight leaving for Larnaca in Cyprus in a little over an hour. He bought himself a ticket then found a payphone and called London. No one was in the office yet so he left a message for Maria to contact Karin Visser at the Nicosia Grand Hotel and warn her that she was in serious danger and to lie low until he could get to her. Then he made his way through security and to his gate.

The plane was old and had no on-board phones. His ankles, wrists, stomach and thighs began to stiffen and throb from the chaffing and bashing they'd taken last night, so he walked up and down the aisle to stop them stiffening. The pacing made him fretful. The Grey Wolves had been notoriously well represented among the large community of Turkish army veterans who'd relocated to Northern Cyprus after partition. If Asena really was their leader, a single phone call from her could put Karin in terrible jeopardy. He remembered, suddenly and painfully, his MI6 handler breaking the news about his wife and son. The numbness of that loss, his sky turned black by storm. He was first up on landing, first through the gate. He looked around in case Asena had anticipated his move and sent a welcoming committee, but saw nothing to alarm him. He called London again. Maria was in. She hadn't been able to get hold of Karin, she told him, but she'd left a message for her at her hotel's front desk. He headed out the main doors, waved over a taxi. The driver tossed away his unfiltered cigarette. 'Where to?' he asked.

'The Nicosia Grand,' he said. 'How long?'

'An hour,' grunted the driver. 'Best part of.'

'Ten extra euros for every minute under fifty,' said Iain.

The driver grinned and plugged in his seatbelt. 'You're on,' he said.

III

They'd had to clear the SUV of weapons before crossing the border into the Republic of Cyprus. Unfortunately, that meant arriving empty-handed for the job. Emre pulled up across the street from the Nicosia Grand Hotel then went into a supermarket to see what he could improvise. Tape for her mouth, a plastic bag for a hood, rope for her hands and feet, a selection of kitchen knives to make her docile. Plus a packet of Polos for himself. He paid with cash, went back out to the car. 'Any sign?' he asked.

'Nah,' said Rageh. 'But I've got us a better picture.' He turned his laptop around to show him a photograph of her modelling some pitted old sword for the camera.

'Not bad,' nodded Emre. 'I'd do her.'

'After me, you would,' said Yasar.

'Fuck yourself. But I'll let you watch, if you're good.' He called the hotel switchboard, had them put him through to Visser's room. It rang six times then switched him to voice-mail. She was out. He sucked noisily on his mint as he looked around. The street was too busy for an easy snatch. If she was considerate enough to go walkabout, they could tail her and pick her up the moment she left herself vulnerable, hold her in the SUV. But what if she returned to the hotel? He rapped the window for Yasar's attention, nodded at the Nicosia Grand. 'Go get us a room,' he told him. 'Somewhere to keep this cow until Asena gets here.'

Yasar shrugged. 'Why not hold her in her own room?'

'Because that's the first fucking place people will look when she goes missing, you idiot.'

'Oh, yes,' said Yasar.

'And get one with a double bed. Might as well have some fun while we're waiting.' He popped another mint then looked around once more, enjoying the sunshine on his face. Lights changed at a junction ahead. Traffic slowed and stopped. Across the street, a tall young woman with straw-coloured hair and a bulky red bag between her feet was watching a bank branch a couple of doors down from him. He turned back to Rageh. 'Give us another look at that picture,' he said. Rageh tapped a key and held up his laptop. Emre looked from the screen to the woman and back to the screen again. Then he grinned broadly.

No question. No question at all.

Bitch was here.

IV

The car was different this morning, a white Renault sedan. As best Zehra could tell, the men were different too, though she didn't get close enough to make certain. But there could be no doubt they were part of the same enterprise, whatever that might be.

She shuffled past them to the end of the road, turned right. Then she went in search of a payphone. 'Excuse me,' she said, when the woman answered. 'There's something terrible going on.'

'Your name, please.'

'They're breaking in right now,' said Zehra. 'They've been sitting outside his home for three days already, but now they're breaking in. That poor old man. I dread to think what they'll do to him.' She talked over the woman's questions, describing the car and giving the address before putting down the phone. Then she found herself a vantage point from which to watch.

Turkish Cyprus being what it was, there had to be a chance that these men were official in some way. This at least should answer that for her. The three squad cars took five minutes to arrive. They approached at pace from both directions, pulling up either side of the Renault to box it in. Doors flew open. Everyone got out. She could see the Renault's occupants angrily protesting their innocence. One of them went chest to chest with a policeman. Pushed himself, he pushed back. A mistake. At once, he and his two companions were spun around and frisked and cuffed, then bundled into two of the police cars and driven away.

The third car drove up to the house. The two officers pounded on the door, cupped hands to peer through windows. They conferred briefly then got on their car radio. One of them fetched a crowbar from the trunk, pried open the front door. They went inside for a minute or so, came back out shaking their heads and laughing. One called in a report on the car radio while his colleague did his best to fix the jamb. They wrote a note of explanation or apology then got into their car and drove off.

Dust settled. Silence returned. Minutes passed.

Zehra circled around to the citrus grove, half expecting at every moment to be challenged, then made her way up to the house.

THIRTY

I

Karin's gentle flirtation with the branch manager of the Société Genève had caused her a minor headache. Not only did she suspect he now was watching out for her, he also knew the serial numbers of the two boxes she'd rented. She therefore waited across the road until she saw him emerge from his office to welcome a prosperous-looking couple and take them off for a private consultation. The moment his door closed again, she hoisted her red vinyl bag to her shoulder and hurried across.

Two cashiers were free: a cocksure young man with gelled hair who started chewing phantom gum when he saw her, presumably because he thought it made him look cool; and a woman with pendant gold earrings and kindly eyes. An easy choice. 'Miss Visser, isn't it?' said the woman. 'Marcus told us you might be in.'

'Is he around?'

'He's with customers right now, I'm afraid. You could wait for him. Or I could take you down myself?'

'Could you? That would be great.'

They went to the office with the keys. The woman took out a register. 'What number, please?'

'Seven A,' said Karin. She showed her key then handed over her passport. The cashier filled out the register then turned it for Karin to sign. They went downstairs together. 'I hope this will all fit in one box,' said Karin, patting her bag. 'I did rent two, but I want to save the other one for my next load.'

'Ah,' said the woman. They went inside, opened 7a. The cashier removed her master key. 'I'll leave you now,' she said. 'Call me when you're finished.'

'Thanks.' She waited for the door to close then set the bag down, unzipped it. Inside were cheap paintings and china swaddled in bubble-wrap that she'd bought that morning to simulate an inheritance. She transferred most of it to her box but kept a painting and a fruit bowl back. She zipped her bag up again, closed the lid of her safety-deposit box, then slid it most – but not quite all – of the way in.

She went across to Rick's box, number 16a. She crouched before it and placed her palm upon it, like an expectant parent feeling for the kick. How much would this particular baby be worth? Half a million euros? A million? Her heart suddenly began beating uncomfortably fast, her mouth went dry. She stood back up, took several deep, long breaths and walked around the table until she was calm again. She double-checked her pockets. In her left was Rick's key. In her right was her own second key, for box 13a. *You can do this*, she told herself. She went to the door, knocked on it. 'Excuse me,' she called out. 'Could you please come back in a moment?'

'Of course.' The door opened. The cashier smiled. 'Yes?'

Karin gestured at her bag, the tell-tale lumps of the painting and the fruit bowl visible in it. 'I feel like such a fool,' she said. 'It won't all fit. I'm going to need to use my second box.'

'No problem.' She held up her master key. 'What number?'

The moment was upon her. The exact situation she'd hoped to engineer. Open Rick's box and wait for the woman to leave then simply switch its contents with those in her own, still-open box. Then come back at any time to take the whole lot away. But a strange thing happened as she took hold of Rick's key in her pocket. Her shoulder muscles went weak on her; she felt nauseous. She became starkly aware of consequences: the shame her mother would feel; the disappointment of her father. The certainty of jail and the ruin of her prospects.

'Madam?' asked the cashier anxiously. 'Are you all right?'

Karin's body knew before her mind did. Her heart-rate slowed; her hands began shaking slightly with the release of tension. She couldn't do it. And not because she was too moral. No. It was because she simply lacked the guts. She let go of Rick's key and took out her own second key instead, held it up. 'Thirteen A,' she said.

The cashier smiled quizzically. They unlocked the second box. Karin waited until she was alone again then went down on her haunches. The knowledge that she was both more venal and less courageous than she'd imagined was dismaying yet perversely also a relief. She put the remaining items and the red vinyl bag itself into her second box, closed them both. Then she allowed herself another minute to compose herself before returning to the door and asking to be let out.

II

The coded messages sent out by Asena were received by senior Grey Wolf commanders around the country. They, in turn, passed the word on to their local units. In apartment buildings and lock-ups all across Turkey, small groups of tough young men gathered, joking excitedly about the adventures ahead. They pulled on T-shirts with ridiculous socialist slogans, and filled their day-packs with banners and balaclavas, with cans of spray-paint and rocks and other missiles, then set off in jubilant spirits to join their local rallies.

A more senior cadre of Grey Wolves had tougher tasks. Over the preceding few weeks, they'd visited local shops and department stores looking for those with large stocks of flammable goods and no sprinkler systems. They'd bought bulky boxed goods from these, had carefully opened their cellophane wrappings and replaced their contents with home-made incendiary devices. Now they took them back to where they'd bought them, surreptitiously replacing them on the shelves. No one checked your bags on the way in, after all; only on the way out.

As for the commanders themselves, they loaded the explosives they'd taken from the forest lair back onto vans and trucks, then drove them to multi-storey car parks, railway stations, street markets and other designated spots. And, finally, in a disused warehouse on a run-down industrial estate outside Ankara, five men of quiet purpose stripped down a horse-box in the livery of the Ankara mounted police, then oiled it and checked it all over one final time, as though their lives depended on it.

III

The girl Visser was inside the bank twenty minutes, plenty of time for Yasar to get them a room in the Nicosia Grand then rejoin them outside. She no longer had her red bag when she came out, and she looked in something of a daze. She waited for a break in traffic then hurried across the road and into the hotel. They went in after her. She headed for the lifts but the receptionist called her over, handed her a message. She ripped the envelope open as she went to the lifts. Emre ushered her in ahead of him. 'Which floor?' he asked, as Yasar and Rageh got in behind him.

'Ten, thanks,' she said.

Yasar's room was on the third floor. Emre punched the buttons. It was one of those ones with doors that take forever. He hit the button irritably to make them close. Visser frowned and looked oddly at him. Emre tried a reassuring smile but for some reason it didn't seem to reassure her. She made abruptly for the closing doors. He grabbed her by her arm and threw her violently back against the mirrored rear wall. Then he clamped a hand over her mouth and pressed his knife against her throat. Her face drained of colour; her eyes went wide with terror. Emre grinned. Nothing thrilled him quite like the fear of a pretty woman. They set off upwards, reached the third floor. The doors slowly parted. Yasar

301

looked out then gave the thumbs-up and hurried on ahead to open his room for them.

'One sound, bitch,' Emre warned Visser. 'You understand me?'

Her nod was barely perceptible, but enough. He looked out. A maid's trolley was heaped high with used sheets and brushes, but there was no one in sight except for Yasar, beckoning from the far end of the corridor, right down by the fire exit. Stupid fuck could have got something closer. He put one hand on Visser's arse, pressed his knife into her tit with his other, then fast-marched her along the corridor.

A burst of TV laughter from one of the rooms gave him a start. He glanced around. The pain in his foot when the girl stamped on it was indescribable. He yowled to wake the dead. She tore herself free of him, fled through the fire-escape doors. A blink of stillness as Rageh and Yasar stood there open-mouthed, unable to believe he'd been bested by a girl. 'Get her, you idiots,' he yelled, hobbling towards the fire-doors. 'Get her.'

THIRTY-ONE

I

Huge crowds had been expected in Taksim Square. But not this huge. Marchers kept pouring in by the thousands, the tens of thousands, and the bridges and the approach roads and arcades were thronged as far as the eye could see. There were thousands of policemen too, many already dressed in riot gear, and dozens of empty paddy-wagons waiting for arrestees. Yet the mood was buoyant. And why not? It was spring, it was sunny, it was Friday. There was free music and treats for all the family: iced drinks for the children, roasted chestnuts and charred corn cobs dandruffed with salt.

There was purpose in the air too. These were proud people. They didn't ask for much. They harboured no wild ambitions for wealth. All they wanted was a fair wage for their hard work, enough to live on and raise their families. But fair wages weren't the norm any more. The economic crisis had been bad enough; the recent bombings been worse. Tourism was devastated. Property prices had slumped. New construction projects had been mothballed, multitudes of workers laid off, undermining wages elsewhere. And don't even mention the price of food and fuel and all the sneaky tax hikes that the politicians had thought they could slip through without anyone noticing.

Even so, they might have borne it had they felt their troubles were being taken seriously. They didn't. The new Prime Minister seemed sympathetic enough, but he was hapless; he didn't have the balls. And the rest of his cabinet were a venal lot, career politicians in it for what they could get their hands on. So, for all the good humour, there was an edge to the singing that made the police nervous. And that nervousness gave the marchers extra voice, and made them bang their pots and pans all the louder, for it was a fine thing to be a part of such a vast movement, a fine thing to feel this kind of solidarity with so many good people just like themselves.

Surely, this time, someone *had* to listen.

II

The stairwell was tight and poorly lit, the stone steps polished and slippery. Karin grabbed the rail to turn the corner, but she was going too fast and her ankles slipped from under her and she crashed into the wall and went tumbling. The double doors above her burst open again and two of the men came charging through together, followed by the third, limping badly but pointing his knife at her in promise of horrific revenges. She hauled herself up by the rail, ran down another two more flights only to take another tumble. Her hard heels were ideal for impressing bank managers and stomping the feet of abducting thugs, but hopeless for taking polished stairwells at speed. She kicked them off, ran on barefoot. Swing doors ahead. She punched through them and stumbled out into the hotel's dining room, fighting to keep her balance. The place was empty except for an early lunch table giving orders to a waiter. They stared blankly at Karin as she raced past. One of the men closed up behind her, scrabbling at her shoulder, his wheezing sounding perversely like strained laughter. She crashed through more doors out into the hotel foyer. The receptionist was talking to a man who looked miraculously like Iain. He saw her and came racing over. She swerved at the last moment and he clubbed the man with his fist, sent him tumbling to the ground. But the man staggered back to his feet and then his two friends burst through the dining-room doors, and she grabbed Iain by his wrist and dragged him out of a side door into the hotel's car park. There was a narrow alley to its rear. They fled down it onto a side road, jinking left and right until finally they reached a fringe of park across from the Old City and she couldn't run any further and she stopped and put her hands on her knees and looked fearfully around, expecting the men to appear behind them. But they didn't. 'What the hell's going on?' she gasped. 'What are you doing here? Who were those people?'

He ignored her questions, gestured instead across the park at Nicosia's Old City, a minor labyrinth of narrow streets and alleys. 'There might be more of them,' he told her. 'We need to get off the street as soon as we can. They'll be looking for couples. So you go first. Briskly but not too fast. I'll be directly behind you. If you hear me shout, do exactly what I tell you. Okay?'

She felt conspicuous without her shoes, but she began walking and didn't look around. They reached the Old City without incident, went through a gate into a cobbled alley of tourist shops and pavement cafés. There was a boutique hotel ahead, its courtyard ablaze with baskets of blooming flowers. A woman with fleshy arms and a plastic red apron was clearing plates and cups from a table. 'Do you have rooms?' asked Karin.

'We're a hotel,' she said, frowning down at Karin's bare feet. 'Of course we have rooms.'

'Terrific,' said Karin, as Iain arrived behind her. 'Then perhaps you'd show us one.'

III

The jamb had splintered beyond easy repair. Zehra barely had to lean against the front door for it to give. She slipped inside, closed it behind her. Her overpowering first impression was the smell, as though something had died beneath the floorboards. No wonder the police had laughed and left in such a hurry.

The note they'd left was a terse invitation to call the local station. She left it where it was, set straight to work. She photographed indiscriminately, not sure what might prove significant. There were pale patches on his walls where pictures had once hung. The furniture was old and shabby, crudely mended with black tape. Several of his floor tiles were broken and his oven and refrigerator were almost as old as Zehra's own. His cupboards contained a few jars and tins of food, but nothing fresh. His study was lined with learned-looking histories in a variety of languages. She photographed their spines. His desk drawers and filing cabinet were empty. Either he'd packed everything up before he'd left, or someone had beaten her here.

The wooden lean-to against the side of his house proved to be his workshop. Rakes, spades and mattocks were lined up against the wall like irregular soldiers, while saws and chisels and hammers hung from pegs. He had a number of electrical and motorized tools too, all of which looked old and very well used, other than a heavy-duty hand-drill still in its original box, along with a selection of drill-bits whose perfect black finish suggested they'd never been used at all – except for the largest, which was already worn down to the grey steel beneath, and which was lightly powdered with cement dust, as though he'd used it to dig up his floor.

Upstairs, now. Yellowed walls in his bathroom, an unflattering mirror, smears of black-spot mould in hard to reach places. No toothbrush, toothpaste or soap. The first bedroom was so dusty that it couldn't have been used in months. A cobweb caught in her hair. She brushed it off. A matching set of wheeled suitcases stood against the far wall, except that the two largest of them were missing, to judge from the patches of dust-free floor. Nothing in the wardrobe but a cardboard box containing several empty picture frames that perhaps explained the pale patches on the walls downstairs.

The next room along was clearly where he'd slept, though it lacked personal touches. Surplus hangars in his wardrobe and empty spaces in the drawer beneath both suggested he'd packed for perhaps three or four days, certainly not enough to justify two large suitcases. And she couldn't find any socks or underwear, which was odd. She looked around. His bed was covered by a tatty white spread that dropped almost to the floor. She checked beneath it, one side and then the other. Yes. There were two drawers in the bed's base. The first contained his missing underclothes; the second was half filled with photographs and documents, print-outs from the Internet and handwritten letters in multiple languages, some of which were still in their envelopes. Perhaps these were the missing documents from the desk and filing cabinet downstairs, or perhaps whoever had taken those had simply not found these. She sat on the bed and skim-read a few of the letters. His name appeared to be Yasin Baykam. He had a sister in Istanbul. He'd been at loggerheads with some local farming commune over who should pay for the—

Something banged loudly outside. She went to the window. An old truck was passing along the road. Her nerve was shaken, however. It was time to leave. She fetched the smallest of the wheeled suitcases and packed all the photographs and documents into it. It was so heavy that she had to bump it downstairs one step at a time. She closed the front door behind her then ducked her head and hurried back through the citrus grove, dragging the case after her like a sulking child.

An army Land-Rover drove by just as she reached the road. Her heart went crazy on her. They were sure to stop and ask her to explain her flustered appearance and odd behaviour, demand to see inside the suitcase; but they simply gazed past her as if she wasn't there. Nothing in this world was quite so invisible as an old woman in widow's black struggling with a suitcase. Normally, this would have infuriated Zehra. But sometimes, she had to admit, it had its benefits.

THIRTY-TWO

I

The uniforms and helmets were copies rather than the real thing, but you'd have needed a close examination to tell. They had no badges or tags, of course, though that wasn't the give-away it might have been, because it was standard practice among riot police to remove or cover up anything that could identify them on days like this, precisely to avoid being caught by some do-gooder with a camera-phone.

They chose a young man with a union banner, a pronounced limp and lips reddened from drinking pomegranate juice from a fat-mouthed bottle. He had soft plump features and the wary eyes of the picked-upon. They seized him and dragged him down an alley cluttered with bins and black bags into a boarded-up shop. They punched him to the ground and kicked him in the stomach and face while their comrade filmed through a broken window so that it would look like some random passer-by had stumbled upon the incident by chance.

The young man soon fell unconscious. They carried on kicking him anyway, then left him for dead. They uploaded the footage anonymously onto YouTube and the unofficial Facebook page for the Day of Action, then sent out alerts and links on Twitter and other social media. Within an hour, it had been viewed over 100,000 times; and those who hadn't yet seen it had been told about it through the grapevine. And suddenly there was a new edge to the chanting in the squares.

Suddenly there was anger.

II

The concierge showed them to a snug double with powder blue walls and pink-and-white chintz bedclothes. She took their passports to copy and tried to tell them about breakfast. Karin thanked her and hustled her out the door. Then she turned to Iain. 'Okay,' she said. 'What the fuck's going on? Who were those men? What did they want with me? And what are you even doing here? You're supposed to be in Egypt.'

'I ran into these guys last night. Friends of theirs, at

least. They pretty much admitted they were the ones behind Daphne. They wanted to shut me up before I could go public.'

'Shut you up? You mean . . .?'

He nodded but didn't elaborate. 'I got away from them. They threatened to come after you if I blabbed. I tried to warn you but I'd lost your mobile number so I caught a flight here then had a colleague call you at your hotel.'

'They left a message with reception. I was reading it when those guys jumped me.' She sat heavily on the bed. 'Jesus. What do we do? Do we go to the police?'

Iain grimaced. Going to the police would inevitably lead to the whole story coming out, including the taxi-driver locked in his own boot. That was certain to bring a shit-storm down upon his head unless he could first find a way to establish his innocence. 'It's not that simple,' he told her. 'They're bound to call the Turks to check our story. But these people have got good connections in the Turkish police.' His bruises had stiffened; he winced as he sat beside her. 'And if they find out where we are . . .'

She frowned at him. 'What's up? Are you hurt?'

'How do you mean?'

'The way you grimaced just now. And when we were running earlier.'

'Like I said, I ran into these people last night.'

'Take off your clothes,' she said.

'Now you're talking.'

'You have injuries,' she said severely. 'They need attention.'

'They're fine.'

'Show me.' He shrugged and stripped off his shirt, revealing the welts on his forearms and wrists, the bruising on his chest. Karin's initial shock hardened into anger. 'Stay here,' she said. 'I'll be back in a moment.'

'You're not going out,' he said. 'Not on your own.'

'Those cuts will infect.'

'I don't care. You're not going out on your own.'

She sighed, relented. 'I'll ask the concierge for a first-aid kit.'

He sat on the edge of the bed, gingerly pulled off his trousers. His socks had glued to his ankles with blood and other seepage. He went to the bathroom to wipe away the worst of it. Karin returned. He wrapped a towel around his waist and went back out. She held up a red first-aid box in mock triumph but stopped smiling when she saw his ankles. 'Those fuckers,' she said. 'I *hate* them.'

'It's not that bad,' he told her. 'Truly, it isn't.'

She had him lie on his back on the bed then sat beside him and attended to his feet. She swabbed them with cotton wool and iodine, rubbed in antiseptic cream, covered them with gauze and bandage cut from a roll. Her back was to him, her T-shirt tucked into her waistband, tautening each time she leaned forwards, emphasizing the ridge of her spine, the strap of her bra. The way Tisha had looked after him in hospital had played a big part in his falling for her: that potent combination of concern and not taking any of his shit. Without thinking, he placed his hand upon Karin's lower back, began caressing her with his thumb through the thin cotton. She glanced around at him. 'Stop that,' she said.

'Sorry,' he said, taking away his hand. 'Damned thing has a mind of its own. It can be really embarrassing sometimes.'

'I'd imagine.' She finished his ankles, turned to face him. She rested a hand on the bed the other side of him to take her weight as she checked his chest. Wisps of hair spilled forwards over her eyes. She tucked them back behind her ears. She took a tube of heat-rub from the first-aid kit, squeezed a thin white worm of it onto her fingers, massaged it in to his chest, making his heart go hot. A little double crinkle appeared between her brows whenever she concentrated. Her eyes were a slightly paler blue than he'd remembered. She locked her elbow to take her weight so that her arm was bent slightly beyond the straight. Light freckles ran down to her wrist before dispersing into the darker tanning of her hand. She had silver rings set with semiprecious stones on many of her fingers, but not on all. 'So do you have a boyfriend back in the States, then?' he asked.

She smiled but shook her head. 'Nathan kind of made it impossible.'

'Good,' he said.

She laughed at his directness. 'It wouldn't work,' she said. 'Like I said the other day, I don't do flings any more. And we live halfway across the world from each other.'

'I thought you were going back to Holland.'

'I'm thinking about it. I haven't decided yet. It depends where I can get work.'

'Come in with me,' he said. 'I'm about to set up on my own. We can pool our skills, set up the world's first Homeric-themed business intelligence agency. It'd be our edge. Our USP.'

'Someone must have tried it before,' said Karin. 'It's so obvious.'

'That's what they say about all the breakthrough ideas.' He put his hand on her waist, stroked her with his thumb. She didn't stop him this time but rather put her hand on his as if intending to remove it, but then simply kept it there. There was uncertainty in her expression, that old struggle between appetites and good intentions.

'Are you serious?' she asked. 'About setting up on your own?'

'I was,' sighed Iain. 'Until that fucking bomb went off.'

'What difference would that make?'

'My colleague Mustafa, the one who was killed. I promised him I'd see his wife and daughters okay. Only it turns out my bastard boss scrapped his life insurance.'

'You can't blame yourself for that.'

'I recruited him to the fucking company. So yes I can. But that's beside the point. He was my mate, I gave him my word and that's the end of it. And it's not as if I can't afford it. I earn a good whack, I own my own place and I've got savings. It'll just set my plans back a bit, that's all. Unless I can come up with something clever.'

She still had her hand on his. Now she drew it slowly up her side to her chest. He looked up at her in surprise. 'I thought you didn't do flings any more,' he said.

'I lied,' she said.

III

Even wheeled as it was, the suitcase was too heavy for Zehra, especially as the pavement was so broken that she had to lug it half the time. The cheap handle made her fingers swell and turn alarming colours. She found a bench by a children's playground then set the suitcase on the ground in front of her and rummaged through it. But the chaos of photographs, letters and documents overwhelmed her. She didn't have the right kind of mind for it. Her son Taner would be able to make sense of it, but he was in prison. Professor Volkan would too, but he was under house arrest.

She struggled back to her feet, trudged to the nearest bus-stop. The first bus took her to Famagusta's central bus station, then she caught another out along the Salamis Road. 'Who is it?' asked Andreas irritably, when finally he answered his buzzer.

'It's me. Zehra. Taner's mother. I need you to look at something.'

'I'm busy,' he told her. 'I've got classes to prepare. Papers to mark.'

'Please,' she said.

Andreas sighed heavily. 'Fine. Come on up.' He buzzed her in. She took the lift to the top floor. A sulky young woman with dishevelled hair was waiting by the doors. *Some classes!* thought Zehra. *Some papers!*

The lock was on the latch. She went in. Andreas was boiling the kettle at his kitchen counter, wearing only a loosely knotted blue-and-white silk kimono. 'This better be important,' he said.

'Put some clothes on,' she told him. 'Don't you have any shame?'

He vanished into his bedroom, came out a minute later, still barefoot, buttoning up a black shirt that he tucked into crumpled cream slacks. 'What the hell?' he asked, when he saw her decanting the suitcase onto his floor.

'These came from the house of the man in that picture,' she told him. 'His name is Yasin Baykam. He had something to do with the bomb they're blaming on my son. And you're going to help me find out what.'

318

THIRTY-THREE

I

They lay in bed together afterwards, turned to face each other. Iain told her more about what had happened since the police had come for him in Antioch: his interrogation, his deportation, his time in Israel, his afternoon with Mike.

'How did that go?' Karin asked him. 'Did he get anything from those samples?'

'It's going to take longer than I expected. Though there was some pollen. From here in Cyprus, as it happens.'

She pushed herself up onto an elbow. 'From where, exactly?' she asked.

'Some place called Salamis. Ever heard of it?'

Karin laughed. 'Of course I've heard of it. It's one of the great sites. In fact, I was going to go visit it with Nathan. It was founded by a Trojan War veteran, you see.'

Iain gave a wry smile. 'Except don't tell me: the dates don't fit, right?'

She looked curiously at him. 'Why do you say that?'

'Your boss wrote a note to Mike to go with the samples. He said you were all closing in on your Virgil Solution. I couldn't figure out what he meant. But then I realized. What's Virgil famous for? For Dido and Aeneas, the impossible lovers who lived four hundred years apart. Impossible, that is, unless the conventional chronology is fucked up. That's what you think, isn't it, you and Mike and Nathan? That the Dark Ages never happened. That's why there's no trace of David or Solomon in Israel, and how Homer described the Trojan War so accurately, and how the Hittites and Phoenicians and those other cultures all picked up so precisely where they'd left off before. You think Dido and Aeneas really were lovers, don't you?'

Her expression was hard to read, as if torn between discretion and an eagerness to share. 'Not exactly,' she said.

'Not exactly?'

'There really was a Catastrophe. There really was a Dark Age. We simply think it didn't last anything like as long as most people claim. But even if we could cut out 350 years, which is pretty much the upper limit, Dido and Aeneas still couldn't have been lovers. Though they *could* have known each other.'

'I don't get it. Why all the mystery? Why not just tell me?'

Karin sighed. 'Because you learn not to. It's considered crank history, you see. An extreme variant of it was once proposed by this crazy Russian psychiatrist called Velikovsky who also blamed the planet Mercury for destroying the Tower of Babel and Jupiter for Sodom and Gomorrah. So no one's ever had to engage with our arguments. All they've ever had to do is point at Velikovsky and sneer at us. But our arguments are *strong*. That doesn't make them right, of course, but it surely makes them at least worthy of refutation. But of course the people who matter can't admit even that much. To do so would be to admit that all their ridicule was unwarranted, which would be humiliating. So they exclude us from their academy instead. They ignore our papers and try to pretend we don't exist.'

'So I'm in bed with a crank, huh?' grinned Iain. 'Cool.' He kissed her, threw back the duvet, grabbed his towel from the floor. He paused at the bathroom door, turned. 'And no going through my stuff this time,' he said, gesturing at his holdall. 'We know how that ends. Watch TV or something instead.'

II

The signs had been there, in the minutes leading up to it, that the dam had been about to burst. The chants in Taksim Square had turned increasingly belligerent. Small surges of demonstrators towards the police lines, almost playful to start with, had grown in frequency and aggression. Parents who'd hoped for a fun and cheap day out grabbed their children's hands and headed briskly for the exit roads. And the police stepped up their own preparations too, putting on masks in anticipation of tear-gas, picking up their shields and batons.

A man holding a placard was shoved from behind by a youth in a Fenerbache scarf. He stumbled into one policeman and his placard hit another. They laid into him with their batons. He staggered off a few dazed paces, blood streaming from his forehead, then collapsed in an ugly heap. A roar went up. A volley of empty bottles and other litter was launched at the police, with rocks and other nastier missiles mixed in. Skirmishes broke out, turned quickly into running battles. Mounted police charged from one side; tear-gas canisters were fired from the other. Pandemonium took hold as panicked people tried to get away. A throng crushed up against temporary barriers set up to seal off a shopping street. The pressure proved too much for them, they gave way. The crowd spilled down it like a river in full spate. Most simply wanted to get to safety but others saw a chance for easy pickings. Plate-glass windows were smashed, clothes and jewellery grabbed. The steel shutters outside a large department store were jemmied up while a TV camera crew filmed it live for the news.

Police reinforcements were urgently summoned. But reports were now streaming in of trouble elsewhere. A builders' merchant was on fire in Beşiktaş; a carpet shop in Üsküdar. Cars had been upturned and set ablaze all across the city. The Interior Minister went on television to assure the nation everything was in hand, but the split-screens showed the truth of it: the worsening mayhem in Taksim Square; a TV helicopter circling a city block on fire; young men with their faces hidden by hoods and scarves calmly looting an electronics store while police officers stood helplessly by.

And all that was before the bombs started going off.

III

Iain came out of the bathroom pulling on his last clean shirt to discover that Karin had indeed turned on the TV. A news channel was showing bewildered people covered in cement dust emerging from smoke, so that his first thought was that it was more footage from Daphne. But then he realized that this was something new. He sat on the bed beside her. 'Where?'

'Izmir,' Karin told him. 'But there's been one in Bursa too. And you should see Istanbul. The whole country's on fire. What the hell's going on?'

'I don't know,' said Iain. 'Not for sure.'

She looked sharply at him. 'But you think you do?'

Iain hesitated. He didn't much want to open the door onto that part of his life; but she had a right to know. 'Do you remember, when you were a kid, a scandal in Holland about things called Stay Behind Organizations?'

'No. What are they?'

It would sound crazy if he came straight out with it. He had to give her some background first. 'Okay. It goes back to the end of World War Two. We'd defeated Hitler, only to be faced with Stalin instead. Churchill fully expected war. It needed to be prepared for. Resistance groups had proved their value against the Nazis, even though they'd been set up on the hoof. Think how much more effective they'd have been if we'd been able to set them up in advance.'

'Stay Behind Organizations,' murmured Karin.

'Our enemies were communists,' said Iain. 'Our natural allies, therefore, were nationalists and ultra-right-wingers – pretty much exactly the same people we'd just been fighting. We brought likely prospects to England, taught them how to identify and recruit others, raise funds, make bombs, assassinate and sabotage. We effectively wrote the handbook of modern terrorism then gave it to them. When we Brits ran out of cash, the CIA took over. They weren't scared only of the Soviets invading, they were equally nervous that some European country would vote the communists into power and so bring down NATO from within. Their response was something called the strategy of tension. It involved having their pet Stay Behind Organizations run high-casualty bombing campaigns then blame them on left-wing terrorist groups – of which there were plenty, mind you. The idea was that the situation would get so out of hand that the public would demand the restoration of security, whatever it took. That would give the army the perfect excuse to step in. They'd arrest a long list of left-wing politicians, academics, trade unionists and writers, and the bombings would magically stop.'

Karin looked horrified at him. 'Are you serious?'

'Yes.'

'How do you know all this?'

Iain sighed, reluctant to admit that for years this had been his own life, and that he'd been proud of it too. For the curse of it was that it always seemed to start with honourable intentions, with a refusal to watch passively as good people suffered under terrible regimes. But the violence needed to overthrow those regimes poisoned everything. And so, one day, you'd walk unexpected into a compound captured by men you'd trained yourself only to find them standing among the executed corpses of their former enemies, and their young families. For no one back home ever seemed to learn the bitter truth of it: that the enemy of your current enemy all too often simply became your next enemy. 'It's public domain,' he told her. 'It came out in the early 1990s. The Gladio investigations. Every country in Western Europe had its own version, including Holland. But they never got all the way to the bottom of it. Too many powerful people and institutions were implicated. Besides, there was no real appetite for it. The Cold War had been won, you see. It was history.'

Karin looked bleakly back at the TV. 'Oh hell,' she said.

IV

It was a curiously telling way to learn about a man, looking through his photographs of himself and his friends. By that light, Zehra didn't much warm to Yasin Baykam. The only thing to be said in his favour was that at least he'd taken them down and hidden them in his closet; as though he'd grown ashamed of the man he'd once been.

It was easy to work out which ones had been in the picture frames. They were backed with card, and mostly had dates and locations pencilled upon them. She examined one now: black and white, unevenly faded, starting to curl up a little at the edges, revealing the dried yellow glue beneath, and exuding a faint yet evocative chemical smell. In the next, six young men were sitting around a campfire in a clearing in a forest, roasting chunks of meat on skewers. Now they were marching down a city street, parading the banners of the Nationalist Movement Party and carrying placards demanding war with Greece. He and three friends then held their forearms up for the camera, showing off matching tattoos of grey wolves. Now he was in army uniform, a rifle in one hand, his other draped around the shoulders of a young woman struggling not to show her fear. Then a very different shot, Baykam standing sheepishly alongside a stick-thin teenage girl, an older woman with a broad flat nose and an older version of himself that could only be his father. Home on leave. When she saw where it had been taken, she tapped Andreas on his arm. 'Look,' she said. 'He came from Antioch.'

Andreas had made discoveries of his own: a sheaf of handwritten letters on distinctive thick yellow paper. 'Did you read these?' he asked.

'They're in foreign.'

'They're from the daughter of the family who used to own his house.'

'Ah,' said Zehra. There'd been a plague of these pests since the border with the south had been opened. They came to gawp at your house and make pointed comments about the improvements you'd made, trying to make you feel guilty for building a new life after having been chased out of your own childhood home. 'And?'

'The first one is very formal. Merlina introduces herself. She lived in his house as a young girl. She has her own children now. With his permission, she'd love to show them where she grew up. But these later ones . . .'

'Yes?'

He held up another letter, a colour photograph pinned to its top corner. Yasin Baykam looking faintly bewildered, surrounded by a family of five, all smiling broadly for the camera, the little boy standing in front grinning crazily and giving two thumbs-up while his elder sisters each held gifts of food they'd brought. Zehra's heart gave an unexpectedly powerful thump as she looked at it, at the thought that even a man like this could find a new family after he was grown old. She gestured at the photographs spread out on the floor. 'These used to be on his walls,' she said. 'He must have taken them down before these people came to visit. Then he never put them back up again.'

'Men of violence often mellow as they grow old,' nodded Andreas, getting onto his hands and knees to look at her photos. 'They come to regret the things they once did. Imagine that you'd been a fiercely nationalistic Turk, the Greeks your sworn enemies. You'd defeated them on Cyprus, you'd taken one of their houses as rightful booty. But now the former owners come to visit. And they're nothing like what you've imagined. They're nice. They're warm. They bring you pies. And, despite yourself, you *like* them. That would have to shake your view of the world, wouldn't it?'

'That's why he went to see the Professor,' murmured Zehra. 'He wanted to make amends.'

Andreas was still glancing over her photographs. Suddenly he froze. 'I'll be fucked,' he said. He rested his weight on one hand and reached across to turn one of the photographs around to face him. It showed Baykam standing in front of a tank with a tall, good-looking officer, a bandanna around his forehead. 'It's the Lion,' he said. 'I'll swear to God that's the Lion he's with.'

Zehra shook her head. 'The who?'

'The Lion of Famagusta. General Kemal Yilmaz. Turkey's Chief of the General Staff himself.'

THIRTY-FOUR

I

General Yilmaz had hand-picked every member of the team overseeing that day's deployments from his Ankara command centre. Using the growing chaos as excuse and cover, they sent increasing numbers of units to take control of arterial routes, to guard key buildings and the homes of Turkey's ruling elite. The vast majority of these units were unaware that they were participating in a coup, but they hadn't been chosen at random. They'd been chosen because Yilmaz had reason to believe their first loyalty was to the uniform, not the government.

His buzzer vibrated in his pocket. He checked Asena's message then beckoned Major General Hüseyin Yazoğlu aside. 'You're in command, Hüseyin,' he told him. 'You know what to do.'

'Yes, General. We won't let you down.'

He walked briskly back to his private office, established a secure line. Asena was waiting for him. 'You do realize I have work of my own today?' he asked drily.

'There have been developments,' she told him. 'Black got to his girlfriend before we could. It's possible they'll go public. And something else: an incident outside that Famagusta house you wanted watched.'

Yilmaz's heart clenched like a fist. 'An incident?' he asked. 'What kind of incident?' He swivelled almost subconsciously in his chair as he listened, until he was facing his ego-wall, dozens of photographs of himself with some of the world's most powerful people. But the photograph in pride of place actually showed him on his own: a young officer, at the turret of his tank, leading his squadron south to Famagusta, his wife's golden silk scarf knotted around his forehead, trailing him like a mane in the wind. He hadn't even noticed the photographer. She must have been crouching by the side of the road. But, two weeks later, this photograph had adorned the front cover of one of Turkey's bestselling news magazines, in celebration of their triumph over the Greeks. They'd captioned it 'The Lions of Famagusta'. But only one lion had been visible, so that was what he'd become, to the envious joshing of his comrades. The Lion of Famagusta! And the photograph had become iconic. It had come to symbolize victory. *He'd* come to symbolize it. And because a lion was brave and fierce and handsome and noble, he'd come to personify those virtues too.

The woman with the dyed blonde hair. The youngster squinting fearfully up at him through his horn-rimmed glasses. He scowled at them until they went away again. Everyone had ghosts. His were more persistent than most, that was all.

'There's no danger,' Asena was saying. 'The police have already let our three men go. And it's not like there was anything left in the house anyway. I had Emre and his men go in that first night, remember? They swore to me they cleared out all his papers, so there's nothing left to link him to you. Besides, it's almost certainly a coincidence. I wouldn't even have bothered you with it except that—'

'Almost certainly a coincidence,' he said. '*Almost certainly a coincidence.* An anonymous tip-off today of all days. The house left unwatched so that anyone could have waltzed in. And you think it's *almost certainly a coincidence?*'

'My love,' she said. 'If you're so worried, let me help. I'm in Cyprus myself now. Tell me what needs doing and I'll—'

'No.'

'But—'

'No.' Yilmaz touched fingers to his desktop. For forty years, he'd lived in a kind of denial, pretending it had all happened to someone else, that it was a scene from a movie he'd once watched. Yet, somewhere deep inside, he'd always known this day would come. 'You concentrate on finding Black and the girl before they can go public. Leave Famagusta to me.'

'My love,' pleaded Asena. 'You need to stay in Ankara. Who knows what may come up? But if you just tell me what—'

'I said leave Famagusta to me.' He ended the call before she could argue further, then sat there brooding. He'd accepted, from the beginning, the possible failure of their enterprise. He could endure that kind of disgrace, as well as the life imprisonment or even execution that would surely follow, just so long as Turkey understood that he'd acted out of principle, to avenge the humiliations inflicted upon the army by corrupt politicians and a crooked justice system.

But this was a very different kind of disgrace, and it terrified him.

He didn't need to panic, however. The commander of the Turkish forces in Famagusta had already doubled Varosha's perimeter security at his request. He could have him redouble it. But that would provide only a temporary fix. He needed something more permanent. And he'd have to oversee it himself. In part that was because he'd never have full peace of mind unless he'd witnessed it for himself. It was also because he needed to be there to make sure no one sneaked a look before they closed it up. But mostly it was because it had all happened so long ago that he'd forgotten where it had taken place, and only by returning there in person could he hope to find it again.

At first glance, it seemed crazy to go tonight, what with everything so in flux. But in fact it was the perfect opportunity. Hüseyin had the command centre, and could be trusted to handle things until he was next needed, which would be when the time came for him to address the nation and explain what they had done. But that wouldn't be until tomorrow morning at the very earliest. And, with Turkey on fire, no one would look twice at unusual events in Cyprus tonight.

Yes. It was time to bury his ghosts.

The decision made, it became a matter of logistics, of planning, of execution. After a lifetime in the army, these were second nature to him. He drew up a list of everything and everyone he'd need. Then he picked up his phone and started making calls.

II

The news reports out of Istanbul and Ankara were so distracting that Iain had to mute the TV to let himself think clearly. 'Turkey was always a special case,' he told Karin. 'It was a *major* strategic prize during the Cold

War. Muslim but secular. Straddling Asia and Europe. A key NATO member both because of the size of its army and as a first line of defence against the Soviets. But it was also large and poor and vulnerable to promises of communist nirvana. So the Stay Behind Organizations there were bigger and busier than most. And the most notorious of them was that ultra-nationalist group I mentioned the other night.'

'The Grey Wolves,' said Karin.

Iain nodded. 'The woman last night pretty much admitted she was one of them; which is strange, because we all thought they'd largely disbanded. At their peak, they were *very* closely tied not only to the police but even more so to the army. In fact, they were almost their black-ops wing. They financed themselves with bank robberies, protection rackets, prostitution rings, that kind of thing.'

'You're not serious.'

'But by far their biggest source of income came from controlling the Balkan route, which is how most Afghan heroin is trafficked into Europe.'

'You're not fucking serious.'

'Afraid so. And they were political too. They were *very* closely tied to the right-wing establishment, what's known in Turkey as the Deep State. They were deeply involved in the coups in 1960, 1971 and particularly 1980, which was a classic strategy of tension operation, multiple mass-casualty attacks blamed on left-wingers that gave the generals the perfect excuse to step in and arrest whoever they liked.'

'And you think that's what's going on now? That someone's setting up a coup?'

'Coups are a bitch to pull off,' he said. 'The more people you involve, the more likely someone is to blab. Yet you need a big enough presence that people will accept it as a done deal or you'll find yourself in a civil war. So the secret is to make it look like something else. For example, you degrade the security situation so badly that people *want* you to put troops onto the streets; for another, you make their lives so shitty that they'll cheer any change of governance. Think of how the Egyptian army got rid of the last two presidents: the perfect templates for your modern coup.'

'How long have we got?'

He gestured at the TV. 'Looks like they're going for it right now. Maybe because today was always the day, but maybe they've freaked out that we're onto them.'

'We have to do something,' said Karin. 'We have to tell someone.'

'Who?' asked Iain. 'They just deported me, remember? I have zero credibility. I don't have any great contacts in the government; and either the police or the army are behind it. Or maybe both of them together.'

'You must know someone.'

'No one I trust completely. And if we go to the wrong people and they tip our friends off, they'll come after us, hard.'

She looked at the TV again: two lines of bodies were covered by dusty white sheets outside a railway station. Her expression hardened. 'We have to at least try.'

Iain nodded. He could think of one person they could take this to. Someone predisposed to believe them, someone who understood Turkish politics, had useful contacts and was surely uninvolved in any coup. Best of all, someone certain to be at home, less than half an hour's walk away. He stood, turned off the television. 'Let's go get our passports back,' he said.

'Why?'

'Because we've got a border to cross.'

III

It was Andreas who insisted that they tell Professor Volkan of their discovery. They couldn't call him, for fear that his phone was tapped, so Andreas volunteered to drive. Zehra's delight at saving herself a bus-fare didn't last long, for Andreas drove at such terrifying speeds that she clutched her door handle and closed her eyes until thankfully they arrived in Nicosia and had to slow for other traffic.

The policeman on duty outside Volkan's house patted Andreas down but waved her through. The Professor was surprised to see them. She locked herself in a bathroom to retrieve the photographs from beneath her skirts then joined them in the study. 'Your friend from the rallies is called Yasin Baykam,' she told him. 'I took these pictures from his house. Look at this one of him as a young soldier.'

Volkan frowned down at it. 'So?' he asked.

'Look again,' said Andreas. 'Look who he's with.'

He took it to his desk, turned on his lamp. He squinted at it for maybe four or five seconds then suddenly stiffened. He looked up at them both. 'It can't be,' he said.

'It is,' said Andreas. 'I checked it against that photograph of him in the tank. You know the one. He's even wearing the same bandanna.'

Zehra checked her watch as the men talked. Katerina would be breaking up from school in a few minutes. She needed to leave now or she'd be late for her. She cleared her throat for the Professor's attention. 'Andreas said you'd be able to use these pictures to get my son out of jail.'

Volkan sighed. 'Are you really still so desperate to get rid of Katerina?'

Zehra drew herself up to her full height, such as there was of it. 'Taner is only in jail because of you. God alone knows what they are doing to him there. I want him out because he is my son and because his daughter misses him and I have to go meet her now after school, and I want to be able to give her good news.' A little fire drained out of her. 'I want to tell her that her father will be home soon.'

Volkan's expression was unreadable for a moment or two. Then suddenly he marched around his desk and enveloped her in a great hug. '*There* she is, at last,' he said. 'My beautiful Zehra.'

She wriggled her shoulders. 'Let me go!' she protested.

He laughed and took a pace back, held her by her shoulders. His smile was charged with an extraordinary warmth and she understood suddenly why rash young men like her son would risk prison on his behalf. 'Taner will be home soon,' he assured her. 'I guarantee it. And please tell your granddaughter from me that it's largely thanks to you.'

THIRTY-FIVE

I

While Karin bought herself a pair of plimsolls, Iain borrowed her mobile to call his London office. He referred Maria to his address book then told her which of his Cypriot contacts might know the home address of Metin Volkan and asked her to call him back as soon as she'd found it out.

It was a short walk to the border, a pedestrianized alley in which two men in blue overalls with long-handled rollers were whitewashing away graffiti, while a border guard with hooded eyes lost a private battle against the urge to yawn, then shifted weight from leg to leg.

Iain's recent troubles in Antioch might have earned him a place on an immigration watch-list, so he and Karin joined different queues. The woman officer glared at him.

But then she glared at everyone. She held his passport beneath a scanner then stamped it like it had jilted her. Then she turned her glare onto the family behind.

Maria came through with Volkan's address. They Googled directions then hurried along cobbled streets as shadows inched up facing buildings. Everything was shabbier this side of the border, at least until they crossed the road into an enclave of expensive homes. A policeman was standing outside one of the front doors. Iain took Karin by the hand and walked up to him. 'Is Professor Volkan at home?' he asked in Turkish.

The policeman grunted. 'What's it to you?'

'I used to be his student.'

'He's got someone with him.'

'Please. This is my fiancée, Karin. I've told her so much about the Professor, she really wants to meet him. And we're only here for the day.'

The policeman didn't look convinced but he knocked all the same. Then he knocked again, more loudly. There was shuffling inside, then the door opened. 'Yes?' asked Volkan irritably.

'It's me, Professor,' said Iain, speaking rapidly to prevent Volkan from interrupting him. 'Iain Black. And this is my fiancée Karin. I've told her so much about you. She insisted we come to meet you.'

His smile was forced, his eyes elsewhere. 'Charmed,' he said. 'But I'm afraid this is a very bad—'

341

'Please, Professor,' said Iain. 'Five minutes.' He switched to English. 'It's not only to meet Karin. I've also got a question about my thesis. On the Deep State, you'll remember. On the Strategy of Tension. On how bombing campaigns were blamed on innocent parties to facilitate a coup.'

The professor stared hard at him for several seconds. 'Iain Black,' he said. 'You used to wear a goatee.'

'I was a student. Students do crazy things.'

'How good to see you again. And your fiancée. Karin, wasn't it? Come in. Come in.' He held the door wide for them, closed it behind them. Then he folded his arms. 'You have one minute,' he said. 'Please tell me what this is about.'

II

Zehra did her best to make it to the school before the end of Katerina's day, but her legs were tired and wouldn't obey her, and she found herself arriving a full twelve minutes late. Fortunately, there was still a knot of children, teachers and parents there, though the flutters of panic didn't go away until she saw Katerina with another girl and an elegant looking woman in long blue skirts and a gorgeous cream jacket. She hurried straight up to them to explain herself, but she was wheezing too hard to speak.

'You must be Katerina's grandmother,' said the woman. 'So nice to meet you at last.'

Zehra nodded and tried a smile but still she couldn't speak. 'I thought I was going to miss her,' she managed finally.

'You mustn't worry,' said the woman. 'Everyone's late from time to time. Someone will always stay around until everyone's collected who should be. And it's been a pleasure to spend time with Katerina again. Especially as I don't suppose we'll be seeing her so much from now on.'

'How do you mean?'

The woman smiled brightly. 'Oh. We're the ones who usually get to look after her when your son is away. But now that you're back, I don't suppose we'll be needed so much any more. Which is a real shame for us, because our girls get on so well together.'

Zehra looked blankly at her. 'You look after Katerina when my son is away?'

The woman smiled warily and screwed up her nose as if she sensed she'd made some kind of mistake, but wasn't sure what. 'Someone has to, right?' she said. 'All the travelling he does. And what with everything else.'

Zehra thanked her then took Katerina by the hand and led her off along the pavement. Her cheeks were flushed, her heart was roiled. Her wretch of a son had tricked her! And, to make matters worse, Katerina's guilty expression made it perfectly clear that she'd been in on it too.

'Don't be upset,' begged Katerina. 'He was just sad you wouldn't talk to him. He missed you. *I* missed you. I had a grandmother and I'd never even met her. Anyway, we were worried that you were lonely.'

Zehra looked away. It took her a few moments to compose herself, then she looked around again. 'Me lonely?' she said. 'Get away with you, you little scamp.'

'Please don't tell him I told you,' said Katerina. 'He can get really angry, you know.'

'Not with me, he can't,' said Zehra. She settled her hand upon Katerina's head and looked both ways to make sure the street was clear before they crossed. Then she bought them each an orange-flavoured iced-lolly, and they licked them in companionable silence as they walked together back through the park and home.

III

One minute won Iain and Karin five. Five earned them an invitation into Volkan's study, where he introduced them to another man tapping away at his smartphone. The fortuitousness of their timing quickly became apparent. They shared stories, suspicions, discoveries. Theories were mooted. Some failed. Others gained traction, were revised and honed. The room grew dark enough that Volkan turned on the wall-lights, reflections sharpening in the window panes.

Volkan took it upon himself to sum up their progress, like the natural chairman he was. He put his index finger on a photograph of Yasin Baykam. 'What do we know about this man?' he asked rhetorically. 'We know he served alongside Turkey's current Chief of the General Staff, who led the advance into Famagusta as a young tank officer back in 1974. We know he used to be a member of the Nationalist Movement Party, whose youth wing was notoriously close to the Grey Wolves; and that he and his friends had grey wolves tattooed upon their forearms. We *think* that his sympathies mellowed with age and may have changed altogether after meeting the former owners of his home and farm. We know he came to one of my meetings two months ago, but held back. And that he then came to another meeting last month, and this time offered to help.'

'What changed between the two meetings?' asked Iain.

'The bombs grew worse,' said Volkan. 'As did the backlash. They destroyed any hope of Ankara agreeing to hand back Varosha. And yet people still blamed us for them.'

'So let's assume that was the real purpose of the bombs,' said Karin. 'To make Varosha politically toxic. And Baykam realized this somehow. Maybe he recognized the methodology, or maybe one of his old Grey Wolf friends confided in him, not realizing his sympathies had changed. So he came to see you speak that first time, perhaps to assess whether he could trust you or not. But he wavered. Then the bombs got worse and he came back.'

'Why not just tell me what he knew?' asked Volkan.

Iain shook his head. 'It's one thing to disagree with or even go up against someone you once fought alongside,' he said. 'But no soldier would ever turn in a former squad-mate.'

'Okay,' said Karin. 'Baykam asks you how he can help. You tell him you need money. He's not rich himself, but somehow he knows where there are artefacts.'

Andreas nodded. 'Famagusta's dotted with old caves and burial chambers. My great-grandfather used to hunt for them when he was a kid.'

'He also needs to sell them,' said Karin. 'So he does his homework then contacts my old boss and the Bejjanis and invites them to Daphne to bid.'

'Why Daphne? Why not here?'

'Misdirection,' said Karin. 'I can't speak for Bejjani, but Nathan knew his stuff. Give him a decent thread to follow, he'd likely have found the site for himself in no time.'

'And Baykam grew up in Antioch,' added Andreas. 'He'd have felt at home there.'

'Okay,' said Iain. 'But the antiquities police got onto him somehow.'

'Not onto him,' said Karin. 'Onto Nathan. He almost got caught buying on the black market last time he was here. I'll bet they had him on some kind of watch-list.'

Volkan stood up, a little agitated. 'Yes. They set a team to watch him. They followed him to Daphne then discovered he was there to meet Baykam. But Baykam once served in the same tank as the current Chief of the General Staff. In Turkey, you don't go around arresting old friends of the Chief of the General Staff, not if you value your career. So they notified him as a courtesy. For some reason, this news spooked Yilmaz so badly that he ordered the Daphne hotel bombed before Baykam could be arrested.'

Iain frowned. 'Why not just spike the investigation?'

'He's army,' answered Volkan. 'He has no jurisdiction over the police. Besides, if we're right about this, they were running a bombing campaign anyway. It would have been two for the price of one.'

Iain nodded. 'So he has Asena bomb the hotel and blame it on you guys. But then I send footage of her and her friend to the police. There was a military intelligence officer at my interrogation. I'll bet he tipped off Yilmaz, who set her after me. And they also decided to launch their coup at once, before word of it could get out.'

Volkan nodded soberly. 'And your evidence for this?'

'It's how it happened,' said Iain. 'Something like it anyway.'

'Maybe. But your evidence? There are far too many

347

holes in this story for us to take it public and get heard, let alone believed, on a day like today. Where are these artefacts you mentioned? How did Baykam get his hands on them? Why would the Lion care? What's it to him if someone he knew forty years ago got arrested? You have to understand: General Yilmaz is a hero in Turkey. A national icon. Above the fray. And who are we? A bunch of trouble-makers with every incentive to invent stories to clear our names or promote our causes. If we're to get people to believe us, we'll need to give them proof.'

'And how the hell do we get that?' asked Karin.

No one answered. Energy seeped from the room. It was Andreas who finally spoke. 'Zehra took a whole suitcase full of papers from Yasin's house, not just these photos. I didn't see anything else in them, but then I didn't know half this stuff at the time. So maybe we missed something.'

Iain nodded. 'Let's go look,' he said.

THIRTY-SIX

I

The main rally in Ankara was being held in Güven Park, as close as the public could get to the seat of power these days, now that the government quarter had been enclosed by high perimeter walls and its new ring of steel. But the chanting was all the louder because the protesters knew that the Office of the Prime Minister lay just a hundred metres the other side, and that Deniz Baştürk was there right now, holding a crisis cabinet.

Riot police tried twice to turn Şükrü away, claiming that the Güven Park entrance was closed. But he pointed to the livery of his horse-box and told them he had orders to bring it here. He kept his hand on his horn and the crowd parted with ill grace. A young man with ridiculously hairy eyebrows stood in front of his bonnet and yelled taunts. Someone banged his window with a battered saucepan, making him jump. He revved his engine hard and pressed on until he was through the last of them, into the narrow stretch of no man's land that separated them from the lines of riot police behind their steel barricades, their helmets on and their Perspex shields held at the ready.

They opened up the barriers for him. He gestured thanks as he drove by. There was a gap of perhaps twenty metres behind them, then the road funnelled through a chicane of concrete blocks to reach a pair of concrete and bullet-proof glass bunkers that squatted either side of the triple-barred security barrier and the two sets of tyre shredders. He pulled up, ratcheted his handbrake, turned off his engine. He wiped his palms on his trousers as he jumped down, throwing a resentful glance at the thugs still yelling back down the street. 'Idiots,' he muttered, handing his licence, ID and paper-work to the duty officer. 'I could have had horses in the back for all they knew.'

'I'd have paid to see that. A couple of police horses going berserk on their arses.' He nodded at the horse-box. 'What's the story?'

'It did its rear axle,' shrugged Şükrü. 'We put a new one in this morning. They told us to take it to Alparslan Türkeş. Alparslan Türkeş told us to bring it here, to your mounted police barracks.'

'No one told us.'

'Can't you call someone?' He opened his door and grabbed a form off the passenger seat. 'They gave me this number for authorization.'

The man took it back inside his booth. But he came out a minute later, shaking his head. 'Can't get hold of anyone. Everything's so fucked up today.'

'Hell,' said Şükrü. He looked back at the increasingly rowdy protesters. 'Then can I at least leave it here? They don't pay me enough for me to drive back through that mob.'

'Let me take a look.' He checked the cab first, then used a mirror on a stick to inspect the undercarriage. Şükrü unbolted the rear of the horse-box and lowered it into a ramp. They went up inside together. Two stalls, both empty. A pungent smell of horses, a few wisps of straw on the floor. Loud cheers from the mob made them glance around just as a first missile was thrown, a plastic bottle of yellowish liquid that smacked into a riot shield then sprayed the police with a golden shower.

'Shit,' said the policeman. 'This is going to get tasty.'

'What do I do?' asked Şükrü.

'You'd better go on in. You know where the barracks is?'

'Where that school used to be, right?'

'That's it.'

Şükrü closed up the horse-box, climbed back into his

351

cab. They raised the barrier for him, removed the shredders. The buildings here had imposing yet drab façades,
expressions of the power that lay within. He turned right.
The mounted police barracks was along the second road
to his right. He drove past it, went instead into a half-
empty car park and found a quiet corner in which to
park. He took the Thermos flask from his lunch box,
uncapped it, then held it down by his side to slop the
cold sludge of coffee inside in spatters onto the ground.
Asena had told him it was an old wives' tale that it would
fool sniffer dogs, but he was of the firm opinion that
those old wives knew a trick or two. He slapped the
side of the horse-box then walked south, mingling with
the suits leaving work for the day, all seeking to avoid the
Güven Park protests. He offered his papers but was waved
straight through. He walked a little way down the street
before he made the call. 'It's me,' he said.

'Are they in?' asked Asena.

'Yes,' Şükrü told her. 'They're in.'

II

They left Professor Volkan to his house arrest and headed
for Famagusta. With Andreas pushing his old Citroën up
against the natural limiter of its engine rattle, and the
windows rolled down against the fumes, conversation

was hard. Karin had opted for the back seats. The road was flat and fast and faintly hypnotic, while the beams of oncoming traffic threatened a mild head-ache. She folded her arms and stared at the dark ridges of the Five Fingers to her left and fell to brooding.

The last two weeks of his life, Nathan had been like a kid on Christmas Eve. At the time, she'd put it down to general excitement about their upcoming trip. But knowing what she now knew, it had to have been because of what he'd hoped to buy. In which case, surely his behaviour during those two weeks would offer clues as to what that was. The books and articles he'd chosen to read, the topics of the conversations he'd started and steered.

'A penny for them,' said Iain, glancing around.

'I'd be ripping you off,' she warned.

'I'll take that risk.'

'Fine. Then I guess I was thinking about names.'

'Names?'

'Do you know how history worked back in Homer's time?' She had to talk loudly to make herself heard over the engine and passing traffic. 'I mean the Greeks didn't have the kind of established framework we take for granted: no chronologies or history books, nothing like that. Writing had been lost; there weren't any inscribed monuments to speak of. They had oral history, that was all, and little way to test the accuracy of their stories.'

She lurched forwards suddenly, as Andreas hit the brakes for a speed-camera on the junction ahead, then rocked back again. 'A lot of those stories were wrong in some way. They got exaggerated for propaganda purposes. They became garbled from being passed on too often. Or maybe the world simply changed around them, so that they didn't make sense any more. So they got tweaked an awful lot to make them more fun or satisfying or coherent.'

'What's this got to do with names?'

'Names were a leading source of confusion,' she told him. 'That's largely because the Greeks pretty much took it for granted that people and places with similar names were connected to each other. Take Salamis, for instance. The old city up on the coast ahead, where your pollen came from. It shares its name with an island near Athens off which a famous sea-battle was fought. So the ancients would have expected the two places to be connected somehow. And indeed they are. A prince from the island of Salamis went to Troy with the Greeks; but his brother was killed during the fighting and he couldn't face returning home alone. So he came to Cyprus instead, and founded a new Salamis.'

'Sounds plausible.'

'The prince's name was Teucer. Which is where it starts getting really tangled, because the original founder of Troy was also called Teucer. So clearly the Teucer from

Salamis had a connection to the Trojans. And yes, it turns out that his mother was the sister of the Trojan King, Priam. So in effect, he was half-Trojan himself, fighting against his cousins. And there's another connection too: his followers – the ones who settled here in Cyprus – were known as Teukrians because of him. But the Trojans were also called Teukrians, after their own founder Teucer.'

'Okay,' said Iain doubtfully.

'Take our old friend Aeneas, for example. Virgil calls him Aeneas of the Teukrians. Aeneas, as you know, was the legendary founder of Rome. By a curious coincidence, a number of historians believe the Cypriot Teukrians to be the ancestors of the Etruscans, who we know actually did found Rome. They have remarkable cultural similarities; and their DNA seems a fairly close match.'

'Huh.'

'Carthage is another interesting name. It's a corruption of *Qart Hadasht*, Phoenician for "new city". Yet the Phoenicians built new cities all over the Mediterranean. It was what they did. The place we know today as Carthage, the one in Tunisia, is simply the one that prospered. But we know for sure from ancient records that there was at least one other Carthage. And it was here in Cyprus. Most people think it was probably a place called Kition on the south coast, near where you flew in today, because that was the most prominent Phoenician settlement on the island. But actually there's no proof of that, and there are traces of Phoenicians all over the island, including at Salamis.'

'I still don't see—'

'According to legend, Dido didn't sail straight from Tyre to Tunisia. She stopped off along the way. In Cyprus. Some sources say it was to pick up wives for her crew. Others say that she settled here for a while, maybe even founded a new city here. A new city that, almost by definition, would have been called Carthage.'

Iain squinted at her. 'Are you saying Dido's Carthage is *here*?'

'I don't know,' said Karin. 'I'm thinking out loud is all. But what I do know is that if Dido did indeed found her new city here, and it was other Phoenicians who went on to found the new city in Tunisia, then when this Carthage failed, all of the stories initially associated with it would later have been re-attributed to Tunisian Carthage instead, because that's how it worked back then. And get this: According to legend, one of the reasons Dido fell so hard for Aeneas was that she was obsessed by the Trojan War. She even commissioned a marble frieze of it for her palace, depicting its great battles and heroes. But guess how she first got so fascinated by it? It was because she'd met a Trojan War veteran when she was a young girl, and he'd beguiled her with his stories. A veteran who'd been in Tyre to ask permission to start a new settlement on Cyprus. A new settlement he wanted to call Salamis.'

'Teucer,' murmured Iain.

'Teucer,' agreed Karin. 'So when Dido went on the run from her brother, what better sanctuary than here with her old friend Teucer?'

Iain nodded. 'You think that's how it happened?'

'No,' she said. 'The dates don't work. I'm thinking out loud, is all. But you have to admit it's a curious coincidence of names. And here's another, while I'm at it. I think I told you that Dido was a folklore name. So we've always thought that maybe she was really known as Elissa, because she was sometimes called that too. But guess what: Cyprus wasn't called Cyprus back then either. It was known as Alashiya or Alisa, after its most prominent region. And if Dido settled in that region, couldn't that be how she got the name? As queen of Alashiya.'

'And that region was where?'

Karin tapped Andreas on his shoulder. 'Have you ever heard of a region of ancient Cyprus called Alashiya?' she asked.

'Of course,' he frowned.

'Where is it?'

He waved his hand at the night-time lights of the city of Famagusta that lay scattered like embers before them. 'Here,' he said.

THIRTY-SEVEN

I

Fifty years before, Famagusta had been one of the busiest port cities in the eastern Mediterranean. But the Turkish invasion and occupation had led to such severe trade embargoes that it was now a faint shadow of its former self.

The *Dido* was moored between pleasure boats in its old harbour, cables clinking in the light breeze. There were lights on in the Port Authority building, and two old men were playing backgammon in the harbour café, while the occasional pop of a flashbulb revealed some tourist taking night-time photos from the city's ancient walls. But that was about it. Butros Bejjani stared south towards the dark shadow of the Forbidden Zone. 'You're certain about this?' he asked. 'There's no mistake?'

'There's no mistake, Father,' Michel assured him. 'The woman Visser is not only back in Turkish Cyprus, she's on her way here right now. And Black is with her. He borrowed her phone earlier to make a phone call.'

Butros sighed. He'd hoped they'd have time to explore Varosha at their leisure. But it wasn't to be. Visser and Black had clearly made the same deductions he had, which meant he now needed to adapt his plans accordingly. This was no discussion for an open deck, however, so he led his sons to his cabin and closed the door behind them. 'Well?' he asked. 'Any ideas?'

'I say we let them make their move,' said Michel. 'Maybe they already know where it is, in which case we can track them on Visser's phone.'

Butros shook his head. 'If they were foolish enough to take a phone into Varosha, which they're not, its signal would give them away instantly. The army would be onto them in no time. Anything else?'

'Maybe we should turn them in,' said Georges. 'Get them out of our way.'

'No,' said Butros. He'd liked Black, and didn't wish him or Visser harm. He merely intended to beat them to the site. 'What if they talk? We'd lose our chance.'

'Then let's make a deal with them. Pool our resources.'

'And what if *they* turn *us* in?' scoffed Michel. 'Anyway, we have all the resources we need. What can they offer?'

It was a valid point. One of the benefits of uncommon wealth was the ability it gave you to acquire expensive and sophisticated equipment at short notice. Butros had had a truckload of it delivered that same afternoon: cell radio sets, night-vision goggles, inflatables and much else. He gave himself a moment to think. His original plan had had two phases: reconnaissance and recovery. In phase one, Georges was to have led a small team over Varosha's perimeter wall to search the derelict city, night after night, until finally they found the site. In phase two, they'd go back in on the inflatables, taking video-cameras and a satellite modem with them, so that Butros would be able to watch it all live from the *Dido*'s bridge, and decide which pieces they should take and which they should leave. Then they would carry their booty out to the inflatables and away.

Yet this plan, while prudent enough, had always been unsatisfying to Butros. To assess an artefact properly, you needed to touch it, hold it, weigh it, smell it, taste it. You had to feel what it did to your gut. Besides, if he was right about all this, it was Dido's palace they were talking about. *Dido's palace*. A discovery that would go down in history. More than anything else in the world, he wanted to play his full part in it.

His heart began beating a little faster when he realized what he was going to do. It was in the nature of banking that you came to assess everything in terms of risk. But where was the fun in that? He smiled as he turned to Georges. 'We're going in on the inflatables tonight,' he said. 'And I'm coming with you.'

II

The lift was out of order, no matter how many times Andreas pressed the button. 'Is that how it works?' asked Karin sweetly. 'You just hit it hard enough?'

Andreas grunted. 'That's my understanding.'

The stairwell was gloomy with fire-escape lighting. They passed another couple coming down, exchanged wry greetings. Andreas was wheezing hard by the time they reached his floor. He put his hands on his knees and gave himself half a minute to recover. 'What kind of a fool buys a top-floor flat?' he sighed, fishing out his keys and letting them in.

His floor was strewn with papers. They set straight to work. It was Andreas who found the paper-clipped pages of an old street-map printed out from the Internet. 'Varosha,' he said. 'But from before the Turkish invasion.' He fitted the eight pages together into a strip two wide by four tall, the seafront to the east, the modern city to the west and north. The scale was large enough to name consulates, shops, hotels and other buildings of interest, and there were pencil jottings in the margins.

Rear of hotel
Car park
Perimeter wall, industrial estate?
Two yellow buses
View of Church roof
At least one street in from the sea

These notes were reflected on the map itself. The churches had rings around them, as if someone had placed a glass over them, then drawn around it. And the hotels one street or more in from the sea were highlighted in pink marker pen, while the top four of them had been crudely scratched through.

'Imagine you were one of the first soldiers into Varosha during the invasion,' said Iain, 'but you haven't been back in since. There's a place you want to find, but your memory of it is hazy. It was a little way inland, there was a hotel nearby, a pair of buses in a car park. And you could see a church roof. The place is now under military occupation so that you can only visit it at night and at considerable risk, so that you have to minimize torchlight and blundering about. What do you do?'

'You find yourself a map,' said Karin. 'You make a shortlist of places to check.'

Iain nodded. 'Then you cross them off as you go along. That's why the rings around the churches and the highlights are neatly done, but the crossings out are so rough. Because Baykam did them on the hoof.'

Karin put her finger on the next hotel down. 'Until he found what he was looking for, at least. Then there'd have been no further need to scratch anything off, would there?'

A frisson ran through Iain as he looked down. The Daphne International Hotel hadn't been bombed merely to kill Yasin Baykam, say in punishment for some breach of Grey Wolf security or protocol. No, it had surely been bombed to stop Baykam from revealing the location of this Varosha site. Which meant that there was something in there worth the murder of Mustafa and all those others.

Andreas was still staring down at the map. 'Do you know how Famagusta got its name?' he asked.

'How?' asked Karin.

'It's from the Greek word *ammochostos*. It means "buried beneath the sand".'

Iain nodded. 'Then let's go dig it up.'

III

Frustration had piled on top of frustration for Asena these past twenty hours. The fiasco in the desert, Visser's escape from Emre, her Grey Wolf team arrested in Famagusta, an afternoon wasted searching Nicosia for Black. Now, to cap it all, the turmoil in Turkey had persuaded the government to close its airspace until security could be restored; and while that was testimony to the success of their enterprise, it meant that her flight back home had been cancelled, stranding her here in Cyprus.

She sat with folded arms in the cramped rear of the SUV as they headed east to their safe house. The radio was on, provoking cheers every time some new outbreak of trouble was announced. Tiredness got to her. She'd have fallen asleep except that her head kept knocking against the window, jarring her back awake. A haze of memories enveloped her instead. Twenty-one again, and in a different car, heading with her father to some swanky soiree for the Fourth Army's top brass, her mother having backed out at the last moment with the usual profession of nerves.

Asena had been studying modern history at Bosporus University at the time, and while not quite mutinous enough with liberal ideas to refuse to escort her father, she'd been quite liberal enough to punish him with a sulk. Her ill grace had lasted until he'd introduced her to the Lion. Tall, golden-haired, unbelievably beautiful in his uniform. Late forties, but didn't look it. Their first conversation had lasted perhaps a minute and to this day she only had the vaguest idea of what they'd said. Yet, by the end of it, by the end of those sixty seconds, her heart had set itself on him.

They reached a roundabout, turned left, headed north out of Famagusta.

He'd fallen for her too. She'd known that instinctively. The difference was, he'd tried to fight it. His wife had been sick with a degenerative disease, and he'd been too loyal to leave her or even betray her. He'd therefore avoided Asena, had refused to take her calls. So she'd concocted an essay on the Cypriot campaign as an excuse to interview him, and had asked her father to set it up. Her father had outranked the Lion back then; he'd been unable to say no. She'd sat beside him at his desk as he'd gruffly pointed out landmarks on a flapped-out map. She'd edged ever closer to him. Their thighs had touched. She'd placed her hand on his leg to support herself while leaning over to look at how he'd outflanked the northern mountains. Then her hand had slipped. Thus had begun a period of squalid joy. He'd been too well known in Turkey for the usual business of country hotels; nor could he visit her at her digs. One of his friends on secondment overseas had lent them his apartment. How well she'd come to know it, and the others that had followed. He was marked out for great things. Promotion had followed promotion. She'd built her life around him, taking jobs wherever he was posted, even dating a series of plausible young men both to give them cover and to get her parents off her back. One of these, a shudderingly narcissistic young officer called Durmuş Hassan, had asked her to marry him, but his proposal had so transparently been intended to gain favour with her father that she'd laughed in his face.

The Lion's wife had fallen sicker. The term had been uncertain, the final outcome not. They'd pledged their futures to each other the moment he was free. But then they'd been blind-sided by the notorious Sledgehammer investigations, in which hundreds of senior Turkish officers had been arrested and charged with plotting a coup on evidence so flimsy that it would have been tossed out of any self-respecting court; except that it was never about justice or a coup, it was all about the government grabbing the army by its balls, and then slicing.

Her own father, absurdly, had been among the accused; and the key witness against him had been her old suitor Durmuş, taking vengeance for her rejection of him by concocting malicious lies about covert planning meetings. She'd testified in her father's defence, but no one had believed her. She'd gone to the Lion instead, but he'd been as helpless as she, for any officer who tried to defend his comrades was instantly added to the charge sheet. He'd begged her to be patient, had confided her that the fightback was already underway, that he was leading it himself. But it would take time. There was a vast quantity of work to be done, not least in finding someone to rebuild and then lead their shadow army of

Grey Wolves, for their ability to create covert mayhem was a necessary precondition of success.

Still furious about her father, Asena had volunteered herself for the job. He'd refused even to countenance it. The chances of discovery were too high. It would involve unspeakable acts, not suitable for his future wife. And she was too precious for him to risk. Instead of arguing further, she'd bought herself a handgun and had gone to wait outside Durmuş's Istanbul apartment one frosty morning. She'd called out his name as he'd emerged, so that he'd know by whose hand nemesis was come, then she'd put twelve hollow-point rounds into his chest and face, one for each year of her father's sentence. Thus had begun her new life as Asena, leader of the Grey Wolves, the Lion's liaison and right-hand.

They turned right off the main road. An estate of holiday homes, quiet with the off-season. They pulled up behind a white Renault saloon. Doors opened. She shook herself from her reverie then followed the others through the cactus garden and inside.

THIRTY-EIGHT

I

The suspension of the horse-box had been stiffened to suppress excessive movement. The undercarriage had been lubricated to minimize creaking. An observant passer-by might still, however, have noticed its fractional rocking or heard the faint squeak of metal on metal as a series of bolts were drawn beneath the floor, then a metal panel was lifted up and slid to one side.

But there were no passers-by.

The horse-box settled again. There was silence for perhaps half a minute. Then a man sat up slowly and broke a glow-stick, enough to see by but not enough to be seen from outside. It gave a greenish tint to his hand and wrist as he set it down, as though in sympathy with how he felt inside, for it was no joke lying for two hours in a fume-filled, poorly ventilated and overheated space some thirty centimetres high – a space, what was more, that he'd had to share with three other men.

Haroon moved away from the floor panel, stretched his cramped legs. Erol now emerged. Samir and Mehmet. When all four of them were safely out, Haroon and Erol went to the wall that separated the main body of the horse-box from the back of the driver's cab. They pushed hard against it and the internal locking mechanisms released. Two large, flat panels now swung outwards, revealing shallow cavities filled with grey packing foam that had been precision cut to accommodate weapons, munitions, clothing and other equipment.

In silence, they removed and distributed this equipment. They closed the panels again then stripped to their underwear and began to dress. The body-armour and the bomb vests first. Then the uniforms, jackets, boots and caps of Special Protection Squad officers. Assault rifles and spare clips. Handguns, grenades and enough military-grade explosives to blast their way through bulletproof glass and reinforced doors.

Ideally, tonight would happen on the front steps, for maximum visual impact. But they'd take it inside if they had to.

The glow-stick faded. Darkness returned. Haroon put in the earpiece of a digital radio and tuned it to the news. The crowds in Güven Park had apparently been dispersed by the police, but the riots were ongoing elsewhere. He shared this bulletin with his comrades, then they settled down to wait.

II

There was little breeze tonight, but Butros wouldn't have ordered the masts rigged even had there been. They needed to keep as low a profile as possible. He stood on deck as they left their mooring and passed out through the harbour mouth, headed east-south-east out to sea, off for their supposed night of fishing. Then he went into the bridge, where Michel was at the helm. 'Any more news on Visser and Black?' he asked.

'They haven't moved,' Michel assured him.

'Visser's phone hasn't moved, you mean.'

'Sami's sitting outside the apartment building,' said Michel. 'The moment anything happens, he'll let us know. But I must tell you, Father, I don't like this. It's too big a risk, your going in. Think what it would do to the bank if you were caught. Think what it would do to the family.'

'We're doing this,' stated Butros flatly. 'That being the case, we need someone there familiar enough with Phoenician history and material culture to make good decisions about what to bring out. That effectively means me. However, you have some small expertise in this area.

If you're genuinely so concerned about my being caught, you could lead the team in yourself, and both Georges and I could stay behind. That way, only one member of the family would be at risk. How about that for an idea?'

Michel flushed. 'This is foolishness, Father. This whole thing is foolishness.'

Butros nodded to himself. 'I won't make this decision for you,' he told him. 'But, if you choose to stay here, I assure you I will go with Georges.'

Silence stretched. It went on so long, it was clear that Michel had got the double message. 'If that's what you think best, Father.'

'Yes.' He went back out on deck. For years he'd tried to convince himself that his son was merely prudent, as befitted a banker; but the hard truth was that he was a coward. He gripped the rail tight as they left the shore behind. The old harbour dwindled to a twinkling of coloured lights. Georges and his team had unpacked the two black inflatable dinghies on deck and now began pumping them up. They were eight-seaters, and only six of them were going in, but they needed both in case they found the site and had to bring out artefacts. They secured them with ropes then lowered them over the seaward side. They made splashes like silvery soft felt. They climbed down the ladder onto them. Water sloshed around the bottom so that his feet quickly grew wet and cold, almost as if with fear. They attached the outboards, passed down packs that were bulky not just with their comms and night-vision equipment, but with more old-fashioned supplies too: torches, cameras, emergency medical kit, coils of rope both to climb down into the site and to hoist up artefacts. They also had food and water to last them for a day or two should anything happen to trap them ashore. A final check then they hunkered down and let go the ropes, drifting to a stop behind the *Dido* as she burbled sweetly on her way. They lay still in their inflatables for a full two minutes, lest some diligent sentry was watching from the shore. Then Butros murmured the word and they sat up carefully, turned on their electric motors and puttered quietly for the beach.

The water was dark yet faintly florescent in places, perhaps from algae. Though the chop was light, inevitably they all took their share of splashes. The inflatables soon smelled of fuel; his lips smacked of salt. Headlamps lit the roads to their right before being eaten by the black hole of Varosha, a mere silhouette of darkness. Yet he remembered it well from their earlier approach. A thin strip of sand in front of a jagged wall of beach-front ruins, their guts exposed and dangling, red flags fluttering weakly on the roofs of the tallest hotels in a feeble assertion of Turkish sovereignty. The rusting cranes behind that surely would soon topple.

They turned their engines down to a mutter as they neared the beach. The waves were so weak they barely broke at all. It would be reckless to leave unnecessary footprints on the sand so they burbled south to a crumbling pier where pleasure boats would once have moored. They hitched the inflatables to it then climbed a rusted ladder and made their way ashore. He glimpsed movement on the beach but wasn't unduly alarmed. It was so long since people had used this beach that birds and turtles had taken to nesting here.

Their first task was to establish a communications link. Georges set up the modem a little way inland from the pier. It sought out and quickly connected to its geostationary satellite, providing them with an encrypted, high-bandwidth link to the *Dido*'s bridge, where Michel was monitoring local army and police radio channels for any signs that their incursion had been detected. Nothing yet, he assured them, and still no sign of Visser or Black, but he'd contact them the moment anything changed.

They couldn't move the modem without breaking its satellite link. They could, however, link their cell radios to it. These were tactical, ultra-high-frequency models based on an British army design, with a range of around 250 metres in built-up areas that made them all but invisible except to the most sophisticated of scanners. Yet they could work in relay, too, so that by dropping them off at intervals, like breadcrumbs in a children's story, they could extend their effective range to well over a kilometre.

All the packs were now ashore. They hoisted them to their shoulders then pulled on their night-vision goggles and slipped stealthily into the lost city of Varosha.

III

The lift was still out of order, but at least gravity made the stairs easier on the way down, allowing Andreas to brief them on Varosha as they went. Superficially, it appeared almost impregnable, what with the sea to its east, army garrisons to its north and south, and check-points and guard-posts along its western flank – a lightly used road that ran all the way south to a closed border with the Cypriot Republic. It had high walls topped with barbed wire and festooned with menacing signs showing soldiers with guns that warned people not even to photo-graph, let alone intrude.

'So how do we get in?' asked Karin.

'Easily,' he assured her. For one thing, Varosha was huge. They were only interested in the northern third themselves, where the resort had been. But the Forbidden Zone as a whole was a rough oblong several kilometres long and over a kilometre wide. That was a lot of ground to watch. More to the point, nothing had happened there for over forty years, other than for a few incursions by mischievous children and reckless thrill-seekers. It had become such a burden and an embarrassment that people barely even acknowledged its existence any more. Its perimeter walls had crumbled and even collapsed. The wire had stretched and sagged and snapped. Such repairs as had been made at all were shoddy efforts of corrugated sheets and nailed planks that had themselves fallen apart, making it absurdly porous. And so the guards yawned away their days and made tired jokes about the world's most closely protected nature sanctuary.

They stopped en route for supplies: dark clothes, torches of varying power, a compass, some water and energy bars, matt-black packs to carry it all in. Then they continued south until they were driving alongside it. The crumbling wall to their left looked as easy to clamber over as Andreas had promised, but the road itself was another matter. Instead of a deserted lane, army Jeeps and trucks were driving by every thirty seconds or so, their headlights on full beam. 'Shit,' said Andreas, turning onto a side road, pulling in and dowsing his lights. 'I've never seen it like this.'

'Never?' asked Iain.

'Never. Nothing like.'

'Are they here for us?' asked Karin.

'Why else?' asked Iain.

'All the trouble in Turkey,' she suggested. 'Maybe they don't want it spreading to Cyprus.'

Andreas shook his head. 'Then they'd be in the Old City or up by the University. Not down here.'

'So what do we do?' asked Karin. 'Do we wait until they're gone?'

'When they're gone, all that will mean is that we're too late,' said Iain. 'We need to do this while it can still make a difference. But we don't all need to go in. No offence, guys, but I'd be safer on my own. I'm trained for this shit. It's what I do. I'll take the camera, find this place, explore it and film it. Then we'll reconvene and decide what to do next.'

'Find it, explore it, film it,' said Andreas drily. 'That's a lot for one person to handle with half the Turkish army on their back. Besides, there's more to journalism than footage, even these days. A story like this, you have to know how to frame it so that people will believe it, so that it will gain traction. I *teach* that shit. I'm coming with you.'

Iain shook his head. 'If they catch me, there's a chance they'll just deport me again. You they'll fuck for sure.'

'I don't care,' said Andreas, with unexpected intensity. 'This is *my* town. *My* country. I've been covering politics here my whole life. But sometimes covering it isn't enough. Sometimes you have to pick a side.'

'Okay.' Iain turned to Karin. 'Then you stay here, keep an eye on things. If it goes to shit, kick up a fuss for us.'

'No,' said Karin.

'No?'

'No, I'm not staying safe back here while you two go

in. Professor Volkan is quite capable of kicking up a fuss for all of us. But I'm coming with you.'

'Seriously, Karin,' said Iain, 'the more of us there are, the more likely we are to—'

'The more likely we are to find this thing,' she said. 'Look at us. Three people with a few scribbles on a map and a matter of hours to prevent a coup. No moon to speak of and we can't risk torches. We'll be down on our hands and knees looking for this fucking place, so we'll need all the eyes we can get. Besides, what do we know about it? The only thing we know is that it has some kind of Phoenician or Trojan War connection. What if that proves significant in some way? I know that stuff. Do you?'

'Yes, but—'

'Enough,' said Karin. 'If you two are both going, then I'm going too. I mean, Jesus, if they don't spot Andreas vaulting the wall, they're not going to spot me.'

'Hey!' said Andreas. But then he shrugged ruefully. 'She's got a point.'

'Good,' she said. She nodded back along the road at the perimeter wall of the Forbidden Zone. 'Then let's stop wasting time and get in there.'

THIRTY-NINE

I

The raucous atmosphere in the safe house quickly grated on Asena. The mayhem in Turkey might be a cause for quiet satisfaction, but not for celebration. They were supposed to be patriots, not vandals. Besides, there was a long way yet to go and it felt like they were tempting fate.

She was jittery for another reason, too. Not fear of failure but rather of success. If all went well, the Lion would soon be Turkey's new leader. Perhaps even by tomorrow. But what about her? Under her old name, she was wanted for questioning about the murder of Durmuş Hassan. A new identity was easily attained, a new face from a Swiss clinic, but explaining their relationship was certain to be problematic. It could be accomplished if the Lion wanted it badly enough. But would he? As head of state, he could have his pick of women.

And she wasn't as young as she'd once been.

She pushed herself up out of her chair, went next door. A dining room turned to storage, the walnut table and six chairs shoved against the walls to make space for the team's luggage and supplies, weaponry and surveillance equipment, plus several cardboard boxes stacked with papers and electronics.

Four days before, the Lion had called her in an uncharacteristic state of agitation. A meeting had been due to take place shortly in the Daphne International Hotel, he'd told her, and it had the potential to cause perhaps fatal damage to their enterprise. She was to send a team, without delay, to take out the entire hotel, then blame it on Cypriots. At the same time, he'd also asked her to assign another team to watch a particular small farmhouse on the outskirts of Famagusta to get early warning of anyone sniffing around. And to send the team in, if they thought it safe, to strip the house of its documents and computer equipment.

She hefted a box onto the table. It was filled with those hanging folders designed for filing cabinets, now sagging shapelessly. The first was fat with academic papers; the second with photographs of Phoenician and Mycenaean artefacts. There were bills and bank statements, catalogues of farm equipment, letters from a veterans' organization.

The second box was filled with hardware: an old laptop, a mobile phone with a broken fascia and a missing battery, an antique television remote control, a GPS handset, various CDs scrawled with black marker pen. She turned the laptop on, ran a search of recent documents. No activity at all for a week, and little of interest before that. She tried the CDs. They contained his accounts. To judge from them, he'd barely scraped a living.

The safe house had no broadband, but then she didn't need it to check his browser history. The last site he'd visited was departure information for passenger ferries from northern Cyprus to the Turkish mainland. Before that, the home page of the Daphne International Hotel. Further back still, multiple searches of men she'd never heard of, and of one that she had: Nathan Coates, victim of the Daphne blast. And now combinations of words such as "donor", "collector", "Dido", "Troy", "Phoenician", "millionaire", "black market" and the like. Plus other searches of "Varosha" in combination with "hotel" and "car park" and "church".

Her chair creaked a little as she sat back. She closed her eyes and let her mind go to work, trying to put herself in Baykam's shoes so that she could imagine what he'd been after and how he might have gone about it. It was ten minutes before she abruptly opened her eyes and muttered a curse at her own obtuseness. She took the GPS handset from the box to check if it kept records of recent activity. A small thrill ran through her when she saw it did. She watched raptly as it drew a beeline for her right into the dark heart of Varosha. Then it simply vanished.

She held the handset against her lips. When first they'd started out on this endeavour, she and the Lion had pledged each other total trust and loyalty, for that was their only hope of success. Yet, when he'd called her to ask her to bomb the Daphne hotel, he'd refused to tell her why, he'd begged her not to press him. Because she loved him, she'd made that promise. But, because she loved him, now she needed to know.

II

Michel Bejjani was on the bridge when Sami called in to let him know that Visser, Black and some unknown friend were on the move. He called again to tell him that they'd driven to a local mega-market to do some shopping, then a third time that they were heading further south towards Varosha. On each occasion, Michel immediately contacted Georges.

'Anything else happening?' asked Georges, his voice breaking up a little thanks to the relay of cell radios.

'No,' said Michel. 'Nothing else is happening.'

The *Dido* could comfortably accommodate twenty-four

passengers. On a windy day, under race conditions, it took a dozen trained crew to get the most out of her. Yet, on a calm night like this, sails furled and away from shipping lanes, her state of the art communications, navigation and propulsion systems made helming her from the bridge easy, even for one person on their own.

If you choose to stay here, I assure you I will go with Georges.

Michel leaned back in the captain's leather chair and resumed the game of solitaire he was playing on his iPad. There was no one to watch him, yet it was a matter of pride to look completely relaxed. He was a banker, after all. Masking one's true feelings needed to be second nature. But, in truth, anger had been pulsing in rhythmic waves inside him ever since his father had delivered his verdict, soft explosions of oddly comforting warmth.

He moved a black jack onto a red queen.

It would serve his father and brother right if they were caught on this crazy mission of theirs, especially with Black and Visser clearly on their way into the Forbidden Zone themselves. Boldness was all very well, but in their line of work prudence always won out over the longer term. Prudence and the ability to turn challenging situations to advantage.

He'd programmed the radio to skip from channel to channel every few seconds, going through a rota of local police, army and emergency services channels. Half an hour before, activity had suddenly picked up with the Famagusta traffic police issuing a series of alerts about various unscheduled army convoys due to pass through the city. As best he could tell, they were headed to the army base at the northern tip of Varosha, just a few hundred metres from where his father and brother now were. Chances were it was coincidence, nothing to do with them. They already had enough on their minds. It was best not to worry them unnecessarily.

He turned over another three cards. Then he sat there, chin resting on his fist, and pondered his next move.

III

The patrols were too frequent and the road too exposed for them to risk hopping the wall here. Andreas therefore drove them back north to where Varosha began its seaward turn, then parked in the forecourt of a shabby apartment block. The modern city and the Forbidden Zone were pressed right up against each other here, making it easier to cross the wall unseen. It would mean a longer walk on the other side than they would have liked, but there was no help for that.

Iain made them go through their packs and pockets a final time, ensuring they had everything they might need, but no more. They locked up the Citroën and walked alongside the perimeter wall as if returning from a night out in the Old City. Headlights swept over them. Karin raised her forearm to shield her eyes. They waited until the vehicle had passed then slipped down an alley into a derelict industrial estate. They talked among themselves as they went, so that they might plausibly claim that they were merely lost should they encounter a guard-post or patrol. But there was no one there. The light was poor, just stars and a low sliver of crescent moon. A pair of warehouse doors hung loose. A rusted car with an open bonnet and no wheels sat on crumbling breeze-blocks. A cat screeched at them then jumped down from a green container. And a stack of broken pallets were heaped against an old wall topped with razor-wire. Iain climbed up this accidental ladder, peered over the top. 'All clear,' he murmured.

Andreas nodded unhappily at the pallets. 'Is this the only way?'

'It's your city,' said Iain.

'Okay,' said Andreas. The pallets proved more solid than they looked. They gathered at the top then straddled the rusted razor-wire and dropped themselves down the other side.

They were in.

The moonlight was weak; Karin had to put her other senses to work. The soft scurry of night-time creatures; the pungent yet not unpleasant smell of rot. They made their way along a broken road, old tarmac ripped by wild bamboo and cacti. But the pavement was little easier to negotiate, flagstones that see-sawed violently beneath their tread, the treacherous tripwires of creepers. They reached a junction. The signpost had fallen onto its side, but Iain knelt beside it and used his weakest torch to check the street names and consult their map. He pointed to his right. 'That way.'

A bird whirred up in front of Karin, sending her heart into overdrive. They turned into what once must have been a chic boulevard of pavement cafés and expensive boutiques, but which now resembled the set of a post-apocalyptic film. The road was so thick with dust that they couldn't help but leave a trail of footprints in it. An Italian restaurant with a tattered red-and-white awning had tables set for meals never taken. Once-fashionable clothes had fallen to rags on shop dummies that lay like corpses in their windows. The cars and vans parked along one side had been stripped by time and now squatted like stalking cats on flattened tyres. Fallen telephone wires slithered across the road like giant snakes.

Their first hotel proved a bust. A swing was creaking on rusted chains in a children's playground outside, and a few spaces were marked out for parking; but there was no church in sight, no buses or industrial estate. They were making their way to the next hotel when Iain held up his hand and they all stopped dead. Karin strained to hear whatever it was he'd heard, but there was nothing, and finally he beckoned them on again.

The next hotel didn't fit Baykam's criteria either. Not from the front, at least. A side road opened out behind into a misshapen square largely used for parking, to judge from the faint traces of white lines just visible beneath the dust. But what really caught her eye were the two abandoned buses and the high wall with badly weathered double gates that suggested some kind of industrial site beyond. And there was an alarming dip in the car-parking area, she noticed, where it had evidently suffered from subsidence. Perhaps that was why it had never been developed.

At the foot of this dip, two large sheets of corrugated iron had been pinned in place by chunks of masonry and an old cement mixer. The iron screeched like fingernails on a blackboard as they dragged them aside, revealing a great mess of roughly set concrete below, like so much scar-tissue in the original tarmac. The concrete was clearly of poor quality, for it was riven through with cavities. Someone had recently attacked one of these cavities with a drill, widening it to the size of a manhole cover. They'd also hammered a steel spike into the tarmac nearby, and tethered one end of a rope ladder to it. The rest of the ladder had been fed through the hole and vanished into darkness.

They'd found it.

Iain knelt beside it, reached his torch down inside, turned it on. The stratification of the modern city: a top layer of concrete held up by what appeared to be planks of wood laid across wire-mesh. Beneath this, more concrete, then hardcore, then compacted sandy earth, then dark and cavernous space.

Iain's teeth flashed palely as he grinned. 'Okay,' he said. 'Who wants to go first?'

Behind them, a man cleared his throat to alert them to his presence then stepped calmly out of the night. 'I think that would be me,' he said.

FORTY

I

They were saying on the radio that the Prime Minister was still locked in his crisis cabinet, but his aides had promised he would come out soon to address the nation on the day's tumultuous events. Haroon passed on this news in the rear of the horse-box. He felt a strange mix of fear, elation and resolution as their moment drew closer. Most of all, however, he felt righteous.

Haroon and his three companions had little in common with their supposed allies in the Grey Wolves. They'd each been recruited specifically for this one job; and their primary qualification for it was their willingness to die. For his own part, Haroon wasn't even Turkish. He was Syrian. And a doctor. He'd finished his studies just a matter of months before the onset of the Arab Spring, then had won a coveted position at an Aleppo hospital. When his childhood sweetheart Mina had agreed to marry him, his life had looked set. A promising career, a beautiful wife, a nice apartment and the hope of better things in Syria and across the Arab world. But then that spring of hope had disintegrated into a summer of violence and the Syrian civil war.

As a doctor, he'd done what he could to tread the fine line between factions. He'd treated everyone brought to him in the same way, had left the questions to others. His caseload had grown heavier and more severe. Every day had brought new trauma victims, and, as the embargoes had begun to bite, their stocks of essential drugs and equipment had dwindled and then given out altogether. His life had become an exhausted blur of eighteen-hour shifts. He'd come to hate those, on both sides, who'd kept the carnage going. Only in his brief respites with Mina had he felt remotely human.

He'd come across the trolley in a downstairs corridor, a white sheet draped over it. He'd passed so many of them, he wouldn't have given it a second thought, except that the left shoe had been partially visible, a woman's shoe, dark blue with a gold buckle, a worn sole and a poorly mended heel. He'd gone numb as he'd noticed the third trimester bulge. In disbelief, he'd pulled back the sheet covering her face.

They'd showed him the proof of it. A Turkish rocket

fired from a Turkish launcher by insurgents trained in Turkey for the proxy war being waged from Ankara to buy regional advantage with the lives of women and their unborn children. Even thinking about it made the hatred well afresh in his heart, and overflow.

Fine lines were for other people now. Haroon wanted blood.

II

The man was silver-haired, slightly built and wearing tightly fitting black clothes, while a pair of night-vision goggles hung loose around his neck like some grotesque medallion. 'Who the hell are you?' demanded Karin.

'My name is Butros Bejjani, Miss Visser,' he told her, his voice low and level and with an unexpected hint of amusement in it.

'The *Dido* man?'

'That's not how I would choose to describe myself. But if you like.'

She could see shadows in the darkness all around them. 'What are you going to do with us?' she asked.

Bejjani gave a little laugh. 'Nothing, I assure you. We are not those sort of men. Ask your friend.'

Iain nodded. 'They try to be sometimes. They're just not very good at it.'

'We were good enough to follow you tonight,' said one of the shadows, stepping forwards into view.

Karin recognized him instantly. One of the two men who'd taken the table behind her in that Antioch café. 'Oh, hell,' she said, realizing too late why her bag had seemed to shift position, and how they'd managed to track them so easily.

'What are you here for?' Iain asked Bejjani.

'The same thing you are,' said Bejjani. 'Though we, at least, have a legitimate claim.'

'Sure!' scoffed Iain.

'I assure you,' he said. 'What lies beneath us came originally from my city of Tyre. It was stolen from us three thousand years ago. We are here to take it home again.'

'If it's been here three thousand years,' said Andreas, 'I'd say it already is home.'

Karin nodded. 'And whatever's down there, it's too important to be locked away in the vault of some private collector.'

'It won't be. I give you my word. I intend to donate everything I take to my national museum. Can you say as much?'

'We're not here for loot,' said Iain.

Bejjani frowned. 'Then what are you here for?'

Iain turned his torch on for just a blink, to illuminate the gash in the ground. 'Why don't we go down there, and maybe I can show you.'

III

Asena pocketed the GPS handset, a torch and the keys
to the SUV, then told the others she was heading out for
a while. Traffic was tailed back all the way along the
Salamis Road so she cut through the Old City instead,
then drove south along the Varosha perimeter.

There were alarming numbers of army vehicles on
patrol. She wondered whether it was the Lion's doing. It
didn't deter her so much as whet her curiosity all the
more. She checked the GPS handset and parked near
the same entry point Baykam had used. She loitered
patiently in the shadows as one army patrol after another
crawled by, until at last there was a long enough gap
between them for her to hurry across the road, vault the
crumbling wall and drop down on the other side.

It quickly grew dark away from the headlights of the
road. She had to concentrate so hard on her footing and
the GPS that she would have blundered into the clustered
group had she not heard them talking just in time. She
stopped instantly, crouched low. A pair of rusting yellow
buses were parked near a high wall. She looped around
them to give herself cover as she went in for a closer
look. One of the group briefly turned on a torch to
illuminate a fat black gash in the ground, and the reflected
light was enough for her to recognize Black and Visser
in discussion with several men she didn't know.

Whatever the Lion was so frightened of, it surely lay down that shaft in the earth beneath them. And it seemed equally certain that these people were here to find it so that they could somehow wield it against them, hoping to derail their coup even at this late stage. She had to stop them. But she couldn't do it alone and unarmed. She retreated quietly out of earshot. Then she began to run.

FORTY-ONE

I

Iain led the way down the rope ladder, his torch strapped around his wrist. The shaft was narrow at the top but then it widened abruptly and he found himself hanging in open space. The rope ladder twisted and yawed, his torch throwing uneven light upon the walls, eliciting eerie shadows from distant walls and disturbing bats from their roosts to whirr and shrill around him.

A hummock of rubble came into view below, presumably deposited by the collapse of the car park. He stepped off the ladder onto it, flashed his torch upwards three times to give the next person their signal to descend. Then he looked around. He was in the corner of an ancient colonnaded chamber. The hummock fell away on three sides, but on the fourth side the gap between it and the wall had been filled with sand so pale and fine that it must have been fetched from a nearby beach and then dumped. It had leaked away at the sides in luminous glaciers, exposing the bonnet of a large vehicle. He knelt upon its front grille, wiped its windscreen with his forearm. The frame was buckled and the glass an opaque sea-green, but it had done well to survive its fall at all.

Butros arrived beside him. 'Is this what you wanted to show me? An old bus?'

For answer, Iain picked up a heavy clump of fallen masonry and smashed the windscreen. Glass shattered into pebbles and fell away inside. He shone his torch down within. Bejjani rested his hands on a windscreen strut to peer down. When he realized what he was looking at, he grimaced and shook his head. 'All yours,' he said. 'I want nothing to do with it.' He turned his back emphatically and made his way across the mound and down into the main part of the chamber.

Karin stepped off the bottom rung. 'Is it what we thought?' she asked.

He gave a nod but then gestured at Butros. 'Why don't you go with him? We need to find out more about this place. You can keep him honest while you're at it.' She looked unhappy at leaving this unpleasant duty to him and Andreas, but she saw the sense in it all the same. Iain waited until she was gone then turned to

Andreas, who'd now joined them in the site. 'Ready?' he asked.

'Ready.'

The bus was resting on its rear, wedged between the mound of rubble and the corner of the chamber. Its angle of repose meant that the rows of passenger seats offered themselves like rungs in a pair of ladders leaned side-by-side against a wall. He put a foot on the steering wheel then lowered himself gently down onto the back of the driver's seat. It creaked and turned beneath his weight, but held. He took a moment to settle himself then stepped to one side and shone his torch down again for Andreas to film.

'What the hell happened?' muttered Andreas.

'War,' said Iain.

It was easy to understand, from a psychological perspective, why the bus had been buried beneath sand; yet it had proved counterproductive all the same. The sheath of sand had kept the bus so sealed and dry that the high heap of corpses lying at the foot were remarkably well preserved. Skeletonized, certainly, but covered with parchment skin in places, heads of black hair, fleshy lips and noses, their bones still articulated, disconcertingly human in their synthetic jackets, leather shoes and the like. Festooned with watches, bracelets and necklaces too, presumably hoping to take what they could carry out ahead of the Turkish advance.

'Get their IDs,' said Andreas.

'Thanks, mate.' He stepped down onto the top rung of seats. The desiccated plastic and foam crackled like forest twigs beneath his foot. The seats were welded into the chassis and so were mostly solid; but one had buckled and it gave way like a trap-door when he trod on it, so that he would have fallen had he not grabbed the luggage rack in time. Disturbed sand whispered like restive ghosts as it trickled to lower levels, then settled back to silence. He reached down into pockets and bags, passing any wallets and purses he found up to Andreas, who checked them for identifying documents then filmed them and read the names out aloud for his microphone.

One wallet caught in the lining of a stiffened leather jacket. In trying to tug it free, Iain only managed to disturb the heap of bones so that they collapsed a little into the cavities created by their own previous decomposition, like a macabre game of pick-up-sticks. Something rolled into view. He had to reach down to pick it up. It was small enough to fit snugly into his palm, heartbreakingly young. A girl, to judge from the few accreted strands of long black hair. Perhaps three or four years old. And the hole in her dome neatly drilled, execution style, by someone standing above and behind, aiming down. He held it up for Andreas, who filmed in silence. For no commentary was needed, not for this.

II

Kemal Yilmaz trotted down the steps of his army transport onto the runway of Gefitkale Airport. 'A great honour, General,' said Colonel Zafer Ünal, when he reached the foot. But the fractional lift of his eyebrow made a question of his greeting.

'We'll talk on the way,' Yilmaz told him, striding across the tarmac to the waiting staff car and small convoy of trucks for his entourage, fifty men he'd handpicked for their toughness and loyalty. 'Have you made the arrangements?'

'Ten dump trucks at your disposal, sir. Filled with sand and hard-core, as instructed. I've also ordered all our stocks of quicklime and cement to the Varosha garrison. They're coming from all over so I don't know how many trucks that will be exactly, but we should know by the time—'

'Water? Mixers?'

'Six fifteen-thousand-litre water tankers are being filled right now, General. I have put another two on standby, just in case. Six cement-mixing trucks are already—'

'I asked for eight.'

'We only had six to hand, sir. The other two are on their way down from the north. They should be with us in an hour.'

'Mechanical diggers? Lighting? Pumps? Pipes? Power? Communications?'

'Everything on your list.'

'And the drivers?'

'Returned to barracks, sir.' He tried a small smile. 'I must confess, we're all very curious about the nature of—'

'What about Varosha itself? Any activity?'

'We doubled perimeter patrols, as instructed, when you called me earlier this week. We doubled them again earlier today. There have been no reports of any activity. But Varosha is large and easy to infiltrate. If you tell me what it is that you're—'

'No. What about from the sea?'

'Again nothing. And very little activity in the ports to speak of either.'

He stopped to look at him. 'Very little?'

'Famagusta is a port city. There is always traffic coming and going. I could ask the harbour-master to send us through a full list, if you wish.'

'Do so.' They reached the staff car. The driver saluted as he opened the rear door for them. Yilmaz ushered Colonel Ünal in ahead of him, climbed in alongside him. It was roomy in the back, glassed off for privacy and with the seats in facing banks. He beckoned to Ragip to join them, then motioned for him to sit opposite Ünal. Ragip wasn't the biggest of his men, but the scarring around his left cheekbone made him the most intimidating. The door slammed shut, enclosing them in its muffled cocoon. He smiled at Ünal, trying to get a sense of him. In a conspiracy like this, knowing who one could trust, and how best to approach them, was the secret to staying alive. A faint shimmer of perspiration showed on Ünal's forehead; but then the evening was warm. And was there a glint almost of eagerness in his eye? The glint of an ambitious man sizing up an opportunity. 'Colonel,' he said. 'I am sure you have been following with distress the reports today from Istanbul, Ankara and elsewhere.'

'Of course, General.'

'You are a patriot, I know. A patriot with a great future. I say that with confidence, having read your file.'

'Thank you, General. It's very kind of you to—'

'No true patriot could watch what is happening to our beloved country without having their heart torn.'

Hesitation this time. 'Yes, General.'

'Your commanding officer was arrested several years ago, as part of the Sledgehammer investigations, and charged with conspiracy to commit treason. The evidence used to convict him was a mockery. So-called transcripts filled with anachronisms, contradictions and other impossibilities. Police officers lied. Witnesses changed their statements. Transparently forged documents were allowed as evidence. And all this in spite of the fact that he was a hero who'd dedicated his life to our nation's security and well-being. That is correct, isn't it?'

'I am a simple soldier, sir,' said Ünal unhappily. 'I wasn't present at the trial so I can't speak to—'

'We are all soldiers, Colonel. *Turkish* soldiers. As such, we have been charged with a terrible responsibility that the soldiers of other countries do not bear. I assume you know what that responsibility is.'

'The Constitution is—'

'The Constitution!' scoffed Yilmaz. 'It changes with each new government. What matters is what was *meant*. As leaders of the army, we are the ultimate guarantors of our secular democracy. If we ever see it endangered, it isn't our privilege to act; it's our *duty*. And when a government flouts the rule of law this flagrantly, it can no longer be considered democratic.'

'The new Prime Minister is a good man.'

'The new Prime Minister is a *weak* man,' said the General. 'He thinks sitting on a horse is the same as riding a horse. It is not.' He turned to face Ünal more directly. 'He has had months to institute changes, if he so wished. He has instituted nothing. But changes are coming anyway, Colonel. They're coming *tonight*. Changes that will restore our nation's honour, integrity, justice and pride. My question to you is this: do you want to be part of those changes? Or are you one of those to stand back while others do the necessary but dangerous work, and only afterwards applaud?'

The blood had drained from the Colonel's face. He

looked bleakly around the staff car. Ragip smiled at him, a smile to render incontinent a stronger man than Ünal. He dropped his eyes in shame. 'I want to be part of the changes, General,' he said.

'Good,' smiled the General. 'Then may I be the first to congratulate you.'

'Congratulate me? On what?'

'On your promotion, Brigadier General. On your promotion.'

III

Maybe it was her knowledge of what was in the bus, but Karin felt more on edge down here than she had even in the derelict city above. Stones kept getting in her shoes, making her limp. The sculpted walls came almost to life in their staggered torchlight. Fragments of ancient stone and mortar fell from exposed sections of roof, making the whole chamber seem precarious. And maybe it was. Sites like this could survive millennia if undisturbed; but the moment their seal was breached, allowing in fluctuations in temperature and humidity, their structural integrity began to go.

She shone her torch around the chamber. It had something of the look of a church, with its vaulted roof, its colonnades of marble pillars along either flank, the passages and chambers that lay beyond. The roof was lower than a church's, however, though in part that was because the pillars were buried to their waists in sand and other debris, either by slow accumulation or pushed into the bedrock beneath by the sheer weight of earth above, like so many tacks pressed down by a cosmic thumb. And all the other evidence suggested this hadn't been a place of worship but rather some kind of banqueting hall. A marble tabletop that ran down its spine had long since toppled, of course, and now was mostly buried; yet it kept resurfacing, like some sea-serpent turned to stone by a glimpse of gorgon. Old benches lay either side, stone legs and traces of charred wood. Scorched bronze tripods and cauldrons stood against the walls, while warped metal and shattered earthenware bowls, vessels and utensils lay scattered everywhere in the sand and dirt.

The arches that flanked the hall on either side would presumably once have led to other rooms, courtyards or maybe even gardens, but most were now blocked by masonry, earth and sand, preventing their easy exploration. Butros had his men spread out in search of interesting artefacts. Many of the pieces proved to be Mycenaean, Cypriot or Egyptian. True to his word, he ordered those to be left behind. The majority, however, were Phoenician, and these he had carried to the hillock of rubble so that Faisal, left on guard up above, could hoist them to the surface for later transfer to the boat. This process underway, Butros took Karin by the arm. 'The friezes,' he said.

'I'm sorry?' she frowned.

'The friezes. From the video.' It took him a moment to realize she had no idea what he was talking about. 'You haven't seen the video? Then how did you find this place?'

She smiled. 'That's a long story. But what video? What friezes?'

'You're a Homer scholar, correct? Then come with me. You're in for a treat.' He led her deeper into the site, navigating confidently, almost as though he'd been there before. Then he pointed his torch up to illuminate a panel of white marble that ran around the top of this section of the chamber. Parts of it had fallen away, while others were blackened from the soot and scorching of an ancient fire, yet the scene he picked out for her was both intact and easy to make out: a handsome youth handing an apple to a woman while two other women watched from the cover of trees.

'The Judgement of Paris,' murmured Karin.

Bejjani smiled with vicarious pleasure and turned his torch onto the section of frieze opposite, in which a fearsomely built warrior was taking food with an older man, while two pairs of oxen grazed nearby. Achilles and Priam negotiating the return of Hector's corpse. A third panel now, a battle scene, the dead and injured lying everywhere, while the gods watched on as though it was all an excellent entertainment. Tears pricked at the corners of Karin's eyes. As a young girl, she'd been so captivated by Homer's epic stories that she'd dedicated her life to them. Yet not for one moment had she ever envisaged playing a part in a discovery like this. 'It's Dido's palace,' she said. 'I can't believe it. We've found it. We've really found it.'

'Yes.'

The passage ahead was partially blocked by the broken pieces of a toppled column packed about with sand and earth that they had to clamber over. The floor beyond was broken. A vast slab of white marble had fallen in to reveal a staircase it once had covered. They had to squeeze between it and the old steps but it quickly opened up beneath. A labyrinth of low passages had been hacked out of the limestone bedrock, the open doorways either side leading to small chambers filled with extraordinary treasures: amphorae as tall as she was; smaller storage vessels still sealed and painted with marvellous designs; gorgeously decorated fine-ware; exquisitely carved ivories on shelves cut from the rock; wooden chests of gleaming necklaces, rings and other jewellery. An armoury of bronze and iron swords and shields. Cauldrons, tripods, platters, bowls and other vessels dulled by dust. She picked a dowdy goblet up from the dusty floor. Its weight so surprised her that she wiped it on her sleeve then shook her head in disbelief at the unmistakeable gleam.

'I don't get it,' she said. 'If Baykam wanted money so badly, why bother with an auction? Why not simply melt this down?'

'Would you melt it down?' asked Butros.

'Of course not,' she said indignantly. 'It's history.'

'Our friend didn't set up the auction merely to sell us a selection of these pieces,' he told her. 'He set it up in order to sell us the location of this place too. I think he feared for its safety should Varosha be handed back. And what do your late employer and I have in common, after all? We're both known for looking after the artefacts we buy, and for donating them to museums. That's why he chose us.'

They ventured on. Wherever they went, however, footprints in the dust invariably indicated that Baykam had been there first. They came across a pair of bronze doors that had fallen from their hinges at the head of a long, downward passage. The gradient was so gentle that the top steps were only lightly covered in sand; but the further down they went, the deeper this covering grew, turning it into a ramp of awkward footing, shrinking their headroom so severely that they soon had to stoop and then to crawl. Karin's eyes grew raw with dust, she fought a cough, she scraped her scalp on the limestone ceiling, but at last she and Butros emerged into a square antechamber with another pair of bronze doors in the facing wall, only their top halves exposed. They were decorated with floral and geometric motifs, and the handles set in them suggested that they were designed to be pulled rather than pushed open, so that their bases were pinned shut by the weight of sand. A small trough in front of the left-hand one suggested that Baykam had tried to scoop away the sand in order to open it, but it was so fine and dry that it must have trickled back almost as fast as he'd cleared it, and so he'd given up.

Karin grinned at Butros. Butros grinned back. A fine thing to be one of the very first people into a newly discovered site of such extraordinary importance, one that had lain hidden for nearly three thousand years. But being one of the very first wasn't the same thing as being actually the first. Not the same thing at all.

They rested their torches on the sand then set themselves to work.

FORTY-TWO

I

It was a quirk of Turkish law that, while firearms themselves were lightly regulated and widely owned, silencers
were fiercely prohibited. Guns could be used legitimately
for defence, after all. But who except a murderer would
need a silencer? There was only one, therefore, among
the safe house's small arsenal, specially adapted to fit a
Kilinç 2000 semi-automatic. Asena fitted it then held it
out. It made the pistol cumbersome and hard to aim,
and there was only a single fifteen-round magazine for
it; yet she took it for herself all the same, then stuffed
handfuls of spare 9mm rounds into her pockets and the
pouches of her pack.

The others had by now changed into suitable clothing.
She made them choose weapons for themselves, then

all nine of them piled into the SUV, sitting on each other's laps where necessary, so that she could brief them on the way. She emphasized how critical this mission was to the success of their larger project and assured them their targets were unarmed. But in truth they needed little encouragement: the mayhem on the news had put them in the mood for some action of their own.

The army was still crawling over Varosha like ants at a picnic. She sent the Wolves one at a time into the gaps between patrols, then followed in after. She led the way by memory. They drew close. She motioned for quiet then fitted the silencer to her Kilinc and crept forwards. There was no one in sight by the shaft mouth and she feared that she was too late, that they'd found what they needed and already left. But in the thin moonlight a low heap of strange artefacts came into view, along with a pale rope ladder that vanished through the gash in the ground. Then, even as she strained her eyes, she heard the scuffing of a boot and a man emerged from the shadows, muttering to himself and walking bow-legged as he zipped up his trousers. She sank slowly to the ground, took the Kilinc in both hands and aimed it at him. He was too far away for a sure kill, however, especially with an unfamiliar gun; and she couldn't risk winging him lest he shout warning to his comrades below. She willed him closer but he seemed to sense something awry. He stopped, squinted around him. He took a pace towards her, then another, peering into the darkness. His night-vision goggles were hanging loose around his neck and he had a radio strapped to his belt. When he reached for both at the same time, she knew that she was rumbled. She aimed at his chest and pulled the trigger even as he whirled around and sprinted towards the gash, yelling warnings as he went. She kept on firing until he cried out and went down hard, tumbling into the shaft, his yells of alarm turning into a shriek of terror that ended abruptly in a thump.

She ran to the mouth, looked down. A ballet of torch-light beneath as his companions came to see what had happened. Her immediate instinct was to haul up the rope ladder and maroon them down there. But what if they had some other way out? What if someone heard their cries for help? Maybe it would do as a last resort, but she owed it to the Lion to try for a more final solution.

She popped out her magazine, refilled it with rounds from her pockets, clipped it back in. Her pack gathered around her. Bulent was the least mobile of them, not yet fully recovered from last night's tumble in the SUV. 'Stay here,' she ordered him. 'If things go to shit, pull up the ladder and leave. Understand? The rest of you, follow me.' She took two deep breaths to steel herself then she grabbed the rope with her left hand and swung herself around and began her fast descent down the ladder into the site, firing at anything that moved.

II

The crisis cabinet had entered its fourth hour when Deniz Baştürk finally accepted that his premiership was over. It was partly the way in which his Interior Minister had just cut him off so rudely while he'd been talking, but it was more how none of his colleagues even blinked at it, not bothering with even the pretence of respect any more. Power had so clearly passed from him that they were all intent on manoeuvring for advantage or at least for the avoidance of blame.

All day long, Baştürk had been fighting on two fronts, both to restore order across Turkey and to keep himself in office. In conceding the loss of this second front, if only to himself, he freed himself to focus on the former and more important task. The relief of this, of being able to do what was right, re-energized him and gave him back some moral courage. He slapped the table loudly for attention, but Iskender Aslan kept on talking. He slapped it again and kept on slapping until the room finally fell silent. People looked curiously at him, as though they thought he'd finally completely snapped. He pointed at the Deputy Prime Minister, then at his

Ministers of Interior and State. 'You three stay. Everyone else out.' He stared down anyone who tried to challenge him and, rather to his surprise, they all complied. He waited for the door to close. 'My congratulations,' he said, when only the four of them remained. 'And my commiserations too.'

The Deputy Prime Minister squinted at him. 'I beg your pardon?' he said.

'My premiership is over,' said Baştürk. 'We all know that. I will stand down the moment order is restored, and one of you three is certain to succeed me. So I would like to congratulate that person. On the other hand, at least one of you will have their career and reputation destroyed. So I offer that person my commiserations.'

The Secretary of State shifted uneasily in her seat. 'Prime Minister?' she asked.

'When I go, I will use my resignation speech to take at least one of you down with me. *At least* one. You know I can, if I so choose. And I do so choose. I tell you now, if any of you, either directly or through your surrogates, continues to put your own personal prospects above the national interest during the next few days, *I will destroy you*. I give you my word on it.' He met and held their eyes in turn until it was clear that they all believed him. 'Good,' he said. 'Then let's call the others back in and sort this fucking mess out.'

III

Iain and Andreas were still at work on their dispiriting exhumation when they heard shrieking above and then Bejjani's guard crashed into the mound and tumbled down its side and came to settle on the bus's bonnet, his head, shoulder and right arm hanging through the empty windscreen, his cell radio clattering down the bus seats until it landed among the bones.

Andreas instinctively shone up his torch, but Iain grabbed his wrist and pulled it back down again, turned it off. 'Not a sound,' he said. 'And wait here.' The seat frames creaked as he climbed, but he couldn't help that. No need to check Bejjani's man for a pulse. His skull was smashed like an egg dropped on a kitchen floor, leaking albumen and yolk. He heard voices above and then saw the rope ladder twirl into an elegant double helix as a figure in dark clothes began to clamber down. A couple of Bejjani's men, rushing into the chamber to investigate the ruckus, were foolish enough to shine up their torches, revealing the descending figure as Asena, but also offering themselves up as targets. Gunfire popped. The men shouted with fear and then with pain and shock and dread as her bullets found their targets.

She reached the rubble mound, stepped onto it. She had her back towards him and he might have risked rushing her except for the fallen body blocking his way.

And then it was too late, her friends arriving down after her, all with handguns of their own. He retreated quietly back down inside the bus, moving as slowly as he could. The old metal still creaked treacherously, however, as he shifted his weight from seat to seat. Torchlight converged upon the bus' bonnet above him.

There was a beat or two of silence before Asena spoke. 'With me,' she said.

IV

They'd reached the western fringe of Famagusta when the shipping list arrived. Yilmaz scrolled through it on Colonel Ünal's smartphone. He wasn't expecting anything, had only asked to see it to keep the good Colonel on his toes, but one of the moored boats was registered to a Butros Bejjani, the very man Iain Black had claimed in his interrogation that he'd gone to Daphne to watch.

It couldn't be coincidence.

'This boat the *Dido*,' he said. 'Where is it now?'

'In harbour, I assume, sir,' said Ünal, taking back his phone. 'Do you want me to double-check?'

'Yes. I want you to double-check.'

The Colonel made the call, posed the question. He looked more than a little troubled at the reply. 'They've gone out,' he reported. 'Night fishing.'

'Night fishing!' scoffed Yilmaz. 'I want them found at once. I want them boarded.'

'On what grounds?'

'On the grounds that I've just given you the order, Colonel.'

'Yes, sir. I'll oversee it myself, sir.'

'I'll have two of my men help you.'

'No need, General.'

'I insist,' said Yilmaz. They'd reached the base while they'd been talking. The trucks, mixers and tankers he'd ordered were all there, parked in neat ranks. Yilmaz had briefed his men on their assignments during the flight and they now made their way directly to their vehicles then arranged them into working clusters. The staff car would be unequal to the broken terrain ahead so they switched to an open Jeep instead. Ragip took the wheel then led their convoy through the final check-point and into Varosha itself, while he stood up beside him and held onto the top of the windscreen even as he looked out over it at the ruined city.

Inevitably, it took him back to his previous arrival here, forty years before, at the turret of the lead tank. They'd expected stiff resistance on their advance, had themselves met only boys with shotguns. Not that the place had been deserted, just that the speed of their breakout and advance had caught everyone by surprise. Villagers had gawped from balconies and shops. Turkish

Cypriots had waved and cheered while Greeks had slunk into the shadows. When they'd reached the coast road, tourist sunbathers had stood up on the beaches, then had laid back down again. Their biggest problem had been all the people wanting to surrender to them. They'd told most of them to make their own way south, but they'd taken prisoner all likely looking Greek Cypriot men of fighting age, plus any women and children too stubborn to leave them. They'd had to commandeer a bus to hold them all, then a second and a third.

The Varosha road was of fair quality near the base, but it quickly disintegrated. They lurched and bumped their way over buckled tarmac and spinneys of intrusive vegetation. He began to recognize buildings. He tapped Ragip's shoulder to have him stop. The convoy came to a halt behind them, their array of beams lighting up a street of derelict shops and cafés. Yes, he remembered driving down here before. It had been empty that day too. Word of their advance had evidently reached this section of town, at least.

A truck that had been delivering cement to a building site ahead had simply been abandoned in the road, blocking their further progress. He could have shunted it aside with his tank, but he'd been under strict orders to avoid wanton damage where he could, especially if it was liable to be photographed or even filmed. He'd therefore checked his maps for an alternate route, and had turned inland instead.

At the time it had seemed the smart move. With the benefit of hindsight, however, it had proved the worst decision of his life.

FORTY-THREE

I

The bus had creaked. Asena was sure of it. There was someone inside it. In which case they needed to be dealt with now, before they could launch a counter-attack. She reloaded her magazine then removed her silencer and stowed it in her pack, for there was no need for it down here, and it was cumbersome. She knelt carefully upon the bonnet. The windscreen had been smashed in. She counted to three, then moved with controlled speed, pointing her torch and Kilinç down simultaneously, her finger trembling on the trigger.

A second passed. Another. 'What's down there?' asked Emre.

His question brought her back from her mild daze, staring down at the grim ossuary below. 'Nothing,' she said.

'Nothing?' he asked, coming to look for himself.

'Stay back,' she ordered, half-raising her gun.

He spread his arms out wide. 'Okay,' he said, looking at her like she'd gone crazy. 'It's nothing.'

She gestured vaguely at the expanse of main chamber. 'Get to work,' she said. 'This place won't clear itself, you know.'

'What do we do with anyone we find?'

'What do you think?'

She waited till he was gone, issuing orders to the others, then looked back down inside the bus. When she'd set out with the Lion on this hard course, it had been a matter of honour for her, of fighting the gross injustice perpetrated against her father and his fellow officers. Her targets had been traitors or liars or at least legitimate combatants. But wars weren't clean; their borders blurred, collateral damage became inevitable. And violence abraded you; you grew inured. So one day you found yourself parking a truck bomb outside a Daphne hotel and murdering over thirty innocent people. And all that kept you going then was the belief that your end justified your means, because at least you'd had right on your side when you'd started.

·The bus creaked again. Maybe it was merely settling after earlier intrusions. Or maybe Black or one of his friends were laying low, hoping that the sight of the killing field beneath would spook her off. If so, they didn't know her very well. She reached her right foot down upon the steering wheel. From there she stepped down onto the back of the driver's seat. The metal groaned softly. She could smell sweat. She didn't feel afraid so much as heightened, her every sense working at its peak. She shone her torch down the aisle, then above and below the parallel lines of bench seats. Uncut diamonds of windscreen glass glittered amid the skulls and bones beneath, like some gruesome pirate treasure. But she could see no sign of anyone hiding. She lowered herself carefully onto the back-rest of the topmost passenger seat, knelt upon it, risked a glance over its back at the space between it and the seat beneath. It was large enough to hide a man, but it was empty, as was its companion across the aisle.

Gunfire erupted in the main chamber; hoots of triumph. 'Got one,' shouted out Emre, for her benefit.

Her heart began to clatter. These seats were awkward, an invitation to ambush. She knew how rash it was to take it on alone, but she owed it to the Lion not to let these others see his shame. She took hold of the luggage rack to steady herself. She reached a foot across the aisle, then bestrode it. She crouched to check under the seats she was standing on. All clear. She made her way methodically down the bus in this way, seat by seat, until she was almost down to the bones. The frame of the next seat had buckled and wouldn't take her weight. And was it her imagination playing tricks, or was that breathing she could hear, pregnant with fear, beneath her right foot? She remembered the speed with which Black had surprised her in the desert, a snake striking.

Never again.

The seats had metal frames but their backs were of toughened plastic. Enough to slow but not to stop a 9mm round. She shone her torch about her, hoping to get a better fix on him, but the reflections were all too indistinct. She shifted her right foot out of the way then aimed down. Without the silencer, the noise of the triple discharge in such a confined space half-deafened her. But the real shock was Iain Black erupting from beneath her left foot. She turned her gun on him and pulled the trigger again but too late, he was too fast for her, he seized her wrist and wrested the gun from her. She cried out and tried to clamber away from him but he grabbed her by her ankle and pulled her down so hard that she tumbled into the bones beneath, and something about it terrified her and she screamed with primal fear, as if the demons of hell itself were clawing at her and dragging her in.

No sympathy from Black. He put his foot square on her face then sprang from seat to seat up the aisle to the windscreen and out. She followed him a little groggily, arriving up top to find him already engaging her Grey Wolves. One against seven. It should have been no contest. And, to her great dismay, no contest was exactly what it proved. A trained soldier against thugs with guns: the difference between them was shocking to her. The way he moved, with such pace, precision and purpose, while her own men seemed glued by fear to their defensive positions, or tried to hide behind each other, or gave themselves away with torches and panicked bursts of wasteful gunfire, as if unable quite to come to terms with the notion of a target with the effrontery to shoot back. She saw Emre fall first, then Tolgay, Ali and Uğur, Black taking their guns to use against the rapidly dwindling survivors when the Kilinç's own magazine ran out, until finally the shooting stopped and silence returned.

Torches lay at haphazard angles on the floor, rolling back and forth in search of their angles of repose. By their confused light, Asena saw Emre lying motionless a few metres away, his gun by his hand. She crept over the rubble for it but Black was too sharp for her, he picked it up and aimed it at her, but calmly, to subdue rather than kill. She knelt and raised her arms above her head, sensing that he wasn't the kind to execute a surrendered woman, willing to bide her time in case the tables should turn once again.

And they did, quicker than she'd dared hope. For Bulent, God bless him, must have witnessed it all from up top, and he began to haul the rope ladder upwards at that moment, stranding the lot of them down here inside.

II

Michel Bejjani was on his tenth game of solitaire when he glanced out the port window at the distant shoreline. Despite her sophisticated systems, the *Dido* had obviously shifted orientation in the last minute or two, for he could see headlights on a stretch of seafront that previously had been—

He felt sick suddenly. He got to his feet, traded his iPad for a pair of field-glasses, took them out on deck, brought them into focus. A long line of vehicles was heading south along the old Varosha promenade. It surely had to be the convoy that had been gathering in the army base. It was one thing to overlook some ambiguous traffic police chatter. There could be no excuse for ignoring this. He hurried back inside, tried the radio. His brother didn't answer. He tried again and kept on trying, so frantic now that he only noticed the roar of helicopter blades when they turned to thunder above him. He ran back out on deck. Instantly the boat was flooded in brilliant white light, the beams so dazzling that they virtually blinded him, leaving him with only the haziest impression of soldiers abseiling down onto deck as he fumbled his way back into the bridge and pawed at the radio, shouting useless warnings into the ether. Someone yelled at him to stop. He cried out one last time. But then something clumped him unbelievably hard on the back of his head and he collapsed in blackness face first upon the floor.

III

The convoy slowed down and spread further apart as it headed along the road towards the square. Great care was needed here. And no one knew that better than Yilmaz himself. They'd driven in close order and at pace on his last visit. The road had been good, the area deserted, they'd had forward positions to establish. He'd noticed a slight spongy feeling beneath his tracks as he'd driven across the square, though he'd made it safely enough. But the combined weight of all the tanks and buses behind him had proved too much for it. A splintering thunderclap that he'd heard even above his engine. He'd looked around to see a great black void where part of the car park had simply collapsed, obscured a moment later by an almost volcanic eruption of dust and debris. Instantly, it had been every driver for himself. Some had tried to reverse away. Others had spurted forwards or to the side. In such unbelievable chaos, a blessing that there'd only been the one collision. Unfortunately, that one collision had involved a tank driving into a bus, crushing its rear end beneath one of its tracks. The prisoners on the bus had understandably panicked; they'd poured out of its ruptured doors. Several of his men, perhaps unnerved by the collapsed car park, had mistaken this self-preservation for an opportunistic mass escape, and so had opened fire. The prisoners had tried to scatter, but all the roads out of the square had been blocked by tanks and troops. And the tensions of the day, the lifelong loathing of Greek Cypriots sharpened by weeks of propaganda, had led to a bloodbath in which all his men had participated. Even he had become infected by the madness. He'd gone back intending to stop it, but had found himself drawing his pistol and taking part in it instead. The red mist, he'd heard it called; and it described it sweetly. There was something both compulsive and cathartic about it, exacerbated by the knowledge that this would be your one chance to unleash the animal within, to do the stuff of nightmares, to rub raw against nature herself. It had felt righteous. It had felt beautiful. But eventually there had been no one left in the square to kill, and the fervour had drained away, leaving only corpses.

Not all the prisoners had tried to run. A few, mostly women and children, had stayed terror-stricken on the buses. His men had hauled them out. No one had ordered them to kneel, but they'd knelt all the same, ululating with grief and the faint hope of mercy. The most difficult decision of his life by far, but they'd been witnesses, he'd had no choice. And he could comfort himself that at least he'd had the courage to do it himself.

Afterwards, they'd needed to get rid of the evidence. The new sink-hole in the square had offered the obvious solution. They'd piled the bodies into the part-crushed bus, had pushed it backwards down the hole. It had somehow wedged itself between the newly fallen rubble and an old wall. Driven by an odd mix of propriety and shame, he'd ordered sand fetched from the beach and poured down through a chute taken from the building site. Baykam had gone below to guide it, which was when he'd discovered the litter of artefacts. He'd begged an hour to pillage the place, but reinforcements had already been on their way, they'd had no time to spare. While some of his men had sluiced down the square of blood and bullets, others had looted a builders' merchant for girders, scaffolding poles, doors, planks, fencing and the like that they'd lashed together into a giant raft to lay across the shaft mouth as a base on which to pour newly mixed cement. An improvised solution, sure, yet it had lasted forty years, and would surely have lasted longer had Baykam not got greedy. But now that it was open again, it was only a matter of time before someone else found it and he was ruined. For while it was considered a fine and necessary thing for a statesman to issue orders that would inevitably lead to the deaths of ordinary people, either directly or as collateral damage, it was another matter altogether to pull the trigger yourself.

That way lay disgrace. That way lay The Hague and a war-crimes trial.

He was here to make sure that could never, ever happen.

FORTY-FOUR

I

Karin and Butros had been joined by Georges in their efforts to clear the sand away from the bronze doors when the first shots cracked out. So absorbed was she by the task that it took her a moment to register the noise and then to realize what it was and what it might mean. She glanced at Butros for reassurance, but got none. Her heart seemed to freeze inside her. Iain was by the shaft mouth; she turned and scrambled for the ramp.

Georges grabbed her by her arm. 'No,' he said. 'Not till we know what's going on.' He picked up his cell radio and spoke urgently into it, calling on his men to report. But none of them did.

'The *Dido*,' said Butros.

Georges tried then shook his head. 'No use,' he said. 'We've lost the satellite.'

More shots now. Clusters of them. Butros flinched with each one, knowing his men were exposed and unarmed. 'We have to go,' said Karin. Georges nodded. He put on his night-vision goggles and led the way back up the ramp. Karin followed closely after him. In the perfect darkness, she had only sound to go by. They reached the top of the ramp and hurried towards the banqueting hall. Sustained bursts of gunfire grew ever louder; she could hear shouting and shrieking. Now she could see stutters of light ahead; but then they suddenly stopped. Georges held up his hand for her to stay back. He crept forwards, peered out into the chamber. He muttered a soft curse then pushed himself up to his feet and walked out. Karin went after him. The relief of seeing Iain standing there, aiming a gun down at a kneeling woman, was dizzying to her. She hurried over to him and put her hand on his arm for the re-assurance of touch. 'Andreas?' she asked.

He shook his head. 'In the bus. I think he's been hit. I haven't had time to check yet.' He turned to Georges, crouched by one of his fallen men, then nodded at the woman. 'Keep an eye on her.'

'I'll do better than that,' said Georges, his voice taut with rage. He picked up a dropped gun and aimed it at her chest, his arm trembling as he steeled himself.

Iain pushed down his hand. 'I thought you weren't those sort of men.'

'They killed Ali and Faisal. They killed Kahlil and Youssef.'

'Even so.'

Georges scowled angrily. But then he exhaled and the tension left him. 'So what do we do?'

'I don't know yet. We need to see to Andreas first.' He bound Asena's wrists behind her back with a strap from a dropped pack, then went with Karin to the bus, knelt on its bonnet. 'Andreas,' he called out.

The man himself poked his head out from his hiding place, like a wary tortoise. 'Thank God,' he muttered. 'I thought you were them.'

'Are you hurt?'

'My leg,' he said.

'Don't move. I'll come down.' But right then a rumbling noise, much like an underground train passing in a neighbouring tunnel, made him look up. Dust, grit and earth shaken loose from the ceiling danced in their torchlight. The noise faded for a moment then returned more loudly. The shakes grew worse, dislodging stones, earth and clumps of rock that landed in puffs of sand and dust all around them. Vehicles were arriving above. *Heavy* vehicles. In a militarily restricted zone like Varosha, that could only mean one thing.

Alone among them, Asena seemed to glow. 'It's the Lion,' she exulted. '*Now* you're for it.'

II

It was well past Katerina's bedtime, but Zehra couldn't bring herself to send her to bed. She was too mesmerized by the news pouring out of Turkey to miss even a minute of it; mesmerized by the sense of its connection to Andreas and Professor Volkan, by the sense that it would have consequences for her son, and thus for Katerina herself. But, for the life of her, she couldn't figure out what that connection was, or what those consequences would be.

The studio switched again to outside the Prime Minister's residence. A doorstep press conference was expected at any moment. But then it had been expected at any moment for at least the past half hour, and nothing had yet happened. The camera panned around to show a vast bank of journalists waiting there, like a pack of hounds champing for their prey. And one of the reporters at the front was busy checking her smartphone in the exact same way that Andreas always did.

Forty years Zehra had spent out of the world. Forty years in which technology had kept marching on without her. That was a lot of catching up to do. But they always said there was no time quite like the present. She turned to Katerina, munching salted sunflower seeds on the sofa beside her. 'I don't suppose you've ever heard of something called Twitter, have you?' she asked.

III

The call from Colonel Ünal reached General Yilmaz as he approached the square. He had to clamp his headphones against his ears to hear. The *Dido* was seized, Michel Bejjani arrested. And he was already talking his mouth off about how his father, brother and others had infiltrated Varosha in search of some mysterious Phoenician treasure.

Not such a shock, therefore, to see the heap of artefacts, the corrugated iron sheets, the rope ladder, the figure cowering in the shadows, trying to hide from the sudden dazzle. Ragip saw him too. He jumped down and raced across the square, his gun drawn. He scragged the man by his collar and brought him back to the Jeep. The man was ashen with terror, wondering what to say to save his life. He chose shrewdly. 'General,' he said. 'Such an honour. Asena told us you—'

'Asena?' Yilmaz waved Ragip out of earshot. 'What's Asena got to do with this?'

The man nodded vigorously at the shaft mouth. 'There were people down there. She said we had to stop them. For your sake. For the cause.'

Yilmaz felt hollow. He could see it all. 'She's down there now?'

'I offered to go with her. She made me stay up here, to trap them if things went wrong. There was a gunfight. It didn't go well.' He spread his hands helplessly. 'I only did what she'd ordered me to do.'

'And Asena, you idiot? What happened to Asena?'

'She's down there still. I think they took her captive.'

'They?'

'The man from Cairo. Iain Black. His girlfriend Visser too. And others we didn't know.'

Yilmaz nodded. Black must have pooled forces with Bejjani somewhere along the way. 'And they're armed, you say?'

The man looked around the square, visibly awed by the number of troops and their hardware. 'A few handguns only. Nothing like you.'

Yilmaz nodded. He'd planned to bury the site forever without having anyone go down. He could still do so and be back in Ankara before morning. But that would mean sacrificing Asena. A man sometimes learned ugly truths about his own true nature when faced with decisions as stark as these. But Yilmaz was gratified to discover that this time it went the other way. He beckoned Ragip back over. 'Your twenty best men,' he said, gesturing at the shaft mouth. 'You're going in.'

FORTY-FIVE

I

There was no time to treat Andreas with the care appropriate to his wound. Iain tore his shirt into strips to bandage his leg then hoisted him up the ladder of seats to the top, where Karin helped haul him out. His trousers were sodden with blood; he bit back a yelp each time he put any weight on his foot. They took the long way round, staying clear of possible lines of fire from the shaft mouth. Butros had arrived to join them, was surveying his dead men with horror and dismay, while Georges covered Asena with a gun in one hand even as he tried in vain to get a signal on their various cell radios with the other.

'Any joy?' asked Iain.

Georges shook his head. 'When Faisal fell, it must have broken our relay.'

433

A long-shot, but worth a try. Iain clambered back down the bus to retrieve and then check Faisal's dropped radio. It was still working, but it had no signal either. The bleak truth settled over him. They were trapped down here, cut off from the outside world, the Turkish army parked above their heads. 'What now?' asked Karin.

'We make things hard for them,' said Iain. 'You lot have explored this place. Is there anywhere we can hold them off?'

'Those doors,' said Georges, glancing at his father. 'If we could get behind them . . .'

Iain saw it from the corner of his eye, a metallic teardrop falling down the shaft. He yelled for everyone to get down, grabbed Andreas and Karin and hauled them to the ground either side of him. The loudness of the explosion, the brightness of the flash even through closed eyelids, he diagnosed it instantly as a stun grenade, of no direct danger itself but a sure sign of danger imminent. A second detonation, a third, then a beat or two of silence. He risked a glance around even as a cluster of yellow ropes dropped down the shaft, bounced briefly before hanging there like creepers in the rain forest, then dark shadows abseiling fast down them, silhouettes bulked up with body-armour, assault rifles at the ready.

He picked Andreas up, threw him in a fireman's lift over his shoulder, then grabbed Asena by the arm before she could sneak away. 'Run,' he yelled at the others. And they ran.

II

Under other circumstances, Deniz Baştürk would have been heartened by the new spirit of cooperation and even enthusiasm in the cabinet room. Just a shame that he'd had to write and then sign four copies of his resignation letter to bring it about. Nevertheless, for the first time, there was a genuine focus on dealing with the protests and riots. Not that agreement was straightforward, even now. Some argued for showing understanding of the demonstrators' grievances. Others demanded a crackdown and ruthless retribution. The usual compromise emerged. Make examples of the worst hooligans and anarchists while quietly letting marginal cases slide. Then flood the streets with uniforms and stamp down ruthlessly on anything that sniffed of trouble while simultaneously announcing a package of measures to boost employment and relieve the worst poverty and hardship.

He had no part in this conversation. No one asked his opinion or even spared him a sympathetic glance. He had become a ghost. Six months in office, and it wasn't just allies he lacked, it was friends. In truth, the only person to become anything of the sort during his tenure was General Yilmaz. And if there was any silver lining to this situation, he reflected, it was that the Chief of the General Staff wasn't a member of the cabinet, and therefore not here in person to witness his humiliation.

III

General Yilmaz waited apprehensively for Ragip to report back on the success or otherwise of his assault. At last he came on the radio. 'The main chamber is secure, sir,' he said. 'No resistance and no casualties. But there were bodies already down here.'

Yilmaz braced himself. 'Any women?'

'No, sir. But my first two men down saw people running, including at least one woman. And there's a blood trail. We'll find them soon enough. What do you want done when we do?'

Yilmaz hesitated. This situation was too tangled yet delicate for delegation. He needed to oversee it in person. 'Wait there,' he said. 'I'm coming down.' He turned to Nezih, his project manager for tonight's works. 'You know the plan,' he told him. 'Use the approach roads for parking. Keep as much weight off the square itself as you can. But be ready to start pumping the moment we're back up.'

'Yes, sir.'

Abseiling was beyond him, so he tossed the rope ladder back down the shaft then sat awkwardly on the broken ground and felt for a rung with his left foot. He took a firm hold then twisted himself around and began his descent. It was a shock to him both how awkward and how taxing he found it. Appearances mattered hugely in the army. You had to look capable. That was why he'd taken to dying his hair these past few years, to improving his diet and adopting a strenuous exercise regime, even to paying annual visits to a discreet Swiss clinic. But then one day you had to climb down a rope ladder and you realized you were old.

The bonnet of the bus was exposed, its windscreen gaping. His heart sank at the thought of all the people who might already have looked inside. But then he'd been living with that fear for forty years. Almost from the 1974 ceasefire, the international community had urged Turkey to hand back Varosha as a gesture of goodwill. Under other circumstances, he'd have lain low and hoped to find anonymity in the general fog of war. But that photograph of him had made anonymity impossible. Besides, it hadn't been just him and his men who'd stood to lose from discovery of the bodies, it had been the reputation of the whole army too, even of Turkey herself. With great trepidation, therefore, he'd requested a private interview with his commanding officer. It had been the most uncomfortable half hour of his life, choking on his confession like on a stuck bone. Thankfully, his CO had seen where he was going, had stopped him before he could reveal it all. A man experienced in war as well as peace, he'd known how fickle the public could be, how quickly they'd come to declare abhorrent the very tactics for which they'd so recently clamoured. And the next Yilmaz had heard was that Varosha was being permanently sealed off, without real explanation, under the direct command of the Turkish army. And so it had remained ever since, despite the occasional prodding of some new UN initiative, until Baştürk had become Prime Minister and signalled his willingness to treat. What choice had he had then but to destroy that willingness with bombs? No choice at all.

He reached the bottom rung, stepped onto the mound. 'Well?' he asked.

Ragip snapped out an uncharacteristically sharp salute, as became this whiff of combat. 'We've found them, sir. There's a long ramp or staircase at the far end of the site. They're trapped in some kind of chamber at its foot.'

'Good,' nodded Yilmaz. 'Show me.'

FORTY-SIX

I

Nothing was said, but by the time they reached the antechamber, Iain was the acknowledged leader of their small band. He gagged Asena to prevent her from yelling out their position or tactics then gave Andreas a gun to cover her with. He set Karin, Georges and Butros to clearing the bronze doors as a possible further fallback, then he himself returned a few feet back up the shaft and built a defensive rampart of rubble and sand to hide them and to offer cover for returning fire.

A first flash of light at the top of the passage. The sudden dazzle of a directly pointed torch. He expected the attack at any moment after that, but as the minutes passed and nothing happened he began to fear instead that they wouldn't even bother. A few judiciously placed explosive charges in the main chamber would bring this whole place down, burying them and the bus for ever beneath countless tons of rock and sand. But then a man called out from the top of the passage. 'Asena?' he shouted. 'Are you there?'

'Who's asking?' answered Iain.

'My name is General Kemal Yilmaz,' said the man. 'You're Iain Black, yes?'

'What's it to you?'

'Is Asena with you?'

'Yes.'

'Let her tell me that for herself. If we're to make a deal, I first need to know she's alive.'

Iain nodded at Andreas. He ungagged her to let her speak. 'I'm alive, my love,' she shouted.

'Let her go,' said Yilmaz.

Iain almost laughed. 'Sure,' he said.

'I have fifty men with me. We have body-armour, assault rifles, stun grenades, CS gas and time. What do you have? No one even knows you're here. And don't think your comrade Michel Bejjani will save you. He and his boat are both now in our custody. Negotiation is your only hope. Let Asena go and we will leave you here unharmed. You have my word on it.'

'Your word!' mocked Iain.

'My word,' he insisted. 'As a Turk. As a soldier. I swear this on my life, my service, my country, my honour, on everything I hold dear: release her and we leave. These old treasures mean nothing to me. All I want is Asena and your oath of silence. You have one minute, starting now. Choose wisely.'

'He wouldn't dare attack,' murmured Georges. 'Not while we've got his girlfriend.'

'He'll attack,' said Butros. 'He has no alternative.'

'And you honestly think, if we give her to him, that he'll just leave us here unharmed?' scoffed Andreas. 'Have you forgotten already those poor bastards on the bus?'

'That was forty years ago,' said Karin. 'People change.'

Everyone looked at Iain. The casting vote. But his heart was heavy. In life, he knew, there sometimes were no winning moves. He turned to Asena. 'Your boyfriend,' he asked. 'Is he a man of honour?'

'He is the Lion,' she said.

Iain nodded. 'I think it's our best bet, guys. We can't hold them off, not with three handguns and a couple of dozen rounds.' He glanced back at Asena. 'Unless you've got more in that pack of yours.'

'No,' she said.

He pushed her down in the sand, rummaged through her pack. A water bottle and some energy bars, her silencer, a hunting knife and a spare torch, but three dozen extra bullets too. 'You lie pretty well,' he said, zipping her pouches back up. 'Were you lying about your boyfriend too? What man of honour would lead a coup against his own government?'

'They started it,' she scowled furiously. 'They wanted all the power for themselves and so they deliberately destroyed good men. They called them traitors. They called my father a traitor! *My father!* All he'd ever done was serve his country and yet . . .' She shook her head, blinked back tears. 'They asked for everything they're going to get tonight, believe me. Tonight is *justice*.'

Iain frowned. There was something too emphatic about her words. That was when he realized. 'You're going after the Prime Minister himself, aren't you?' he said. 'Assassinate him and maybe his cabinet too, then declare a state of emergency and step in. Arrest all your enemies and stop the bombing and everyone will hail you as saviours.'

'We *are* saviours.'

'Sure,' scoffed Iain. 'They'll write songs.'

'We didn't start this,' she said.

Iain nodded. Their minute was up. He jerked his head at the passage. 'Go on, then,' he said. 'Fuck off.'

She didn't hesitate, she scrabbled away his crude barrier then crawled off up the passage. 'Don't shoot,' she shouted, her soles a pale flicker in the darkness. 'It's me. It's me. I'm coming.'

'Your turn now,' called out Iain. 'Get out of here.'

'We're leaving,' said Yilmaz.

There were grunts and scrabbling noises, but they quickly faded into silence. 'I don't believe it,' muttered Georges. 'They've really gone.'

'For the moment,' said Iain.

'You think they'll be back?' asked Karin.

He shook his head. 'I know men like Yilmaz. They'll tell you solemnly that honour means everything to them. And so it will, until it actually threatens to cost them something real.'

'What are you saying?'

'I'm saying he picked his words carefully. He promised to leave us here unharmed. He said he had no interest in all this old stuff. But he never said we'd be free to go ourselves, or to take these artefacts away with us. And why is he even here tonight? I'll bet you anything he came here to seal this place up before it could get rumbled. And nothing he just said would stop him from sealing it up with us still inside.'

A few beats of silence. It was all too horribly plausible. 'Then why the fuck did you let her go?' demanded Georges.

'Because he'd have come for us if we hadn't. We'd have been screwed, trust me.'

'We're screwed now.'

'Maybe,' he said. 'Maybe not.'

'Maybe not?' asked Butros.

Iain allowed himself a faint smile, calibrated to give them hope, though not too much. 'I sneaked one of your cell radios into Asena's pack while I was rootling around in there. With a bit of luck, once she's up top again, we'll get our satellite link back.'

II

The front door of the Prime Minister's residence opened and aides came out to check the podium, microphones, lighting and other arrangements. A sure sign, apparently, that the man himself would be out any moment. Haroon knew he should wait until he was, but suddenly he'd had enough of this cramped darkness so he gave the word to his companions and they opened the rear doors from within and climbed down.

It was late and dark and there was no one else in sight. None of them had been here before but they'd all watched hours of reconnaissance footage, and knew exactly where they were and which way to head. They stretched their cramped limbs and shared words of exhortation and encouragement as they checked their own and their buddy's weaponry and other equipment one final time.

They were ready.

On the radio, the Prime Minister's front door opened again. Only this time he did come out, followed by several senior ministers. He made his way to the podium and began to talk. Haroon took out his earpiece and his radio. He wouldn't be needing those any more. They set the timers running on the incendiary charges in the cab and beneath the false floor of the horse-box, partly to deprive investigators of easy clues about their methods and associates, but mostly to burn their own bridges so that none of them would weaken and turn back.

'Head shots, remember,' said Haroon, for every security officer between here and their destination would be wearing body-armour as standard.

'We know what we're doing,' said Erol.

They set off. A year before, this whole government quarter had been open to the public and so there'd have been armed police on every corner. But since they'd encased it in its new ring of steel, there'd been less need for heavy security inside. There was just one checkpoint, therefore, between them and the Prime Minister's offices, outside which he was currently talking to the media. They reached a corner. Haroon lay on the pavement and looked around it, scoping it out through his night-sight. Six armed policemen were standing in front of a pair of heavy-duty security gates. Only two of the six were on full alert, however; the other four were watching the ongoing press conference through gaps in the gate, cracking jokes about it amongst themselves. He let Erol, Mehmet and Samir each take a look, then he gave orders as to who would take out who. They concealed their assault rifles for the time being then fitted silencers to their handguns and tucked them into their belts. Then they made their way briskly but without menace around the corner and out onto the street.

They were a hundred metres away before the first

policeman noticed them. He alerted his comrades and they all turned to look. Haroon waved cheerfully to them and they recognized their uniforms, and they relaxed again. Haroon and Mehmet walked shoulder to shoulder in front, giving Erol and Samir, their best marksmen, the cover they needed to take out and raise their handguns unseen behind them. When they were close enough, Samir gave the word and they stepped abruptly to the side. The suppressors worked so efficiently that the first two guards were down and dead before the others even realized the danger they were in. By which time, of course, it was too late for them too.

They dragged their bodies into shadow, retrieved their assault rifles. On the other side of the security gate, the Prime Minister was assuring the nation that the day had been an aberration, a one-off; that Turks could go to bed that night confident that morning would bring the restoration of order. Haroon allowed himself the smallest of smiles. For the first time since his life had been torn apart that harrowing day in his Aleppo hospital, he felt something approaching peace.

FORTY-SEVEN

I

Andreas was losing too much blood to move again so Iain gave him one of their two remaining cell radios and instructions on the story he needed to tell. Then he set Butros and Karin to clear the doors while he and Georges headed back up to the banqueting hall with the other radio, to make a relay of it and so maximize their chances of a signal.

The last of Yilmaz's soldiers were climbing up out of the site when they arrived. The rope ladder snaked upwards after them, marooning them inside. Iain's heart sank, though it wasn't exactly a surprise. Arc-lamps sprang on around the shaft mouth, throwing a halo of bright white light upon what looked almost like snow on the rubble mound. Iain cautiously edged forwards, looked upwards. The shaft had been significantly widened;

the snow was freshly drilled cement dust. A fat yellow pipe now wriggled like some grotesque maggot down through the mouth, then a second and a third. Engines started, making the roof thrum. The maggots cleared their throats and coughed out spatters of thin grey slurry. Then they began to vomit in earnest, torrents of watery cement thundering down onto the mound, splashing down its sides and spreading quickly around the chamber.

Iain checked the radio. No signal. He moved closer to the shaft but there was still nothing. The concrete was already washing around his calves. They didn't have time to waste. He stepped out into the circle of light, though he knew he was putting himself into possible lines of fire. The hint of a signal at last, but it vanished as quickly as it had come. He needed to get higher up. He began climbing the hummock, fighting his way through the heavy waterfalls of slurry. He reached the top and held the cell radio above his head.

Muzzle flashes up top. Automatic gunfire churned the ground beside him. He lost his footing as he tried to get away and fell hard, was swept down the mound in a deluge of concrete. His elbow hit a rock; the radio spilled from his grasp. He fumbled frantically for it but it was swallowed by the slurry and further bursts of gunfire chased him from the circle of light before he could retrieve it.

'What now?' asked Georges, coming to help him to his feet.

Iain looked around. The concrete was already almost up to their knees; they had no time to fetch or find another radio. And unless they could find some way to stop it here, it would quickly stream down to the antechamber, where it would catch Karin, Butros and Andreas utterly defenceless.

A marble column fallen across a passage mouth gave them something to work with. They built a barrier of rock and stone upon it, packing the gaps with sand and earth, racing against the bath of concrete filling so rapidly on the other side. They completed their makeshift dam just moments before it would have been over-topped. The pressure, however, was so great that almost at once it began to bulge. Cracks appeared and started dribbling slurry. They patched it as best they could, added ballast to thicken it, though both of them knew in their hearts that their frantic labour wouldn't save them; that even if they somehow held the concrete at bay, all they were actually doing was walling up their own tomb from within.

II

Katerina had fallen asleep on the sofa with her head on Zehra's lap. It felt good to have her lying there and Zehra couldn't tear herself away from the spectacle of

Turkey on fire, not with a new story breaking every few minutes and now the Prime Minister himself at the podium.

Something beeped. She looked around but saw nothing so she put it from her mind. It beeped again, then for a third time before she realized what it must be. She carefully lifted up Katerina's head and set a cushion beneath it. Then she went into the kitchen. Katerina had earlier set up her son's mobile phone to alert her to any tweets from Andreas. She'd left it here when she'd done the washing up. But now it was buzzing and its fascia was alight and she picked it up and read the message on its screen:

> Chief of the General Staff Kemal Yilmaz is planning a coup against the Turkish government tonight **#stopthecoup**

She read it again, in disbelief. Then the next one and the ones after it.

> He intends to assassinate Prime Minister Deniz Baştürk and other members of the cabinet **#stopthecoup**

> He will use these assassinations as a pretext to declare a state of emergency and take charge **#stopthecoup**

He will arrest anyone who protests and accuse them of being behind the assassinations, bombings and unrest #stopthecoup

But in fact he and his associates are behind all of it, including Daphne and today's violence and riots #stopthecoup

He is in Varosha, right now, trying to kill me and my associates so that we can't get this news out #stopthecoup

But I have documents and photographs to prove all these allegations, and more. I will publish links to them beginning now #stopthecoup

Please retweet this as widely as possible and alert everyone you know who can help #stopthecoup

Zehra stared at the small screen, the accusations, the links to evidence. For a moment or two, she felt completely numb, as though her nervous system didn't quite know how to process it all. But then an intense, illicit, sick, sweet thrill ran right through her, like how she'd always imagined adultery must feel.

She went back through to the sitting room, shook

Katerina by the shoulder until she woke, yawning and rubbing her eyes. 'What is it, Grandma?' she asked.

'I need to retweet something to your father's friends,' Zehra told her. 'Show me how.'

III

The noise around the square was extraordinary, what with the generators, cement mixers and pumps all working flat out, plus the rumble of emptied trucks and tankers heading off to be refilled. Asena and Yilmaz had to walk off a little way to find privacy and relative quiet in which to talk. She longed to embrace him, to thank him properly for risking so much to rescue her from Black and his friends, and thus proving in the most categorical way possible his steadfastness and love; but his men were everywhere, leaning against walls, smoking and drinking from water bottles; and while they were fiercely loyal, many were also staunchly conservative in their social outlook and disapproved of open displays of affection, especially on an operation like this. So she held herself back.

They had access to the Internet via a tablet computer and a mobile communications mast. They found a quiet courtyard in which to watch the Prime Minister spouting his usual platitudes. 'I told you it was all he had,' smiled Yilmaz.

'Yes,' agreed Asena. She slipped her hand into his. Their breathing fell into rhythm as they watched. All these long years of planning. All these long years of sacrifice, hardship and loneliness.

Any moment now.

Any moment.

FORTY-EIGHT

I

Yasemin Omari, star political reporter for Channel 5, ever on the lookout for the killer question. It was how you made your name in this business, making the great and good stumble and look foolish. On days as chaotic as this, the best tripwire was news too fresh for them even to know about, which was why she ignored the Prime Minister's bromides and kept checking her twitter-feed instead, even while jostling for position to be called on for the first question.

A new topic was trending crazy fast: #stopthecoup. She scrolled quickly through the backlog of tweets and the links to all the photographs and other evidence. Her eyes widened as she read; her mouth fell further and further open.

Link to article about the police team killed in Daphne while investigating Yasin Baykam for selling antiquities **#stopthecoup**

Photograph of Kemal Yilmaz with Yasin Baykam by their tank, Cyprus 1974 **#stopthecoup**

Photographs of exhumed victims of the Varosha massacre, along with IDs and other documents **#stopthecoup**

She glanced either side to see if anyone else had got it, but the fools were all fixated on the Prime Minister. One part of her mind automatically started trying to frame her knowledge into the most devastating possible question. But another part was shouting at her that, if there was anything to these tweets, some seriously bad shit was about to go down right here, right now, for all that they were deep in the heart of the government quarter's *cordon sanitaire*. She looked around, was reassured to see the six bodyguards flanking the Prime Minister and the four additional state security policemen who'd just passed through the security gates and were now walking briskly towards . . .

Something about them chilled her, their bulked-up silhouettes or perhaps their slightly stiff-legged gait, as though they'd each rolled their right ankle. But they couldn't all have rolled them. Then she realized that they were walking that way to conceal the assault weapons held down against their legs. And she began, almost despite herself, to scream.

II

With a politician's instinct, Deniz Baştürk sought instantly to make a joke of the woman's shrieking. But he faltered when he saw Omari's expression and he followed her gaze to the four policemen advancing so purposefully towards them. They realized they'd been spotted. They bellowed chilling war-cries and began to charge, raising their assault weapons as they came, firing indiscriminately into the small throng of ministers, bodyguards and aides clustered around his podium. Everyone screamed. Everyone tried to scatter in different directions, knocking into each other and falling over, the crash and clatter of dropped microphones and cameras.

Amid this pandemonium, only Baştürk remained immobile, frozen by a mix of fear and incredulity. As well, then, that his bodyguards were trained for this. Two of them grabbed him by his arms and swept him up the steps and inside, closing the door behind him. But there were people stranded defenceless out there, aides and journalists yelling in terror as they scrambled to get in after him, so he himself opened the door for them, helped them inside. A flurry of bullets rattled the wall. He could hear the single cracks of handguns as the rest of his bodyguards began the fight back. He risked a glance out. Perhaps two dozen men and women were lying dead or injured in the street and on the steps leading up to—

A blinding flash; a deafening blast. Too big for a grenade; surely a suicide vest. The shock created a momentary lull. The injured recognized their opportunity and began to limp and hobble and crawl brokenly for cover, leaving just seven others behind. Six of them looked beyond help; but Yasemin Omari, she of the man-trap questions, was wailing in pain and fear, clutching her shattered left hip with one hand and futilely trying to claw herself to safety with the other. Baştürk didn't even think, he simply sprinted down the front steps and into the road, scooped Omari up then ran back to safety. A long burst of automatic gunfire along the street sounded terrifyingly close. The wall ahead of him puffed with multiple impacts. He closed his eyes, as though that could somehow protect him, and tried to duck down low. Something punched his arm and span him around and he dropped Omari even as he stumbled back inside. The door slammed behind him and he was instantly surrounded by bodyguards and others, all shouting at each other to step back and give him space. Two of them picked him up and carried him upstairs to the nursing suite where he had his weekly check-ups, yelling for a doctor; but no doctor appeared and he was too impatient for news just to wait there so he tore himself free of them and made his way to the communications office, hoping to find out what the hell was going on.

The five flat-screen televisions around the walls were each tuned to different news channels, muted and running subtitles. The various anchors and reporters were clearly as bewildered by events as he was. The initial numbness of his gunshot wound quickly wore off; his arm now began to ache unbelievably. A staff nurse cut away his jacket and shirt sleeves while he stood there, exposing the ugly mess of flesh and blood beneath. He thought her name was Selda but he wasn't certain and he didn't want to offend her by getting it wrong. But he had to say something. 'Will I live?' he asked, softening the question with the ghost of a wink.

She coloured as she looked up at him. If he hadn't known better, he'd have thought her starstruck. 'Straight in and out, sir,' she said. 'You'll need to see the doctor, of course, but you'll be fine.'

'You're Selda, yes?'

'Yes, sir.'

More gunfire outside. Wishful thinking, perhaps, but it sounded further off. And more answering cracks now; reinforcements were arriving. Another lull. In the corridor outside, he could hear a journalist breathlessly reporting that he himself had witnessed the Prime Minister being shot; that he was believed critically wounded and perhaps already dead. He stormed out to tell him in no uncertain terms to stop making shit up. Another loud explosion made the building tremble; they all ducked instinctively.

'That's two down,' muttered someone.

'Two to go,' said another.

He led his strange entourage into the cabinet room, Selda still dressing his arm. State, Interior and the Deputy Prime Ministers were already there, making phone calls, trying to find out what they could. He felt strangely exuberant and had to caution himself that it was only shock playing tricks on him, that he mustn't let it go to his head. 'What's going on?' he demanded. 'Who are these people?'

'We're not sure,' said State. 'But they're saying Yilmaz is behind it.'

'Yilmaz?' It was like he'd walked into a glass wall. 'No. It's not possible.'

'That's what they're saying. They're saying it's a coup.'

'Where is he?'

'Cyprus.'

'Cyprus?'

'Apparently he flew in earlier with fifty men and met a convoy of trucks and led them into Varosha.' He gave a grimace. 'They're saying on Twitter he's trying to cover up some old massacre.'

Baştürk sat heavily. The one policy on which they'd clashed; the handback of the lost city. Suddenly he saw it all. 'Get him for me,' he said icily. 'On the radio. On the phone. I don't care.'

'We're trying. He's not answering.'

'Then send people in to arrest him. I don't care what it takes. Just do it.'

Interior nodded soberly. 'Yes, Prime Minister. I'll do it now.'

FORTY-NINE

I

Yilmaz and Asena watched the whole débâcle live on the tablet. The journalist and her shrieks leading to the botched initial assault, the ensuing confusion and gun battle, their hopes reviving briefly on talk of the Prime Minister's death, only for the man himself to dash them with his angry refutation. Then the whispers started. Reporters relaying rumours of an attempted coup involving one of Turkey's most admired men. His own name hinted at then finally spoken aloud. Suggestions of an old atrocity. And, apparently, the whole business exposed by a journalist tweeting live from somewhere beneath Varosha itself.

Rage coursed through him, a rage so intense and sweet that it was almost a pleasure in itself. He turned on his heel and marched back towards the square. Perhaps Asena guessed his purpose for she grabbed his arm and tried to hold him back, but he shook her off so violently that she stumbled and fell. He strode across the broken, pitted concrete and glared down the shaft mouth at the fast-rising lake of slurry below. Everything he'd worked and planned for. All the sacrifices he'd made. To have it end like this, brought down by Black and those others, those *little* people, these *insects* . . . Drowning was too good for them. He suddenly wanted them pulped beneath his feet. He wanted them *crushed*.

The trucks, tankers and mixers were parked prudently on the approach roads and around the perimeter of the square. But he had no more use for prudence. He waved the drivers into their trucks, tankers and mixers, had them start their engines and trundle forwards. Not realizing what he planned, they drove trustingly out onto the square, increasing massively the strain on the ancient pillars below. He felt the ground begin to give under his feet, he turned and hurried away. A terrible splintering noise and half the square simply sheared off and plunged several metres down before juddering to such a violent stop that the shock wave threw him tumbling, while a great geyser of cement spurted up through the shaft high into the sky, the grey lava spattering all around him like something from the End of Days.

II

Iain was working with Georges to strengthen their dam when it happened, an earthquake, everything he'd ever imagined an earthquake to be, the world itself a thunder-clap. The roof above the banqueting hall must have been brought down, either by accumulated stress or by sabo-tage. Countless tons of earth crashed onto the Olympic swimming pool of slurry, slamming it into every available nook and cavity. Their puny barrier swelled out towards them. Cracks turned to crevices, liquid cement squirting through. Then it was simply swept away altogether.

No need to tell Georges to run. They were already fleeing together down the passage, bumping into walls, tripping over steps. The concrete, fortunately, had thick-ened enough to slow it, while the numerous side-chambers acted as release valves. Yet still it came after them, like some remorseless monster from the movies, the collapsed ceiling pressing down upon it like a massive plunger. They reached the top of the ramp, yelled warning to Karin, Butros and Andreas. Their headroom shrank, they got down onto elbows and knees, spilling into the ante-chamber in a confusion of torchlight.

The bronze doors were still closed. The look on Karin's face tore at his heart; no time to explain or even say goodbye, he took her in his arms and held her tight and then the slurry was upon them, swallowing them up, the pressure building and building, unbelievable, unbearable. He thought he was gone when he felt something snap and the bronze doors burst and they spilled out into the open space beyond, tumbling down steps as the glutinous grey liquid splashed and bubbled around them like some giant geothermal pool.

It took Iain several moments to recover his senses. The only light was a soft glow from a torch three-quarters submerged in the cool lava. He grabbed it and wiped its bulb, gave them light to crawl exhausted up a step in the floor then turn panting onto their backs, coated head to foot in the sludge like so many casts of Pompeii victims come back to life. He turned the torch on the broken bronze doors, through which the slurry was still oozing. Then he shone the torch on the walls and ceiling of this new chamber.

There was silence, except for their strained breathing. 'For fuck's sake,' said Andreas at last. 'What *is* this place?'

But no one had an answer.

III

The storm of slurry quickly rained itself out. Yilmaz walked cautiously forwards to the edge of the collapsed section of square, looked down. Remarkably, its surface was still largely intact, albeit riven with massive cracks and fissures, and tilted at an angle so that all the tankers and trucks were now sliding towards its low point, like balls on a wonky pool table. Grey slurry bubbling up from beneath was already forming a shallow pool that the dazed surviving drivers had to wade through to reach the pit's ragged walls, which they now began scrambling up.

Something creaked and then groaned behind Yilmaz. He whirled around to see the rear wall of an old hotel simply collapse like a dropped sheet before smashing into shrapnel upon the ground then tumbling in a waterfall over the edge of the new sink-hole, battering his men even as they struggled to safety.

The rage passed, as it always did. He felt small and cold. While some of his men ran forwards to help their comrades, others stared at him with open loathing. The unwritten army contract: your men would die for you, but they wouldn't be killed by you. He was trying to think of some way to win them back when he heard noise above, the clatter of rotor-blades. Spotlights sprang on, dancing over the square like the build-up to some much-hyped sporting event. Colonel Ünal's helicopters had a new assignment. His men instinctively scrambled to take up defensive positions, but all he could manage himself was a forearm up to shield his eyes, his feet pinned to the spot by age and an oddly obstinate sense of dignity.

Asena appeared at his side, her hair blowing wildly

from the copter's downdraught. The expression on her face was charged with understanding and shared pain, a mother at the bedside of her terminally sick child. It felt like the sharpest imaginable knife being slid between his ribs. 'This isn't over,' he insisted, having to shout to make himself heard. 'We have the Fourth Army camped around Istanbul and Ankara. We have units outside all the key buildings. I'll get onto Hüseyin. We'll make arrests of our own. We'll seize the television stations and Parliament. If we can hold out till morning, we can create a stand-off and then who knows.'

She reached up to stroke his cheek. 'My darling,' she said.

He felt his shoulders sag, his gut. Their plan had been to decapitate the regime then use the ensuing chaos to seize and consolidate power. But the regime hadn't been decapitated and there was no ensuing chaos. To carry on now, therefore, would be to spill unnecessary blood, and yet still lose. They'd always vowed never to become those kind of people. It took him several seconds to accept this, to realize the implications of it, to see the only path that remained open. He took out his pistol, stared balefully down at it. Oddly, it wasn't the prospect of pain or oblivion that bothered him at that moment quite as much as the inevitable disfigurement of it all. Vanity had ever been his great weakness. 'I can't do it,' he told her. 'You'll have to do it for me.'

'For both of us,' she assured him.

He nodded and kissed her forehead. Tears prickled his eyes, regret for what might have been, for the terrible things they'd now write about him. How narrow the gap between patriot and monster. 'The Lion and the Wolf,' he said.

She pressed the muzzle against his temple. 'The Lion and the Wolf,' she agreed.

FIFTY

I

The new chamber was vast and bizarrely shaped, like something from a surrealist nightmare. The doorway through which they'd spilled stood at the top of a flight of steps that widened as they led down to an open atrium in which the slurry was pooling fast, thickened by all the sand it had picked up on its journey through the site. They'd already hauled themselves out of this onto a second flight of steps, facing the first, that led up to a large platform with sinuous walls and further staircases; while above them a ceiling swooped low in places but elsewhere soared so high that Iain's torch beam barely reached it.

It took Karin a few moments to work out that this was because it wasn't a normal chamber at all, but rather a cavern in the limestone made to look like one, its natural contours left largely untouched, but its walls smoothed down then skimmed with plaster or cut with niches for the countless oil lamps and other ornaments that gleamed and twinkled in the torchlight.

That they were trapped here was immediately obvious, yet Karin felt unaccountably calm. She helped Iain carry Andreas up to the upper platform, where they laid him on the ground. Beneath the dust and sand, the floor was tiled with squares of pink and white marble. Against the far wall, two divans slouched either side of a low bronze table. There were frescoes in the plaster, though too dusty to make out. It was all astonishingly well preserved, as though shut up for a matter of decades rather than millennia.

Georges came to join them. He'd fished two packs from the sludge and now unpacked them to see what supplies they had: two large bottles of water, a selection of snack bars, a first-aid kit, a coil of red mountaineering rope, a spare torch and fresh batteries. Iain took the first-aid kit over to Andreas, set about cleaning and redressing his leg. For his part, Butros took the spare torch and went exploring. Karin went with him. At the top of a short flight of steps they found a bed on a raised dais set in an alcove in the rock. They both stopped dead for a moment, unable quite to believe what they could see. The bedstead's gilt frame was inlaid with ivory and strung with woven ropes covered by desiccated and shrunken skins, while twin headrests of carved and painted wood lay at the far end. But that wasn't what had frozen them. What had frozen them was the skeleton that lay upon the skins, and the pitted bronze sword that ran through its ribcage, as though they'd impaled themselves upon it, as Dido had supposedly done.

The walls around the bed were skimmed with plaster and finished with a narrative of paint. Butros returned back down the steps for the surplus bandage and a bottle of water. He moistened the bandage then wiped the panels down. The water brought the old pigments vividly to life. In the first, a queenly woman and her retinue were welcomed ashore from a fleet of ships. The next showed a great feast, the third a hunt. In the fourth, a man and woman held hands in the mouth of a cave. Beneath them, in surprisingly crude letters, like initials carved by lovers into a tree, two sets of Phoenician characters. 'Queen Alyssa, daughter of Belus of Tyre,' murmured Butros, running his finger beneath them. 'Aeneas, son of Teucer of Salamis.'

Karin closed her eyes. How simple explanations could be. Dido's Aeneas not the warrior of Troy himself, but simply named in his honour, as so many people had been: yet a Teukrian of Salamis rather than Troy. And everything else that followed had been just the usual confusion of names. She took a pace back, the better to study the wall as a whole, the whole cavern chamber. 'It's the legend,' she murmured.

'Legend?' asked Iain, coming to join them.

'How Dido and Aeneas became lovers. They went out hunting together. A storm blew up. It separated them from their retinues. They took refuge in a cave.'

'A cave?' Iain frowned and looked around. 'Are you saying *this* cave?'

'Dido is one of history's greatest romantic figures. Is it so hard to imagine her building her palace here precisely *because* it was near this cave? Or maybe she simply needed somewhere discreet to meet him. But you're missing the point.'

'Which is?'

She pointed at the doorway through which they'd arrived. 'That staircase was cut through forty metres of bedrock. *Straight* through. But how could Dido possibly have known they'd find this place at the bottom *unless she'd already visited it*?'

'There's another way in,' nodded Iain. 'There has to be.'

'Then what are we waiting for?' said Georges. 'Let's find it.'

II

The four gunmen were accounted for, the *cordon sanitaire* declared secure. Seventeen others were dead, including the six policemen whose bodies had been found by the security gates. Twenty-one others were being treated for gunshot wounds and shrapnel injuries, and five of them were considered critical.

But it could have been so much worse.

Deniz Baştürk had had a buzzing in his ears since the first blast. What with the high levels of ambient noise, he had to watch people's lips closely as they talked to understand what they were telling him. Mostly, they were telling him to go to hospital. He brushed these suggestions off. The nation had never needed its leader visible as much as it did right now. Besides, heightened security meant restricted access even for medical personnel, and others clearly needed treatment more urgently than he. Yasemin Omari, for one. He walked alongside her as she was stretchered out to an ambulance, her eyes woozy with morphine. 'Don't think I'll go easy on you just because of this,' she said.

He laughed and patted her hand. 'I don't,' he assured her.

The exchange put him in oddly good spirits, though he knew better than to let it show. He went back up to the comms room. In the chaos, it was their best source of news. One channel kept showing a clip of him running out into the street to pick Omari up. He was surprised and somewhat dismayed by how fat and ungainly he looked, by how slowly he moved. He'd thought at the time he was breaking land-speed records. Another channel showed him berating that journalist for suggesting he was dead, while Selda swabbed his arm.

It felt strange to watch himself like this.

Shouting below. His wife had arrived. It would take more than an emergency lock-down to keep her out. He hurried down to meet her, all dressed up for Orhan's concert. Her face was glistening as she wrapped her arms around him. Then she stood back with a reproachful look. 'I heard it all on the radio. What were you *thinking*? For Omari of all people!'

'They'd have killed her.'

'And?' He couldn't tell whether she was joking or not, suspected she wasn't quite sure either. She hugged him again, even tighter. 'They said you were dead,' she told him. 'I was so scared.'

'How do you think I felt?'

They laughed together. It felt good. But it wasn't to last. There was a tap on his arm and he looked around to see Gonka, his senior aide. 'Prime Minister,' she said soberly. 'There's something you need to see.'

'Just tell me.'

'I really think you need to see this for yourself, sir. Please.'

He sighed and took Sophia's hand, followed Gonka back up to the comms room. It had become crowded, yet people edged away from him a little, as though he'd somehow become toxic. He felt the chill of premonition. The screens were no longer showing footage of him. They'd switched to live feed from Istanbul's Taksim Square. It had been completely cleared earlier by the police, but protesters were now flooding back in, at least two hundred thousand already, if he was any judge, and thousands more arriving every minute, waving banners and flags, Turkish and union and regional and football and others, raggedly bellowing out some vaguely familiar slogan that he couldn't quite make sense of, what with his hearing still impaired. His heart sank to his boots. It never finished. It never fucking finished. Tonight, of all nights, hadn't he earned a break?

Everyone was looking strangely at him, even Sophia. She let go his hand and took a pace back. He had the sense that people were expecting him to say something pertinent, but he didn't have the first idea what. 'What's that shit they're chanting?' he asked.

Gonka frowned at him, as if she suspected he was pulling her leg. Then she realized he was serious. 'It's your name, Prime Minister,' she told him gently. 'It's your name.'

III

It was Iain who found it, playing his torch over the gallery roof. 'There!' he said, illuminating a narrow gash in the rock perhaps fifty feet above.

'Christ!' muttered Karin. 'But how do we reach it? How did *they* reach it?'

A good question, for the wall wasn't just smooth, it angled back in as it rose. And there was an overhang directly below the cleft that promised few if any holds. With time, good light and the right equipment, Iain might have made the traverse. Without them, it was impossible. Yet there must have been a way up somewhere. He turned his torch on the facing wall and found the answer: pairs of peg-holes that ascended in a spiral until they stopped directly across the cavern from the cleft: holes into which scaffolding poles would once have slotted, supporting a staircase and presumably a bridge. He stood beneath the gash then paced out the distance to the facing wall. He made it thirteen feet. He tried to visualize leaping it from a standing start.

'It's not possible,' said Georges. 'It can't be done.'

'Then give me a better idea,' said Iain sharply. He checked their coil of rope: thirty metres long, steel eyelets in both ends. He replaced it in the pack then slung it on, pulling the straps as tight as they would go. His shoes were wrong for climbing. He kicked them off. The slurry was rising remorselessly beneath them. He tucked the torch into his waistband and went to the wall.

'Be careful,' said Karin, touching his wrist.

'Count on it.' The holes had no lips but he could anchor himself in them by making fists of his hands. His feet were too wide for most of them so he had to take his weight upon his toes. The first section was fast, even so, with the cave still bellying out. With a foot in the lower hole of a pair, and a fist in an upper, he'd feel out the next set of holes, then heave himself up and across. Then he'd reset himself and start again. The wall soon turned vertical, however, then began to slant back in. The strain built incrementally upon his shoulders, neck and calves. But he kept going and finally he reached the place where the staircase finished, where a bridge would once have crossed the cavern to the cleft in the facing wall. He anchored himself then twisted around to shine his torch at it. It was tall, narrow and jagged, with the promise of more open space behind. He shone his torch either side then up at the roof, but could see no way to climb around or across to it. 'How's it going down there?' he called out.

'The concrete's still rising,' said Georges, doing his best to keep his voice level, not entirely succeeding.

'Okay,' said Iain. There was nothing for it. He rested his torch carefully in one of the peg-holes, angling its beam to illuminate the gash. Then he turned himself carefully around, resting most of his weight on his right heel. Now that he was up here, in this awkward posture, it was clear to him that he couldn't hope to leap directly to and through the cleft. The best he could hope for was to grab its bottom lip then haul himself up. He closed his eyes to visualize in his mind how it would go. He rehearsed it until he had it fixed. Then he braced himself, bent his legs and leapt.

He crashed into the facing wall. The impact was much harder than he'd expected and it left him winded. He flailed with his hands for grip but the rock was smooth and there was nothing to hold onto and he began slipping remorselessly down so that he knew he was about to fall. He clawed crazily at the rock with everything he had, with his feet and hands and chin and knees and elbows, and somehow he gained traction and heaved himself up through the mouth and inside before turning to lie there on his back, panting mightily, his heart hammering.

It was half a minute or so before he'd recovered enough even to look around. He'd left his torch on the other side of the cavern, of course, so that the light in here was minimal. But he was lying in a shallow well at the foot of a slanted, narrow shaft that vanished into complete darkness above him. The rock was raw here, not smoothed as in the cavern beneath, but jagged with juts and knobs. And there were steps cut in a steep spiral in the shaft's walls.

He started climbing. It quickly turned black as pitch. He continued upwards for perhaps thirty feet until he bumped up against something solid. He felt above him, a blind man learning a new face. A pair of wood and metal trap-doors had been laid flat across the shaft's full width, and were held in place by two locking-bars. He tried to wrest these free, but they were too tightly wedged.

He set his back against a wall and stamped one with his foot. Nothing. He kept at it until he was rewarded by a hint of give. He went at it even harder and suddenly it fell loose and clattered free to the foot of the shaft, bouncing out the gash and crashing to the floor fifty feet below. The trap-doors creaked and lurched fractionally downwards, allowing trickles of sand to fall upon his face; and something mighty stirred and groaned above him, a giant rousing himself after a long slumber. And he had a sudden and convincing intuition at that moment, of a city under siege, its Achilles heel a cave system leading to its underbelly. Simply concealing its entrance wouldn't be enough. It would need to be buried so deep beneath sand and earth that no one would ever find it. If so, then releasing the second locking-bar would bring the whole lot down upon him, crushing him beneath it.

He climbed back down to the foot of the shaft, seeking some cunning way to give himself a chance. But if he used the rope himself, and it went wrong, Karin and the others would be stranded on the cavern floor until the concrete claimed them. He knelt on the ledge, leaned out, called down to them. Georges turned on his torch. They were standing on the bedstead, the highest place in the chamber, yet still the slurry was lapping around their knees.

He was out of time.

The deaths of his wife and son had been the most brutal experience in Iain's life. It hadn't just been the overwhelming grief of bereavement itself, it had been the mixture of guilt and self-loathing and falling short that had come along with it, and which he'd never quite managed to shake off since, irrational though it was. For he'd always seen it as his fundamental role in their family to keep Tisha and Robbie safe, whatever it took. And so what use was he? What possible use was he?

There was a knob of rock at the foot of the shaft. He knotted one end of the rope around it then tested it to make sure that it would hold. When he was satisfied, he threw the other end down to Georges. 'Stay where you are for the moment,' he told him. 'There's a blockage I need to clear first.'

'A blockage?' asked Karin.

'Wait until I come back here, or until it's all finished spilling out. Then climb up and we can get the fuck out of here.'

'What about you?'

'I'll be fine,' he told her. He could hear the slightly tinny note of falseness in his voice, so he didn't hang around to argue. He climbed briskly back up to the trap-doors. It was difficult to get leverage on the second bar. The way the doors had lurched down had pinned it even more tightly into its slots. He'd need to relieve the pressure on it somehow. He turned around so that his back was against the wall then bent his legs and straightened his back and pressed his hands and head up against the trap-doors, like Atlas carrying the heavens. He breathed in deep to flood his bloodstream and muscles with oxygen, then he gave it everything, straining to straighten his legs, a weightlifter going for gold. The locking-bar loosened a fraction, enough for him to knock it away with his elbow. The trap-doors instantly burst open, releasing a torrent of dry sand. He grabbed the wall and clung gamely on for a second or two but the deluge was too much, it ripped him free and sent him tumbling down the shaft, helpless as a child caught by a freak wave. The sand already fallen at least buffered his landing, but instantly he was pinned beneath the extraordinary weight of the continuing cascade, like some vast grain elevator in full spate. Within moments he was buried so deep that an eerie silence fell. He was lying on his front with his back bent and his arms up to protect his head, creating a tiny pocket of air beneath him. He tried to move an arm or leg, but he simply couldn't. The weight upon him was so crushing that it was all he could do to breathe.

A minute passed. Another. The air turned sour. A headache started and quickly grew fierce. He began to feel dizzy and knew it wouldn't be much longer. An image came unbidden to him then, of Tisha and Robbie the last time he'd seen them alive, cheerfully waving him off after his final leave. He knew it was only his oxygen-depleted brain playing tricks, but the way they were waving felt like forgiveness; it felt like letting go. And the burden of having fallen short that he had been carrying around all these years finally lifted from him, leaving him feeling almost weightless. A voice began whispering in his ear. He tried to ignore it but it wouldn't go away. It kept telling him that it wasn't his imagination, that the weight of sand truly had lessened. And suddenly he realized the significance of that, that the torrent must not only have poured itself out, but also have spilled out of the cleft onto the cavern floor, leaving only a relatively small mound of it above him. With his last reserves of strength, he wrenched himself around. He began to scrabble at it with his hands and it was so fine and dry that it parted easily now and then he was breaking clear of it and gasping for air even as Karin, digging down to him from above, cried out in relief and threw her arms around him and hugged him with a fierceness that was almost a declaration in itself.

They lay there together for a while as he recovered. The shaft rose high above them, offering a miraculous glimpse of night sky. And then, astonishingly, a helicopter, drawn perhaps by this inexplicable new sink-hole in the ground, passed clattering overhead; and its searchlights caught him and Karin for the briefest moment in its twin beams, as they basked in the relief of it, in the sheer physical joy of being utterly spent, yet still alive.

EPILOGUE

Nicosia, four days later

The sun was out, making rainbows on cobbles slick with soapsuds. Across the square, waiters were laying tables for lunch, stiff white cloths and heavy steel cutlery and fat glasses for water and wine. Karin felt an immense contentment as she watched them. What a pleasant life, to move from café to café with the sun, holding hands with Iain.

She felt fifteen again. Fifteen, and in love.

Every so often, someone would notice her or Iain and do a double take; but less than yesterday, in turn less than the day before. *Sic transit gloria mundi*, as her old professor would have put it. *Thus passes the glory of this world.*

A waiter sashayed through tables to bring them new drinks. Grenadine for her, orange juice for him. Alcohol was somehow redundant. They clinked out a toast, eyes meeting over the top of the ice-misted glass. Another thrumming of the strings. It was absurd. But that wouldn't last forever, and then what?

Iain, seemingly, had no doubts. He was possessed of a new serenity since their ordeal beneath Varosha, as though he'd put old ghosts to rest. He talked of their future together as a settled thing. At dinner the night before, he'd explained how he'd reconfigure his flat for her. 'This is ridiculous,' she'd protested. 'We've only known each other a week.'

'So?' he'd asked.

At times his certainty thrilled her. At others it made her wary. It meant she'd have to be the sheet anchor, the rational one. And there was plenty to be rational about. Money, for a start. Good jobs were hard to come by in her field, and her debt wouldn't retire itself. Iain waved all that aside. But damned if she'd live off him; damned if she would. She drained her grenadine, put down the empty glass, got to her feet. 'You know that thing I have to do.'

He nodded. 'You sure you don't want company?'

'I'm sure.'

'Later, then.'

She stooped to kiss his cheek. She liked it when he

didn't shave. It was a brisk fifteen-minute walk from the Old City to the Société Genève. No sign of the manager. But then she'd timed it for his lunch-hour. The way the tellers glanced at each other suggested they'd been gossiping about her amongst themselves. The cocky young man was free. She walked straight up to him and told him what she needed. He led her to the back office for the master key and to register her details. But his composure failed him on their way down to the basement. 'So that was pretty cool,' he grinned. 'You and your friends in Famagusta.'

'I guess,' smiled Karin. Maybe it had looked so from the outside. From the inside, cool was about the last word she'd have chosen. Watching Iain climb the wall and then make his leap across the cavern had been a kind of torture; and she found it almost impossible even now to think about that avalanche of sand he'd brought down upon himself; her mind would baulk and flinch away from it, she'd have to think of something else, something soothing.

Courage was odd like that, the way it came and went. It perplexed her, for example, that so soon after losing her nerve in this same bank vault a few days ago, she'd managed to fight her way free from those Grey Wolf thugs, then had insisted on going into Varosha with Iain and Andreas. Had she changed so dramatically in so short a time? She didn't think so. But how else to explain it?

The cashier tapped in the pass-code, pulled open the vault door. She went directly to 7a. They crouched to fit in their keys and pull it slightly ajar. 'I hope this is the right box,' she said.

'I'm sorry?' he asked.

'I have two of them. I thought I knew what was in each, but now I'm worried that I might have mixed them up.'

'No problem. As long as you brought both keys.'

'Let me check this one first. I think I got it right.' She waited until he'd left and the door was closed behind him, then she checked her watch. Two minutes should be plenty.

She leaned against the wall as she waited. News had come in a torrent these past few days. Revelations about Yilmaz, Asena and the Grey Wolves had kept Turkey riveted. The Bejjanis had returned home to condemnation and acclaim. And Deniz Baştürk had seized the opportunity of his stratospheric approval ratings to fire his cabinet and replace them with people loyal to himself. Only Andreas had reservations, it seemed, tweeting from his hospital bed about the dangers of a weak man with a mandate.

The second minute passed. She called the cashier back in. 'I feel such a fool,' she told him. 'It must be in my other box.'

'No problem,' he said. 'What number?'

Five days before, in this same vault, she'd faltered at this juncture. She still stood to lose everything she'd stood to lose then, plus this time Iain too. Yet the thought of the possible cash inside the box bolstered her; or, more specifically, the good things she could do with it: she could provide for Mustafa's widow and daughters; she could help Iain set up his new company; she could pay off her debts and start a new life in London, a life she craved, a life she deserved. Without a qualm, therefore, she took Rick's key from her pocket and held it up. And in that moment she realized that she'd been thinking about it wrong. Courage wasn't about one's ability to handle fear.

No. All courage was, was having something that mattered more.

AUTHOR'S NOTE

There is always a risk, with stories like these, of plots being overtaken by real events. Even as I was finishing my first draft, the Gezi Park protests started in Taksim Square in Istanbul then spread quickly across Turkey. And, shortly afterwards, the Egyptian army ousted its second president in less than thirty months. This book contains echoes of both episodes, but as it was substantively completed before either took place, any parallels are genuinely coincidental.

I grew up on the Greek myths and legends; I must have read my children's editions of the *Iliad* and the *Odyssey* a dozen times each. I've long hankered, therefore, to write a book based on the Trojan War, and what happened to its heroes in its aftermath. But discovering the truth about Troy is surprisingly hard, not least because of the impenetrability of the ensuing Dark Ages, and the radically different theories about them. That, essentially, is where the chronological and archaeological ideas at the heart of this book came from. For anyone interested in learning more about them, I'd warmly recommend Peter James' *Centuries of Darkness* or David Rohl's *The Lords of Avaris*.

A note on place names. Much of this book is set in Cyprus, where towns and cities typically have different names in Greek and Turkish. To make life as easy as possible for readers, I have used anglicized versions of the more familiar Greek names throughout – most notably Nicosia instead of Lefkoşa, and Famagusta rather than Gazimağusa – even in situations where the characters involved would likely have used the Turkish names.

My thanks – as ever – to my agent Luigi Bonomi, to my editor Sarah Hodgson at HarperCollins, and to my copy editor Anne O'Brien, who each helped make the book significantly better than it otherwise would have been. I'm also deeply indebted to all those who so generously shared their knowledge and time with me during my research and on my travels. Finally, I'd like to thank my friend Clive Pearson, who first drew my attention to the mysteries of Dark Ages chronology, and who was kind enough to read an early draft of this book to check for the usual mistakes. Any that remain are, as ever, mine and mine alone.